Children of the Sultan

Jonathan van Bilsen

The takeoff was perfect and Captain Anderson asked First Officer Taylor to turn off the seat belt sign as the aircraft continued to climb. Taylor reached for the switch and flipped the toggle, causing the lamps in seat belt signs around the aircraft to be extinguished. The familiar chime accompanied the procedure.

It was the last sound any of the two hundred and thirty people aboard Trans World Airlines, Flight 800 would hear. None of the people onboard the ill-fated jetliner witnessed the blinding, white flash and deafening explosion, for they would all be unconscious the moment the airplane blew apart.

From a distance, a gigantic fireball was visible from the ground. The loaded fuel tanks exploded simultaneously like a fiery volcano erupting and spitting out its flaming insides. It was an unprecedented event. One that would be recorded in the annals of American history.

Novels by Jonathan van Bilsen:

A Past With No Future

Iberian Betrayal

Children of the Sultan

The Crimson Mask (1999)

For more information contact us at
(416) 709-1907 or visit us on the World Wide Web at
WWW.shady-vale.com

Children of the Sultan

Canadian Cataloguing in Publication Program
van Bilsen, Jonathan, 1950-
        Children of the Sultan

ISBN - 0-9680432-3-2

        1. Title

PS8593.A53834C44 1998 C813'.54   C98-900966-1
PR9199.3.V36C44 1998

Copyright 1998 by Jonathan van Bilsen

All rights reserved under international Copyright
Conventions. Published in Canada by
Shady Vale Publishing
65 Front Street West
Suite 0116, P.O. Box 40
Toronto, Ontario M5J 1E6
(416) 709-1907

Edited by: Ellen Murphy

Mass Market:
First Edition: September, 1998
Printed and Bound in Canada

"I look to the world with an open heart full of pure feelings and friendship."

Mustafa Kemal Atatürk, 1933

TURKEY

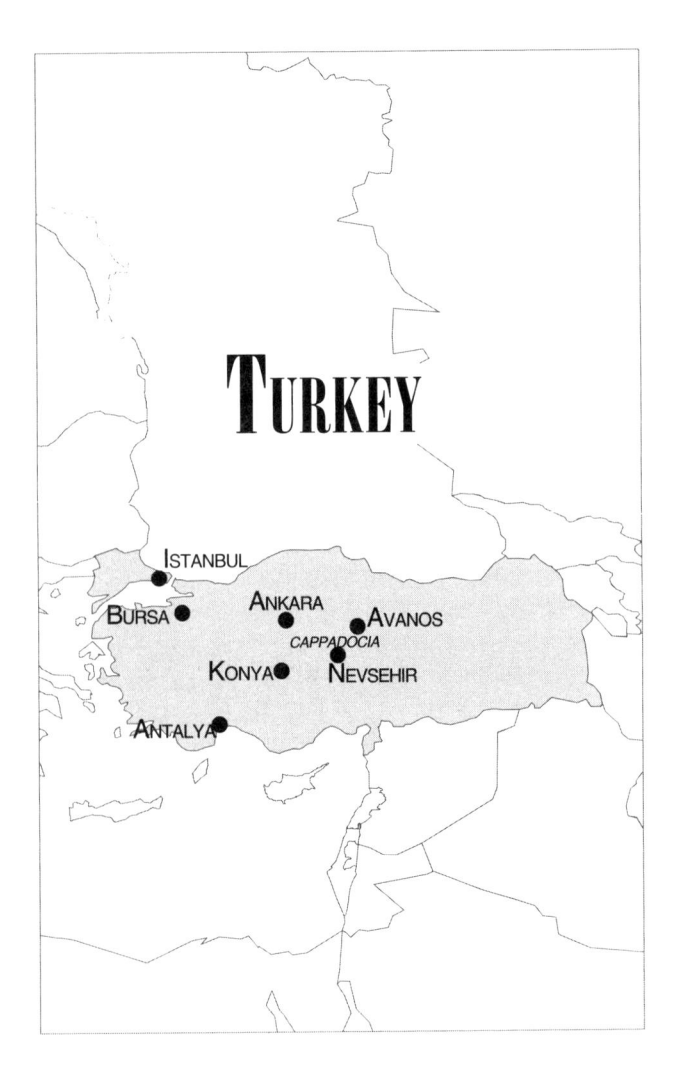

- Istanbul
- Bursa
- Ankara
- Avanos
- *Cappadocia*
- Konya
- Nevsehir
- Antalya

Prologue

Captain Charles Anderson stepped into the cockpit of the TWA 747. The air was still, as the plane sat silently at one of the gates in New York's Kennedy Airport.

A moment later he was joined by his co-pilot. "Good morning Dan, looks like a great day for a flight," greeted the Captain.

"I guess," Dan Taylor replied solemnly. Captain Anderson sensed his co-pilot's spirits were lower than usual, but decided to let it go for now. Instead he removed the checklist folder from its compartment under the seat and began the mundane chore of verifying that each item on the register was in perfect operational order.

Twice Captain Anderson asked Dan to verify a switch and both times his co-pilot's mind was elsewhere. For the safety of the aircraft, passengers, and crew he knew it was time to intervene.

"What's the matter Dan? You seem to be a thousand miles away."

Taylor's thoughts jolted back to the reality of the present. "Sorry Charles," he replied. "I had another row with Kathy this morning. She feels she has no life."

Dan Taylor had been married about six years and was the father of four sons. There was a great deal of tension at home because of his job and the amount of time it caused him to be away from his family.

The co-pilot of the 747 enjoyed his lifestyle and had, for a number of years. His wife had known this when she entered the relationship but, as with any young couple madly in love, problems, such as the ones she now faced, only happened to 'other people'.

It was a common hazard among career pilots and one Captain Charles Anderson was familiar with. "It's tough buddy and there's no easy way around it."

"I know," Taylor replied, shaking his head. "I don't know why she can't understand. I told her to get a housekeeper but she just gets more upset. I tell you, sometimes... if it weren't for the kids..."

Anderson smiled as Taylor vented his frustration: "Anyway, let's get back to work. You know what the boss is like if we're late taking off." Anderson continued reading the checklist and Taylor verified that all controls were active and operational.

The two officers finished their checklist when the flight engineer entered the cabin. "Good morning," he said, removing his uniform blazer and hanging it behind the door. As he sat at his desk he briskly rubbed his arms saying, "Boy it's cold in here, guess I shouldn't have worn short sleeves."

"You'll warm up in no time and be cursing it", the Captain said with a smile. The flight engineer went through his own series of checks and verified that everything was in order.

"Dan why don't you radio the tower and tell them we're ready?"

First Officer Taylor engaged the radio and made the necessary communication.

"Did you check this thing for cracks?" the flight engineer asked.

"That's a good one, Tony. I know I can always count on you for a laugh." Anderson smiled, although he did not really think it to be humorous. Aircraft safety was a major concern to pilots. Every airline was facing cutbacks resulting in less maintenance, causing potentially disastrous effects as the world's air fleet continued to age. Although it was not something airline personnel talked about openly, it was always in the back of their minds.

A moment later the door to the cockpit opened and the smartly dressed TWA flight Purser entered the cabin. Her maroon skirt and perfect white blouse looked stunning against her tanned face and natural blonde hair. "The crew is ready, Captain. With your permission we'll begin boarding passengers in a few moments." She waited for his reply, thanked him, and closed the door behind her as she stepped into the first class compartment. Picking up the phone she relayed instructions to the ground crew. Turning to another attendant she said, "Looks like it's going to be another packed flight."

"Doesn't matter to me! Seven hours from now I'll be on a four day leave in beautiful, romantic Paris."

"Sounds nice," the purser said heading downstairs toward the main door of the wide-bodied plane.

"Hi Janet," a male attendant, standing beside the door, said.

"Hello James. Everything all right?"

"Seems to be," the man replied.

The passengers began to walk through the connecting arm as they entered the fuselage of the aircraft. The two attendants stood at their posts beside the door and greeted the row of people, directing them to their seats.

The procedure went quickly as most of the passengers were tourists familiar with air travel. They had arrived early, eager to start their vacations and obediently followed the instructions of the uniformed attendants.

Janet escorted a couple with a little girl to the bulkhead seat in the centre front section of the aircraft. She offered a pillow to the woman and smiled at the child. She returned to the door and checked the clipboard listing any special situations. There were three vegetarian meals and one kosher request. There was also a person who required wheelchair assistance.

The passengers appeared the same as on any other flight. The cross-section of people included young couples, elderly patrons, and the usual assortment of good-looking men who made it their duty to harass flight attendants in an effort to boost their own egos.

An elderly man, accompanied by his younger wife, was the last to board the plane. A member of the ground crew signed the necessary paperwork and said goodbye to the flight attendants. When the attendant left the aircraft, Janet picked up the telephone receiver and spoke with the lounge to ensure everyone boarding had done so.

"We're waiting for two people," was the reply.

"Where are they?" she asked, efficiently.

"They have been paged and apparently have checked in… wait, I see two people running toward us. It must be them. I'll send them through as soon as possible."

"Are we still waiting for people?" James

asked.

"Yes. Just two and they're on their way," Janet replied.

He looked at his watch and sighed. "That'll be a first, we'll actually leave on time." Both attendants smiled as the two men dressed in business suits and carrying overnight bags hurriedly stepped onto the plane.

"Could we put these anywhere?" one of the men asked.

"You'll have to put them in the bins over your seats, sir," Janet replied. "Unfortunately all of the coat closets are full." The men shrugged and walked along the aisle to their seats. As all of the passengers were accounted for, Janet radioed the Captain and confirmed she was about to close the door.

"It's all yours," Captain Anderson said. "Have a good flight... and I hope they're easy on you today."

"Why should today be any different?" Janet replied, jokingly.

She performed a quick check through her section of the aircraft to ensure everyone had their seat belts fastened and their seats in an upright position. She nodded to a flight attendant at the rear of the aircraft, indicating that she should begin pre-takeoff instructions.

The airplane began to roll away from its parking spot at the gate of New York's Kennedy Airport and taxi toward the active runway. The sky was blue and the winds were light, ensuring a safe, smooth takeoff.

They were ninth in line to leave and as the plane turned the corner, the captain asked the flight attendants to take their seats.

The aircraft picked up speed and began to shake as the massive, metal carrier barrelled along the runway, bouncing as it encountered various dips and cracks in the aging pavement. As the plane picked up speed, the passengers could feel the thrust pushing them back in their seats. People were gazing out the windows, their eyes filled with excitement over the journey they were about to take.

The giant 747 was pushed away from the loading gate and began it's pre-flight journey to the runway. The sky was clear blue and the winds were light. It would be a good day to fly.

After what seemed like an eternity the front of the plane finally broke free from the strong grip of the land below. As the nose pushed skyward, the rear section was forced to follow and the metal giant soared upward defying the laws of gravity and reaching for the tranquillity of the endless sky beyond.

The takeoff was perfect and Captain Anderson asked First Officer Taylor to turn off the seat belt sign as the aircraft continued to climb. Taylor reached for the switch and flipped the toggle, causing the lamps in seat belt signs around the aircraft to be extinguished. The familiar chime accompanied the procedure.

It was the last sound any of the two hundred and thirty people aboard Trans World Airlines, Flight 800 would hear. None of the people onboard the ill-fated jetliner witnessed the blinding, white flash and deafening explosion, for they would all be unconscious the moment the airplane blew apart.

From a distance, a gigantic fireball was visible from the ground. The loaded fuel tanks exploded simultaneously like a fiery volcano erupting and spitting out its flaming insides. It was an unprecedented event. One that would be recorded in the annals of American history.

1. The Organization

Francis Sun was a large man, especially by Asian standards. He stood just under two metres and weighed well over one hundred kilograms. His overbearing manner was in itself an intimidation to the subordinates who served him. Although he appeared gentle in nature, he was capable of making harsh, ruthless decisions. Today his face had a lifeless expression. He looked weary, almost defeated, as if the weight of the world were resting heavily on his broad shoulders.

He waited with great patience, seated upright and facing the front of the first class cabin in the British Airways 757. He glanced at London's Heathrow Airport and watched baggage handlers rapidly scurry to load the various shaped suitcases onto the conveyor belt only to be swallowed by the massive belly of the steel-hulled aircraft.

Further along the outside of the terminal building, dozens of aircraft were standing obediently, waiting their turn to be released to the freedom of the sky. Francis Sun had not spent a great deal of time in London on this trip. He had traveled extensively during the past week and was tired. It seemed only yesterday that he was sitting in a similar seat on another wide-bodied plane, leaving Hong Kong for New York.

His business took him around the world in a manner to which most people were unaccustomed. He traveled in ultimate luxury, staying only at superior class hotels, dining in elegant restaurants, and enjoying the finest wines from around the world.

The organization he worked for was not listed in the Fortune 500 group and had no symbol on any Stock Exchange. There were no annual reports and board meetings were never publicized. It was one of the most profitable global entities of the modern world. Their field offices were never luxurious and were always attached to small, unassuming businesses. Francis Sun headed up one of the most powerful, well-organized criminal networks in the world.

His organization, for which there was no

name, did not deal in petty crimes or activities commonly carried out by the Mafia or similar syndicates. He also refused to be involved in terrorist acts such as those performed by the Black Panthers or the Red Brigade. Their causes were questionable and their actions unprofessional. The main goal of his company was to provide impartial services to governments and industry around the world, services for which he was handsomely rewarded.

As of late, he was involved in high level negotiations with major multinational corporations to offer his organization's services in the field of industrial espionage. He cared little for global economy, national or international security, nor the well being of any individual. He worked for only one goal, to improve the financial position of what he considered to be his corporation.

He constantly remained detached from all emotional bounds and his results were proof that his well-planned, expertly carried out actions were extremely successful.

Francis Sun was very proud of the role he played in securing financial success for himself, his family, and his people around the world. His network spanned the far regions of the globe and contacts had been set up in nearly every country. Only he was familiar with the vastness of the entire system and he made a point to keep such information away from the hands of his operatives. He personally negotiated every transaction and dealt only with people whom he knew, respected, and felt he could trust.

Establishing his organization during his early twenties, nearly thirty-seven years ago, it quickly developed a reputation for getting results which governments and corporations could not attain through standard, legal methods.

On this occasion, however, he was greatly troubled. Events had taken place and he was not in a position of control. His mind wandered back to a sunny morning several days before. In his own luxurious office high atop the Tudor building, overlooking Victoria Harbour in the city of Kowloon he had been preparing for a meeting with representatives of the Chinese government. They were to discuss his organizations role now that the take over of Hong Kong by the People's Republic of China was to take place.

Confusion ran rampant throughout the business community of Hong Kong in anticipation of what was to come. Wealthy citizens were leaving the country by the hundreds and establishing new roots in North America. Francis Sun had no intention of leaving his beloved homeland; he viewed the political upheaval as an arena in which he would be able to do battle and surface successfully.

As he sat at his uncluttered African teak desk, the telephone, the only tool he needed to run his business, chimed twice; an indication his secretary wished to speak with him. He lightly touched one of the keys and spoke quietly. Moments later the massive door opened and an attractive, dark haired woman, in her late forties, entered. She stepped softly across the thick, cream-coloured carpet and stopped when she reached the desk. Francis Sun stared at her, a signal he was ready for her to speak.

They had worked together for nearly twenty years and, although she was aware of many of the activities which took place within the walls where she now stood, she never once suggested concern about the immorality of the deeds performed by Francis Sun's organization. The secretary knew her superior was a methodical man who appreciated undisturbed time to quietly plan strategies and to calculate responses to queries with great sincerity.

"I have received an urgent telephone call from Mr. Wu," the secretary said. Francis Sun's facial expression showed no emotion as his secretary continued to speak. "Mr. Wu wishes to meet with you, and he considers it to be most important."

Again the older man's face showed no sign of anxiety. His dark brown eyes stared directly at his secretary and the smooth, light skin on his face remained impassive. His lips parted slightly and he inhaled before he spoke.

"I shall see him in one hour," he said in a monotone voice. Upon the completion of his words, he allowed his gaze to drift sideways, viewing the harbour from his spectacular vista, outside the large, floor to ceiling, darkly tinted windows.

His secretary knew this was her superior's

way of saying the conversation had come to an end. She quietly departed his office.

Exactly an hour after the last interruption the telephone chimed. Francis Sun went through the ritual of answering the call and was informed by his secretary that Charles Wu had arrived.

"Send him in," Francis Sun said, solemnly.

A moment later Mr. Wu entered. His frail body leaned forward as he shuffled toward Francis Sun. His aging frame no longer filled out his neatly pressed, old, navy suit and worn white shirt. Untrimmed, black hair, artificially dyed in a 'failed' attempt to hide his age fell stiffly about his face and neck. His facial lines were deep, and sad, pale eyes revealed that time had not been particularly kind to this elderly man. He spoke as he entered the room.

"It's very good to see you again Francis."

"Welcome my friend. Please sit down." Francis Sun motioned to one of the two, high-back, brown leather chairs facing the desk.

As Wu seated himself, Francis Sun turned to a teak credenza behind him and entered several digits on the keyboard of a computer system, causing the screen to go blank. Wu had not been able to read the confidential information on the monitor.

"What is it that is so urgent, my friend?" Sun asked.

"To the point," Charles Wu said, knowing the man across from him had always been adamant about people being direct in their conversation, "I received a telephone call from a friend connected with a senior post in the American government. He referred to the recent airline catastrophe involving the Trans World Airlines Flight off the coast of the eastern United States." Charles Wu paused momentarily, fidgeting slightly.

"Would you care for a cup of tea?" Francis Sun asked, realizing his associate was nervous about the conversation about to take place. "Perhaps a glass of sherry?"

"A glass of sherry would be most appreciated," Wu replied.

Francis Sun stood and absent-mindedly brushed imaginary creases from his grey, silk-clothed suit, as he walked to a small closet in a corner of his office. He opened a door and removed two stemmed glasses as well as a full lead crystal decanter. He poured the sherry into the glasses, replaced the bottle, and handed Charles Wu his drink. In a further effort to ease the tension that Wu seemed to feel, Francis Sun sat in the second high-backed chair, next to his friend and raised his glass to suggest a toast.

Charles Wu thanked him and continued with his story.

"My contact informs me the Americans believe the plane was shot down by a surface to air missile which, they feel, was launched from a boat somewhere off the eastern coast of New York." Charles Wu paused to gather his thoughts, at the same time sipping his sherry.

"Why are you telling me this?" Francis Sun asked.

Wu continued. "As you are aware, no one is claiming victory for the disaster. The American CIA, however, believe it to be a group of Kurdish rebels." Again Charles Wu began fidgeting in a nervous manner. His actions were beginning to agitate Francis Sun.

"Why are you telling me this?" Sun asked again, maintaining a soft-spoken voice.

"Well, it seems," Charles Wu was visibly stammering. "It seems," he continued, repeating himself, "that they claim your son is involved." The frail Asian sighed with the last word he spoke, as if relief had finally come, brought on by the conclusion of his formidable news.

Francis Sun sat silently and stared at his guest, who continued to fidget slightly, but not as noticeably as when he was speaking. "What did you say?"

"The United States is blaming a terrorist group for the downing of TWA Flight 800," Wu repeated. "They believe your son to be directly involved."

Francis Sun could not believe what he had just been told. Holding his composure and showing no outward sign of emotion he quietly said, "I thank you for this information." He stood, still holding his untouched glass of sherry. Charles Wu gratefully accepted the cue to leave the room.

Only after the door had been tightly shut did

Sun allow a gust of air to escape from his lungs. Slowly he walked around his desk and angrily realized the tension that suddenly over took him. Inhaling deeply and releasing the air slowly he felt great discomfort and confusion. Staring out the window he began asking himself questions. Firstly, what basis did the Americans have for assuming his son to be involved in this wildly contrived plot? Francis knew his son; he was convinced he would never allow himself to become involved in a crime of this magnitude.

Francis Sun and his wife had three children. Thomas Sun was the eldest, his only son and his father's pride. A recent graduate from one of the finest universities in New York, he developed an aptitude for business and economics. He was aware of the nature of his father's business and knew he was being groomed to one day take over the organization. Thomas had assisted his father on several occasions and was well aware of the influence and respect others had for him.

He knew he had to act quickly to secure his son's safety before he was arrested by the American government. Picking up his phone, he dialed a number and waited as the phone rang twice. When he heard the simple "yes' he said, "This is Francis Sun."

The tone of the recipient's voice changed dramatically to that of a subordinate nature. "Yes, sir. How may I help you?" The people who worked with Francis Sun knew he had no time for the formalities of small talk.

"I want to know where my son is." It was a statement. There was little inflection in his voice.

"I understand. I will contact you shortly." The subordinate understood the directness of Francis Sun's demand.

"You will be able to reach me at my office number. I will await your call and will be here for thirty minutes."

Francis Sun contemplated telling his wife but decided to defer the unpleasant task until he had more concrete information. He rang his secretary and asked her to bring him a cup of tea. His mind was troubled with a concern that only a father could have for a son whose life was in grave danger.

After a short knock, the secretary entered the office. She carried a silver tray, supporting a Rosenthal tea service. She carefully placed a cup on the desk directly before Francis Sun and filled it with freshly brewed green tea. Using a sterling silver sugar spoon, she scooped precisely one half a spoonful of brown, raw sugar and allowed it to fall into the steamy, hot liquid. She rested the spoon on the saucer, removed the two sherry glasses from the desk, and placed them on the tray.

Francis Sun did not move during the ritual performed by his secretary. When she finished he nodded his head ever so slightly and briefly smiled at the woman. She sensed a sadness about him but knew conversation was not expected. Picking up the tray she left the room securely closing the door behind her.

The telephone rang, startling the usually composed leader of the giant corporation. He instructed his secretary to put the caller through immediately.

"Yes?"

"I have very little news to report, sir," the caller replied. Francis Sun frowned at the news being presented to him. The caller continued. "We cannot account for your son's whereabouts in the past forty-eight hours."

"Where was he last?" the concerned father asked.

"He was last seen in Istanbul."

Francis Sun was slightly shocked by the statement. He assumed his son was in the United States. He was unaware of his recent travel arrangements. "Do you have a contact for me?"

The caller replied and Francis wrote the information on a small notepad, which he always kept in his inside jacket pocket.

At the completion of the call Francis Sun rang his secretary and asked her to make arrangements for him to fly to Istanbul with a stopover in New York. He also asked that his car to be brought to the front of the building.

Leaving his office he stopped at his secretary's desk to pick up his travel arrangements. Thanking her he walked to the elevator. His thoughts were all of the son he cherished and his anticipated succession as the next leader of his organization. An event such as this could destroy the years of planning and grooming that Francis Sun had so meticulously orchestrated.

When the elevator door opened he stepped out, deep in thought he did not hear the greeting from the security guard and made his way through the busy, marble lined foyer of Hong Kong's finest office building. A uniformed chauffeur stood waiting beside the white Rolls Royce Corniche and immediately reached for the twenty-four carat, gold plated door handle to allow his employer entry into the luxury vehicle.

Not a word was spoken. The driver knew after many years of dedicated service that if no directions were given he was to deliver Francis Sun to his home. Today was no exception.

As he reminisced about his son he was brought back to the present by a British Airline, flight attendant offering a pre-flight beverage. Francis Sun ordered a cocktail and checked his watch to calculated the time difference till his meeting in Istanbul with Davud Kurvesh, one of his associates. He had extended his trip by stopping in New York to meet with one of his colleagues to look into the possibilities of his son being involved in the downing of the TWA flight 800. He believed there was little chance of Thomas' involvement but he was also convinced the crash was no accident.

The American people had been told it was

quite common for passenger jets to be used for training missions by anti-terrorist soldiers, therefore explaining the plastic explosive residue lodged deep within the creases of the cloth covered seats. The American public believed what their media told them, not because it was true, but because they desperately needed to believe.

Francis wondered if his son had gone underground in Turkey. He was greatly concerned, as any father would be, realizing the grave danger his son was facing.

Looking at his watch he was thankful there was little time left before the plane departed from the busy Heathrow airport. The flight attendant brought his drink and a dish of roasted almonds and placed them on the small table within the armrest of his seat.

Sitting next to Francis was an elderly lady who was already asleep. For this he was grateful, as he did not wish to engage in conversation. Several people straggled onto the plane, carrying various pieces of luggage while studying their boarding passes to see where their seats were located.

He was annoyed at the ill-prepared passengers who left things to the last minute and were responsible for the delay of others. He did not notice a dark haired youth in blue jeans and leather jacket, as he wandered onto the airplane and made his way past the first class cabin, toward economy.

At last the familiar announcements were made, and the airplane readied itself in preparation for its takeoff and four-hour journey across Europe to the Middle East and Turkey, gateway to Asia and once the centre of the Ottoman Empire.

2. JSJS

Standing in the aisle, Quentin Wright, waited patiently while an elderly lady placed her belongings in one of the overhead bins of the British Airways 757. Behind him other passengers grew anxious, waiting to get to their seats. Manoeuvring herself into the seat she smiled apologetically at Quentin as she sat down. He found his seat and settled himself in. His row mates seemed to be conversing in what he thought was Italian. Realizing conversation would be limited he began to think about his own life and although he was only in his late twenties his life had been far from normal.

To Quentin's eye many of the passengers seemed to be businessmen traveling to Istanbul to secure transactions. Others were tourists en route to visit the ancient historical land and still others were native to the Middle East with their traditional Muslin head coverings.

Born in New York City, Quentin's father suddenly deserted his family without a trace when he was six years old. Very soon he and his brother were moved, by their mother, to Sydney, Australia. At first he spent a great deal of time wondering about his father but as time went on the memory began to fade and the pains healed.

Bernard Lawson, his mother's companion, filled the void by providing them with a very wealthy and happy existence. The boys wanted for nothing. They traveled extensively and attended the finest schools.

Bernard Lawson had bought a house in the resort town of Port Douglas, a two hour boat ride from the Great Barrier Reef. Scuba diving, snorkelling, and frolicking in the ocean became favourite pastimes of the newly formed family.

Quentin's mother seemed happy with their new life and, although Quentin had asked her upon several occasions, she refused to speak of his father other than to offer bitter comments about his desertion of the family.

Quentin was never able to understand why his father would do such a thing. They had always maintained a close relationship and enjoyed their lives. He failed to understand the motives behind his father's strange and unaccountable actions.

It was not until Quentin's twenty-second birthday that his life took a dramatic change. He had just graduated from college and his mother had organized a small gathering attended by his numerous friends. Suddenly, without warning, two people from America appeared at the door. There had been periods of loneliness in Quentin's mother's life. She enjoyed Bernard Lawson's company but, from time to time, she missed her friends and some aspects of the past. She had long desired to communicate with some of her old friends from New York City and finally made an effort to contact two of them. Davey and Yasmine Reid were planning a trip to Australia and welcomed the invitation to visit and possibly surprise her son on his birthday.

The reunion had been enjoyable; however, the next morning, during a breakfast rendezvous in Sydney's tourist district, Davey and Yasmine Reid explained to Quentin the truth about his father's strange disappearance.

Davey was shocked to hear Quentin had been misled from the truth by tales of his father's wrongdoing. Although the short, cherub-faced New Yorker did not wish to be involved, he felt Quentin had a right to know the truth. It did not take much prodding by Quentin to convince Davey to reveal the events, that actually occurred.

He explained about Quentin's mother having had an affair with Bernard Lawson and being caught by Quentin's father, Phillip. Devastated by the event he aimlessly wandered the streets of New York for several days trying to deal with the shattering situation. When he returned home, his wife had taken his two sons and vanished. There was no forwarding address, no note of explanation, and no indication where they had gone.

Phillip quit his job and searched desperately for his loved ones. He received a Visa statement in the mail and saw a charge, which had been posted in Vienna. Phillip became wild with excitement and eager at the prospect of following what he believed to be a substantial lead, and possibly being reunited with his sons. He acted in haste and was gravely disappointed when, after an eight hour plane journey the lead vanished as he discovered the company responsible for issuing the Visa chit was only the head office for a New York branch, a store where Phillip himself had shopped only days before.

As he was about to return to New York, he made the acquaintance of someone employed by the United Nations. The two men spoke and after some discussion, Peter Alexander, the UN representative, offered Phillip a potential career with an international investigation sector of the United Nations. Phillip accepted the position and, after a rigorous training program, became a field agent traveling the world. It was a great opportunity, or so Phillip thought, to look for his two sons.

After hearing the shocking story Quentin decided upon graduation from university, to join a travel organization and became a tour manager, escorting senior citizens on luxurious vacations around the world.

This provided Quentin with an opportunity to search for his father. Sparks of hope were continually extinguished, as the results led nowhere. One day, while wrapping up a tour, he received a telephone call from Davey Reid in New York. Davey had come across information, which could possibly lead to an address for Quentin's father, Phillip Wright.

Quentin had immediately followed the lead and learned his father was living in a small English village outside of London. He made a decision to make contact with Phillip Wright.

It was a tremendous shock for father and son to meet but the reunion did go well. Quentin and his father looked remarkably alike. Both were just under six feet and both had thick, wavy hair. Thanks to hotel fitness rooms Quentin was in excellent physical shape.

Phillip still worked with the International Security Investigations Sector of the UN (ISIS) but now had a job at the home office in London. His responsibility covered Europe and the senior position meant much less traveling. His hair was just beginning to grey and he was starting to show signs of regular meals, a slower pace of life, and his age.

Quentin liked Phillip's new wife, Lana.

Eight years younger than Phillip with a pleasant and positive personality, she ran a successful antique shop and tearoom near their home in the village of Cowden-In-Kent.

During the initial reunion, Quentin had decided to stay only a few days in order to catch up on lost time. During his stay a resident of the village was kidnapped. The incident became an international affair involving Iraq and Portugal. Quentin had been flung into the web of intrigue, but with the help of his father managed to walk away a hero.

It was during this time that Quentin gained respect for his father and his work, which led him to inquire about the possibility of joining ISIS.

The decision was made without Phillip's blessing. He knew the kind of life in store for his son if he was to become an agent. After sitting in cars and abandoned buildings waiting and watching suspects, he knew the glamour associated with international espionage quickly fades as the reality of mundane, thankless work is realized as well as the ever present danger.

Phillip never questioned the capability of his son, but was more concerned with his own selfishness of constant worry. There was, however, no reasoning with his new-found son and Phillip knew he had to place his personal concerns aside.

Phillip's influence secured Quentin an opportunity of gaining admittance into ISIS and, after spending a year of rigorous training, the protégé was finally allowed to participate in a field assignment. Thus began his present career

As the plane left Heathrow, Quentin realized he knew very little about his assignment but felt excited and confident about his ability as an ISIS agent.

ISIS trained him thoroughly in every survival technique possible. He could use any kind of weapon from a revolver to automatics and rifles. He quickly achieved a black belt in the art of Kung Fu and learned to survive in the wild without any 'comforts'. He was trained in all types of covert actions from underwater rescue to hostage-held aircraft. He also learned to follow orders and that he was only part of a very large organization. He would do as instructed; make contact with the British Consulate office in Istanbul as soon as he arrived.

Quentin did very well and both he and his father enjoyed their conversations about ISIS and his training. Many times they talked into the early morning hours creating a lasting bond between he and his father.

In the first class section Francis Sun enjoyed his meal and the numbing effect of a couple of glasses of red wine. His journey had been long and tiresome. He departed from Hong Kong remembering the saddened eyes of his loving wife as she begged him to return their son safely to her. He promised but silently was not sure. He flew to New York looking for information about the crash and then onto Istanbul via London. The time was consumed with thoughts about his son. How Thomas Sun could be involved in this cruel act of terrorism was beyond his understanding.

Quentin was enjoying the trip and the time went by quickly. He was surprised to hear the landing preparations being announced. He wished he had been able to speak with his father before leaving but Phillip had been busy and he left word with Lana.

"Be careful," she had said. "Istanbul sounds like a dangerous place."

"I will," Quentin had replied. He smiled as he reminisced about the conversation. Lana was sweet and, though he was a newcomer to her life, she had accepted him with open arms.

Phillip put down the phone and began to read a file which had been laid out before him.

He had only scanned the first paragraph when his secretary called him on the intercom. "Mr. Wright, your wife just telephoned."

Phillip thanked the girl and dialed the appropriate digits. He knew Lana only called him if an urgent matter required his attention.

"Hi, what's up?"

"Nothing serious," Lana began. "Quentin just called to say goodbye. He's off on his first assignment." Phillip was surprised, for he had not been told of his son's first project.

"Assignment? Where did he call from?"

"Heathrow," Lana replied. "I thought you knew. He's heading for Istanbul."

"Istanbul?" he questioned. "I didn't know." He said goodbye to Lana and immediately dialed another number.

"James?... it's Phillip. Do you have a moment?" Phillip asked. "Thanks I'll be right there." He hung up the phone and headed for the office of James Richardson.

Greeting James Richardson's assistant he walked by her desk, knocked on the office door, and went in when he heard his familiar voice.

"Hello Phillip, I wondered when I'd be hearing from you."

"Why Istanbul? He's not ready for the Middle East!"

"He's ready -- besides it's a simple assignment."

"It doesn't matter. You could have told me."

"It's none of your concern," the man facing Phillip replied.

"James, he's my son! That make's it my concern!" he said, visibly upset.

"Phillip, you can't get involved in every assignment he goes on."

"I know, but this is his first." Phillip recovered his business tone, but did not allow his anger to ease up while he spoke. James Richardson was a senior member with ISIS responsible for new recruits. He showed compassion as he listened to Phillip's angry outbursts. The two had known each other a long time. It was Richardson who trained Phillip and gave him his first start over twenty years ago. Although he held a higher rank than Phillip, he decided to let him blow off steam. At last, when he sensed Phillip's anger diminish, he interjected.

"Look," he began. "I know how you feel and I also know you are not thinking rationally. You know he has a job to do. This is the career he chose and he works for this organization, not for you."

"I know," Phillip said, in a softer tone. "It's just that I would have liked to have known beforehand."

"It would not have made any difference," Richardson said. Phillip sighed and nodded his head in agreement.

"What sort of job is it?" he asked.

"You know that's confidential, Phillip. I can't tell you."

Phillip expected this answer as soon as he asked. An agent's assignment was part of an intricate puzzle, the pieces of which were scattered. Quite often, the field agent was not aware of the overall game plan and performed a function only because he was told to do so.

James Richardson rose from his chair and waited for Phillip to do the same. He told Phillip he would report any updates as he received them. Phillip thanked him and departed, contemplating his next move. Returning to his own office, he picked up the telephone and dialed his immediate superior, Peter Alexander.

Peter was approximately Phillip's age and had been responsible for recruiting him twenty-one years ago. They had become close friends and it was Peter's recommendation that put Phillip in the home office in London.

Phillip had once saved Peter's life and although it had never been mentioned, he always felt indebted to Phillip.

Peter Alexander was a senior executive officer in ISIS. His abilities were legendary in ISIS for planning and organizing assignments and people. He developed a network throughout the organization enabling him to lay his finger on any piece of information at any given time.

"Phillip. What can I do for you?" Peter asked, in his proper British accent.

"Do you have a minute?"

"Of course. Come on up."

Phillip told his receptionist where he would be for the next little while and left his office. He took the lift to Peter Alexander's floor, walked to his office and knocked on the door.

"Come in, come in," Peter Alexander replied.

Phillip entered the large, well appointed office. One wall was lined with shelves filled to capacity with books ranging from policy manuals to literary classics. Rich, warm panelling gave the room a warm, studious atmosphere. A large oak desk stood regally near the middle of the room and behind it in a leather tufted chair, sat Peter Alexander.

"How have you been keeping?" Peter asked, motioning for Phillip to sit in one of the burgundy chairs facing his desk.

"Very well, thank you."

As Phillip walked across the thickly piled carpet he noticed a file sitting on Peter's desk. On it were the letters 'QW' followed by several numbers. He sat in one of the comfortable wing chairs and faced his superior. Peter smiled, as he noted Phillip staring at the folder with his son's initials boldly typed on the front. The lines at the corners of his eyes grew deep as his face displayed a compassionate grin. His silver hair was thick and neatly combed. His cream coloured suit was neatly pressed and his silk tie and shirt were a perfect match

"If you think I don't know why you've come to see me you must think me a fool!" Peter said, smiling as he spoke. "I knew you'd be interested in your son's whereabouts the moment you called, so I took the liberty of getting his file."

"I'm extremely concerned about Quentin," Phillip replied. "I don't want to make this a habit but because it's his first assignment, I'd certainly like to know what he's up to."

"Most understandable. That's why I've got his file. You know we're breaking the rules by doing this."

"I know and believe me, I appreciate it very much."

Opening the file before him, Peter went on, Quentin's case involves the TWA flight that crashed off the coast of New York several months ago. He paused to ensure Phillip recalled the incident then continued. "It appears there is information which led the Americans to believe it was a sabotage operation and not a mechanical defect."

"I thought they ruled out all forms of sabotage. Wasn't it determined to be a fault in the aircraft?," Phillip asked.

"That's what the media was told and that's what the American public ended up believing. The truth of the matter is the airplane was shot down by an AEGIS missile, apparently launched from a surface launcher."

Phillip sat quietly, listening to the explanation of events. "Of course nothing was publicized and it took a great deal of time to establish what is now known to be the actual order of events." Peter went on, "First they assumed it was engine failure. Later plastic explosive material was found and was dismissed as the result of a military training mission prior to the flight. Then some paint scrapings similar to those used to paint BQM-34 missiles was found. After piecing together most of the plane it was decided that a missile penetrated the tip of the wing causing the plane to explode."

A knock on the door interrupted the account

of events.

"Come in," Peter said.

A pleasant, older woman entered carrying a tray with a silver tea service and two cups.

"Thank you so much Mrs. Jackson." Peter said. Nodding and with a smile, she placed the tray on the oak side table and poured tea for both of them. They thanked her again and then waited until she left the room before Peter continued.

"At long last, after following numerous leads, the FBI received a tip that Kurdish rebels were involved."

Phillip looked surprised. "They haven't been active in a long time."

"I know. As a matter of fact when I heard the news, I didn't believe it either. The FBI put their best men on it. They had assistance from the CIA as well as the Iraqi government who, to this day, still denies harbouring members of any rebel groups. They followed up lead after lead but the terrorists involved were professional and it seems no one came forward to volunteer information.

"Suddenly, last week, there was a breakthrough. A boat rental provided a vital link to the downing of the aircraft."

Phillip looked curiously at his friend. "A boat rental?" he asked softly.

"Yes. Apparently someone rented a boat and kept it moored off the coast of Long Island." Peter referred to his notes from time to time, refreshing his knowledge of the events.

"I'll certainly give the FBI credit for their thoroughness. The boat was capable of being used to launch a Surface-To-Air missile. An accelerated search provided several leads. The only one that seems to fit is a long shot and they've asked for our help, as it has now become an international affair.

"Are you familiar with a fellow by the name of Francis Sun?"

Phillip thought for a moment and shook his head. "No, I don't believe I am."

"Francis Sun heads up an organization from the Orient which is one of the world's best kept secrets. They specialize in industrial espionage. He's been at it for at least twenty-five years, maybe more."

"What does this have to do with Quentin being in Istanbul?" Phillip asked.

Peter Alexander sensed Phillip's impatience. "This man's son is the one who rented the boat. The very fact that the kid is in Istanbul makes us nervous. If he gets into the hands of the Kurds, we'll have a tough time capturing him.

"We've also learned that Francis Sun, the boy's father, is in London. I don't know what his involvement is but whatever it might be, I don't like it."

"Do you think he's responsible for the crash?"

Peter Alexander shook his head. "No, I don't think so. It's not his style. I think he's just concerned about his son."

"So what you're saying is it's Quentin's job to locate this kid before the Kurdish rebels get him," Phillip said.

Alexander nodded his head. "That's it." He closed the folder and Phillip knew the meeting had ended. There was nothing further to be discussed and

Phillip understood. As he stood Peter added, "We've assigned our best agent in Turkey to assist Quentin. I don't know if that makes you feel any better, but it should alleviate some of the stress you're experiencing."

Shaking hands, Phillip thanked Peter and left the office. Walking back to the lift his thoughts were of his son who was just beginning to experience some of the same things he'd experienced during the last twenty years. He knew Quentin was well qualified to work as an ISIS agent. The thought, however, did not bring him peace of mind.

3. İnci

The aircraft descended over the colourful and heavily populated city of Istanbul with it's numerous mosques and their towering minarets. The smog covered city seemed to be bursting with a population of thirteen million people and probably almost as many cars polluting the air.

Quentin departed from the aircraft with his bag. Grateful he didn't have to line up and wait for luggage, he made his way through the airport to the first available cab and instructed the driver to take him to the Holiday Inn Crowne Plaza.

The driver did not reply but guided the cab

from the parking lot on to the main thoroughfare, leading into the city. As they drove, Quentin noticed several gigantic billboards, each advertising American cigarettes. The concept of a cowboy lighting a Marlboro was apparently quite appealing to the Turkish public. The advertising seemed to be effective, for as they passed one of the signs, the driver removed a cigarette from a package kept beside him and lit it, inhaling the smoke deep into his lungs. Quentin smiled as he noticed the similarity of the driver's brand with that of the posters along the road.

The vehicle sped along the street and changed direction when it approached a traffic circle. The traffic was very heavy and Quentin wondered if it was due to the time of day or if it was always this congested. He decided to refrain from engaging in conversation with the driver, for the man had not spoken one word since he had stepped into the vehicle. No doubt the tenseness of driving a taxi along the busy streets of this overpopulated city would be enough to occupy the man's mind.

It did not take long for the taxi to arrive at the entrance of the large, North-American hotel -- a gigantic tower of at least thirty stories pointed skyward as if to defy gravity. The grounds surrounding the building were beautifully maintained with colourful flowers and shrubs.

The taxi stopped at the entrance to the lobby. An attendant hastily opened the rear door. Quentin paid the driver and thanked him. Again the man failed to respond. Quentin shrugged his shoulders and walked into the hotel.

Once inside, he was surprised by the security metal detector set up at the main entrance. A uniformed porter was posted next to the device, but paid little attention as Quentin walked through it. There were no lights or sounds. He wondered if the device was operational at all.

Scanning the lobby he thought to himself how North American it appeared; no character and certainly no Turkish influence. The massive walls were a boring, off-white beige colour with a few, very large paintings depicting, also boring, ocean scenes. Turquoise couches were positioned in the centre of the lobby surrounding a glass top coffee table. Along one wall a marble covered check-in counter stood with several uniformed employees behind attending to guests of the hotel. Straight ahead he noticed a double elevator which rose skyward on the outside of the building.

He walked to the counter where a uniformed, young lady politely greeted him. While waiting for his room to be assigned he noticed, among others, a large Asian man dressed in a grey business suit also checking in. He then headed to the elevators and waited only a few moments before the door opened and he stepped in. Checking his watch he was glad he still had an hour before his meeting with Mr. Davenport of the British Consulate.

Entering his room he immediately checked

the bathroom and closet. It was a ritual learned during his training with ISIS and one his father had drummed into him. Phillip had relayed an incident many years ago when an intruder had hidden in the shower stall of a hotel, and had attacked him, nearly causing him to lose his life.

When satisfied he was alone, Quentin threw his duffel bag onto the bed and noticed a light flashing on the telephone. He lifted the receiver and dialed the operator. After a moment, the attendant relayed a message from his father.

Quentin thanked the woman and wondered why he had not been handed the message during check-in. Phillip hadn't left a telephone number so Quentin assumed his father would be in his office.

Before placing the call he opened the mini bar in his room, removed a bottle of Heineken Beer, and filled one of the Pilsner glasses located above the bar. He returned to the night table, sat on the bed and called his father.

"It didn't take you long to figure out where I was," Quentin said.

"We're well organized," Phillip chuckled. "I wanted to make sure you were okay, and to tell you to call me, should you need any help."

"Thanks. I appreciate it." Quentin was sincerely grateful for the opportunity to speak with his father. It somehow made him feel less alone in this far away city. "There is one thing you can tell me."

"What's that?"

"What am I supposed to be doing here in

Istanbul?"

"What are your instructions?" Phillip asked, answering Quentin's request with another question.

"I have to report to someone at the Consulate."

"I'm sure they'll fill you in. You know I can't go into details. Turkey is not under my jurisdiction."

"I understand," Quentin said, subconsciously nodding. "Who is it I report to?"

"A guy named Amr El Hab. I've worked with him a number of times, in fact we trained together twenty years ago. You'll like him, he'll cut you lots of slack."

At the termination of the call, Quentin replaced the receiver into its cradle and glanced at his watch. He had approximately forty-five minutes before he was to meet his counterpart in Turkey. He decided to take a shower in a further effort to eliminate the odour of smoke that seemed to have attached itself to him. Excitement, along with a hint of fear, ran through his body. He was apprehensive of the future and the unknown.

Francis Sun splashed cold water on his face in an effort to refresh his tiresome body. The time for his rendezvous in the lobby bar of the Holiday Inn Crowne Plaza was approaching. He entered the glass-lined elevator and sighed deeply, for he knew the days ahead would not be easy ones.

He walked several steps to the open bar in

the lobby of the hotel and scanned the patrons. It was the first time Francis Sun would meet the men who were about to assist him, but he immediately recognized their stereotypes in a corner of the bar.

As he approached the table, the men stood as a sign of respect.

"I am Francis Sun," he said, softly.

"My name is Davud Kurvesh," one of three men said extending a thin, bony hand to greet the large Asian. He was at least twenty-five centimetres shorter than Francis Sun and a poorly fitting dark suit and black, greasy hair combed in a style popular during his youth in the fifties accentuated his cheap appearance.

"These are my two associates Mr. Kwok and Mr. Seleng."

Francis Sun nodded and sat in the remaining vacant chair. He did not make an effort to greet Davud Kurvesh's assistants. Kurvesh continued. "Mr. Kwok is from Mainland China and has assisted me many times before."

Mr. Kwok was over weight with a short but strong and stocky build. His double chin bulged over the collar of his dark turtleneck sweater and the rest his body overflowed his chair. He sat silent and expressionless. One could compare him to a statue were it not for an occasional blinking of his eyes.

A waitress appeared, dressed in a brown and pale blue uniform and asked Francis Sun if he would care for a beverage.

"I would like a soda water please." He glanced at a table positioned near the window, which held a variety of sweets. "May I also have a slice of that brown, marble cake, please?" The server frowned slightly, as her English was limited. She walked to the table and pointed at several cakes before Francis Sun nodded. She smiled and returned to a small counter.

Francis Sun was anxious about any news the three men before him had, but spoke only a few calculated words. "What news have you of my son?" he asked, directing his attention at Davud Kurvesh.

"Mr. Seleng has been a great asset in this matter." Seleng sat quietly as Davud Kurvesh spoke. "He has followed a trail which was left, inadvertently, by your son since his arrival in Istanbul a few days ago." Although Seleng was small in stature, he was extremely muscular and was by far the youngest of the three. He worked out regularly and the muscles in his neck and arms were visible. He wore a short-sleeve, dark-green golf shirt as well as a tan-coloured windbreaker neatly placed on the back of his chair.

Francis Sun casually looked in the direction of Seleng but said nothing. His face was void of emotion.

Kurvesh continued. "We obtained immigration records which show that your son arrived the tenth of October. He flew from New York via London. We believe he knows people in Istanbul.

We found a Visa receipt which your son had used at a local restaurant

"When you first alerted us, we contacted our network and began an in-depth search of Istanbul.

"One of the waiters remembered your son, as well as the person he was with, a member of a well-known Kurdish gang in the area. They are not a threat, and are usually used as messengers by other gangs. We located the man and when we followed him, discovered he had arranged a meeting between your son and some Kurds in the Dolmabahçe Palace, this afternoon."

"Where is this palace?" Francis Sun asked.

"It is approximately forty-five minutes from here. It is on the other side of the Bosporus, in Asia."

Francis Sun was not aware of Istanbul's split between Europe and Asia, and a confused look prompted Kurvesh to explain further. "The Bosporus divides Europe from Asia and slices directly through the northwest corner of Turkey."

Francis Sun nodded his understanding of the explanation. "And where is my son now?"

"Ah, that is a problem. When we arrived at the Dolmabahçe Palace, it was closed. We attempted to enter but were confronted by a group of guards who refused us admittance." Although Davud Kurvesh was a native of Turkey, his English was excellent. "We are doing everything possible to locate your son."

Although Francis Sun showed no visible signs of displeasure, he was extremely upset and immensely deflated by the news. While listening to Davud Kurvesh, he thought the matter of finding his son would be a simple one. He was now concerned that perhaps this would be a far greater task than first anticipated. "What exactly is the nature of your plan?" he asked.

"We are searching the entire city of Istanbul. Our network is so vast that it would be extremely difficult, if not impossible, for one to leave this city without our knowledge. We are following all possible leads and are checking on every Kurdish rebel group with which we are acquainted. We believe your son is involved with one of them. Their intention more than likely would be to hide him underground."

"How difficult will it be to locate him?" Francis Sun asked.

"That, unfortunately, is a question I cannot answer. Perhaps it would help if you explained your son's dilemma."

Francis Sun pondered the question. He raised his hands to his chin placing his fingers against each other. After a long, methodical pause, he spoke. "My son has been wrongfully accused of participating in a plot against the Americans."

"What is the nature of this plot?"

"Why do you need to know?"

"We do not wish to pry. We are only concerned that it would help us search for a specific group of individuals he may be involved with."

"It was an act of terrorism for which no one has taken responsibility. There is no indication Kurdish rebels were involved and definitely nothing which points to my son's collusion."

"What is the nature of the act of terrorism?" Davud asked, fearful he might be crossing a line which delved into his employer's personal life.

Again, Francis Sun stared at Kurvesh before answering the question. His initial intention had been not to reveal the nature of the alleged crime for which his son was being sought; however, it appeared he had little alternative. "There was an attack on an American aircraft several months ago. The plane was shot from the sky and all its passengers were killed."

Davud Kurvesh looked at his accomplices, but said nothing. He turned his gaze back to Francis Sun and inhaled before he spoke. "Are you referring to the TWA crash of last July?" he asked. Francis Sun nodded his head. "We knew the downing of the aircraft had been a terrorist act and suspected it to be Kurds. They certainly had reason for the action. What I don't understand is your son's involvement! He is certainly not Kurdish."

"Why do you say the Kurds had validity in their action?"

"You must understand, Mr. Sun, that Turkey is a strange country and has extremely radical, political groups. I have lived here all of my life and every day is a learning experience for me. We are a country divided in two. Most consider the west to be the more civilized part of the country. The eastern half is inhabited by Kurdish groups, which originated in Turkmenistan and Iraq. The Turkish government pays little attention to the Kurds and, in many cases, refuses to give them any type of social assistance. Their reasoning is that Iraq constantly sends groups of Kurds into Mesopotamia and eastern Turkey to perform violent acts of terrorism. They then retreat back to Iraq, leaving the world with the impression that the Kurds of Turkey, who are by nature peace-loving people, are responsible.

"Our new government is extremely religious and favours the Muslims. They denounce the violence and blame our people in the eastern half of the country. They even went so far as to call on the Americans to assist them in combating terrorism.

"The Americans of course had no choice, but to assist. Turkey was, after all, extremely helpful to them during the Gulf War. They launched many Patriot Missiles from sites in our country.

"The Americans sent in marines who caused havoc within the Kurdish villages. The action was totally uncalled for and was nothing more than an act of aggression, resulting in the hatred of Americans by the Kurds. Vigilante groups formed and vengeance became the only concern people had. The one thing which has always kept the Kurdish rebel groups weak, was a lack of unity. The methods chosen by the Turkish government, aided by the Americans, however, gave the people a reason to unite and face a common enemy.

"Those of us who are aware of the political background were extremely surprised that only one airplane was targeted. We expected far greater terrorism around the world.

"How was your son involved?" Kurvesh asked.

"My son was not involved. He was merely a scapegoat and is being wrongly blamed." There was anger in Francis Sun's voice.

"Of course," Kurvesh replied, not wishing to aggravate the man who was currently responsible for his income.

"When do you anticipate finding my son?"

"I believe we will do that within the next three days," the Turk replied, confidently. "Providing, of course, we do not have any hindrances."

Francis Sun raised an eyebrow for he knew there was more to this statement than merely its words. "Explain these hindrances to me," he said, in a businesslike manner.

Davud Kurvesh appeared slightly nervous, visibly upsetting his superior. He felt, however, it was necessary to relay all potential problems to the man who sat quietly before him. "I have two concerns: the first is that we must find your son in the next two or three days. It will take the Kurds that long to transport him to Eastern Turkey where I fear we may never find him. The Kurdish network is so vast and the people are so secretive, it would be almost impossible to track him down."

"What is the second concern?" Francis Sun asked.

"The second is..." Kurvesh hesitated before continuing. "The second," he repeated himself, "is while we were searching for your son, we ran into an agent we believe works for the United Nations."

"Also looking for my son?"

"I believe so."

Francis Sun was surprised. "What is your intention with respect to this agent?"

"We are not certain. We will allow no interference in our operation." Davud Kurvesh was hesitant and Francis Sun did not appreciate his indecisiveness.

"Perhaps you should put someone on this agent full-time in the event they have connections which will locate my son before you do."

"That is an excellent idea," Kurvesh exclaimed. "We will do that. In fact, we will put Mr. Seleng on that detail immediately." He paused a moment and smiled, being rather pleased with his recent decision. "Where will you be in the event we have to reach you?" he asked.

"You can contact me here. I will not leave until my son has been found." As soon as Francis Sun completed his statement, he rose from his chair. The waitress arrived with his order just as he was about to leave. "Could you please have this sent to my room?" he asked in a soft, polite manner.

The girl nodded and after asking for his room number, returned to the kitchen. Francis Sun left the lobby bar and walked to the elevator. He would attempt to enjoy his snack, make several telephone calls, and try to relax, as much as he could under the circumstances.

Quentin towel-dried himself as he stepped from the shower. He ruffled through his duffel bag in an effort to locate some clean clothes. He threw on a pair of denim jeans blue plaid shirt, and grabbed his leather windbreaker. The temperature in Istanbul, this time of year, was not what Quentin had envisioned. For unknown reasons, he expected the climate to be hot. Instead, it was a chilly seventeen degrees Celsius. He made a mental note to study the climate of an area before his next assignment.

Quentin looked around the room before departing to ensure he had not forgotten anything. He was about to exit when he realized the address for the British Consulate office was in his duffel bag. He returned, grabbed it, and left the room.

Several taxicabs were waiting patiently at the entrance to the hotel. As Quentin stepped onto the sidewalk, one of the cabs immediately pulled forward and stopped directly before him. He slid into the back seat and gave the driver the address of the government building.

The driver gave the thumbs up sign and slammed his foot on the accelerator, spinning the steering wheel to exit the drive of the hotel and turn onto the main road. It was evident that he had made this trip many times in the past.

Evening rush hour congested the road and

Quentin sat back enjoying some of the sights along the way. It seemed almost every other building was a mosque until they approached the Bosporus Strait. There the concrete structures were replaced by small, canvas covered kiosks where a variety of merchants sold various goods, most of which dealt with fish products of one sort or another.

Water traffic was extremely heavy on the strait, linking the Black Sea to the Sea of Marmara. Quentin's taxi passed by two U.S. Navy destroyers as well as hundreds of fishing boats, dozens of oil tankers, and a mixture of pleasure craft.

"Lots of boats," Quentin said.

The driver turned his head slightly over his shoulder and nodded in agreement. "Many ships. Big oil tankers will be sitting here for six maybe seven weeks before they may go ashore. Permits are hard to get." Quentin nodded his head. The driver continued. "You are American?" he asked.

"No," Quentin said, smiling slightly. "Actually, I'm Australian."

"Ah," the driver expressed. "ANZAC."

"No, no. Tourist." Quentin replied.

"No tourist. ANZAC Memorial in Çanakkale."

Quentin had no idea what the man was speaking about and decided to nod his head as if he understood. He thought it better not to make any further conversation.

Dusk was beginning to settle over the city and Quentin could make out several large mosques silhouetted against an orange sky. They passed old ruins, some of which appeared to be remnants of a stone wall which had once surrounded the fortress city of Constantinople.

The driver expertly manoeuvred the cab through the curved streets of the downtown area, coming to a halt before a two-storey, white stucco building protected by a black, wrought iron gate. There were two white cement pillars, which supported a metal barrier. On each of them was a wooden plaque, which displayed the British coat of arms. A flagpole supported the Union Jack halfway between the gate and a building. As with many countries that maintained embassies in Ankara, Turkey's capital city, a greater flurry of activity in Istanbul demanded large consulates.

Quentin paid the driver and mentally tried to convert Turkish lira into British pounds. Finding it quite confusing, he decided he would calculate the exchange rate later.

As he approached the wrought iron gate, two sentries, dressed in green British military uniforms stepped from guardhouses within the confines of their property. One of them spoke through the gate at Quentin.

"May I help you, sir?" the young soldier asked, politely.

"Yes. I have an appointment with Mr. Davenport," Quentin replied. He reached into his pocket to remove his passport and in so doing the second guard clutched his rifle tightly as if preparing to use it. Quentin realized the uniformed soldier thought he was reaching for a gun and smiled, slowly removing his hands, which contained his passport.

The first guard reached through the gate and Quentin handed him the passport. He studied it carefully and motioned to his comrade to open the gate.

The man did so and Quentin entered. One of the soldiers led him to the front door of the building and escorted him inside. He was greeted by an older, uniformed gentleman seated behind a desk, "May I help you sir?" the man asked with a proper British accent.

"Yes, I have an appointment with Mr. Davenport. My name is Quentin Wright."

"One moment please." The man ran his finger along a sheet of paper with several names and telephone numbers. He dialed a number and in a moment said, "I have a Mr. Quentin...," the man looked up, "...Wright here, to see Mr. Davenport." Quentin nodded approvingly as the man remembered his name.

"I will," the commissionaire replied. He turned his attention to Quentin. "If you will follow this corridor to the end and turn right, you will see several doors. I believe the second one is marked with Mr. Davenport's name."

"Thank you very much."

"One more thing," the man said, as Quentin was about to leave. "May I have your passport please?"

Quentin removed his passport from his pocket and handed it to the older man. He walked along the corridor and entered the door marked 'Edward Davenport'.

A young, dark-haired girl sat behind a worn metal desk and appeared agitated by a problem caused by her computer. Upon seeing Quentin, her expression immediately changed and she asked, "May I help you?" She spoke with a slight accent. Quentin did not believe it to be Turkish. Perhaps Spanish, he thought.

"I have an appointment with Mr. Davenport." Although Quentin tried to sound as businesslike as possible, his casual attire and youthful appearance presented a more carefree image.

"Your name?"

"Quentin Wright," he said. "I'm with ISIS," he added, proudly.

"One moment, please." The young woman lifted the telephone connecting her with her superior in the adjacent office. Quentin noticed the black nail polish which seemed to accent her naturally tanned skin. "You may go in," she said, as she motioned to a door on her right.

Edward Davenport sat upright in his large, comfortable, leather chair behind a massive desk. The office was neat and tidy with dark, wood-panelled walls. A red, Turkish-wool carpet covered most of the floor space and a recently painted portrait of Queen Elizabeth hung next to the British flag. Directly behind Mr. Davenport were floor-to-ceiling bookcases, filled to capacity with various books and souvenirs, no doubt obtained on state visits with foreign dignitaries.

When Quentin arrived in the office, Davenport rose. He extended his hand and smiled, seemingly pleased to meet the ISIS agent. "My name is Edward Davenport, Mr. Wright. I trust you had a safe journey?"

"I did, thank you very much."

"Would you care for tea?"

"I don't suppose you have coffee?" Quentin asked. The moment he spoke the words he realized he would probably offend the dignitary before him.

"Of course. I keep forgetting you are Australian not British." Davenport picked up the receiver and asked his secretary to bring them tea and coffee. He turned his attention to Quentin. "I must tell you, I think you people are doing a wonderful job. In countries such as this, where there is constant unrest, it is important to have a worldwide organization concerned about the well-being of the average citizen."

Quentin felt as if he were listening to an election speech. He began to wonder about the role of Mr. Davenport.

"We are meeting with another member of ISIS, who should be along in a few moments."

"Do you know who he is?"

"Let me see." The man fumbled through a notepad on his desk. "Ah yes, here it is. His name is Inci Arzu. Come to think of it, I've never heard of him."

A moment later there was a soft knock on the door. The attractive woman, who sat outside of Davenport's office, entered carrying a tray with two cups. She walked toward the desk and placed Mr. Davenport's tea directly before him. She passed the other cup, a cream coloured mug, directly to Quentin. "I did not know whether you took milk or sugar," she said, and placed two plastic milk containers and a packet of sugar on the desk before him.

"Actually I take it black, thank you," Quentin replied.

The woman smiled, removed the milk and sugar containers, and left the office. She had no sooner closed the door when again she knocked and entered. Quentin and Davenport turned to face her one more time.

"There is someone here to see you, sir."

"Is it Inci Arzu?" Davenport asked.

"Yes sir, it is."

"Well, show him in."

Quentin detected a puzzled look on the secretary's face, and seconds later realized why.

"Good afternoon, I am Inci."

Davenport stared, without saying a word. His mouth parted slightly. "Of course, of course. Come in. Do sit down. Would you like a coffee?"

"No thank you." Inci Arzu was nearly the same height as Quentin with neatly trimmed, straight, shoulder length, auburn hair. She wore tight fitting jeans and a brown, checked blazer under which she had a white, loose fitting, T-shirt. She was thin but shapely and Quentin was quite taken by the beautiful woman before him.

He stared deep into her large, blue eyes and noted how striking the features of her face were. Her lips were full and her complexion appeared bronze. She smiled when she noticed Quentin staring.

"Is something the matter?" Inci asked, directing her question at Quentin.

"No, of course not. I just didn't expect a woman."

"That is all right. I did not expect a boy." She smiled as she spoke.

Quentin felt a flare of anger shoot through his body at the condescending remark but immediately shrugged it off and returned the grin. He knew he would have to work with this woman and he certainly wanted to get along. Deep down, he was quite pleased at the prospect.

Davenport had recovered from the shock and sat behind his desk sipping his tea. He looked at his watch, "Perhaps we should get down to business," he said. Inci sat in a chair beside Quentin and they both focused their attention on Edward Davenport. He removed an envelope and began to relay its contents to the twosome before him.

"I have here a letter from ISIS explaining your involvement, Inci," he began. "You are familiar with some of the facts."

Davenport looked at Inci who was about to speak. "Yes," she began. "I received an order to get as much information as I could on Thomas Sun. Apparently he is wanted by the United States government. He arrived in Turkey four days ago. I do not know who he is or why they want him."

Davenport continued. "There is no mention in here as to why they want him either, but I suppose it doesn't matter."

"What are we to do with him when we catch him?" Quentin asked.

"Deliver him to the U.S. authorities. I believe the rest of the information you already have." Davenport directed his statement at Inci.

"Yes. As I mentioned, he entered the country four days ago from the U.S. He is quite naive, for he used a Visa card to pay for a restaurant bill yesterday. I contacted my office and was told to wait until you arrived." She turned her gaze to Quentin.

"I guess we should plot some sort of strategy. Perhaps we can talk on the way back to my hotel." Quentin did not wish to discuss this matter further in the presence of Edward Davenport. For some reason, Quentin thought the man would not keep a secret. Inci noticed Quentin's concern and rose from her chair.

"That would be fine," she replied.

They both thanked Mr. Davenport for his courtesy and assistance. On the way out, Quentin smiled at the secretary who continued to do battle with the computer before her.

The commissionaire returned their passports to them and the twosome walked through the large, black doors, along the path and through the iron gate. They waited on the sidewalk until a cab appeared.

"I wonder why we used the British Consulate?" Inci asked. "It does not make sense when it is an American matter."

"Probably because ISIS's head office is in London and we have more access to the British government than anyone else."

"You are not British are you?"

"God no. I'm Australian," Quentin replied, smiling as he spoke. "I was born in New York but moved to Sydney when I was six. I don't tell many people I'm American." Again, he smiled.

"That is probably wise in this country or for that matter, anywhere in this part of the world." She paused for a moment as the taxi neared. She raised her arm in an effort to flag it down and as the car came to a halt Quentin opened the back door, waiting for Inci to enter first.

"Are you staying at the Holiday Inn?" Inci asked. Quentin nodded and she relayed the directions to the cab driver, speaking in her native Turkish.

"How long have you been with ISIS?" she asked.

"About a year. This is my first assignment."

"I'm impressed," Inci said. "I hope it will

be memorable for you." She smiled.

"Not too memorable, I hope," Quentin said. They both laughed. "How about you?"

"Seven years now," she replied.

"Always in Turkey?"

"Yes. I love this country and its people. We are undergoing so much internal destruction, I feel it's important to do what I can to prevent as much of it as possible." She paused a moment before continuing. "You must have strong connections within ISIS to be given this type of duty as your first assignment."

Quentin looked confused, for he never thought much about the nature of his assignment. "My father works in the home office in London."

"Of course," Inci looked as if an awakening thought had just struck her. "You are the son of Phillip Wright."

"Yes I am," Quentin replied. "Do you know my father?"

"My superior has made reference to him upon several occasions."

"Of course. Amr El Hab."

Inci nodded when Quentin mentioned her superior's name.

"I should be on good behaviour. Otherwise you might tell your father." She laughed as she spoke.

"I don't think that'll be necessary. As long as you do as I say and don't get me into trouble." They both laughed and Quentin felt he would get along well with this person who had much more experience than he. A thought struck him as the taxi sped through the downtown streets of Istanbul. "Have you had dinner?" he asked.

"No," Inci replied. "Why do you ask?"

"I thought that perhaps we could go to the restaurant where Thomas Sun left his Visa chit. Maybe someone remembered him and can give us a lead."

"That's a good idea. I was planning on contacting them first thing in the morning but your idea makes sense." Inci turned her attention to the driver and gave him new directions to the popular restaurant.

The taxi made several turns as it whisked along the dark streets. Quentin was pleased with the arrangements and felt he would enjoy his first assignment. His eagerness was like that of a young child attending his first day of school, apprehensive but excited.

4. The Trail

"We will get out here," Inci said to the driver, as the taxi pulled up to the curb." It is a short walk and very difficult for cars." She paid the driver and waited for a receipt. They stepped from the car and walked along a short alleyway turning left on to a small street, which took them to the Cavasoglu restaurant.

"I noticed you took a receipt from the taxi driver. I was under the impression we didn't need to show proof of our expenses," Quentin said.

"We do not as a rule but I do it whenever I can I have never been questioned in all the time I have been here."

"Makes sense," Quentin said, nodding his head approvingly.

Entering the restaurant they walked up a flight of stairs where the formally dressed, maitre d' greeted them by giving Inci a big hug. The two spoke in Turkish then Inci turned to Quentin and said, "This is my good friend Mr. Kurran. He is responsible for the best food in all of Turkey."

Quentin extended his hand and the maitre d' shook it vigorously.

"I'm afraid I'm slightly underdressed for your establishment," Quentin said, referring to his denim jeans.

"That is not a problem, my friend. Come with me. I will seat you at the best table we have." The maitre d' led them through the establishment toward a corner table. Different rooms, each of which catered to various sized groups, divided the restaurant.

Quentin waited to sit down, as Mr. Kurran held out a chair for Inci. At the same time he snapped his fingers and immediately a neatly dressed waiter appeared. Speaking to him in Turkish the waiter hurried off toward the kitchen.

"That is not necessary," Inci said.

"I know, but it is my pleasure. Please enjoy your meal" He smiled, tipped his head slightly, and returned to the entrance of his establishment.

Inci smiled. "He has ordered us a bottle of wine with his compliments."

"That was very nice. You seem to know him quite well."

"I have been doing business in this country for a long time, and I have always made a point of being friendly and helpful whenever I can. In turn, I have built a large communication group of people I can depend on. A network, I believe you call it." Quentin nodded his head, impressed by this extremely attractive woman sitting across from him.

Pictures of Turkey, during the Ottoman Empire, decorated the beige painted walls of the restaurant. Sultans draped in luxury sat in large palaces or on horseback, leading their men into battle.

"I did not bring up Thomas Sun or the Visa receipt to the maitre d' yet. I wanted to wait for a few minutes to build a comfortable relationship."

"I agree a hundred percent," Quentin acknowledged. "Do you have the receipt with you? I'd like to take a look at it."

Inci picked up her small, black purse and opened it, removing the Visa chit. She handed it to Quentin. Although it was a photocopy, the information was clearly visible. Quentin shook his head. "How could anybody be so stupid? Sun knew people would be after him, yet he leaves a trail like this behind."

"I asked my office to get information on his background. They sent me this passport photo of Thomas Sun, The rest of the information will be faxed to me this evening or tomorrow."

"You speak English extremely well. Where

did you learn it?" Quentin asked, as he placed the receipt in his pocket.

"Most of it is from school but, like you, I was trained with ISIS in England. I spent two years there."

Her accent intrigued Quentin. He made a mental note to avoid sounding like a schoolchild on a first date with this girl.

The waiter came with the bottle of wine and placed two glasses on the table. He filled Quentin's slightly and asked him to sample it.

"I'm certain it'll be fine. Please go ahead and pour." He hated the formalities associated with such pompous acts as wine tasting. Ninety percent of people who sampled wine had no idea what they were looking for and those who did would know the wine from the list provided. During his travels over the last few years, Quentin had opportunities to taste some of the world's finest wines and had never in his life been served a bottle which had to be sent back.

The waiter nodded and proceeded to fill their glasses. He handed them each a menu and spoke to Inci in Turkish.

Quentin had no idea what the two were saying. The conversation seemed to centre on the daily specials. The waiter removed the menus and retreated to the kitchen, leaving Quentin with a confused look on his face.

"Because you are not from this country, they will put together a sampling of various foods on which their reputation has been built. It will be enough for the two of us. I am sure you will enjoy most of it."

"Thank you very much for your consideration."

"You do not have to be so formal with me Mr. Quentin Wright," Inci said, smiling as she spoke. She lifted her glass and held it in front of Quentin. He returned the toast and the two of them enjoyed a sip of the finest wine Turkey had to offer.

"It comes from Cappadocia," Inci said. "It is in the centre of the country and is known worldwide for its fine wines. Perhaps after this assignment, if you have time, you will visit the region."

"I must confess I know very little of your country."

"We are a country of deep history. St. Nicholas was born in Turkey and the Virgin Mary died here. Saint Paul, the Apostle, preached in Ephesus and John the Baptist lived here as well."

"You seem to know a lot about Christianity considering everyone in Turkey is Muslim."

"I have changed my religion. I was born Muslim but have turned Christian. I find their teachings easier to follow, also more believable."

"That must have gone over well at home?"

Inci laughed. "That is, as you say, an understatement. My mother was devastated. I am the only girl with two brothers. They, of course, are Muslim, as is ninety-eight percent of the country."

"Does anyone else in your family work for

ISIS?" Quentin asked.

"No," Inci replied. "My father and two brothers are doctors and my mother was a nurse. I am the black sheep of my family." Again she laughed.

"I'll bet you lead a more interesting life than they do?"

Inci nodded, still smiling.

"Where in Istanbul do you live?" Quentin asked. "Let me know if I'm being too nosey."

"Not at all. I'm always on the go so it's nice to sit and enjoy a good meal, a glass of wine, and some conversation." She took another sip of the wine while continuing. "I live in Izmir, three hours south of here."

Quentin was unfamiliar with the city and was slightly embarrassed when he learned Izmir was the third largest city in Turkey.

The waiter approached the table with a trolley containing at least half a dozen covered dishes. After placing them in the centre of the table, topping up their wine glasses he departed saying, in Turkish, he hoped they would enjoy their meal.

"This looks great," Quentin said as Inci and he began to remove the silver coloured covers.

"These are cabbage rolls stuffed with rice."

"It looks good." Quentin picked up several pieces of buttered chicken, vegetables, a spoonful of thin flakes of boiled lamb, and spoonfuls of rice. The accompanying pita bread was freshly baked.

"I could get used to this," Quentin said as he dove into the food. "I didn't realize how hungry

I was until I smelled this stuff."

Halfway during dinner the waiter returned and asked Inci if everything was satisfactory. She told him how they were enjoying it and when he asked if they cared for another bottle of wine, Inci turned to Quentin. "He wants to know if we would like more wine?"

"I don't think it's a good idea. I have a habit of falling asleep at dinner tables when I drink too much."

Inci smiled and spoke to the waiter declining the wine. She said a few more words and he departed.

"What was that all about?" Quentin asked.

"I asked him to send the maitre d' so we could ask him about the Visa receipt." Quentin nodded and took another sip of the rich, red wine.

The maitre d' returned to the table shortly. "I trust everything is well with your dinner?" he asked. He was concerned that perhaps he had been summoned to discuss a problem.

"The dinner is excellent," Inci replied.

"We have something we would like to ask you." Quentin began. "Were you working last evening?"

"I was, yes," he replied.

"There was a man in your restaurant. He was Asian and in his early twenties. This is his photograph." Quentin handed the photo to the maitre d'.

The man studied it closely and frowned. "I

am afraid I do not know this man." He looked up at Inci and Quentin. "You say he was here yesterday?"

"Yes," Inci replied. "He may not have been alone."

The waiter shook his head from side to side and rubbed his chin. He could not recollect meeting the man in the photo.

Quentin removed a copy of the Visa receipt from his pocket and handed it to Mr. Kurran. "This was how they paid."

The maitre d' studied the Visa chit and nodded. "Let me check yesterday's receipts. We still have them here. I will return in a moment."

"That is very strange," Inci said. "He sees everyone who comes into this restaurant."

They were pondering the problem when the maitre d' returned. He was smiling from ear to ear. "I have good news for you, my friends," he said, as he approached the table. "You were right. They were here but not last evening. It was during the day." The news elated Quentin and he felt the basis of his assignment was beginning to form. The maitre d' continued. "One of our waiters served them. I have asked him to come upstairs and meet with you. He should be here shortly."

"That's terrific," Quentin replied. The maitre d' left, and Inci and Quentin resumed their dinner.

"I hope he has some good information for us," Inci said.

Moments later the maitre d' returned, followed closely by a young man dressed in similar attire to the waiter who had been serving Inci and Quentin. He introduced the man, but spoke in Turkish, as the waiter knew no English. Quentin listened for key words as Inci and the waiter conversed.

He felt the Turkish language was similar to Arabic and could not make out any of the words. He continued eating and waited patiently for the conversation to end.

"I am sorry," the maitre d' said, directing his attention to Quentin. "My friend does not speak English. But I believe your news will be good." Inci thanked the waiter and waited for him and the maitre d' to depart before relaying the news to Quentin.

"Thomas Sun was definitely here yesterday," Inci began. "He was not alone."

"I figured that, judging by the amount of money on the Visa receipt," Quentin interjected.

"The person with him did not look like the type of person who would eat in this restaurant. His hair was uncombed; he was wearing dirty blue jeans, a red shirt and a torn green jacket."

"It almost sounds like you're describing me."

Inci smiled. "Thomas Sun looked very much like his photograph. He wore a suit and his hair was neatly combed."

"Any idea where they might have gone?"

"The waiter said they stopped speaking

every time he approached but, at one point, he noticed a brochure for the Dolmabahçe Palace.

"The what?"

"The Dolmabahçe Palace. It's a museum now displaying the luxurious life of the Sultan Kings. It's a very famous tourist attraction."

Quentin was impressed and again felt slightly embarrassed at not having heard of this obviously famous, landmark. "Does the waiter think they might have gone there?"

"I asked him and he was not sure. It is the only clue we have, so perhaps we should follow it up."

"Most definitely. Do you think it is still open tonight?"

"No. It is only open until six o'clock. But we can go there first thing in the morning."

"What do you think we might find?" Quentin asked, naively.

"I suppose we can take Sun's photograph with us and ask the staff if they recognize him. I know it is a long-shot but it is the only thing we can do." Inci sipped her wine before she continued speaking. "There is more," she said, as Quentin looked up. "The waiter said three men were here about two hours ago asking similar questions."

Quentin halted eating. "What do you mean?"

"They were inquiring about Thomas Sun."

"I wonder who they might have been?"

"The waiter told me that they showed him a photograph which was identical to the one we have."

"That's interesting," Quentin replied. "The one we have is a copy of his passport photo isn't it?"

Inci nodded. "Yes. It is the one I received from my office."

"Did the waiter describe the men?"

"That is a good point. I forgot to ask him. Perhaps we can find out when we leave."

They finished their dinner and enjoyed the last remnants of wine. The waiter asked if they cared for anything else, but both were too full to consider dessert. He brought the cheque to the table and Quentin insisted on paying. He removed enough money from his pocket to include a sizeable tip, leaving it on top of the bill, as Inci and he departed from the room and headed down the stairs.

The maitre d' was greeting guests as they entered the restaurant. He smiled when he saw Inci and Quentin approach. "How was your dinner?"

"Wonderful," Quentin replied. "It is the first time I've eaten in Turkey, but I can assure you it won't be the last."

Inci asked him if they could meet with the waiter one more time.

"Of course, of course. I will get him for you." They waited a few moments and the maitre d' returned with the waiter. Inci spoke to him in Turkish and the man responded.

When he had completed speaking, he bowed slightly and returned to his duties. Again Inci and

Quentin thanked the maitre d', and they left the restaurant retracing their earlier steps.

"What did he say?" Quentin asked, eager to find out any information relevant to this case.

"Two of the three men looked Chinese; the other was Turkish. They dressed very neatly. He mentioned one of the men, one of the Asians, was very large. Not tall but big."

"You mean fat?"

"Not exactly. I think he meant muscular."

"That's great. Let's hope they're on our side." Quentin hesitated a moment. "Do you think they might be police?"

"It is possible."

They found a taxi and went back to the hotel.

"I want to check if a fax has arrived and perhaps you could fax your office to see if they know of anyone else's involvement." Inci said.

"Good idea," added Quentin.

Inci pointed out some landmarks as the cab swiftly returned the twosome to their hotel. Quentin was impressed with her knowledge of the historical aspect of Turkey, and found it extremely interesting, as he had always wanted to learn more about exotic places. He commented on how few women walked the streets, and those who did were always veiled.

"It is the way of the Muslim," Inci said. "Most men do not like their women to be outside for reasons other than shopping. It is customary that women do not allow themselves to be in positions where other men can see them."

"It looks like your country has a long way to go before they catch up to women's lib?"

"Not all women are like that," Inci said. "That is why I get along well with men. Most women, however, will not give me the time of day."

"I don't suppose that would matter a whole lot?"

They both chuckled as the taxi pulled into the entrance to the hotel.

Inci paid the driver and they walked toward the lobby. "Do you know of anywhere I can buy some toiletries?" Quentin asked.

"Yes. There is a shopping mall directly across the street and a fax machine is also located there. I do not like to use the one in the hotel because too many people have access to it."

They walked through the lobby of the hotel toward the elevator. "I will meet you back here in fifteen minutes." Inci said, looking at Quentin for a response.

Quentin pressed the illuminated button for the elevator. "Fifteen minutes it is." At the sound of the familiar chime the elevator door opened and the twosome stepped in. Quentin pressed the button for his floor.

"What a coincidence," Inci said. "We are staying on the same floor."

When the elevator stopped at the twenty-sixth floor, Inci and Quentin stepped into the hallway, each of them turning in separate directions.

"See you soon," Quentin said, as he continued to his room.

He checked the time and decided it was still early enough in the evening to contact his father at home in Cowden.

The telephone rang twice before Lana answered. "Well, what a nice surprise," she said. "How is Istanbul?"

"Different," Quentin replied. "Lots of people and the food is great."

"I guess you want to talk to your father," Lana said. "He's right here." She did not wait for a reply before passing the phone to Phillip.

"How's the spy business?" Phillip asked. There was humour in his voice.

"So far it's manageable."

"Have you met your counterpart?"

"I have. Her name is Inci Arzu."

"I think I've heard the name somewhere, but I've never met her."

"She seems pretty good. She's been with ISIS for seven years and she's still alive. That must mean something. She seems to have heard of you."

"Why do you sound surprised? I am a legend in this business," Phillip said, smiling as he spoke. "What's on your mind?"

"Have you ever heard of a Thomas Sun?"

Phillip did not want to tell Quentin he had spoken with Peter Alexander earlier in the day. He felt that perhaps Quentin would not appreciate his father checking up on him. Phillip felt a twenty-seven year old, headstrong youth would not understand the concern and worry felt by a father.

"I'm sure someone will fill you in soon."

"Do you know what he's wanted for?"

"Don't you?" Phillip asked, somewhat surprised.

"No, I don't. I've only been asked to find him."

"If the agency had wanted you to know, they would have told you. They'll also know the information came from me which will cost me my credibility."

"I understand," Quentin said.

"I'll help you where I can, but it's got to be confidential. I can't stress that enough."

"I won't say a word."

"Well, good luck and remember, call me if you need to."

"I will, Dad, and thanks." Quentin replaced the receiver and checked his watch. It was time to make his way downstairs to meet Inci.

When he arrived in the lobby, he saw Inci seated on one of the large couches in the centre. She stood when she saw Quentin approach.

"All set?" she asked. Quentin nodded and the twosome walked through the doors of the lobby.

"The shopping mall is directly across the street," Inci said as she pointed to a large neon sign of a kangaroo, affixed to a building. "It is a supermarket chain." Quentin nodded his head and noticed the multilevel parking area, which was under construction.

"It must be quite new?" Quentin asked.

"It is very new and designed for tourists, mostly American. The prices in the store are so expensive that Turkish people could never afford to shop there."

Quentin nodded. He then changed the subject.

"Did you receive your fax?"

"Yes. I had a telephone message indicating a fax was waiting for me," Inci replied. "There is a twenty-four hour business centre located inside the plaza."

The road between the hotel and the shopping centre was a major thoroughfare, which led from the airport to downtown Istanbul. It took quite some time before Inci and Quentin could safely make their way across.

Once inside the mall, Quentin noticed designer type shops, with brightly illuminated windows displaying mannequins which wore the latest fashions. One thing Quentin found different, were the armed guards at the entrance of the stores. They passed through metal detectors at the supermarket entrance, and Quentin made his way to the toiletries section. Inci helped him with the pricing, as well as translating the descriptions of products, labelled only in Turkish. After paying at the cash register, they walked several metres to a small shop advertising faxes, mailboxes, and photocopying services.

They entered and Inci spoke in Turkish to the young woman seated behind a counter. She handed Inci a sheet of paper. "It is from my office," she said, reading the fax. "It says Thomas Sun is twenty-two years old and lives in Hong Kong. He has spent a great amount of time in America and was recently involved in some illegal activities in New York State."

Quentin waited for Inci to continue.

"That is all there is," she replied. She paused a moment. "I will fax back and ask them for more information."

She did not wait for a response from Quentin and returned to the woman behind the counter, asking for a sheet of paper and a pencil. She wrote down several questions and asked the woman to fax it to a number which Inci gave her. She settled the account and thanked the clerk for her assistance.

"You must be tired?" she asked.

Quentin nodded, in response to her question. "A good night's sleep would be very welcome," he replied.

The two agents left the shopping centre, crossed the road, and returned to their hotel where they each went to their separate rooms. They decided to meet for breakfast at eight a.m. to plan their day. They both hoped, it would be a day that would bring them some clues to the whereabouts of Thomas Sun.

5. Istanbul

With the sun shining brightly from a clear blue sky, the fall air was already beginning to warm and Istanbul welcomed a new October day. In the Crowne Plaza's main restaurant, Davud Kurvesh was enjoying a cup of Nescafé. He checked his watch several times wondering when the others would appear. Although they were not late, he was slightly perturbed that they were not early.

The hotel was a busy haven for casually dressed tourists making him look out of place in his one and only dark suit. The smell of food was making him hungry but he decided to wait until his associates arrived. He was contemplating calling their rooms when he saw them walking down the large, circular stairway, which led from the lobby into the restaurant.

He stood to greet them. "Mr. Kwok, Mr. Seleng. Good morning, it is good to see you."

The two men acknowledged the greeting and seated themselves around the table. A waitress appeared and asked if they wanted coffee or tea. Both men preferred coffee and Mr. Seleng wondered why they only had 'Nescafé'. Davud Kurvesh explained that it was a delicacy in Turkey and aside from Turkish coffee, it was all they served. It was expensive and refills were charged at the maximum price of nearly three U.S. dollars.

"It must be very good," he replied. His blue jeans and denim shirt did little to conceal his muscular frame.

"Let us try the buffet," Kurvesh said, as he joined Kwok who was already on his way.

The threesome ate in silence, ravenously attacking their food. Finally Davud Kurvesh asked if either of them had been to Turkey before. Neither stopped eating but indicated they hadn't. Seleng swallowed a mouthful and said, "All these hotels look the same to me."

"That is very true," Kurvesh replied. "It is unfortunate that all Holiday Inns are alike."

"It is probably done so American tourists feel at home wherever they go," Seleng added.

Davud Kurvesh had developed a worldwide network of men who assisted organizations to accomplish illegal goals. He had at his fingertips, a selection of individuals who were specialists in various fields. With only a few hours notice, he was capable of putting together a team of mercenaries or a group of assassins. No request was ever declined -- whether in Beijing, Bogota, or Calcutta. He spent many years establishing his network and was quite proud of his organization. He could be trusted and his greatest satisfaction was the successful completion of any job. He was expensive, but that did not matter to people who needed results.

Davud Kurvesh grew up in Libya, although he was born in Istanbul. He had been thoroughly trained for all aspects of terrorist activity at one of Moammar Khaddafi's highly rated training camps.

In his mid forties Kurvesh lived in a modest house on the outskirts of Istanbul. He left Libya twenty years ago and enjoyed the Turkish life style.

He had been forced into hiding for several years, for it was believed that he had been involved in the killing of the Egyptian Prime Minister, Anwar Sadat. It was a false accusation, as Kurvesh was nowhere near Cairo at the time of the murder, but the rumour had added to his reputation, giving him global acceptance in the world of organized crime.

He had never worked directly for Francis Sun, but had been involved with his organization several times in the past. He knew this operation would require the highest level of expertise when Francis Sun telephoned him directly. Mr. Sun said money would be of no concern, and Davud Kurvesh knew the objective had to be met. He hand-picked the two men sitting across from him, knowing they were both extremely experienced in different areas.

Rudy Seleng was born and raised in the Philippines and had, at one time in his life, worked under the Marcos' Regime. He was an expert in various forms of martial arts and trained regularly to keep his body and mind in perfect condition. He was also smart and could quickly analyze any situation.

Wu Fung Kwok was massive allowing his body to expand at its own rate aided chiefly by over eating. In trouble on numerous occasions in Mainland China during Mao Tse-tung's rule, he was now wanted by both the Chinese and Western governments. A quiet individual with the strength of ten men, Kurvesh knew Kwok would be capable of tearing a man apart should it be required.

Both men had one quality which Davud Kurvesh admired and demanded. They were loyal. He knew that both would lay down their lives without question, if it was requested. He worked with them previously and never objected to rewarding them with more money than most men made in a year. He was glad both were with him, as it added security and confidence to his ability. It was at Francis Sun's request he took charge of this operation, for he was seldom directly involved.

"Let us speak of today's events." Kurvesh began the conversation as the threesome finished their breakfast. "I believe we will begin by going to the Dolmabahçe Palace." He took a sip of his coffee before he continued. "Mr. Seleng and I will go there while you," he said, pointing to Kwok, "keep an eye on our United Nations agent."

Kwok looked up. "What information do we have about her?" he asked.

"Her name is Inci Arzu and she works for the United Nations in Istanbul. She probably has the same information we have from Visa and the Immigration department. Her contacts of course, are legitimate, but it appears they are the same as those supplying us with information."

"Do you know where she is?"

"But of course. She is staying in this very hotel."

As Kwok sipped his coffee, he looked up at Davud Kurvesh. The words caught him by surprise. "I thought she lived in Turkey. Why would she be staying here?" Kwok asked, slightly confused.

"She does live in Turkey but not in Istanbul." Kurvesh paused to sip his coffee. "We will assume she has the information about the restaurant Thomas Sun visited yesterday. I'm certain she also knows about the Dolmabahçe Palace. When Mr. Seleng and I go there, we will be on the lookout for her." Kurvesh paused for yet another sip of coffee before he continued. "What I would like for you to do, Mr. Kwok, is to remain in the hotel until she appears. I would like you then to contact me, but do not let her out of your sight. I am certain she will come to the Dolmabahçe Palace, but there is always the chance she may not." Kwok nodded. "Do not, I repeat, do not under any circumstances lose her."

"I will make certain she stays within my sight. I have one question. How do you know she has not already left the hotel?" Kwok asked. He spoke English extremely well for someone who was born and raised in the Orient. His voice had a high-pitched tone but he pronounced the words perfectly.

"I telephoned her room this morning and she answered. I have been here ever since, watching for her. From my seat in the restaurant, I have a direct view of the hotel entrance." Kwok and Seleng glanced through the panoramic window beside them which gave them a clear view of the area by the front door to the hotel. "I would suggest, however," Kurvesh continued, "that you remain in the lobby, so you can follow her immediately if need be. Here is a photo of her." Kurvesh removed a small passport-type photograph of Inci and handed it to Kwok.

Again, Kwok nodded his head in agreement.

"Well, if there is nothing else gentlemen, we will be off." Neither of the two men spoke; the three stood as Davud Kurvesh took the bill and walked to the cashier. Kwok immediately went up the stairs and took up his post in the lobby. The place was a hub of activity with many of the restaurant patrons now making their way through the lobby to identify luggage and board departure buses to their next destination.

Inci applied the last bit of eye make-up, accentuating her big, blue eyes. She brushed her hair thoroughly enjoying the massaged feeling. She rarely had time for such niceties. Fortunately she had naturally tanned skin and although makeup accentuated her features, she was extremely attractive without it's use. To maintain her strength and well proportioned figure, she worked out regularly and watched what she ate.

Inci studied her watch and realized she was to meet Quentin in ten minutes. She had been awake for quite some time, as a wake-up call placed incorrectly had woken her from a deep sleep in the early hours of the morning. If her assignment had been further developed, she would have been concerned by the mysterious call. However, as this case was in its infancy, she knew no one was familiar with her whereabouts, and therefore did not give the matter a second thought.

Walking through the lobby and down the stairs into the restaurant, she glanced around to see if Quentin had arrived. Not seeing him she sat at a table near the entrance. The room was almost empty as most tourists were now gone.

She asked the waitress for coffee and as the girl was filling the white, ceramic cup, Quentin entered the dining area.

"I'll have some as well, please," Quentin said.

"Good morning," Inci said when she saw her partner. "Did you sleep well?"

"Like a baby," Quentin replied. He grabbed the coffee and took a swallow, slightly burning the inside of his mouth. "What's good to eat?" he asked.

"I think you will probably enjoy everything."

"Shall we?" he asked, as he stood, making his way in the direction of the buffet.

Inci smiled and joined him. She was not as hungry as Quentin appeared to be, and decided to stick with a bowl of fruit and some light cereal.

Quentin, on the other hand, piled his plate with croissants, pancakes, two hard-boiled eggs, and several strips of bacon. He placed the food on the table where he was sitting, and returned to the buffet to pour a large glass of apple juice.

"You're going to eat all that?" Inci asked, amazed at the amount of food on the plate before him.

"Absolutely. I didn't eat right yesterday and I'm quite hungry."

"I believe you ate your fair share last evening," Inci said, smiling.

"Well, that was different. That was just to try out the Turkish cuisine." Quentin laughed and began to devour his food.

Neither of the two noticed the large Oriental who had wandered down the stairs into the restaurant, and seated himself at a corner table. He ordered a cup of coffee and sipped it slowly. It was his third cup and he was now drinking only to keep up the pretence.

"So, our first stop will be the Dolmabahçe Palace," Quentin said. Inci nodded, as she filled her mouth with a large piece of juicy cantaloupe.

"What exactly will we be looking for?" Quentin asked.

"I am not sure," Inci replied. "We will talk to some of the guards and if there is a favourable response, we will show them the photo of Thomas Sun. Perhaps someone will recognize him."

"What about those policemen or whatever they were?" Quentin asked.

"You mean the men asking about Thomas Sun at the restaurant yesterday? If they are policemen, it would not be a problem for us, but I somehow suspect they are not."

Quentin looked surprised at Inci's words. "You don't think they were police?"

"Not at all. If they represent any type of authority, ISIS would have been informed, and they would have told us."

"Who do you think they might have been?"

"My guess would be they are working for the American government on an undercover mission to capture Thomas Sun and return him to the

United States."

"That's interesting," Quentin commented as he continued to eat. "What makes you say that?"

"The US is not the type of country that would sit back and wait for something to happen. Americans are a pro-active people; however, they cannot legally enter Turkey to apprehend anyone. They will have to do it illegally."

"Then why are we even bothering to get involved?"

"Only in the off chance, I am wrong." Inci grinned.

Quentin broke into a smile. The attractive woman whom he had just met, intrigued him. Her face appeared very smooth, and her lips seemed moist. Her hair had been neatly combed and framed her face perfectly. Quentin felt slightly flattered when he noticed continuous stares from other male patrons in the restaurant, directed at his breakfast companion.

"How long will it take to get to this palace?" Quentin asked.

"This time of day it will take close to an hour. We must cross the bridge over the Bosporus into Asia."

"Then I guess we should think about going." Quentin paused and looked at Inci's plate. "If you're finished, that is."

She nodded her head and finished her coffee. Quentin signed the bill to his room and they exited the hotel, stepping into the first cab that approached.

Directly behind them was Wu Fung Kwok, raising his finger to motion to the next available taxi. He gave the driver explicit instructions to follow the cab ahead, indicating they might possibly be going to the Dolmabahçe Palace. He insisted they keep a safe distance to avoid recognition, yet remain close enough to ensure not losing the taxi.

Kwok had experience at this type of surveillance, and felt confident he was able to maintain a good trail without being spotted.

Davud Kurvesh and Rudy Seleng stepped out of a taxi in the parking area of the Dolmabahçe Palace. A massive gate, guarded by armed soldiers, greeted the two men as they walked to the ticket office to gain admission to the palatial estate.

It only took moments to purchase the tickets; however, the line-up to enter the grounds was quite long.

"We have no choice but to wait in line," Kurvesh said. He detested the thought of standing behind dozens of tourists who were in absolutely no hurry, but he did not wish to gain unwanted recognition.

The uniformed soldier, guarding the entrance to the palace, stood at attention without movement or change of expression. Several small children were running up to him, giggling, in an effort to cause a reaction, but the trained guard did not succumb.

Through the entrance gate, Kurvesh and Seleng could see the beautifully manicured grounds of the palace and in the distance high walls of pampas grass swayed in the breeze. As the line began to move the two made their way onto the grounds following a winding path leading through beautiful flower beds and neatly trimmed bushes ending at the massive steps of the colossal building. The white marble stones of the building gleamed in the bright sun. Small-paned windows in ornate settings gave the palace a European flair uncommon to Turkish architecture. The large, red flag with crescent moon and white star moved softly in the gentle breeze, adding a contrast colour to the white symmetry of the front of the building.

As the two approached the steps, a familiar chime, indicating a call on Kurvesh's cellular telephone, sounded.

He took the small device from his jacket pocket and flipped it open. "Hello," he said, awaiting a reply.

"This is Kwok. I am in a taxi following our little friend."

"Where are you?"

"I am not certain, I do not recall from yesterday, but our driver seems to believe we could very well be en route to the Dolmabahçe Palace."

"That is wonderful," Kurvesh said. He was genuinely pleased with his ability to predict the actions of this female, Turkish agent.

"There is more," Kwok said, interrupting Kurvesh's pleasure.

"What?" Davud Kurvesh asked, impatiently.

"The girl. She is not alone."

"What do you mean she is not alone?"

"She has someone with her. A man."

Davud Kurvesh paused a moment to gather his thoughts. "Do you know who he is?"

"No. I do not."

"What does he look like?"

"He appears to be in his late twenties and has black hair."

Davud Kurvesh thought about the description but could not pinpoint anyone who it might fit.

"I heard them speaking," Kwok said. "I believe he is English."

"What did they say?"

"I could not make out all of their words, but it seemed they were planning something," Kwok said. "It was very noisy in the restaurant.

Kurvesh ended the conversation and replaced the telephone in his inside jacket pocket. He continued his walk up the stairs deep in thought about the conversation and curious about the young Englishman.

"Is there a problem?" Seleng asked, noting concern on the face of his superior.

Davud Kurvesh remained silent as Seleng asked the question. "I was just a little preoccupied," he said. "It appears our U.N. agent has a friend with her. Kwok believes he is British."

"Any idea who he is?"

"None whatsoever." Kurvesh shook his head as he spoke.

They entered the palace and waited patiently as people lined up and proceeded through the metal detector. The security was extremely high, for Turkey did not have many historical sights, especially in such superior condition as this one.

"Please put your metal objects in this tray," an English-speaking guide said. "Then proceed through the barrier and walk over to where I will be standing." The guide walked to an area in the large hall directly beneath a giant, lead crystal chandelier. Kurvesh and Seleng shuffled forward slowly, as the line passed, one by one, through the checkpoint.

Massive marble columns with ornate cornices at the top, supported the giant room beyond. There were two small alcoves, one at each end of the room. Two grand fireplaces stood majestically in the corners. Precision-cut, small rectangular, mirror tiles, made of very thick glass, covered the upper half of each fireplace. Mid-nineteenth century antiques furnished the room in a European style. A burgundy, crushed velvet material covered two chairs. Domed ceilings had been artistically painted with murals of cherubs and clouds.

"Please proceed to where I am." The guide looked as if he had done this many times in the past and seemed slightly bored by the procedure. "Follow me and please stay on the red carpet at all times. The floors are very valuable and we do not want to scratch them."

Seleng and Kurvesh tried to blend in as much as they possibly could, knowing they already stood out by the mere fact that Kurvesh was wearing a suit.

The guide escorted the group of twenty-or-so tourists along a hallway and up a large staircase bordered by a glass-columned hand rail. Kurvesh and Seleng listened attentively to the guide's narration, at the same time looking for a security guard who might possibly answer questions concerning Thomas Sun.

The tour continued through several rooms, all decorated in lavishly, European styles of the seventeenth, eighteenth, and nineteenth centuries.

Finally, after dutifully staying in a regimental line, Kurvesh and Seleng sneaked away from the group and hid in a small alcove, waiting patiently until their tour was out of view.

"Let us go this way," Kurvesh directed and set off toward the staircase opposite to the way the tour had gone. Seleng followed closely behind, looking in both directions to ensure no one was following.

They walked up the staircase and stopped near the top as they saw a uniformed security guard.

Davud Kurvesh casually approached the man. He spoke in Turkish. "Excuse me," he said, being as polite as he possibly could. "I would like to ask you for some information."

The security guard turned to face him. "I wonder if you might have seen this man yesterday afternoon?" Kurvesh took the photograph of Thomas Sun from his pocket and passed it to the guard. "I will make it worth your while."

The guard looked at the photograph and shrugged his shoulders. "Do you have any idea how many people come through here in a day?" he asked, nonchalantly. "Is there any reason why I should remember him?"

Davud Kurvesh paused for a moment in an effort to gather his thoughts. "Perhaps he was wearing a suit and acting out of the ordinary. He may have looked nervous and may even have been with someone."

"That does not help a great deal." The guard changed his expression slightly. "You are not allowed to be in this area. Please rejoin the group or leave the building," he said in a very militaristic manner.

Davud Kurvesh knew he was not getting anywhere and retreated along the walkway and down the steps.

"Any luck?" Seleng asked.

Kurvesh shook his head. "We must try a different person."

"This could be a very tedious effort."

"I know," Kurvesh said, sighing as he spoke. "We have no alternative. Someone must remember him. It may take us all day, but in the end, it will be well worth it."

"What happens if we run into the Turkish agent and her friend?" Seleng asked.

"It will not matter. They do not know us. If they have more information, they may lead us directly to Thomas Sun. Let us continue along this hallway," Kurvesh said. He pointed in the direction of an entrance leading to a large carpeted hallway filled with paintings of ancient sultan rulers. As they turned the corner, they came face to face with another security guard.

"What are you doing here?" the guard asked.

"We are a little lost, we are looking for someone."

"Well, he is not here."

"The person we are looking for was here yesterday. I have his photo, perhaps you recognize him?" Again Kurvesh removed the photo from his pocket and handed it to the guard.

"Who is this?" the guard asked.

"It is someone we are looking for."

"I do not remember this face. Are you with the police?" the guard scrutinized Davud Kurvesh. He carefully studied the features of the Turkish assassin.

"No, we are not with the police, but I will reward you handsomely if you can help us."

"I am afraid I cannot," the guard said, shaking his head from side to side.

Davud Kurvesh placed the photograph in his pocket and wandered back to where Seleng was standing. Again, he relayed the negative findings to his accomplice. "You were right, my friend. This will take a long time. A very long time."

6. Dolmabahçe

Quentin Wright was taking in all the sights of downtown Istanbul as the taxi sped through the streets.

"Here we are crossing the Bosporus Sea which connects the Black Sea to the Sea of Marmara. That, in turn, leads to the Mediterranean Sea."

"I see you are a tour guide in your spare time," Quentin said, smiling.

Inci returned the gesture. "It is always good to have a career to fall back on," she said, laughing as she spoke.

It was only a few more minutes until the

taxi pulled into the parking lot outside the main entrance to the Dolmabahçe Palace. Inci paid the fare and stepped from the cab. Quentin was directly behind her.

"Wow, this is quite a place." Quentin stood in awe as he looked at the sheer grandeur of the palace before him."

"This is only the outside. Wait until we pass the gate to the main building."

The line-up was shorter than it had been earlier in the day when Kurvesh and Seleng were there. Most of the patrons had entered and were busily engaged in tours.

"You go stand in line," Inci ordered. "I will get the tickets." Quentin stepped into the line, directly behind a group of Muslim women busily engaged in chatter.

Inci walked to the small tick booth and spoke in Turkish to the attendant. Moments later she joined Quentin and was glad the line was moving.

Quentin smiled at the foreboding sentry guarding the entrance. "Doesn't look like he has a personality," Quentin said, mockingly.

Inci stepped through the gate and walked amid the tourists gathered at the entrance to the main house of the palace. Quentin followed closely, his eyes taking in all the sights around him.

"Wow, look at these," Quentin said as he stopped to stare at two giant statues of lionesses maternally caressing their cubs. "It almost looks as if they're out of place here."

"You will find that with most of the artifacts in this palace," Inci replied. "The entire building is furnished with gifts from different governments during the reign of the sultans. There is a large polar bear rug which was donated by the Czar of Russia as well as gigantic ivory tusks from a sheikh of Arabia." She paused a moment to light a cigarette. After she carelessly flung the match onto the grass, she continued her narration. "One room contains the largest chandelier in the world weighing four thousand pounds. It was donated by Queen Victoria of England."

Quentin was impressed by Inci's knowledge of the area and enjoyed listening to the descriptive explanations.

"What did Australia donate?" he asked, tongue in cheek.

"I believe it was a movie poster of Crocodile Dundee." They laughed as they made their way to the base of the steps, leading to the large, palatial mansion. Inci dropped the cigarette onto the stairs and stepped on it, grinding it into the pavement.

"Filthy habit," Quentin said, shaking his head as he spoke.

"Come, let us go."

"Do you happen to have a plan of action, once we get inside?" Quentin asked.

"I thought we would walk up to the guards and show them the photo to see if they recognize

Thomas Sun. I don't know what else we can do?" Quentin agreed and the two agents entered the large, spacious foyer.

Neither of them saw Wu Fung Kwok following at a distance, stopping every so often to view the sights, blending in with tourists to avoid being spotted by the people he was pursuing.

Kwok knew his associates were somewhere in the building, but did not wish to risk telephoning them and interrupting any activity they might be involved in. He continued up the steps and stood outside the main entrance, pretending to be waiting for someone. He wanted to allow the U.N. agent and her friend enough time to gain entry past the security system.

He was glad he had not carried a gun for he would surely be identified by the metal detector, and questioned by the regimental guards next to it. He enjoyed the few moments rest as the morning sun's rays beamed down on him.

Inside the royal estate, Inci and Quentin were subjected to the same, standard procedure witnessed earlier that day by Kurvesh and Seleng.

Once inside they made their way to a palace guide, "Excuse me," Inci spoke in Turkish telling him about Thomas Sun. Quentin handed him the photo. The neatly uniformed, young man had glasses that rested midway down his nose so he looked over them from time to time as he spoke.

"This was yesterday?" he asked. He had changed his conversation to English, realizing

Quentin spoke no Turkish.

Both Quentin and Inci nodded their heads. "Probably yesterday afternoon," Quentin added. "He may not have been alone."

The guide shook his head. "I am sorry. I do not recognize his face. Perhaps he was on an Oriental tour? Have you checked with the lady over there?" he pointed in the direction of a young, Chinese woman who was trying to organize a group of camera-carrying Orientals. Inci and Quentin thanked him for his assistance and stepped to where the Asian guide was grouping her tour.

They repeated the questions and became disheartened at her negative response.

They asked a third person but he was unable to assist them at all, as yesterday was his day off.

"This could be quite the job," Quentin said.

"Unless you have a better alternative, I suggest we keep going."

"Who put you in charge?" Quentin asked, smiling as he spoke.

"Someone has to take the lead."

"Well, aren't we special?"

Inci rolled her eyes and shook her head as she approached another guide. She was just about to ask him the routine set of questions when suddenly, from out of nowhere, she heard someone shouting her name.

She turned in the direction from where the sounds originated and took several moments to recognize the face of the person waving at her.

"Oh my God!" she yelled. "It is my old friend, Maria." She totally ignored Quentin and ran toward the woman smiling at her.

"Maria!" Inci said, extending her arms to hug her friend. "How have you been?"

The two carried on in Turkish and Quentin assumed, from the way they behaved, they had known each other for a long time. The commotion had attracted attention from several visitors to the palace.

Kwok had finally cleared security and was standing quietly in a corner pretending to be part of a tour group. His sight never once left Inci and Quentin.

After what seemed an endless conversation, Inci turned to Quentin and introduced him to her dear friend Maria.

"Oooh! He is very cute." The two women giggled to each other and Quentin could feel himself blushing.

"I need your help," Inci said after the laughter stopped.

"Simply ask and if it is mine to give, I will comply."

Inci nodded to Quentin to pass her the photograph of Thomas Sun. "We are looking for this man. He was here yesterday afternoon."

Quentin assumed by the attire Maria was wearing that she was a guide in the museum.

She shook her head and shrugged her shoulders. "He does not look familiar to me, but I will ask my friends." She wandered over to several of the guides and asked if they had seen the man in the photograph.

Quentin's heart sank at the continued rejection to the only lead they had. Inci too was becoming slightly subdued by the negative response.

Several minutes later Maria returned. "I am sorry, but no one seems to recognize him." Maria sounded sincere when she said she felt bad at not being able to help. "Perhaps we could try some others a little later."

"Thank you so much for your help," Quentin said, as he replaced the photograph in his pocket.

Inci also thanked her friend and they made arrangements to meet for coffee in the very near future. Maria waved goodbye and returned to her tour group who waited patiently in the corner of the large, marble column filled room.

"You seem to be very good friends," Quentin said.

"We went to school together. I have not seen her in at least ten years. I had no idea she worked here."

Quentin changed the subject. "What are we going to do?" he asked. The sound of despair was in his voice.

"I don't know. Perhaps Thomas Sun has not been here at all."

Davud Kurvesh became frustrated at the continuous negative results he was receiving. He began to feel uncertain about Thomas Sun's visit to the Dolmabahçe Palace.

"Perhaps we are mistaken," Seleng said, sighing as he spoke.

"You may be right; however, I felt certain about this place. Why else would he have had the brochure in his hands at the restaurant?"

Seleng shook his head, not knowing how to answer the question.

"I am going to call Mr. Kwok." Davud Kurvesh removed the cellular phone from his pocket and pressed the appropriate digits. He leaned against a wall ensuring he was out of view of the main flow of tourist traffic. "I hope he is not indisposed." The telephone rang twice before it was answered.

"Can you talk?" Kurvesh asked.

"Yes," Kwok replied.

"I hope the telephone did not draw too much attention."

"No. The ringer was off."

Kurvesh paused for a moment trying to understand what Kwok meant. He then realized the cellular phone had a pulsing action which vibrated to indicate a call. "Do you have any news to report?"

"No. The Turkish agent and her friend have spoken to most of the tour guides, but no one seems to recognize the man in the photo."

"It is not right. We must be missing something. Stay with them and let me know what they do." Kurvesh terminated the call and replaced the telephone in his pocket.

"What now?" Seleng asked.
"We must think."

Inci stared at Quentin. "I suppose we have no alternative but to leave," she said.

"That's great but where will we go?"

"Back to the hotel or perhaps the restaurant. Maybe we missed something."

Quentin nodded and the two headed for the exit.

"Wait a minute," Quentin said. "Look, over there."

Inci gazed in the direction to which Quentin was pointing. "What is it?" she asked. "I do not see anything."

Further back the large Oriental had also stopped and was looking in the direction in which Quentin was pointing.

"Over there. In the corner," Quentin continued. "The video camera." It took Inci a moment to realize the point of Quentin's statement.

"Of course," she exclaimed.

"They normally record everybody that comes in. All we have to do is get a hold of yesterday's tape."

"Let me ask my friend, Maria. Perhaps she can help us." The two agents walked back into the large room and looked for Inci's friend. "She must be on her tour already."

"What are we waiting for?" Quentin said.

They walked in the general direction the tours were taking in anticipation of catching up to Maria. They were about to exit the main room and follow a hallway when a security guard approached them speaking in Turkish. Inci answered him and the two carried on a conversation. The guard waved them through, directing them to the party they were looking for.

"What was that all about?" Quentin asked.

"I explained we were part of the tour but because you had to go to the toilet we were left behind." She smiled as she spoke. "He gave me directions to find Maria."

"Thanks a lot."

The same guide stopped Kwok as he attempted to find Quentin and Inci. He, however, was not as fortunate as they had been. He did not know what to say and the guard escorted him back to the entrance.

As he watched Quentin and Inci disappear around the corner, he immediately removed his cell phone and called Davud Kurvesh.

"I believe they have made a discovery. They were about to leave the building when they spotted something. They turned around and raced down a hallway. Unfortunately I lost them. The security guard did not permit me to enter."

"Do you have any idea what they saw?" Davud Kurvesh asked. He was growing impatient.

"I do not."

Kurvesh tried to gather his thoughts in an effort to determine his next move. "You stay where you are. We will come toward you. Perhaps we will meet them. They cannot leave the building unless they pass by you, so do not leave your post."

Kwok complied and replaced his cell phone in his jacket pocket.

"There is Maria," Inci said, pointing to the tour group ahead. The twosome quickened their pace in an effort to catch up to the group of tourists being escorted around the beautiful artifacts of the Dolmabahçe Palace. Inci made her way through the crowd toward the front. Quentin stayed directly behind her, apologizing to people as they bumped their way through.

Maria smiled when she saw Inci approach. "You wish to be part of my group?" she asked, mockingly.

Inci smiled. "Not this time. We wish to know where they watch the videotapes that the security cameras record."

"I do not know. I am certain, however, one of the guards can help you." She looked around. "Come with me." She waved the group forward and as sheep would follow a shepherd, the tourists obeyed.

They entered a large room where a gigantic, crystal chandelier hung suspended from the ceiling by heavy iron chains. Beautiful, mahogany inlaid tables were lined along the walls accompanied by chairs and settees. In a distant corner of the room, resting against a wall beside an alabaster fireplace stood a security guard.

"Wait here," Maria said to Inci and Quentin. She walked to the security guard and spoke to him briefly. He acknowledged her request and seemed thankful for an opportunity to perform a different function.

Maria returned to the group. "Go with him," she said to Inci and Quentin. "He will take you to the area where they view the videos." She returned her attention to the group, and once again began to explain the importance of each relic in the historic palace.

Inci and Quentin walked toward the guard who smiled as they approached. She addressed him in Turkish and he replied in a heavily accented English, primarily for the benefit of Quentin.

"You walk with me," the guard said, and led them along the hallway past Maria and her group of tourists.

Maria smiled at Inci one last time, and Quentin found himself staring at a series of giant, hand painted urns depicting scenes which appeared to emanate from an Arabian Nights fantasy.

The guard led the two along a smaller corridor, which ended with a solid, brown, wooden door. The interesting part about this barrier was there was no handle on the outside. There was no visible method for anyone to gain admittance except from the inside.

"Why is the security so heavy here?" Quentin asked, as the guard knocked on the door.

He turned to face Quentin. "This palace is the most historical sight in all Turkey. We have most valuable artifacts which must be carefully guarded with great concern."

It took several seconds until a uniformed man opened the door. The two officials spoke in Turkish and moments later, Inci and Quentin were allowed entry into the room.

Although the chamber was part of the original palace, it had been recently redecorated with brown, grooved, wall panelling, dropped ceilings, and beige tiles. The walls of the room were lined with wooden bureaus totalling eight in number. Each desk had a person sitting before it, and seven of the eight had computer monitors or television screens placed on them. The last desk had a large switchboard and the person operating it had been outfitted with a telephone headset.

The guard who had escorted Inci and Quentin to the room bade them farewell and departed. Inci began to converse with the man who had admitted them into the security area.

After a few sentences, the uniformed official looked at Quentin and smiled. Inci introduced the man as Veli Kazim, and explained he was responsible for security within the palace.

Kazim made an effort to speak English. "Who is it you are looking for?" he asked.

Quentin was impressed and thought to himself that most people he had come in contact with in Istanbul spoke very good English. Quentin removed the photograph from his pocket and handed it to the guard.

"And why is it you are looking for his man?" Kazim asked.

"It is a matter of national security," Inci stated, in an official manner.

"Are you with the police?"

"No. We are with the United Nations." She removed her passport and showed the guard the page bearing the official seal of the United Nations. Unlike other crime fighting agencies, ISIS used agent's passports to display their credentials. This was done due to the international traveling involved.

Quentin also removed his passport and held it for Kazim to see. The man appeared impressed and acted as if he were suddenly involved in an international incident. "If you step over here, we can review yesterday's tape." He guided Inci and Quentin to a desk staffed by a young woman. In front of her were three small television monitors, each showing different views of the entrance lobby.

Kazim continued his explanation. "This is where we watch and videotape all the people who come into our building. Over here," he said, pointing to the next desk, "is the exact same equipment. We use it as a back up."

"Do you have a lot of criminal activities?" Quentin asked, wondering about the in-depth security system.

"We do not. We wish to make certain that we can watch anything which might occur."

The lady sitting at the desk spoke in Turkish to the guard. He studied the screen and replied. Suddenly, Inci leaned forward and stared at one of the small monitors.

"What's going on?" Quentin asked.

"She says a man has been standing for a very long time in the entrance," Kazim replied.

Quentin leaned forward and squinted in an effort to see the small figure in a distant corner of the entrance foyer. The monitors were fairly large in size; however, because the subject was so far away, it made him appear small. He looked Oriental and quite heavy. Inci and Quentin's thoughts paralleled and they both looked at each other. Without saying a word, each of them knew the other was wondering, if this stranger was the same man who had made inquiries about Thomas Sun in the restaurant the day before.

The two agents continued to study the monitor, but unfortunately the detail was not clear enough for them to be able to recognize the man again elsewhere. The fact that the monitor displayed in black and white also did not help the situation. Quentin noted the man was wearing a dark turtleneck sweater, a jacket, which appeared to be plaid, or tweed, and dark slacks. His short hair gave his head an obese appearance. Quentin filed the information away for later.

Kazim spoke again in Turkish to the lady sitting at the desk.

"We will keep an eye on him and see what he does." The guard walked to a shelving unit, located in a corner of the room and removed a videotape. He brought it back to the desk and touched several keys on a videotape recorder causing a cassette to be ejected. He removed it and replaced it with the one he had just retrieved.

"This is the tape from yesterday afternoon. We will use the back up system to monitor today while you review yesterday's tape. The centre monitor is the one which will display the information." As he spoke he pointed to the middle monitor. The camera had been set up to capture the chest and face of people as they had entered the palace. For medium or long angles, the side monitors were used.

It took several seconds until the tape was rewound. The attendant stood and offered her chair to Inci. She left the room as Inci sat down.

"Are you certain this is all right," Inci asked, not wishing to seem abrasive.

"Yes, most certainly. She is going for a short break. If you need anything, please let me know." After engaging the system, Kazim returned to his desk. The tape began showing images of activity in the lobby of the Dolmabahçe Palace yesterday afternoon.

Quentin sat on the corner of the desk and watched the tape for several minutes. It did not take long for him to realize it would be a tedious effort to sit through three or four hours of video. His motivation was fuelled by the excitement of discovering whether Thomas Sun had entered the palace yesterday. They viewed the images for another few minutes and Quentin touched a small control speeding up the playback. The faces of the people entering the palace were still distinguishable but the motion saved some time.

After several minutes, the lady returned and insisted Inci remain in her seat. Kazim, who seemed to be in charge, returned to where the two agents were watching the videotape. "Would you like a cup of coffee?" he asked. "I am going to get some."

Inci and Quentin thanked him and accepted his offer.

"Just black for me, thanks," Quentin added.

The guard looked at Inci who asked for milk and sugar. He left the room and while Inci continued to glance at the screen Quentin leaned over to the monitor on the desk next to him and viewed the present action in the foyer of the palace.

"Look at this," Quentin said. He leaned over to Inci's videotape recorder and pressed the pause button. Studying the 'live' monitor they saw Kwok standing in a corner of the entranceway to the palatial estate. Two accomplices had now joined him.

It was very difficult for the two ISIS agents to make out the faces of the people. Neither Inci nor

Quentin recognized the three on the video screens before them.

"It could be coincidence. These people could have nothing to do with Thomas Sun," Quentin said.

"You don't really believe that," Inci replied. She studied the monitor closely, squinting slightly in an effort to obtain a better view. "This is mostly a tourist spot. People like these three do not normally come to visit here. It would also be very coincidental that they were here at the same time as us. It almost looks as if they are guarding the door waiting for something to happen."

Quentin nodded in agreement and turned his head when he heard a knock on the door behind him. One of the people sitting at the desk stood, walked to the door, and opened it. It was Kazim carrying a tray with Styrofoam cups each filled with steaming hot coffee. He walked to where Inci and Quentin were sitting.

"Any luck?" the guard asked. He noticed they had paused the videotape recorder and were staring at the one showing the live images of events taking place in the entranceway in the lobby of the Dolmabahçe Palace.

Quentin answered Kazim's question. "We noticed the man, pointed out earlier, has been joined by two others. We were wondering if they were perhaps involved in our activities."

"Well that is easy enough to determine." Kazim turned to the lady sitting in front of the telephones and spoke to her in Turkish.

"Perhaps," Quentin interrupted. "Perhaps if we leave them alone, we can discover what they're up to."

Veli Kazim paused a moment, contemplating Quentin's request. He nodded and again spoke in Turkish to the telephone attendant.

He turned his attention to Inci and Quentin. "We will watch them closely, as you requested."

Inci and Quentin resumed their scanning of yesterday's tape. Again they used the fast forward control to save a little time. The coffee tasted good and seemed to satisfy a craving that was developing in the back of Quentin's throat.

After what seemed an eternity, Quentin thought he recognized something on the videotape.

"Stop!" Quentin said, reaching for the proper control on the recorder. He rewound the machine slightly and again put it into play mode.

"What is it?" Inci asked.

"I thought I saw someone who looked like Sun."

As they replayed the tape Quentin realized he was wrong. It was an Oriental tourist but there was no resemblance to Thomas Sun.

As time continued, there were several more false warnings, mostly as a result of Quentin's enthusiasm.

"Wait a minute," Inci said. "Back up a little."

Quentin halted the controls of the video

cassette recorder. This time as they approached the face of the person they were looking for, Quentin agreed there was an extreme similarity between the image on the monitor and the photograph of Thomas Sun, which he had now placed on the desk.

Using the shuttle control Quentin forwarded frame by frame and paused when he had the clearest possible picture of the man who resembled the photograph. Inci picked up the photo from the desk and held it beside the monitor.

"It's got to be him," Quentin said. "Even the suit looks the same."

Kazim overheard the two ISIS agents and stepped closer. "That does look very much like the photo." He also studied both images simultaneously and nodded his head in confirmation. "Let me print the image. We have a high resolution printer which will give you very good quality."

In a corner of the desk was a keyboard affixed to a small monitor. He entered several commands and a message appeared on the screen, indicating the image had been sent to a printer. "It will take a few moments."

There was a tremendous amount of enthusiasm building up within Quentin. The earlier despair had now been turned into excitement because a potential dead-end had been avoided. Inci shared Quentin's feelings and waited anxiously for the printer to complete its task.

Kazim walked to a corner where the small printer was feeding a sheet of paper into the output tray. He picked it up, studied it carefully, and walked back to Quentin and Inci. He placed the printer's product on the desk directly beside the photograph of Thomas Sun.

"Looks like a good match to me," Quentin said.

"I agree," Inci added.

Kazim also nodded in agreement.

"Do you know what time this would have been taken?" Quentin asked.

Kazim studied the tape and the controls on the videotape recorder. "Four-forty-five, yesterday afternoon."

It suddenly occurred to Quentin that their new-found lead had only confirmed what they thought they already knew. It gave them no indication of Thomas Sun's whereabouts nor his reason for coming to the Dolmabahçe Palace. A sinking feeling worked its way into Quentin's stomach when he realized they once again faced a dead end.

"Let us scan this tape on the other monitor to see if your suspect was alone." Kazim activated a few controls and the tape spun backward, rewinding to a point prior to Thomas Sun's entry into the palace.

"There!" Kazim said, as he pointed to the screen. "There is a man with him."

Inci and Quentin watched the tape as Thomas Sun stepped through the security system at the entrance to the palace and greeted a man who was waiting for him on the other side. He seemed quite pleased to meet his counterpart, a dark haired man dressed in a light coloured, knitted, turtleneck sweater covered with a dark, three quarter length jacket.

He greeted Thomas Sun with a firm handshake and the two wandered into the crowds at the Palace, each looking carefully behind and around to ensure they were not being followed.

"Why don't we scan ahead and see when they leave," Inci said.

Kazim made a note of the tape's position on a piece of paper. He left the two agents the task of searching on the small monitor before them.

It was still a tedious process and while Inci scanned the monitor, Quentin returned his attention to the other desk viewing live transmission. The three men remained in the same place as before, each of them scanning tourists leaving the complex.

He returned his attention to Inci who was still searching the tape. Suddenly the screen went blank. "What happened?" Inci asked.

Quentin noticed the machine had gone into rewind mode. "I think we have come to the end of the tape."

Inci looked around for Kazim and spoke to him in Turkish. The man replied and Inci translated to Quentin. "He said the doors close at five o'clock and that is why there is nothing else on the tape."

"Is there another way out of here?" Quentin asked.

"There are many ways but they are not moni

tored. We are only concerned with the main entry, as that is the way most people come in. Every other door has a guard posted at it."

"So there's no way out unless..." Quentin's word trailed off as the thought occurred to him.

"Unless what?" Inci asked.

"Unless they had an accomplice."

"That is a very strong accusation," Kazim said, defensively. We perform a detailed screening process for all our employees."

It was evident that Quentin had upset Kazim, for he was responsible for security at the Dolmabahçe Palace.

"Let's go back to the location on the tape where they first entered the palace," Quentin directed.

Kazim touched a few buttons and the machine spun into rewind, stopping at the exact location of the co-ordinates noted on the sheet of paper. Quentin paused the recorder at the best possible view of Thomas Sun's accomplice.

"Do you think we could print this out and see if we can get a better resolution?" he asked.

"Yes," Kazim said. He again stepped to the keyboard, entered a few digits, and walked to the printer. He waited several seconds and removed the sheet of paper, returning to where Inci and Quentin were sitting. He handed the image to Quentin who stared at it blindly, not knowing what to look for.

Kazim looked at Quentin. "Will you be requiring anything else?" It was evident to Quentin that his manner had changed. He was no longer the friendly person he had once been, largely due to Quentin's suggestion that one of his men could somehow be involved. Quentin felt badly, but it was a logical assumption and one he had not yet discounted.

The woman whose desk they were using, spoke in Turkish, addressing her superior. Kazim replied and stepped to the desk where Quentin had laid the second print. Inci also rose from her chair and leaned over. The man responded as he picked up the printed image of Thomas Sun and his accomplice.

"What's going on?" Quentin asked.

"This lady says the man looks familiar," Inci replied.

Quentin listened attentively to the Turkish conversation of which he understood not a word.

Kazim rubbed his chin and pondered what appeared to be a question put to him by his subordinate.

"It is possible," he said, speaking slowly.

Quentin was keen to know what was going on and was glad the man had again reverted to English.

"Who do you think it is?" Quentin asked.

"Aynur thinks this looks like someone who worked here about a year ago. It seems she is quite possibly correct."

"Who might that be?" Quentin asked, with

enthusiasm.

"It would have been Ibrahim Trohak. He worked as a guard on a lower floor, near the back of the building." As the man spoke, he realized what was going through Quentin's mind. He felt that perhaps the young ISIS agent had been closer to the truth when he raised suspicion on one of the Dolmabahçe Palace guards.

"Where does that door lead?" Quentin asked.

Kazim thought for a moment before answering. "It leads to our shipping and receiving area."

"Would it be possible for us to exit that way?" Quentin asked, hoping to speak with the guard on duty, at the same time avoiding the three men in the lobby who perhaps were trailing Inci and himself.

"Yes, of course," Kazim replied, in a more pleasant tone.

"Do you have an address for this Ibrahim Trohak?" Inci asked, pointing to the accomplice in the photo.

"I will see." Kazim walked to a desk occupied by a younger man. Inci and Quentin watched as the man seated behind the desk rose and walked to a row of filing cabinets. He opened several drawers and flipped through a series of file folders, extracting one and handing it to his superior.

Kazim returned and spoke to Inci in Turkish. She grabbed a pencil from the desk and wrote down the information he gave her.

Kazim handed the file folder to the clerk and motioned for Inci and Quentin to accompany him. "I will take you myself."

The threesome left the security of the administration office and followed the guard along carpeted hallways, down a flight of stairs, and into an area not visited by tourists.

They met a uniformed man guarding an exit, which led to the shipping and receiving docks. Kazim spoke in Turkish to the guard and the two carried on an in-depth conversation. Inci and Quentin were too far away to understand any of the words. Moments later Kazim motioned them to accompany him through the doors. "He says he saw no one fitting the description I gave him."

Inci and Quentin thanked Kazim for his time and the assistance he had given them. They continued past the loading dock and down a short flight of concrete stairs, which led to an exterior ramp at the side of the palace.

The sky was blue and the sun was shining brightly as seafaring traffic made its way over the Bosporus toward the Sea of Marmara. Inci and Quentin walked along a large, wrought iron fence interspersed with white, ornate, concrete pillars.

"I hope this leads to something," Quentin said. Inci agreed. "I wonder who those three men in the foyer are?"

"I do not know, but if they were following us we have, how you say, given them the slip."

The two ISIS agents smiled as they left the

grounds of the Dolmabahçe Palace to continue their search for Thomas Sun, and follow up what appeared to be a substantial lead.

7. Missing

Inci and Quentin raced from the grounds of the Dolmabahçe Palace glancing over their shoulders to ensure they were not being followed by the three men who appeared to be waiting for them at the front entrance of the palace. There was still a line up at the gate as they made their way through the crowd of tourists.

In the parking area they hailed a cab and instructed the driver to take them to the address they were given. She added a few more sentences in Turkish causing Quentin to curiously stare.

"I asked him if he knew where this address

was," Inci said, as if reading Quentin's mind.

"How far is it?"

"Not far. Maybe twenty minutes."

Quentin paused a moment before speaking again. "I'm puzzled about those three guys?"

"I am also," Inci confirmed, shaking her head. "I wonder if there is someone else tracking Thomas Sun?"

"Or us," Quentin added.

"But why?"

"I don't know. It doesn't make any sense."

The taxi sped along the streets of Istanbul coming to a halt at a red traffic light. The driver engaged his turn signal and turned into a smaller, less populated street. He slowed the vehicle and carefully studied the numbers on the houses, stopping when he arrived at a four-storey apartment building, the top of which was still under construction.

Quentin looked around. "Why are none of these buildings finished? There seems to be a lot of construction."

"There is always construction in Turkey," Inci replied. "People do not have to pay taxes on their house until it is complete. That is why the top floor of buildings is always unfinished."

"Sounds like a good deal," Quentin replied.

The two agents left the taxi and walked toward the white, stucco building. Quentin looked up and noticed each balcony was outfitted with a miniature satellite dish. He smiled at the irony of poverty meeting luxury.

There was no directory of occupants, and Inci and Quentin walked to the first door. Inci banged hard on the worn, wooden door and waited patiently until finally the handle turned and an older woman, visibly placing a kerchief over her head, answered. Inci spoke to her in Turkish and Quentin knew from her expression that she would not be able to help them. Quentin removed the printout from his pocket and handed it to her. Again she nodded her head and closed the door quickly.

"One down, twenty to go," Quentin commented.

"Let us try the next one," Inci said, as she moved along the hall. Again she knocked on the door and waited for someone to answer.

A dark haired man in his mid-forties answered the door and nodded. His eyes squinted as the smoke from a cigarette in his mouth trailed upward slightly irritating his eyes.

Inci asked him if he had seen the whereabouts of Ibrahim Trohak. The man shook his head and closed the door.

"People are not too friendly here, are they?" Quentin said.

"People do not like to talk to strangers, especially ones that ask questions."

They continued their search covering the entire first floor, then walking up the stairs to the second. As they knocked on the last door, a young child, a boy of about ten, greeted them. His hair was short and his large, brown eyes looked up at the two strangers standing before him.

Inci smiled at the youth. She spoke to him in Turkish and he shook his head. She spoke several more words and the boy replied.

Quentin knew something was going on. "What is it?" he asked.

Inci turned and looked at him. "He says Trohak was here and left about twenty minutes ago."

Quentin felt his heart beating rapidly. "Ask him if he was alone." Inci turned and addressed the boy.

Quentin's heart pounded even faster when the boy nodded in response to her question. He rapidly removed the picture of Thomas Sun and held it out for the boy to see.

As the youth nodded, the door was suddenly opened further and an unshaven, dishevelled looking man appeared. He shouted at the boy, ordering him to disappear into the confines of their residence, as he confronted Inci and Quentin. Inci spoke to the man. He began shouting and screaming and slammed the door, causing the walls to vibrate.

"Let me guess," Quentin said. "He's never heard of him." Inci smiled. "Let me try again," Quentin said, and he stepped to the door banging on it with the side of his fist. They waited patiently, but no one came. Again Quentin hit the door with his hand, this time using his knuckles.

A moment later, the door swung open and

the man stood face to face with Quentin. It took a second before Quentin realized the man had an automatic pistol in his hand and was pointing it in the direction of the young ISIS agent.

Quentin was shocked by the action and froze. Inci spoke and the man began to scream.

"Just a minute," Quentin said. "We don't want any trouble."

The man, realizing Quentin spoke English, stopped his shouting and stared at the dark haired youth.

"If you want no trouble why you here?" he asked, speaking in broken English.

"We are looking for this man." Quentin held up the picture of Thomas Sun for the man to see. "We are not with the police."

"I not care who you with. You go or I shoot."

There was something about the way the man spoke which convinced Quentin the time for them to leave had arrived. Until this point, the chase had been a game. The introduction of the firearm, however, had suddenly made it apparent how real and dangerous the situation was becoming.

Inci held her hands up, palms facing the scruffy, overweight, unshaven man, indicating she wanted no trouble. The two agents departed, backing away from the angry individual standing in the doorway. They raced down the stairs and did not stop until they were outside.

"Wow!" Quentin said, sighing as he spoke. "I wonder what that was all about?"

"I guess it is safe to say that he is acquainted with Ibrahim Trohak." Inci paused and looked around. "If only we had skipped breakfast, we might have caught him."

"Hindsight is always twenty-twenty," Quentin said. He paused in an effort to determine what their next move should be. He was just about to speak when Inci interrupted his thoughts.

"Wait a minute," she said. "I have an idea." She walked to the curb and looked in both directions.

"Hey," Quentin said. "Hold on a minute." He stepped quickly to join Inci and the two agents walked across the street in the direction of a man selling roasted chestnuts.

Inci approached the street-side vendor and asked him several questions. After a short conversation, she turned to Quentin. "Where are the photographs?"

Quentin removed the photograph and printout from his pocket and handed them to her. Inci showed them to the vendor who nodded his head and waved his arms as he spoke. Inci turned to Quentin. "He saw him a few minutes ago."

"Which way did he go?" Quentin asked, enthusiastically.

Inci again turned to the vendor and asked him the same question, speaking in Turkish. The man replied and Inci relayed the information to

Quentin. The vendor spoke no English, but smiled at Quentin who returned the greeting. Inci continued the conversation as Quentin removed some change from his pocket. The man pointed in a direction other than the one from which the two agents had come and Inci looked puzzled as she followed the man's finger. She spoke a few more words and pointed, giving Quentin the impression that she was confirming the directions.

At the termination of the conversation, Quentin handed the man the change and motioned to the chestnuts. The man smiled, nodded, and proceeded to scoop a dozen or so of the small, brown, roasted nuts, placing them in a white paper bag, and handing them to Quentin.

"We have to go to the main street," Inci said.

"What was all that about?" Quentin asked.

"The man says Trohak and Sun were definitely there. He remembers them because he saw them yesterday running across the street into the building. Today when they came out, they drove in the opposite direction." She pointed down the street.

"Isn't that away from Istanbul?"

"Yes. As a matter of fact it leads to the small town of Pendik."

"What's in Pendik?" Quentin asked.

"Nothing I am aware of." As Inci spoke, an idea came to her, causing her deep-blue eyes to open wide, and her mouth to break into a grin. "Of course," she said, emphatically. "Why did I not think of this earlier?"

"What?"

"Pendik is a very small town where the ferry to Asia departs from." She pondered her own statement a moment before continuing. "If that is where they have gone, then they are leaving Istanbul and heading inland."

"Why would they do that?" Quentin asked. "Istanbul has thirteen million people. It seems to me it would be a lot easier to hide in a city of that size rather than in small villages."

"You are correct except for one thing," Inci said. Quentin waited for her to continue. "There is an imaginary border between east and west Turkey known as Cappadocia. People on the east are mostly Kurds and have built up an extremely complicated network of terrorist groups. They are aided by Iraq and Iran and are responsible for most of the attacks in the Middle East."

"So what you're saying is if they make it to this... whatever the place is called,"

"Cappadocia," Inci interjected.

"Cappadocia, then we might as well kiss them goodbye."

"It will definitely be difficult to catch them. If they are hidden underground, we may never find them."

"Well I guess we'd better get moving," Quentin said. "What kind of car were they driving?"

Inci stopped. "I forgot to ask," she said,

softly, slightly embarrassed.

"Oh yeah," Quentin said, a hint of sarcasm in his voice. "I guess we'd better go back to your buddy."

The two retraced their steps to the vendor and as Inci asked the question, Quentin took the opportunity to eat some of the chestnuts.

"Let us go," Inci said, as she began walking along the sidewalk for the second time. Quentin followed, but not before commenting to the vendor on the superb quality of the chestnuts.

"It was a yellow Vauxhall," Inci said. "He recognized it immediately because it always sits in front of the building."

"Are you sure the chestnut vendor doesn't work for us?" Quentin said, smiling as he spoke. "He certainly seems to be doing a great job."

The two agents stood on the street corner and flagged the first taxi they saw. The car stopped and Inci slipped into the back, sliding across to leave room for Quentin. She asked the driver to take them to the ferry terminal in Pendik, adding they were in an extreme hurry.

The ride took less than twenty minutes and as they arrived, they noticed the heavy traffic on board the ferry, indicating it was about to leave. Inci quickly paid the driver and the two ran from the cab toward the ticket booth.

"It will leave any minute," Inci said, as she handed the agent enough money for two fares.

They hurried to a small gate, which led to

the ferry and began to panic when they saw the attendant close the barrier, denying entry to any other passengers. Inci began shouting at the attendant who returned her loud demands with several screams of his own. Quentin chuckled slightly as he watched the two continue their confrontation. He continued eating the remainder of his chestnuts and dug his hand into his jacket pocket, removing a twenty U.S. dollar bill. He held it out for the guard to see and as the man caught a glimpse of the money, he ceased his shouting match with Inci. He quickly glanced around, smiled at Quentin, and unlocked the gate, giving them entry to the ship.

"See how simple that was," Quentin said, smiling.

Inci shook her head in exasperation. "If I had done that, they would have put me in jail for bribery." Quentin smiled as they walked on board the vessel.

The ferry had two decks; one was reserved for cars and buses, the other for passengers. It was relatively small and only held about fifty automobiles. As soon as they boarded the boat, the horn blasted loudly, drowning out any conversation people were having.

"How long is the trip?" Quentin asked.

"About twenty minutes," Inci replied.

"I think we should check the cars first to see if they're here," Quentin suggested. Inci nodded and they walked straight ahead to the lower deck. Most of the passengers had gone upstairs to enjoy the view and perhaps have a sandwich.

The fumes from the boat were nauseating, and both Inci and Quentin felt despair as they failed to see the yellow Vauxhall.

"It's not here," Quentin said.

The two stepped quickly to the rear of the boat and looked at the shore, just as the boat began to make its way across the Sea of Marmara.

"Look!" Inci shouted, as she pointed toward the shore. "There he is."

Quentin followed Inci's finger and saw the yellow sedan backing away from a parking spot leaving the ferry terminal. Quentin slammed his fist on the guardrail as he stood helplessly, watching the shore grow smaller while the boat made its way across the channel.

"Do you think he was on to us, and led us here intentionally?" Inci asked.

Quentin shook his head. "I don't think so. I bet if we look around this boat, we'll see Thomas Sun."

"Do you think he dropped him off?"

"What other reason would he have for driving down here and then leaving?"

Inci pondered Quentin's statements and agreed. "Let us look for him then."

They walked up a set of steel stairs, which led to the passenger level. The boat appeared well worn and had been in use for many years. The floors were steel plates, which had been painted a bright orange. The green wooden walls were once new but had suffered from deterioration. People stood along the railing and glanced out over the water at the disappearing shoreline. Minarets were silhouetted against the bright, late morning sun.

Inci and Quentin did a quick tour around the outside of the deck then stepped through the glass doors to the inside cabin.

The seating area was small and packed with passengers, most of whom were enjoying a noon day meal. The smell of food made Quentin realized he had not eaten much in quite a while. "Smells good," he said.

"Are you thinking of eating again?" Inci asked, shaking her head from side to side. "I have never seen anyone eat as much as you."

The two ISIS agents scanned the immediate vicinity and were slightly disappointed when they saw no sign of Thomas Sun. They stepped into the next room and again their search turned up nothing.

Suddenly, without warning, the ship's horn sounded, indicating the vessel had reached its destination.

"Let us line up so we can be off first," Inci said. Without waiting for an answer, she moved toward the front of the boat as it docked on the Asian shore of Turkey.

They continued to scan the crowds for any sign of Thomas Sun. Quentin sighed when they found no indication of his whereabouts. "I don't understand it," he said.

"Let us follow this through," Inci said. "Thomas Sun went to the Dolmabahçe Palace yesterday afternoon and met Ibrahim Trohak. The two of them evidently spent the night at Trohak's flat leaving this morning for Pendik where Trohak dropped Sun off. There would be no reason to do this other than to deliver Thomas Sun to the ferry. He must be on board somewhere." Her comments were interrupted by a loud crash as the metal exit ramp slammed onto the hard concrete of the dock. The gate opened and the passengers were allowed to disembark. There were about fifteen people ahead of Inci and Quentin, and the line moved rapidly.

"Look! Over there!" Quentin shouted, as he watched a young man jump over the railing onto the pavement and run through the crowd waiting to board the ferry. "It's him!"

Quentin did not wait for Inci to respond and he shoved his way through the line of passengers who cursed at his abrasive behaviour. Inci followed and, as they made it to the front of the line, the guard began shouting. He raised his hand, ordering them to stop.

Quentin had no intention of obeying the man and pushed him aside, using the full force of both of his hands. The two agents ran down the exit ramp and darted through the crowd who was now curiously watching the antics of the two ISIS agents.

"Do you see him?" Inci asked, running desperately to keep up with Quentin.

"No!" Quentin shouted, as he ran.

"There he is!" Inci yelled. Quentin stopped

and looked in the direction she was pointing.

Thomas Sun was running across the paved parking area toward a waiting car. The door was open and two men were standing beside it. Quentin charged in the direction of the parked vehicle, jumping over several small, concrete barriers. Inci followed as best she could, trying to keep up with the athletic, Australian agent.

As Thomas Sun neared the parked vehicle, Quentin yelled his name. The Oriental halted, turned in the direction of Quentin, and continued running toward the automobile.

Quentin suddenly stopped when he saw the two men, next to the vehicle, remove firearms from within their jackets and point them in his direction.

"Get down!" Quentin yelled, directing his comments to Inci.

The Turkish agent saw what was happening and immediately fell to the ground, rolling in the direction of a metal waste container. Quentin did the same and as he found security behind a stack of wooden crates, he heard the loud snap of the gun as it released its projectile in his direction.

A second shot was fired, followed by a third. The crowd became aware of the gunshots and began to scream in unison. People scattered in all directions. When Inci and Quentin decided it was safe to surface, they saw the grey automobile speed off in a southerly direction.

Inci ran toward Quentin. "Are you all right?"

Quentin nodded his head. "Yes I'm fine."

"We have to follow them."

Quentin glanced around. "Come with me," he ordered.

He led Inci back to the line-up of passengers waiting to board the ferry. Most of the pedestrian crowd had vanished when the gunfire broke out. People in cars appeared terrified and squirmed when they saw Quentin approach.

He walked up to a small, white car, grabbed the door handle, and violently opened the door. "Get out!" he shouted. The owner of the vehicle, a young man slightly smaller than Quentin, spoke in Turkish but did not leave his car. "Look. I don't have time for this." Quentin grabbed the man by the shoulder and pulled him from the vehicle. "You'll get your car back," he said, as he jumped in the driver's seat. He backed the car and waited for Inci to enter. Her door was still partially open when he accelerated the vehicle, nearly running over its owner who shouted loudly and waved his arms frantically.

"Let us add car theft to our long list of problems," Inci said.

"Hey, what can I do, we have to get him, don't we?" Quentin said, relaxing slightly as the car sped away from the paved parking area, following the direction taken by the grey car and Thomas Sun.

"He must have known we were following him," Inci said, as she reached for a pack of cigarettes from her jacket pocket. Quentin glanced quickly at the movement, not wanting to take his eyes from the road for any length of time.

"If you're going to do that, open the window." Quentin shook his head.

"In Turkey, everyone smokes."

"I guess Trohak must have had a cell phone and the guy at the apartment called him as soon as we left."

Inci agreed. "That is something we must get." She glanced at the dashboard. "Do not drive too fast. We do not want to be stopped by the police. This is a stolen vehicle, remember?"

There was merit in her words. Quentin lifted his foot from the accelerator, allowing the car to slow to a reasonable speed. The adrenaline was flowing within him and he was caught up in the excitement of the chase. "Where does this road lead?"

"I believe it goes to Bursa."

"How far is that?"

"About one and one half hours."

Quentin nodded and continued to concentrate on his driving. "We have another problem," he said. "We're almost out of gas." He glanced in the rear-view mirror and saw no sign of other traffic

"Well, cops or no cops we've got to get them." Quentin accelerated the car to a speed far beyond the legal limit. He kept his eyes trained in front, constantly looking for the grey sedan and

Thomas Sun.

"What time is it?" Quentin asked, not daring to take his hands from the wheel.

"It is nearly two," Inci replied.

The vehicle sped through the countryside in a southward direction in search of the grey sedan. Another twenty minutes passed before Quentin noticed a small, amber light illuminate on the dash. Inci was staring out the front window and failed to notice the gasoline warning lamp.

"Is that it?" Inci asked, as she leaned forward squinting slightly. "That looks like a grey car up ahead."

"I think you're right," Quentin confirmed.

"How much gas do you think we have?" Inci asked.

"I would guess another twenty minutes, half an hour maybe."

"It will be very close. We are sixty kilometres from Bursa."

"Is Bursa a large city?" Quentin asked.

"Yes. It is a very large resort town. People from Istanbul go there for skiing. The mountains attract a great number of tourists."

Quentin looked in the direction of the mountains Inci was referring to and noticed their peaks were covered in snow. "I didn't expect snow in Turkey," he said.

"We always have snow in the winter, especially in the mountain region."

The two ISIS agents continued in pursuit of

the grey sedan and Thomas Sun. The car sped along and Quentin emitted a sigh of relief when they entered the city limits of Bursa. A headache was developing from his intense concentration on driving. He did not want to be spotted by the grey sedan they were following. "I don't think they know we're behind them," he said.

Inci agreed and lit another cigarette in an effort to relieve stress. She was glad the cars were beginning to slow as they entered the more populous area of the city. "Look," she said. "They are turning."

The grey sedan turned into a narrow side street. Inci and Quentin looked on in curiosity. Quentin slowed slightly so as not to arouse suspicion. Suddenly, without warning, their stolen car fell silent as the engine stopped running.

"Well, I guess that's it," Quentin said, as he guided the coasting car to the side of the road. "From here on, we go on foot."

The two left the vehicle and walked quickly to the spot where the grey automobile had turned. They stopped, peered down the narrow, winding street and smiled as they realized it was a private driveway which led to a hotel.

"I guess they're going to spend the night," Quentin said.

"We should telephone the office and see what they can tell us about Ibrahim Trohak."

"There's a store over there," Quentin said, as he pointed along a set of stairs, which led to another road. "I'm going to buy some aspirin and get the license plate number of the grey sedan. Why don't you check in and I'll join you shortly."

"Are we planning to spend the rest of the day here?" Inci asked.

"I don't see why not. I'm starving and tired."

"You are always starving." Inci laughed as she spoke. "It will be easier if we get one room," Inci said. "I will make sure it has two beds."

Quentin laughed. "This could turn out to be fun after all," he said, jokingly.

Inci rolled her eyes and walked toward the lobby of the hotel, being careful not to remain visible. She was not certain if Thomas Sun or his accomplices had seen her or Quentin long enough to recognize them again, but did not wish to take any chances.

Quentin took the stairs and walked down a small, narrow path, which led to a main thoroughfare, bordered by several stores. He immediately saw a pharmacy and purchased aspirin, a bottle of drinking water, and a chocolate bar. He returned in the direction of the hotel and thought that perhaps he should have bought a chocolate bar for Inci. Rather than waste time by returning to the store, he decided to devour his and not tell her.

As he neared the stairway, he glanced in the parking lot and could not believe his eyes. The grey sedan was no longer parked in the spot where it had been only minutes before. He shook his head slightly and scanned the area. Perhaps he was mistaken, perhaps it had been parked somewhere else. No, it was definitely gone. An empty spot was all that Quentin could focus on.

Quentin raced down the steps, ran between parked cars, and made his way toward the lobby of the hotel. He did not see Inci and assumed she had already checked in.

He approached the desk and was greeted by an attractive, young woman with long, black hair dressed in a blue, hotel uniform.

"Excuse me," he said, slightly out of breath from his quick jaunt through the parking lot. "I'm looking for my friend. She checked in a few minutes ago."

"What is her name?" the attendant asked.

"She would have booked the room under Arzu."

The girl behind the desk entered the information on a keyboard and waited momentarily for the computer to respond. "I have no one registered by that name."

"You must have. She was here just a few seconds ago. She has reddish, brown, shoulder length hair, wore blue jeans, a white shirt, and a brown jacket."

"Ah," the girl explained. "I remember her. But she did not check in. She was talking to several men and they left together."

"They left together?" Quentin asked, slightly confused. "Did she appear to be struggling?"

"It is not for me to say."

"What do you mean, not for you to say. Was she struggling or wasn't she?"

"She did not appear to be. Is there anything else I can help you with?" the attendant asked, slightly irritated by Quentin's abrupt manner.

"Was this one of the men she spoke with?" He removed the photograph of Thomas Sun from his pocket.

The girl nodded.

"Thank you for your help." Quentin walked away from the desk and stood facing the exit doors of the hotel lobby. He was totally dumbfounded and had no idea what his next move would be. He felt a wave of nausea race through his stomach as he thought of Inci trapped by terrorists who, quite possibly, were responsible for the murder of two hundred and thirty people aboard a TWA airliner.

8. Fear

Seleng, Kwok, and Davud Kurvesh waited patiently in the foyer of the Dolmabahçe Palace. "It has been a long time," Kurvesh said, after checking his watch. "You are certain they went in there?"

Kwok nodded confirmation.

"I find it difficult to believe they have not come out."

"Perhaps they left through another door," Rudy Seleng said.

Kurvesh thought a moment and nodded his head in agreement. "It is quite possible. If that is the case, however, they would have had help from inside."

"I wonder who could have helped them?" Seleng asked.

Davud Kurvesh leaned against a wall and rubbed his chin as he pondered the question. His eyes never once left the crowd entering and leaving the entranceway to the palace. "If they left by another door, they must have passed a security guard. That is where they would have received help. He paused a moment. "Let us check with the sentries at each door. There cannot be that many."

Kwok and Seleng agreed with their leader's recommendation.

"I would like you to wait here, Mr. Kwok." The expression on Kwok's face showed displeasure at the suggestion; however, he knew better than to challenge the demands of his superior.

"Let us go." Davud Kurvesh hurried off and was followed closely by Rudy Seleng. They were careful to stay hidden from the guides, as unescorted jaunts throughout the palace were strictly forbidden. They attached themselves to a tour group climbing the grand staircase. Although they had become part of the group, they heard none of the commentary spoken by the guide.

At the first opportunity, Davud Kurvesh motioned to Seleng and they darted into a small chamber which led to a larger room. They were careful to tiptoe gently over the parquet floor to avoid making any unwanted noises.

They bypassed the doors they had checked

earlier and were confronted by one which led to the shipping and receiving area. Davud Kurvesh approached the security guard and inquired about two people who might have passed through the exit recently.

The guard questioned the intentions of the men confronting him, but was soon intimidated by Davud Kurvesh's loud voice. The guard, in a muster of strength, opposed Kurvesh and told him to get lost.

The Turkish mercenary leaned forward and in a split instance removed the semiautomatic pistol from the guard's holster. "I will ask you one more time," he said, calmly. "Did two people pass here in the last few hours?"

The guard, stunned by the action and the sight of the weapon, began to tremble and nodded his head slowly.

"Were they a man and a woman?"

Again the guard nodded. His eyes were trained on the firearm, which was pointed directly at his stomach.

"Do you see how simple it is when you cooperate?" Kurvesh asked, sarcastically. "Where did they go?"

"I... I do not know," the guard stammered. The expression on the man's face confirmed he was telling the truth.

Seleng stood by and watched blankly as his superior spoke in Turkish to the guard. He was also shocked by the sight of the gun, for he did not expect Davud Kurvesh to use force in a place as public as this. Surely, he thought, his superior knew one gunshot would bring dozens of guards upon them.

"Was anyone with them?" Davud Kurvesh continued his interrogation.

The guard paused before speaking, knowing he was contradicting the duties he had been trained for. "Yes," he said slowly.

"Who?" Kurvesh's voice indicated impatience and the guard sensed anger. He thought it best to answer quickly.

"My superior," he said, timidly, focusing on the small weapon, which remained pointed at his stomach.

"And where might we find your superior now?"

"In his office."

Davud Kurvesh paused a moment to contemplate his next action. "Take us there," he ordered.

The guard was slightly hesitant but when Kurvesh pushed the barrel of his pistol into the soft, sponginess of the guard's oversized stomach, he decided to reconsider any act of bravery which might have crossed his mind.

The three men walked along the hallway and through a double set of wooden doors. Davud Kurvesh had secured the gun in his belt under his jacket. The guard was perspiring and his blue, uniform shirt showed signs of dampness in the centre of his back.

They arrived at the door, which led to the administration and security area visited earlier by Inci and Quentin.

"How does one enter?" Kurvesh asked, realizing there was no handle on the outside of the door.

"You knock two times and then three," the guard said, nervously. "Please, I beg you," the guard said, trembling, "do not let my boss know that I led you here. He will surely fire me and I need this job."

Davud Kurvesh studied the guard's face a moment and nodded his head, indicating the man return to his post.

Kurvesh and Seleng waited for the guard to leave the immediate vicinity and Seleng was the first to speak. "What did he say?" he asked, not having understood any of the Turkish spoken between the two men.

Davud Kurvesh relayed an abridged version of the conversation. Kurvesh knocked twice, paused a moment, and knocked three more times. It was only a moment before the door was opened by one of the young ladies inside the room.

Kurvesh sprang forward causing the wooden door to make contact with the woman's forehead. The two men leapt through the opening with Kurvesh's gun poised, ready for action.

"Freeze!" Kurvesh yelled, as he quickly surveyed the location of the people inside of the room.

The woman who had answered the door was nursing her wound, which bled slightly. Davud Kurvesh grabbed her by the shoulder and held a gun against her neck. "Who is in charge?" he asked, speaking forcefully.

"I am," Veli Kazim replied. "What do you want?"

Davud Kurvesh moved the gun and pointed it at the guard. "I want to know about the two agents that met with you earlier today."

"I have no idea what you are talking about," Kazim said, bravely.

"Do not tease me. You may think me a fool but I will not hesitate to use this weapon."

"If you use the weapon I will not be able to tell you anything," Kazim spoke in a commandeering way.

Davud Kurvesh smiled and slowly returned the muzzle of the gun to the neck of the girl whose arm he held tightly. "You are absolutely correct," he said, staring as he spoke. "I will therefore shoot this lady." The girl began to tremble sobbing loudly as the stress of the situation engulfed her.

Kazim did not speak and was debating if the armed terrorist before him was bluffing. His eyes were fixed on his opponent, the gun being held only two metres away. He was amazed at Kurvesh's calmness and noticed his face was void of emotion. Kazim could feel beads of perspiration forming on his forehead and knew if something did not happen soon, he would not be able to maintain his composure.

Davud Kurvesh spoke calmly to Kazim. "I will count to three and, believe me, I will not hesitate to shoot." There was something in the way he spoke which caused complete silence in the room. Everyone was stunned by fear. Davud Kurvesh uttered the first number and as he spoke, used his thumb to pull back the hammer of the automatic pistol in his hand. The action made a loud, clicking noise, which echoed as evening thunder would over a tranquil valley. Suddenly, the girl emitted an ear-piercing scream, which caused everyone, including Kurvesh, to jump slightly. Three of the other women in the room broke into tears. One of the men could also be heard sobbing softly.

"Two," Davud Kurvesh said, again speaking calmly. Seleng looked on as a spectator and wondered if his superior would risk being caught. It was a bluffing game. It was a game in which he had been involved several times in the past. He fully understood that the ability to remain calm was the key to a successful result.

Kazim did not move and continued to stare coldly at Davud Kurvesh. He felt his hands shake slightly as perspiration formed in the palms. He could feel a drop of sweat trickling down his forehead, then resting in the softness of his bushy, brown eyebrow.

Davud Kurvesh did not look away from the man's eyes. "Three," he said, and watched as

Kazim's eyes grew wide with fear and rage.

Kazim knew he had miscalculated his action and stared blankly as he heard the sound of the spring within the mechanism of Kurvesh's gun. The terrorist slowly squeezed the trigger.

"Wait!" the Turkish guard, shouted. His scream was drowned by the shuddering crack of the semiautomatic pistol as it released its killing projectile.

Davud Kurvesh instantly swung the gun around pointing it directly at Kazim who had instinctively taken a step toward him. He released his grip of the young woman and did not watch as her lifeless body fell to the floor beside him. Seleng could not believe his eyes and stared at the form lying motionless on the floor, a pool of blood rapidly forming at the side of her neck.

He had killed many times himself, but never found it an easy action to accept. He had been aware of Davud Kurvesh's sinister reputation of achieving his goals at all costs but he had never before witnessed the harsh, cold action the man was capable of.

The noise from the gunshot was a lot quieter than Seleng had expected. He realized Kurvesh had held the gun close to the girl's head muffling much of the sound. The action, however, caused a large exit wound, which left small particles of raw flesh scattered on the floor and against the wall creating a nauseous feeling in the stomach of Rudy Seleng.

"Now my friend, will you tell me what I want to know?" Kurvesh asked.

Kazim nodded and sighed deeply, knowing the two men who had entered the room were not to be underestimated. "Good. I ask you one more time. Who were the two agents who were here earlier?"

"They identified themselves as members of the United Nations organization known as ISIS."

Davud Kurvesh exchanged glances with Rudy Seleng. The name ISIS was unfamiliar to both of the men. "Go on," he ordered.

"They were looking for someone."

"Who were they looking for?"

"They showed us pictures. It was someone who came here yesterday. We checked the videos."

"Did they locate him?"

Kazim hesitated slightly before nodding his head.

"When was this?"

"Yesterday afternoon nearly five o'clock."

"Who was the man?"

"They showed me a photograph. It was a Chinese." Kazim paused a moment. "I do not know his name."

"What was the purpose of his visit?"

"I do not know," Kazim replied. He directed his gaze toward the lifeless form, lying on the ground and felt a sickening feeling develop in the pit of his stomach. "I have told you all I know. Please leave us alone. I cannot tell you anything about them. They left..." his voice trailed off when he realized he had slipped.

"What do you mean 'them'?" Davud Kurvesh asked, picking up on the guard's slip of the tongue. "How many were there?" The guard hesitated a moment. "Would you like me to pick someone who will be my next victim?" Kurvesh asked, glancing around the room at the sobbing individuals huddled closely together.

Kazim shook his head from side to side. "The Chinese was met by someone inside the palace."

"Who?" Again Kazim was silent. "Who?" Davud Kurvesh snapped.

The guard was slightly startled. "It was someone who used to work here."

"Then certainly you must have his name and address?"

Kazim walked to the desk behind him and lifted the file folder, which had not yet been returned to its filing cabinet. He read the name and address in a similar fashion as he had done to Inci and Quentin hours before.

"I would suggest you not telephone the police, for we will surely harm this lady." Davud Kurvesh directed his gun at a short, obese woman standing amid a group of her co-workers, huddled in a corner.

The terrorist took several steps in the direction of the terrified woman and held the gun against her temple. Kazim raised his hands, palms facing outward, in a gesture of surrender.

"Please do not harm anyone else. We will do as you say."

Davud Kurvesh took the woman by the arm and motioned her to accompany him and Seleng as they moved toward the door. Once out in the hallway, the two terrorists, accompanied by their hostage, made their way through hallways and antique-filled rooms toward the emergency exit in the shipping and receiving area.

The guard, who only moments earlier had showed them entry to the security and administration centre, confronted them. The uniformed man, upon seeing the sobbing woman, immediately knew something was amiss. "Now you have gone too far," he said, finding strength he had never been called on to use before.

"I think not," Davud Kurvesh said, as he pushed his gun into the woman's back.

The guard, upon seeing the movement, retracted his comments and opened the door for the gangsters and their hostage.

"If you call the police, she will not live to see them arrive." The guard knew he was not to take the words lightly. He dared not think of what might have caused this aggressive action.

The shipping area was void of people. It was not staffed unless necessary shipments arrived. "Get out of here!" Kurvesh shouted at the guard who was peering through the slightly open door. Upon hearing the shouts, the security guard immediately shut the door.

"We must hurry," Kurvesh said, addressing Seleng. "I am certain the fools will contact the police if they have not done so already." As he motioned for his accomplice to follow, he dragged the woman through the rear entrance of the shipping area, down a flight of stairs, and through the exterior door. He removed the cellular phone from his pocket and entered several digits.

"Kwok." He did not wait for a reply before continuing. "They are not here. Meet us at the main gate, immediately."

The woman was unaware that Davud Kurvesh had placed the gun in his trousers and continued her sobbing as she was led along a path through the serene gardens and sparkling fountains.

Crowds were still entering the palace, making it difficult for them to make their way to the exit. Both men kept looking for their accomplice, Wu Fung Kwok, but could not see him.

When they arrived at the gate, they casually strode past the guard. Davud Kurvesh squeezed the woman's arm tightly as she gestured toward the uniformed sentry.

"What has happened?"

Kurvesh and Seleng both turned in the direction of the voice of their comrade. Kwok emerged from behind a large, concrete pillar used in earlier times as a watchtower. "Who is she?" the Oriental asked.

"I will explain in the taxi."

As they neared the parking area, they raced for the first available cab. "Thank you so much for your hospitality," Kurvesh said mockingly, speaking to the fear-filled woman. He released his grip on her arm and she immediately rubbed the area where pressure had been applied. She stared into the eyes of her captor and displayed a mixture of hatred and fear. Davud Kurvesh expressed no emotion. "Go!" he ordered and did not wait for the woman to race back toward the gate.

The three men jumped in the taxi and were leaving the parking lot long before the woman was halfway to the sentry's guardhouse. "What has happened?" Kwok asked, concerned about the sudden change in events.

Seleng shrugged his shoulders. "I do not know. A great deal was said but none of it was in English."

Davud Kurvesh explained the events and the justification for them. Kwok nodded but showed no signs of emotion. Kurvesh explained how Inci and Quentin had gained information about Thomas Sun and his accomplice. He went on to say he had a name and address, and they were now on their way there. "I doubt very much if we will find Thomas Sun sitting there waiting for us, but as we have no other leads, it is our duty to go."

"Did you feel it was necessary to shoot the woman?" Seleng asked, still slightly shocked by the deed.

"We are professionals and we have a job to

do. If you feel it is too much for you, please advise me now and you will be relieved of your duties."

"No, no. Do not misunderstand me. I am in full compliance with what you have done. It is only because everyone spoke in Turkish, and I did not know what was happening that caused me to be confused."

"Let us speak no more of it." Davud Kurvesh slouched in the front seat of the taxi, relaxing slightly for the first time since the ordeal at the Dolmabahçe Palace had begun.

The taxi raced through the streets on the outskirts of Istanbul heading toward the home of Ibrahim Trohak. The driver slowed his vehicle as he studied the buildings in search of the address given him by Davud Kurvesh. When at last he found the building, he brought the taxi to a halt and waited for the man seated in the passenger seat to pay.

Kurvesh, Seleng, and Kwok entered the building cautiously, unaware of what unexpected dangers they might encounter. They had no idea where to begin and it was Kurvesh's idea to split the search into three, each of them taking one area.

"Be certain to always stay with visual range of each other."

It was evident by reactions encountered from the tenants that their search was becoming a nuisance. None of the three appeared concerned with the verbal abuse they received from the residents.

Davud Kurvesh's emotions were elated

when he was told by an older lady that he was the second person that day to inquire about Ibrahim Trohak. He felt he was on the right track, and knew the two ISIS agents could not be far ahead.

Kwok was the first to approach Ibrahim Trohak's apartment. He paused for a moment before knocking again and when at last someone did open the door, it was only by several inches. Kwok watched, as a face became visible through the small opening in the door. It took the mysterious inhabitant only a few seconds to realize the large, Oriental man in the hallway was looking for Ibrahim Trohak.

With a sudden force, the door was flung shut and Kwok was slightly stunned by the action.

"Here!" he yelled, quickly gaining the attention of Kurvesh and Seleng.

The two men rushed to his aid as Kwok was already forcing his massive weight in sudden jolts against the door.

After several attempts, the persistent barrier gave way and, with a loud, crashing sound, the Oriental was flung through the opening into the room beyond. Kurvesh instinctively drew his weapon and poised it ready for action. There was no one inside the small, sparsely furnished room. Kwok regained his balance and waited a moment for Seleng and Kurvesh to join him. The threesome walked stealthily into the room beyond.

Immediately upon entering they saw seated in a corner, a boy of no more than ten or eleven years of age. The child trembled at the sight of the three men, one of whom was pointing his firearm directly toward him. He said nothing and instinctively looked toward a window. Davud Kurvesh followed the child's gaze and realized the window was open as the white, lace curtains were blowing in the afternoon breeze.

"The window!" Kurvesh shouted. "Get downstairs immediately!"

Seleng bolted into the hallway, down the stairs, and on to the pavement. It took him a moment to realize the window was at the side of the building.

His leather soled shoes slipped on the concrete as he ran around the corner of the building. Regaining his balance he could see, off in the distance of the narrow, tree-lined street, the figure of a man running away from him.

"There he goes!" Davud Kurvesh yelled from the second story window. "Follow him. We'll join you."

With his excellent physical shape, Seleng was able to over take the Turk and wrestle him, face down, to the ground. The Filipino stood and lifted Trohak by the shoulders. There was little resistance as the Turk was well out of breath and bleeding from his injured nose and several cuts on his face. Rudy Seleng noticed a Beretta had slipped from Trohak's holster. He grabbed it and pointed it at the stomach of its owner. The gesture seemed to awaken the senses of the captive who decided to avoid any evasive action.

Seleng waited for Kurvesh and Kwok to appear on the scene. He saw the men running toward him and watched as they slowed their pace realizing the culprit had been captured.

"What is your name?" Kurvesh asked, as he arrived on the scene. There was no answer. "Why are you running away from us?" Kurvesh spoke calmly not really expecting a response. "We know your name is Ibrahim Trohak and we also know you assisted Thomas Sun." Kurvesh waited for a reaction and was not disappointed. The man, still held tightly by Rudy Seleng, looked up at the mention of his name. "Because Thomas Sun does not speak Turkish, I assume you can converse in English. If you assist us, we will be far more lenient with you."

The Turk raised his head and stared coldly at Davud Kurvesh, a gesture of defiance. He curled his lips slightly and spat directly into Kurvesh's face.

Davud Kurvesh felt anger form deep within the confines of his mind but knew that he would not allow himself to be pressured into responding. He had to control the situation at all costs. Slowly he wiped the foamy, spit from his cheek and smeared his hand on the green coat of Ibrahim Trohak. "Search him," he ordered, addressing Kwok.

The large-framed Oriental stepped closer to Trohak. He searched the pockets of the green, quarter-length jacket but found nothing more than several used tissues, a few coins, and a set of car keys. He checked the pockets of the blue denim jeans Trohak wore and after finding nothing, directed his attention to the ankles, in the event a weapon had been hidden under the jeans. Kwok handed the keys to Kurvesh who held them by their round ring, dangling them before the dark, tanned face of Ibrahim Trohak.

"Where there are keys, there must be an automobile," Kurvesh said. "I know you do not wish to help us but I am afraid I must insist. You will tell us everything we need to know. If you refuse, we will kill the boy in your flat." Kurvesh's words had penetrated Trohak's defences. He looked up at the mention of the boy. "Is it your brother, perhaps?" Kurvesh said tauntingly. "I am running out of patience. Where did you take Thomas Sun?"

Again Trohak refused to answer and continued to nurse the scrapings on his face. Seleng had not released his grip and was growing short on patience. He wished their captive would answer the questions. He had witnessed the potential destruction Davud Kurvesh was capable of.

"Kill the boy," Kurvesh ordered, directing his comment at Kwok.

The heavyset man, still slightly out of breath from the recent jog, nodded confirmation of his superior's request. He began to walk in the direction from which he had earlier run and had only gone two metres when Trohak yelled for him to stop.

"I will help you," Trohak said. "Do not hurt

my brother."

Kurvesh motioned for Kwok to return. He faced Trohak. "Where did you take Thomas Sun?" he said again.

"I drove him to the ferry terminal at Pendik."

"How long ago?"

"I returned no more than fifteen minutes ago."

"Do you have an automobile?"

"Yes."

"Take us to it."

Ibrahim Trohak led Kurvesh, Seleng, and Kwok in the direction of his flat. They walked briskly until. Trohak halted in front of the building and motioned to the yellow Vauxhall parked neatly beside the curb.

"This is your car?" Kurvesh asked, somewhat amused. Trohak nodded. "It is very bright." Davud Kurvesh lifted the handle on the door and was surprised the automobile had not been locked. "Get in!" he ordered to his accomplices.

Kurvesh entered the driver's side of the vehicle. Kwok joined him in the front seat and Seleng pulled Trohak into the rear, keeping the Beretta pointed at the man's stomach.

Kurvesh inserted the keys in the ignition and started the engine. He looked at Trohak and asked which direction. He pointed straight ahead; Kurvesh began to drive.

He knew the port of Pendik quite well, but was unfamiliar with the small suburban area where

Trohak's flat was. Once on the main road, he increased his speed, passing several automobiles as he made his way to the sea of Marmara.

The drive was uneventful and there was only a short line-up the ferry terminal. Glancing at his watch Kurvesh wondered when the next boat would depart.

"Wait here," he ordered and stepped from the car, walking toward the attendant's office.

He returned shortly and manoeuvred the car into the line-up, giving them access to the on-ramp. "It will be no more than twenty minutes," he said. "Who will be meeting Thomas Sun at the other side?" Kurvesh asked, turning around in his seat to face Ibrahim Trohak.

"I do not know." It was evident by the expression on Trohak's face he was not lying. "All I know is he is to be met by two men who were to deliver him to Central Anatolia."

Davud Kurvesh looked surprised. "That is quite a distance. Why would they take him there?"

"I have no idea."

"Are they driving directly there?"

"Again I do not know," Trohak said, then added, "Thomas Sun mentioned a long rest and a hot Turkish bath."

Kurvesh pondered the statement a moment. He was familiar with the area and had been to Bursa many times. The best Turkish baths were to be found in the Kervansaray Termal Hotel. "You have been most helpful and to show you we are decent men, we will not harm you." Davud Kurvesh smiled as he spoke. "I must, however, insist you lend us the use of your automobile."

Trohak was about to object when he quickly realized there was not much he could do.

"Let him go," Kurvesh ordered. Seleng stepped from the vehicle and pulled Trohak with him. He pointed the gun at his back and pushed the muzzle against him. "Go," he ordered. "Do not look back and do not stop." Trohak began to walk and picked up the pace as he realized he would live to see another day. He made his way across the street and disappeared among the buildings.

Seleng returned to the car, got in, and closed the door. "What's our plan now?" he asked.

"Now we go to Bursa," Kurvesh answered. "With luck we'll find Thomas Sun and the two agents."

"What are your plans for the agents?" Kwok asked with a teasing grin.

"Kill them, of course," he replied nonchalantly.

9. Abducted

Quentin stood dazed on the steps of the Bursa hotel. Looking out over the parking lot he desperately tried to figure out his next move. The evening air chilled him as he realized he was not sure what would be the best thing to do. Damn! He thought almost out loud.

He quickly decided to follow the grey sedan carrying Thomas Sun and his accomplices, as well as, Inci. Not knowing which direction to go didn't help matters but doing nothing wouldn't either. He headed toward the first of three cabs and said, "I need a cab and I only speak English."

The man smiled, "That is good, I too. Get in. I will drive you."

Relieved about the language barrier he got into the cab and said, "I need to rent a car, one with a cell phone ."

The driver thought a moment as he began to turn the car out of the hotel parking lot. "Ah," he said, as if an idea had just struck him. "I have a very good friend who will rent cars. For a small fee, he will also include a telephone."

Quentin smiled and nodded. "Please hurry."

The car sped along the narrow street, lined with ancient buildings and made its way to the bottom of the road. The driver slowed slightly and looked at a black and white police cruiser, parked randomly in the street. Two officers were huddled near a small, white vehicle, which had been abandoned by the side of the road.

Quentin slid down in his seat, even though he knew the police would not recognize him. He wondered if they realized the car had been stolen, or if they were merely concerned about someone abandoning their vehicle.

"It looks like trouble," the driver said, as he turned his vehicle onto the main street, leading to the centre of downtown Bursa.

"If someone were to leave Bursa by car, where would they go?" Quentin asked.

"It would depend on where they wish to go."

Quentin realized his question had been silly.

"What I mean is, if someone wanted to leave Bursa by car, in how many directions could they go?"

The cab driver thought a moment about the question before answering. "There are two main roads that lead from Bursa. One goes to Troy and the coast, the other to Ankara, the capital of our country."

Quentin sat back and tried to relax in the rear seat of the cab. His mind was tense and the thought of relaxation was a luxury to be reserved for later.

He decided to contact his father as soon as he had access to a telephone. He did not have a good feeling for the layout of the country, and made a mental note to investigate the geography of a country before any future mission.

He could see no reason for Thomas Sun to go to the coast. If he were meeting a ship, it would be easier to board it in Istanbul. Ankara, on the other hand, would take him into the centre of the country. Quentin contemplated his options and decided to head toward Ankara.

He had absolutely no idea what he would look for when he got to Ankara and felt certain the people he was pursuing were now beyond his reach.

His thoughts were interrupted when the taxi driver stopped the vehicle in front of a car rental lot. "You go in and ask for Samir," the driver said. "He will look after you." Quentin thanked the man and showed his gratitude by a sizeable tip. He left the cab, walked between parked cars, and entered a small, concrete block building. A middle-aged man, wearing a slightly stained white shirt and knitted necktie, sat behind an old wooden desk.

He smiled as Quentin entered the room, showing a large, dark gap where a tooth had formerly been. "English?" the man asked.

Quentin nodded. "Yes. Are you Samir?"

At the mention of his name the man rose from behind the desk and walked to greet Quentin, extending his hand in a friendly gesture. "I am Samir," he said, shaking Quentin's hand. "How may I help you?"

"I would like to rent an automobile, as well as a cellular telephone."

"Certainly sir. Will you be needing it for a long time?"

"A few days." Quentin paused a moment then added "I'm in a hurry."

"Of course." Samir realized the social aspect of this transaction was at an end and returned to his desk. He removed a sheet of paper from a drawer, picked up a pen, and began to write.

He asked Quentin the standard questions associated with car rentals and asked to see a his driver's license. Quentin obliged the man by removing his international license, as well as his Visa credit card. Again Samir smiled and thanked him.

It did not take long to process the information and the only formality seemed to be having his Visa authorized. Money is the main driving force in

Turkey, as it is everywhere in the world. Samir led Quentin into an adjacent parking lot and escorted him to a silver-grey, Opel Cadet. He opened the driver's door, slid into the seat and pushed a key into the ignition. After several attempts at starting the engine, the car began to purr. "The gasoline tank is full of fuel and the cellular phone is located in the glove compartment." Samir removed the portable cell phone to verify its existence.

"Would you happen to have a road map?" Quentin asked.

"But of course." The owner of the rental agency dashed back to the building and returned quickly as Quentin familiarized himself with the automobile.

"Here, I have a map of Bursa and this is one of western Turkey. I hope you will find them satisfactory."

"Yes. Thank you very much." Quentin placed the maps on the seat beside him. "Could you tell me the fastest way to the road to Ankara."

"But of course. You are on it," he said, pointing at the road in front of the agency. "This will take you to Ankara. It is E90."

Quentin thanked the man and slowly left the parking lot, driving as carefully as he could to avoid hitting other closely parked vehicles in the lot.

He made his way onto the main street and found the car very easy to manoeuvre. As he started driving, he realized the rental agency was on the outskirts of Bursa. The population grew sparse and traffic was less heavy as he continued on his journey.

As he left the city limits of Bursa, Quentin reached for the cellular phone and dialed the operator. He explained that he wanted to make a long distance call to England. He gave the operator his father's home telephone number and waited patiently while the connection was made.

"Hello." It was Lana's voice.

"Hi there," Quentin said, cheerfully. "Do you miss me?"

"Who is this?" Lana said, mockingly.

"Well that's nice. I'm not even gone two days and I'm already forgotten." Quentin chuckled as he spoke.

"How are you keeping?" Lana asked, when she recognized Quentin's voice.

"Good thanks."

"Are you enjoying the glamorous life of a spy?" Lana asked.

"Nothing glamorous about this job." He paused a moment. "Is Dad there?"

"Hold on. I'll get him. Take care of yourself. Hope we'll see you soon." The telephone line went silent for a few moments and Quentin waited patiently for Phillip.

"Hi. How's it going?" Phillip asked.

"Not too good, I'm afraid," Quentin said, slightly embarrassed. He wanted very much to prove himself in the eyes of his father, but realized he had a lot to learn. He also knew that Phillip Wright would be compassionate, for he had certainly been in the same position many times himself.

"What's up?"

Quentin explained the events leading to his present position and destination.

"Sounds like Ankara is a good idea." Phillip paused a moment. "You don't happen to have the license plate of the car that you're following, do you?"

"No. It happened too fast."

"Maybe that's something you should remember for next time. It's more important than getting aspirin." Phillip was not scolding Quentin, but an important fact had been overlooked, especially since an opportunity to note the license number had existed.

"Point noted." Quentin knew Phillip was helping him and did not object to his father's comments.

"I will make some phone calls," Phillip said. "I'll see if I can find out something about this Trohak fellow and what his connection is." Phillip paused. "I will also contact Amr El Hab. He heads up the Middle East sector for ISIS, and tell him what has happened to Inci."

"I'm not sure if that's a good idea," Quentin said.

"Why is that?"

"He'll obviously think I don't know what I'm doing and probably send someone else in."

"He'll do what he feels necessary to ensure your partner's safety." Phillip spoke sternly. He paused a moment before continuing. "I'll tell you what. I'll hold off with the call until I get this information. I'll talk to you again and then we can decide what to do."

His temporary reprieve relieved Quentin. He felt his inexperience would mean certain replacement and knew ISIS would send in more senior members to help him. It would not only be a severe blow to his ego, but would also put a hold on his career advancement. A wave of guilt overcame him when he realized his selfishness was more important than Inci's safety.

"Do me one more favour will you, Dad?" Quentin asked. "See if you can find out what Thomas Sun is wanted for."

Phillip hesitated a moment. "What difference does that make?"

"It might help me to know where he's headed, or with whom he is involved ."

"I'll see what I can do." Phillip paused. "Call me in twenty minutes. What's your number in case I need to contact you?"

After Quentin gave him the number, the line went dead. He pushed the power button on the cellular phone.

Other traffic was almost nonexistent as Quentin continued his trek. He spread out the road map of western Turkey and tried to find his position. Quentin realized he was heading east. For some reason, he thought he was going south. Turkey seemed to be a larger country than he thought. The surrounding countryside appeared to be more primitive than Istanbul and Bursa.

He continued driving as fast as he dared but found he could no longer view the map as dusk was beginning to set in. Quentin began to think of Inci and wondered how she was doing. It pained him to think of her as a captive of terrorists.

Lana looked at her husband. "Is there a problem?" she asked, as Phillip replaced the telephone receiver. He walked to the kitchen table and joined his wife who had just finished setting out their evening dinner.

"I think Quentin's in trouble." Phillip thought a moment staring at the food before him. "The people he was chasing have taken his accomplice hostage. He's not sure what to do. He has no leads to follow."

"What are you going to do?" Lana asked, knowing Phillip would want to be involved.

"I'm not sure. It's a touchy situation. I don't want Quentin to feel he can't work on his own. On the other hand I know what he's feeling. It's a long time ago but I remember being there myself."

"And who helped you?" Lana asked smugly. Phillip understood her point that he shouldn't get involved. But he was thinking of the many, dangerous times during his own career when help could have eliminated some of the close calls.

"I'm going to phone Peter Alexander and tell him what I know."

Lana nodded as she began to eat her dinner. "That probably sounds like a good idea," she said, knowing her husband would do as he pleased anyway.

Phillip went to the phone, dialed the number, and waited several seconds before the call was answered. He entered a security clearance code and waited for confirmation. Moments later a voice came on the line and asked for his password. Phillip responded with the necessary information and after what seemed an eternity, was put through to the records department. "I need information on a Turkish activist who goes by the name of Ibrahim Trohak." Phillip spelled out the letters and was put on hold while the person at the other end ran the search.

It did not take long for the results to be relayed. Ibrahim Trohak was a member of a Kurdish rebel group known as the 'Children of the Sultan'. It operated mainly in the southeastern part of the country near the Iraqi border. They did, however, have contacts throughout Turkey as well as the Middle East.

Phillip thanked the records clerk, hung up the phone, and jotted down the information on a notepad. He turned to Lana. "I'm just going to call Peter. Quentin is waiting for this." While he dialed the number she picked up his plate and placed it in the microwave until he was finished.

"Is Peter there, please?" It was only because of Phillip's long-term relationship with Peter Alexander that he was able to call him at home for business purposes. Peter Alexander did not have a wife. He lived alone, but had the luxury of a maid to look after his apartment in London.

"Peter Alexander speaking." The voice was very formal.

"Peter this is Phillip. I'm sorry to bother you at home, but it is urgent."

"Not at all. You can call me any time, Phillip. You know that."

"I just received a call from Quentin and he's got problems."

Phillip heard Peter Alexander sigh before speaking. "This should not be your concern," he said. "I thought we agreed you would not get involved."

"I know, but he called me. I'm calling you before I act on this."

"What's the problem?" Peter asked, in a businesslike manner.

They did locate Thomas Sun but unfortunately some of his aides abducted Quentin's partner. I'm sure they'll be looking for him too.

"What do you mean, abducted?" Peter interjected.

"I don't have all of the details, but Quentin asked me to run a check on a specific name. It is someone who is linked to a group of Kurdish rebels calling themselves the 'Children of the Sultan'.

Does that name mean anything to you?"

"Yes it does. They are a very deep-rooted terrorist organization, which operates throughout the Middle East. They were allegedly responsible for training the people who blew up the World Trade Centre in New York.

"If Thomas Sun is involved with them, this could be larger than we first anticipated." He paused then added, "How do you want to handle this Phillip?"

Phillip thought a minute before speaking. "I would like to work as a liaison between Quentin and us."

"I'm not sure," Peter said, hesitating. "I think you're too close."

"But I'm already involved."

After a few moments he responded, "All right. Just remember Phillip, people's lives are at stake. Don't forget... *You Can Not*," he emphasized each word, "let your emotions get involved in your decisions."

Phillip realized he was asking his friend to breach regulations but he was sure he could rely on his years of experience. Thanking Peter, he hung up the phone and turned to Lana who was still sitting at the table.

"What did he say?" she asked.

Phillip relayed his conversation with Peter Alexander, staring at the empty place setting before him.

Lana went to rise but Phillip motioned her

to stay seated and enjoy her dinner. He walked to the microwave and programed it to reheat his dinner. His mind was elsewhere and he was debating whether he should tell Quentin the background behind Thomas Sun. There was no immediate benefit for Quentin knowing about TWA Flight 800, but Phillip saw no reason why Quentin should not be told.

The microwave beeped several times. Phillip removed his plate, walked to the table and sat down with Lana to eat his dinner. She could see and understood that his thoughts were elsewhere. There was little conversation between them.

Davud Kurvesh decided it was time to contact Francis Sun. Dialing the hotel in Istanbul, he was relieved to hear his voice. "Mr. Sun this is Davud Kurvesh."

"You have my son?" He was cut off by his employer.

"Not yet but we know where he is."

"When do you anticipate contacting him?" Sun asked methodically.

"That may not be as easy. It appears he is involved with a Kurdish rebel group known as the 'Children of the Sultan'."

Francis Sun went still at the mention of the terrorist organization. Although he had never encountered them before, he was familiar with their actions and many of the events with which they had been credited. He knew it was a ruthless, terrorist organization made up mostly of Iraqis who had settled in Southeast Turkey. They were responsible for most of the chaos in the eastern part.

In the last ten years, these terrorists had begun to infiltrate Kurdish settlements in Turkey. They initiated car bombings and minor terrorist acts, giving the impression that Turkish Kurds were responsible. The government of Turkey in turn decided to punish its own people by limiting social assistance and eliminating many programs, including education. The Turkish Kurds, not being responsible, began to despise their government and turned to the Iraqis who offered them money, food, and other necessities. The price was loyalty to the Iraqi cause.

An elite team of professional killers emerged from within this band of terrorists and stepped aside from the main group. They were not satisfied with the small time activities performed by the rest of the organization and decided it was time to go after bigger, with more publicized events. They recruited only the fiercest fighting mercenaries and trained them in Libya under the direct supervision of Moammar Khaddafi and his elite army. As the group grew they developed some ideals and philosophies. They blamed the misfortunes of poverty in their country on the government and believed that they had been sold out to the western world.

When the trouble between Iraq and the rest of the world began, the 'Children of the Sultan' had chose to side with the Arabs. Many of the men enlisted in Sadam Hussein's elite Republican Guard and thus further enhanced their skills. During the Gulf War, they aided Iraq in terrorist attacks around the world.

It is believed, by many, that the 'Children of the Sultan' were responsible for the new, religiously oriented government's success in achieving political victory in the last election. Their desire was to adopt the customs of old and go the way of Iran and Afghanistan. They believed in many of the ideals whose origins lay in the Ottoman empire and would be quite pleased if the sultans again ruled their once-great nation.

Francis Sun smiled to himself as he thought of these simple people and their so called ideals. They knew nothing of the real history of the area. The great poverty, the persecution, and the lack of freedom their forbearers endured which started the 1923 revolution in Turkey. How stupidly they overlooked what really happened and how easily they forget the past.

Francis Sun knew there had been many reports linking the 'Children of the Sultan' with the World Trade Centre bombing in New York City. He also remembered reading recently a report that Timothy McVeigh had vacationed in eastern Turkey. There had been no credit given to the Kurds for the Oklahoma bombing but Francis Sun would not be surprised at a possible link.

He knew from experience that a major drawback to dealing with this particular terrorist organization was that it did not seek recognition. They never claimed deeds as their own and maintained a code of silence, which kept them from being known to most of the world. He shuddered to think of the implications arising from his son's involvement with these people. He had to act quickly before it was too late. Once these people swallowed up his son, the chances of being reunited with him would be very slim.

"Hello," Davud Kurvesh said, concerned about the silence at the other end of the line.

"We must meet immediately," Francis Sun said. "Come to my hotel."

"But we are at the ferry dock, about ready to board."

"How far behind my son are you?"

"About two, maybe three hours."

"Do you know where he is going?"

"He is heading for central Anatolia. He will probably stop in Ankara."

"What type of vehicle is he driving?"

"We are not certain."

"You plan to pursue a man who has a three-hour head start in a vehicle, the description of which you do not know, en route to the second largest city in Turkey more than two hundred kilometres away." Francis Sun paused a moment. "Your statements make very little sense. I will expect you in my hotel in half an hour."

Davud Kurvesh stood silently, his mouth

slightly agape, as he heard the familiar click at the other end of the line.

Seleng and Kwok looked to their leader for direction and immediately realized by the expression on Kurvesh's face, that a change in plans had occurred.

"Mr. Sun wishes us to return to Istanbul and inform him about what we have learned, Kurvesh said. Noting the puzzled looks on the faces of his two assistants he headed toward the yellow Vauxhall. Starting the car and waiting for his to accomplices to enter he explained, "Mr. Sun feels we have little chance of locating his son or the two agents because of the lead they have."

The car sped along as daylight transformed into dusk in the age-old city which linked the continents of Asia and Europe.

Quentin again glanced at his watch as he forced the rental automobile to race along the open road toward the capital city of Ankara. He judged his distance to be no more than an hour and decided enough time had passed since he last spoke with Phillip Wright.

He picked up the cellular telephone and again dialed the numbers, putting him in touch with his father. The telephone was answered after the first ring and Quentin thought he detected a slight sound of concern in his father's voice.

"Are you still on your way to Ankara?" Phillip asked.

"I think I am about an hour outside of the city." Quentin paused a moment while he passed an old-modelled pick-up truck, heavily laden with garbage, pieces of which were caught by the wind and blown to the sides of the road. "Did you manage to find anything?"

"I spoke with Peter Alexander and he agreed you should continue. He's quite concerned about your partner, and until we learn anything further, you're in charge."

Quentin was relieved at the news. His biggest fear had been that he would be taken off the assignment and replaced by someone who had more experience. "Well I'm glad to hear that."

Phillip relayed the information he had learned from Peter Alexander.

"Are you familiar with this particular terrorist group?" Quentin asked.

"I've never heard of them, but what I did learn is that they're quite powerful. Their network spreads throughout the Middle East and they've been involved in attacks around the world."

"Could you find out more information about them?"

"I'll contact the archive department and see if we have anything else on them. As soon as I hear I'll call you."

"Did you find out what Thomas Sun is wanted for?" Quentin asked.

"He is wanted in the U.S. for his alleged involvement in the downing of the TWA flight off the coast of New York last July."

Quentin was stunned by the information. He did not realize that the passenger airliner had been sabotaged. "I was under the impression the crash was an accident."

"Apparently not. At first it was thought there might have been terrorist involvement because they found traces of plastic explosives in the seats."

"I remember reading that, but I thought passenger planes were used for training missions by the FBI and CIA."

"That's right. The 'terrorists' story sold a lot of newspapers. Everyone craves that kind of sensationalism. Also remember insurance companies don't have to pay all the claims if it's a terrorist attack."

"So why wouldn't they just tell everyone that it was a terrorist attack?"

"I think the U.S. government decided it would hurt the country's tourist industry if suddenly it wasn't safe to fly in and out of the U.S. anymore."

"What's Thomas Sun's involvement?" Quentin asked, intrigued by this new turn of events.

"Apparently he rented a boat for three weeks prior to the event -- a boat large enough to use as a missile launcher for the AEGIS missiles, the one they believe downed the airliner."

"Wouldn't a lot of people have rented boats?" Quentin asked. "It was, after all, the middle of summer."

"I imagine they would, but it seemed strange that the boat sat in the same place for three weeks, then suddenly disappeared right after the plane was shot down. Also, his trip to Turkey and his father's business cast great suspicion on him.

Quentin smiled and relaxed a bit as he passed a sign indicating he was heading in the right direction for Ankara. "What do you mean 'his father'?" he asked.

"Thomas Sun's father heads up the world's largest industrial espionage organization. He has been responsible for millions of dollars lost by companies because their secrets have been divulged to competitors. Apparently he is known worldwide for his expertise and professionalism. He is wanted by dozens of law enforcement agencies that have never been able to pin anything on him. He lives in Hong Kong. Thomas Sun, the young man you are chasing, is his only son. No doubt he's being groomed to take over his father's business. I'm sure the old man will try anything to get his son back."

A thought occurred to Quentin. "Inci said she thought she was being followed. When we went to the restaurant yesterday to find out about Thomas Sun, the waiter told us someone else was interested in his whereabouts. At the palace, we saw a couple of suspicious people hanging around the lobby. They sure looked like they were waiting for someone. At the time, we wondered if we were being followed. I wonder if they work for Francis

Sun and are on the same mission we are?"

Phillip paused a moment as he reflected on Quentin's statement. "You could be right. Be very careful and don't trust anyone." Phillip hesitated a moment. "Oh, Lana wants to know if you're getting enough to eat?"

Quentin smiled. "Tell her the food here is nowhere near what she sells in her restaurant."

"I will. I'll call our office now and see what I can learn about the 'Children of the Sultan' and anything else I can find. Call me in thirty minutes."

Quentin replaced the receiver and adjusted his seating, trying to find a comfortable position in the small automobile as it raced along the autoroute through Turkey. He replayed all the facts in his mind and attempted to sort them in an order that made some sense. He grabbed a pen from his pocket and began to make notes on a pad of paper, which he had found in the glove compartment. During his training, ISIS had been very specific on separating fact from fiction. Only too often would a person's imagination embellish a fact to the point where it would no longer resemble the truth. He tried to establish a set of details consisting only of factual experiences. He found this difficult to achieve as his mind continued to wander through all possible scenarios.

He was extremely intrigued by his father's comments surrounding the TWA disaster. He tried to picture Thomas Sun sitting aboard a boat off the coast of Long Island preparing for such an attack. His mind also drifted to the terrorist group known as the 'Children of the Sultan'. He thought of Inci and wondered how she was faring in the hands of these paid assassins.

Thinking of her led him to conclude that he had no plan of action for the near future. He had no idea what he would do when he got to Ankara. In the back of his mind, he had hoped to somehow overtake the grey automobile which had a thirty minute lead. Even with his accelerated speed, he had not yet come in contact with the vehicle. Another distressing thought occurred to him. What if it wasn't Ankara where they were heading? What if they were going to the coast instead? He hoped his choice had been correct.

He glanced at his watch and was surprised at how quickly time had passed since his conversation with Phillip. It was nearly thirty minutes and he decided he would call again. Although the traffic had not grown heavier, there was an increase in buildings, indicating he was nearing the capital city of Ankara.

He picked up the cell phone and dialed his father's number for the third time. Lana answered the telephone and asked Quentin several questions about his wellbeing.

"So far I'm OK but it's a lot more scary than I thought it would be."

"I can imagine. I know what your father has gone through for the last twenty years and I still worry every time he goes out of town." She paused a moment before continuing. "Quentin," she said. "You will take care of yourself, won't you?"

"Of course I will. I'm getting pretty good at this stuff." Quentin tried to force a smile, hoping his voice would sound calm, thereby allaying Lana's concerns. He knew his words were not the truth and he was quite frightened at the prospect of pursuing this assignment on his own.

"Phillip will be here in a second. He's just upstairs waiting for a fax to come in. How's the weather where you are?" She asked, in an effort to bring a light note into the conversation.

"It's not too bad. It seems to be getting cooler. I'm glad I have a jacket."

"That's funny. I always pictured Turkey as desert."

"Anything but. The hills are covered in trees, mostly evergreens. The leaves of the others seem to be experiencing a change in colour."

"That's interesting. It's not how I pictured the Middle East."

"It's a beautiful country and I'd like to come back some time for a vacation. There seems to be a lot of history here."

"Well make sure you get through this without getting hurt. Here comes Phillip now."

Quentin waited while Lana passed the telephone receiver to her husband. "Sorry. I was just waiting for a fax from London."

"Did you get any information?"

"This is quite interesting." Phillip read the fax and relayed the information to Quentin. "It states here that the 'Children of the Sultan' was formed about twelve years ago. Their leader is a man named Mustafa. According to this, he's in his late forties and resides in a town called Nevsehir."

Quentin turned on the dome light illuminating the inside of the automobile as he tried to find the town on the map beside him.

"Apparently he's quite ruthless," Phillip continued. "He's a close personal friend of Sadam Hussein, but seems to be two-faced. In his earlier days, he was responsible for helping the Ayatollah Khomeini restore the Muslim way of life in Iran. They also think he's responsible for running guns to the Afghan rebels in their fight against the Soviets several years ago. Apparently he's a hard man to get hold of. He always surrounds himself with dozens of bodyguards. Several agencies around the world have tried to do him in, but without success." Phillip continued to read more of the fax in his hand. "This is interesting," he continued. "Francis Sun was in New York two days ago and left for Istanbul. He's probably there now."

Quentin listened carefully as his father continued to read the information to him.

"I think this is getting a little too far beyond your capabilities," Phillip said, concern in his voice.

"I'm fine," Quentin said, adamantly. "What would you do differently?"

"I'm not sure that I would do anything differently," Phillip said. "But I know I would feel a lot better if there were other agents working with you."

"I'll be fine," Quentin replied. "Right now I've got to find Inci."

"What are your immediate plans?" Phillip asked.

"Ankara is quite large. There is not a whole lot I can do here. I was hoping to run into these guys but that obviously isn't going to happen. I think I'll get a hotel for the night, try to find where this town Nevsehir is, and head that way tomorrow. It seems like that's where they're going."

"That central part of Turkey you're heading to is quite religious. Make sure you don't get into trouble."

"Yes, Dad," Quentin said, mockingly.

"I know, I know. I'm just concerned."

Quentin said goodbye and replaced the telephone set on the seat beside him. He noticed the battery indicator light was flashing and hoped a charger was in the glove compartment.

He continued his drive into Ankara and had to slow his speed as the traffic increased and pedestrians became more predominant.

Ankara was a modernized city with tall office buildings and large apartment houses. The face of the city looked new, and Quentin thought that perhaps the entire city had been planned similarly to the way Canberra, the capital of Quentin's homeland, Australia had been constructed, from a set of blue prints.

He noticed Turkish flags on display everywhere, and several buildings had been covered with gigantic pictures of Atatürk, the statesman who had led Turkey into the twentieth century, away from Ottoman customs. Quentin assumed he had entered into a national celebration of some type. He was amused at the sight of a huge, red flag suspended from a wire attached to two minarets high above a mosque.

He brought the car to a halt at a red light and glanced in all directions at the sights around him. He noticed a large, brown, concrete building, which seemed to be a museum or similar attraction. He saw a sign and realized it was the mausoleum of Atatürk. Tourists were walking along a concrete sidewalk, which led to the entrance. From his vantage point, Quentin noticed the size of the structure was at least one city block. There were a series of buildings, all constructed from large, sandy brown, concrete blocks, which formed a perimeter around a central square. Armed guards, dressed in the navy blue uniform of the Turkish army with white helmets, gloves, and shoulder straps, stood obediently at their posts.

As the traffic signal changed, Quentin continued on, slowly taking in the view of the historical sight. Suddenly, the honking of a car horn behind him caused him to realize that he was driving too slowly. He decided to change lanes and upon doing so, saw a large sign indicating a hotel. He cut across a third lane of traffic and entered into the driveway leading to the fifteen-storey building.

On the green, manicured lawn, stood an oversized, ceramic teapot, which had been tilted forward and was pouring water into a cup of similar size. The entire sculpture was at least five metres in height and was made from small tiles. The fountain was a tribute to the ceramic industry located in this part of Turkey.

Quentin pulled his car into the parking lot near the side entrance of the hotel. Before leaving the vehicle, he grabbed the telephone charger from the glove compartment and plugged it into the lighter socket allowing the unit to recharge.

While approaching the front door to the hotel he made a mental note to let his father know the hotel's phone number. He also hoped the hotel had a good dining room.

He entered the lobby, walked to the desk and gave the clerk all the necessary information to secure a room for the night.

10. Mustafa

The grey sedan slowed and turned into the parking lot of a small hotel on the outskirts of Ankara. Inci sat quietly in the rear seat with Cengiz, one of the two men who had abducted her earlier that evening. During the ride from Bursa her hands had been bound and she grew more concerned at the sexual innuendoes suggested by her captors. At one point he grinned and put his grimy hand on her knee indicating his control over her. She was repulsed. In his fifties and over weight he wore an old T-shirt and a shaggy, black V-neck sweater tucked into his dirty jeans. There was a hideous stale odour about him indicating he had not bathed recently. His smile revealed crooked, yellow teeth stained from his continual smoking of non-filtered cigarettes. His hair was uncombed and greasy and a greying moustache blended into his unshaven face.

The driver, Yalcin, like his partner, was not concerned much about personal cleanliness either. Younger and somewhat larger, his long forehead stood out prominently as he tried to keep his greasy, black hair off his face by continually running his fingers through it. It defied his efforts and fell over one side of his face as soon as he lowered his hand.

Seated in the front seat, beside the driver, was Thomas Sun. The young Oriental was a complete contrast to the two men escorting him. He was wearing the same grey, wool suit, white shirt, and tie he had worn in the photograph taken at the Dolmabahçe Palace the previous day. He sat straight and looked forward, offering little conversation.

Inci assumed he spoke no Turkish and was therefore excluded from a majority of the conversation. His hair was neatly cut and had been kept quite short. He had a cowlick at the part near his hairline, which caused a small tuft of hair to stand straight up. His yellow-tinted skin was smooth and Inci doubted if he shaved every day. He was wearing small, wire-rimmed glasses and she noted his appreciation for the finer things in life. His mannerisms and speech, upon the rare occasion when he did speak, were those of an educated man and, although Inci did not know his connection to the people with him, she felt he was above their status.

The man in the back seat offered Inci a cigarette, which she gladly took. He smiled as he lit a match and held it for her. She inhaled deeply and relaxed slightly and allowed the smoke to slowly exhale from deep within her lungs. Thomas Sun opened his window several centimetres as the scent of the sulphur accompanied by cigarette smoke made its way to the front seat.

"You do not like the cigarettes?" the driver asked, glancing at Thomas Sun.

"I do not," he replied.

The driver turned the automobile into a parking spot near the entrance to the hotel.

"We will spend the night here and continue our journey tomorrow morning," the driver said. His English was good, although his accent was heavy. Every time he spoke, he translated the conversation into Turkish for the benefit of his partner in the back seat who did not understand English.

"You will wait in the car while I make the necessary arrangements for our accommodations," the driver said. He removed the keys from the ignition and departed for the hotel.

Inci was not certain whether his remarks were directed at her or at Thomas Sun. Bits and pieces of conversations had caused her to wonder how much control Thomas Sun had over his destiny.

The man in the rear seat leaned across Inci and rolled down her window slightly, allowing her to throw the cigarette ashes out. She was revolted when he purposely brushed his arm against her breasts as he returned to his position. She gave him a distasteful look and cringed when she saw him smile.

"What is your connection with these men?" she asked of Thomas Sun. The man beside her told her to be quiet but she ignored him and sat upright, poised to listen to an answer, should there be one forthcoming.

For the first time since they had been on their journey, Thomas Sun turned slightly in his seat and glanced over his shoulder at Inci. "These men are my accomplices," Thomas Sun replied.

Inci could feel the discomfort of her captor beside her, as he was unsure of what was being said. "I cannot believe you are mixed up with people like this," she said.

"I do not know these people. They are merely transporting me to a meeting."

"I suppose it was your idea to bring me along."

Thomas Sun had a strange look on his face. "No," he said, slowly. "I do not know who you are, but I know you have been following me." He paused a moment and slowly tilted his head, as a puff of smoke made its way onto his face. "Who do you work for?" he asked.

"Let me ask you the same question?"

"I am here merely on vacation mixing in a little business.

"And what type of business might that be?"

"I am in the mining industry. The people I am meeting are business associates who own mining operations in this part of the world."

"Funny, I don't believe you," Inci said.

"I cannot help that." Thomas Sun paused momentarily. "Now, tell me who you are with."

"I am a nun from the Christian school in Istanbul," Inci said, mockingly. It was the first time since Inci had met him that she saw Thomas Sun smile.

"I am sorry if you are uncomfortable. It is a necessary precaution." He glanced at the man in the rear seat, but showed no emotion. He continued his conversation with Inci. "Do you work for the government of Turkey?" he asked.

"Would it bother you if I did?"

"Your technique of answering every question with a question is tiring."

"Then do not ask any more questions."

Thomas Sun was about to make a rebuttal when the driver returned to the car. He took up his seat behind the steering wheel and smiled at everyone. "We will spend the night here. I have ordered a room with two large beds. Tomorrow morning we will leave very early for our rendezvous with Mustafa."

Thomas Sun raised his eyebrows and stared deep into the eyes of the driver, at the mention of the leader of the terrorists' name. "It is unwise for you to speak of such meetings before our captive."

"I do not think it matters. She will not be alive long enough to know of what we are speaking."

By the look on Thomas Sun's face, he knew that threats such as this, far too often came true.

"Who is Mustafa?" Inci asked.

"That is none of your concern," Thomas Sun replied.

"I have the hotel key," the driver said. "Let us enter quietly. Remember," he said, addressing Inci. "My friend has a gun and it is pointed directly at you. You should also know he would not hesitate to use it." The man turned to face his friend behind him and translated the comments into Turkish.

At the conclusion of the conversation, Cengiz removed the semiautomatic pistol from his pocket and flashed it for Inci to see. Again he smiled. He opened the car door without once taking his eyes from her. As he stepped from the vehicle, he leaned forward and grabbed Inci by the arm, pulling her toward him. She did not resist as the sight of the gun caused fear within her. She knew only too well that bandits such as these had killed in the past, and would do so again without hesitation.

The four walked into the hotel lobby and the driver led them directly to the bank of elevators at the far end. The lobby had not been well maintained and an odour of tobacco hung heavily within the air. The walls had once been painted a bright white, but were now stained yellow and covered with numerous chips where furniture had been carelessly moved. Several neglected plants had been placed around the perimeter of the lobby and appeared to be in dire need of water.

A well worn, Turkish carpet of deep reds and browns covered most of the floor. Around the edges were grey flecked tiles, which looked as if they had not been washed in quite some time. Two beige-coloured couches sat side by side across from the reception desk.

A young attendant, wearing a blue, short sleeved shirt, stood behind the counter and was writing information on a sheet of paper. He glanced up as the four people made their way through the lobby. He smiled when he saw Inci and was taken by her attractiveness. He did not look away from her face, therefore, failing to see her hands, which were still bound. He continued to stare as the party neared the elevator, watching Inci's walk which was accentuated by her tight fitting jeans.

Once inside, Yalcin, the driver pressed the button for the sixth floor and stood back as the elevator made its way upward. When it stopped and the door opened he was the first to step off. Glancing in both directions to ensure no one saw them the group made their way down the dimly lit hall to their room. Opening the door Yalcin entered and turned on the light. The others followed.

Only Cengiz seemed impressed with the accommodations. He went immediately to the small portable TV that was plainly bolted to the top of the shabby dresser and turned it on. Besides the two double beds the only other furniture in the dingy, dank room was a chipped and well worn, stained coffee table and two wooden, straight-backed chairs.

It was evident by the expression on his face that Thomas Sun was appalled by the accommodations. "There is no reason I have to stay in the same room with you," he said. "I believe I will arrange for my own accommodation."

As he began to turn and walk toward the door, Yalcin stepped forward saying, "I do not think that is a wise idea, my friend. It is our responsibility to ensure you arrive safely for our meeting tomorrow. I would not want to see something happen to you." Thomas Sun paused and decided to abandon his intention. "If it will make you feel better you can share the bed with our lady friend."

The statement relieved Inci. She knew Thomas Sun was a decent individual, but she could not say the same for her two captors.

Yalcin spoke to Cengiz. "Turn that thing off," he said, referring to the television which had mesmerized his partner. "Cengiz!" he shouted, causing his smaller friend to swing his head around.

Cengiz had not been paying attention to the conversation and looked at the three other people in the room. He realized Yalcin was not pleased. "I said turn the television off." Yalcin spoke with authority and Cengiz knew his directives were not to be ignored. "Perhaps you should cut the rope around our friend's wrists."

Cengiz walked to where Inci was standing and removed a pocketknife from inside his jacket. He opened the knife and with one flick, cut the rope, freeing Inci's paining wrists. She immediately rubbed them in an effort to soothe the aching, and instinctively stepped back to avoid close contact with the small Turk before her.

"Let us order some room service," Yalcin said. He reached for a menu on the dresser and stepped to the telephone to place an order for food. "Perhaps you should keep a closer watch on our prisoner," Thomas Sun said to Yalcin. He realized Cengiz was again watching television.

The tall terrorist walked to the television and forced his palm against the on/off control causing the television to shake as the screen went blank. Again Cengiz was shocked by the gesture, for his mind had drifted into the confines of the television show.

"I will telephone room service. You ensure our friend does not do anything foolish."

Yalcin placed the call and Cengiz removed the gun from his pocket, waving it in Inci's direction. The ISIS agent trembled slightly at the gesture and as she backed up, her legs made contact with the bed which caused her to fall into a sitting position.

"Ah, you are getting ready for me," Cengiz said, smiling lecherously.

Yalcin finished the phone call and turned his attention to Inci. "Now, my dear friend. Why do we not begin with you telling us your name." Inci refused to speak and directed her gaze toward the empty chairs beneath the window. She made a point of never carrying identification with her and kept her money in her jacket pocket. A purse was a constant hindrance and therefore she had left it in Istanbul.

"So you do not want to be friendly," Yalcin said. Although Thomas Sun did not understand Turkish, he had a general idea of the conversation. "Please. Give me your jacket," Yalcin continued, motioning for Inci to remove her brown, tweed jacket and hand it to him. Cautiously she did so, knowing they would be upset when they found nothing other than cash in it.

Yalcin searched the pockets and extracted a sizeable amount of currency. He looked at the money, then at Inci and smiled. "I guess you know we will keep this. We will consider it a gift from you to us. It will help to pay for your accommodations." He smiled as he spoke.

"Perhaps she is hiding identification somewhere else," Cengiz was quick to add. "Would you like me to search her?" At the sound of his words, Inci stiffened her muscles as tension filled her body.

"It is all I have."

"Perhaps you should tell us your name or my friend, Cengiz, will search you further." The threat was enough for Inci to succumb to his request.

"My name is Inci Arzu," she replied.

"Ah. Now we are getting somewhere. And who is it you work for Inci Arzu?"

"What did she say?" Thomas Sun inquired.

"She said her name was Inci," Yalcin replied.

"And who does she work for?"

"You heard him," Yalcin said to Inci. "Answer him."

Inci did not respond and Cengiz walked toward her, his pocketknife in his hand. He held the knife close to her throat making a gesture as if he was about to cut her. Inci waited until Cengiz smiled. She instinctively raised her hand, grabbed his wrist and, in the same gesture, pulled it across her front. As his body followed the movement, she raised her knee and caught him sharply in the groin. He emitted a fierce cry as pain absorbed him, and buckled over, dropping to his knees on the carpet before her feet. She was about to raise her leg and let her foot make contact with his face, but stopped when Yalcin removed the gun from his jacket and held it level with her head.

"I would not do that if I were you," he said. She stopped and relaxed her muscles causing her body to stand still. Yalcin began to laugh at the sight of Cengiz clutching his groin in an effort to soothe the pain. Thomas Sun also chuckled.

Cengiz realized what had happened and was not amused at being the centre of his associates' laughter. He slowly rose to his feet and his face was filled with extreme anger. He lifted his arm quickly and lashed out at Inci's face, catching her cheek with his knuckles and causing her head to jolt backward.

"That is enough," Yalcin ordered.

"There will be much more of this before I am finished with you," Cengiz said to Inci. She turned to face him and held her hand to the corner of her mouth feeling a drop of blood. She stared coldly into his dark, brown eyes and as she did so, spat directly in his face.

Cengiz became angry beyond control. He raised his hand and wiped the liquid from his cheek. He was about to hit her again when Yalcin yelled at him to stop. "I will say this. The woman has spirit." Yalcin chuckled slightly. "She is far too much of a match for our friend Cengiz." He spoke in English for the benefit of Thomas Sun, who smiled to himself as he watched the ineptitude of the people before him. His father would have dealt with these people in a much different manner. He would not have allowed such amateurs to work for him.

Yalcin again spoke to Inci. "I would highly recommend you tell us who you work with or I will not be so quick to stop my friend from beating you again." Inci thought about what Yalcin had said and decided she had no choice but to divulge the information they requested. She felt it would not make a difference to the situation. "I work with the government of Turkey," she said, lying slightly.

"And what is it you are looking for?" Yalcin asked.

"I was told Thomas Sun is wanted by our government for questioning. My job was to find him and ask him to return with me."

The Oriental addressed her directly. "Who was the other person you were with?"

"He is also with the Turkish government," she replied. She had decided to continue lying as long as her captors remain gullible. "Why does my government want you?" she asked.

Thomas Sun looked at Inci, surprised by her question. "I do not believe that is any of your concern." He was not pleased by the Turkish government's inquiry into his personal affairs. He had wondered who this woman was and why she had followed him. It made no sense for the Turks to seek him. He assumed they had been asked to do so by the American government.

He was a cautious individual, and his father had taught him at an early age to be concerned about anything which appeared out of the ordinary. He was disturbed by Inci's presence. He had been careful in every action he had taken since he left New York. He understood his passport would have identified his presence to customs officials; however, since his arrival in Istanbul, he had been extremely cautious. He grew curious as to how this Turkish agent had managed to trail him all the way to Bursa.

"What I would like to know is who told you of my location in Turkey?"

Inci looked at the Oriental youth. "You were

extremely easy to find," she replied. "You left a trail so easy to spot that I am surprised every policeman in the country is not here." She was trying to create insecurity in Thomas Sun. She did not want to let on, that it had in fact been extremely difficult for her and Quentin to trail him.

There was a look of concern on Sun's face at the remarks made by Inci and he was about to speak again, when he was interrupted by a knock on the door.

Cengiz immediately removed his gun and stared at Yalcin for instructions. The tall Turk silently suggested he relax as he walked toward the door, opened it, and allowed the waiter to enter with their dinner.

Yalcin paid cash for the service, using Inci's money. He left a sizeable tip and the waiter was grateful as he departed.

The dinner was a hot lamb dish with boiled potatoes smothered in onion sauce. A variety of mixed vegetables, cooked very thoroughly and spiced to perfection, accompanied the meat dish. There were two bottles of red wine from vineyards in the central region of Turkey.

The dinner had a delicious aroma, which reminded Inci how hungry she really was. Yalcin scooped several spoonfuls from each dish and put them on a plate. "Pass this to her," he said, speaking to Cengiz.

"I do not see why we have to feed her," the short man said, still upset about the violent attack

Inci had launched on him.

"We must feed her," Yalcin said. "She is, after all, the one paying for this dinner." He spoke in English and glanced at Thomas Sun for a reaction. There was none.

Inci hungrily attacked her food, expecting it to be taken away at any minute. She was fortunate that her host allowed her to eat without disturbance. She was surprised when Yalcin offered her a glass of wine.

The group ate in silence, each member reflecting on events which had taken place in the recent past. Cengiz continued his harassment of Inci and as he dipped his bread in the gravy, looked up and smiled several times.

She ignored his actions and began to think about a method of escape, feeling it would not be too difficult, as these people were extremely unprofessional. The more she contemplated escape, the more objections surfaced. Perhaps she should abandon her idea, opting instead for a possibility to infiltrate the group behind this abduction. She decided as long as her life was not in jeopardy, she would try to learn as much as she could. She could think of no reason for them to keep her alive and could not understand why these men had not killed her by now. She was, after all, a substantial liability. Inci decided to avoid confrontations and listen attentively to everything being said.

It was, however, important to get information out to assure ISIS knew of her whereabouts.

She also thought of Quentin and wondered where he was. Although he was new at his job, she thought him to be extremely resourceful and felt certain he would be following her as best he could. She knew the country and understood there would be only one direction for him to go. Inci was concerned Quentin might not come to the same conclusion. She had no idea how he would find her, but prayed silently for his success.

She thought about different ways of leaving a message but each time she arrived at a decision, she was faced with many reasons why it would not work. She had no pen and cursed the fact that she carried no lipstick. As she was thinking of alternate ways of getting a message out, she noticed a small pen lying beside the telephone on top of the dark brown, wooden bureau.

"Would you like some more?" Yalcin asked when he noticed Inci's plate was empty. His comment snapped her back to the reality of the present situation, and she hoped he hadn't seen her staring at the pen on the dresser. She nodded in response to his question and got up to help herself to some more food.

At first, Cengiz raised his gun and levelled it at her head but Yalcin waved to him, telling him, she would not go anywhere. "It is important for us to be good hosts," he said. There was a hint of sarcasm in his voice, but he honestly believed Inci was not a threat. Thomas Sun sat quietly in the corner of the room eating his dinner. He had not touched the wine and when Yalcin asked him if he wanted a refill of food. He declined. "Are you going to drink your wine?" the big Turk asked.

Thomas Sun shook his head from side to side. "You may have it," he said, quietly.

Yalcin smiled and walked toward him. He lifted the glass, toasted Thomas Sun, and drank the contents in one gulp. Cengiz also decided to have another glass and glanced around for the opener, in order to remove the cork from the second bottle.

Inci realized there would not be enough wine to make her captors drunk, but she was glad they were enjoying it. It would at least dull their senses slightly. She was concerned about Thomas Sun. It was evident by his actions he was worried about her earlier comments. She wondered about his background, who he was, and where he came from. She had no idea why he was wanted by ISIS, but the mere fact that he was caught in a web of intrigue and associated with the likes of Yalcin and Cengiz, indicated he was a player in an illegal transaction of one sort or another. She assumed he was selling drugs or arms.

She waited a few more minutes before deciding to make her move toward the pen. She slowly stood, walked toward the dresser, and placed her plate on it. She stared at Cengiz and Yalcin who both stopped what they were doing and gazed at her. Each movement she made was calculated and she had played, it over in her mind several times in the last few minutes.

"Perhaps I will have a little more food," she said, returning to where she had set down her plate.

"Please, eat all you wish. It is healthy for a young woman to eat," Yalcin said. "Cengiz, get our friend some more wine."

Cengiz looked at his superior and hesitated about performing the task he had been asked to do. Yalcin nodded to him, suggesting he obey.

It was the perfect opportunity Inci had waited for. As Cengiz and Yalcin exchanged glances, she picked up her plate, at the same time extending her fingers several centimetres until she made contact with the pen. The entire action only took a split second and she hoped Thomas Sun was not watching. She had tried, as best as she could, to shield herself from his view. She managed to roll the pen slowly toward the plate and as she picked up the dish, felt the pen within her grasp.

She walked to the stainless steel serving trolley and scooped several helpings of dinner onto her plate. She then returned to her corner of the bed and continued to eat. Her muscles tensed slightly when Cengiz neared her with the bottle of wine. He indicated she lift her glass in order for him to fill it. She leaned forward, picked up the glass from the floor and held it for him to fill. Again he smiled, showing his yellow teeth..

She forced an unwanted feeling of nausea back into the pit of her stomach and began to eat the food in front of her. It was her third helping and she was becoming quite full, but she knew she had to finish this plate to avoid suspicion. As she ate quietly, Yalcin and Cengiz continued to drink the wine and joked back and forth about trivial matters. Thomas Sun remained quiet in the corner of the room and looked out the window at the darkness below.

When Inci felt the time was right, she slipped the pen into the pocket of her jeans to be used at a later time. When she finished eating she again stood and replaced the plate on the dresser. She walked toward the washroom and was about to enter when Yalcin spoke to her. "Where do you think you are going?" he asked.

"I have to use the bathroom."

Yalcin paused a moment and thought about what Inci had said. "Very well but do not close the door. Inci entered the bathroom and pushed the door leaving a small gap as per the instructions of her captor.

"I said leave the door open," Yalcin yelled angrily.

Cengiz walked to the door and pushed it hard, causing it to slam into the side of the bathtub. The sudden action caused Inci to jump as she came face to face with Cengiz who stopped and stared at her partially exposed legs. He smiled when he saw the soft, tanned flesh before him angering Inci. "Get out of here, you pig," she yelled. Her voice was filled with hatred. She reached forward and grabbed the edge of the door and slammed it shut. Cengiz laughed out loud as did Yalcin. Thomas Sun remained serious.

Inci was appalled by the action but realized she could use it to her advantage. While the door was closed she looked around the bathroom and saw a small card on the vanity beside the sink. It was a standard hotel reply card which patrons were asked to complete with their impressions of the service and accommodation.

Inci quickly grabbed the white card and removed the pen. She wrote a short message in Turkish asking whoever read this to call the telephone number of ISIS, which she wrote down. She added her location as well as her presumed destination and that she was in trouble. "Please send help".

She slipped the card under her sleeve, near her shoulder and was thankful she wore a white T-shirt. The material was thick enough that the writing on the card was not visible to the outside. She decided to slide the pen in her boot for she was concerned it would be found if she left it in the bathroom.

She stood and looked in the mirror and was quite shocked at her dishevelled appearance. She tried to straighten her hair slightly, but decided not to put any effort into it. The last thing she wanted was to appear more attractive to her slimy captors.

She left the bathroom and returned to the main area of the hotel room. Cengiz sat on the other bed and smiled as she entered.

"You are a filthy dog," she said. "If you ever touch me, I will kill you."

Her words caused Cengiz to laugh even louder.

"You had better be careful, my little friend," Yalcin said to Cengiz. "This woman is very dangerous and I am certain she means you harm." He laughed at his mocking statement. He directed his attention to Inci. "Would you care for some more wine?"

"No, but apple tea would be good."

"Apple tea sounds like an excellent idea," Thomas Sun said. It was the first time he had spoken since they had begun eating. The incident in the bathroom had taken his mind away from his concerns. Inci thought she noticed a hint of compassion in his eyes.

"Very well," Yalcin replied. Again he walked to the telephone and placed the order for apple tea.

Inci knew she had a twenty-minute window of opportunity before the waiter arrived to deliver the tea. She had to slip the note onto the tray. She noticed the half-filled glass of wine sitting on the floor beside the bed where she had left it. She slowly stepped back and casually touched her foot against the glass knocking it sideways and spilling its liquid on the carpet.

She let on as if the action had startled her and immediately stepped to the trolley, removing a white, cloth napkin. She went back to the spill and dabbed at the carpet in an effort to clean it.

"Leave it," Yalcin said. "One more stain will not make a difference to this carpet."

The time was enough for Inci to make her move. When she had put her body between the wineglass and her three captors, she managed to get the small, white card out from under the sleeve of her shirt and covered it with the napkin. She stood, returned to the trolley, and placed it on top, being careful that it covered the card which contained her desperate plea for help.

Her timing could certainly not have been any more perfect. She had just stepped back from the trolley when a knock came to the door. Cengiz stood and walked toward the entrance, letting the waiter in. The young man, dressed in a white shirt with tuxedo tie and black slacks, looked nervously at the people around him. His appearance looked out of place as his neatly pressed uniform was in contrast to the surroundings of the two-star hotel room. He was unsure what to make of the group and decided his best action would be to quickly pour the tea and leave. He carried a large tray with sugar and cups and placed it on a corner of the dresser. He removed the cap from a small jar and scooped a spoonful of beige coloured crystals, placing them into each cup. From the urn, which he had also brought with him, he poured hot water and stirred the individual mixture.

"You can just leave them there," Yalcin said.

The boy nodded and looked around the room noting Cengiz had left his plate on the floor. Thomas Sun had placed his on the table. He walked over to gather the dishes and sat them on the trolley. A wave of shock riveted through Inci's body as she watched the young waiter pick up the napkins and scrunch them into a ball. When he replaced them on the top of the trolley the white card with her message on it was partially exposed. She knew she had to do something but did not want to bring attention to the trolley. She knew that if anyone looked at the cart, they would surely see her note.

"The smell of that food is starting to make me sick," she said, rubbing her stomach as if she had eaten too much.

Cengiz placed himself directly beside Inci and felt for the gun in his jacket pocket. He touched the trigger, ready to use it, should Inci decide to make an attempt at escape.

Yalcin removed a sizable amount of Inci's cash from his pocket. Peeling off enough liras from the roll to cover the tea and a handsome tip, Inci's heart beat increased as he walked toward the trolley with the money. As the waiter appreciatively accepted the payment, one of the reddish bills fell onto the trolley. Inci stopped breathing when she saw Yalcin's thick hand reach for the bill that lay directly over her note. The waiter speedily recovered the bill. Embarrassed he bowed several times while thanking his patrons for their generosity and pulling the trolley with him, quickly backed out of the room.

Her escape plan successfully initiated, Inci allowed herself to exhale.

"May I have one of those?" she asked, as Yalcin lit a cigarette.

"But of course."

She stood and walked toward Yalcin who held out the package of cigarettes. She took one and waited for him to light it. Inhaling she enjoyed the coolness of the smoke in her lungs and held it as long as she could before slowly exhaling. She was beginning to feel less threatened.

There seemed to be a more relaxed atmosphere in the room and Thomas Sun, who up till now had been extremely uptight seemed to be lowering his defences. Inci assumed they were all becoming tired and wondered if the opportunity for escape might surface. She too began to feel the same exhaustion over taking her and caught herself dozing off.

She opened her eyes and realized she had been asleep. Without moving she glanced at her watch and could see it was nearly three am. All but one of the lights had been turned off and the room dimly glowed with an eerie cloak of orange darkness. Yalcin walked to the bed where Cengiz lay sound asleep and shook him, saying, "It's your turn to watch the girl." His partner woke with a moan and slowly sat up kicking his feet off the bed. Yawning, he rubbed his whiskered face and looked around the room. He stood, stretched again and immediately Yalcin took his place on the bed.

     Inci's back was sore from sleeping in the chair but she felt it was safer than being on the bed. She shifted her body slightly hoping to find some relief from her pain and stiffness and was about to close her eyes when she saw Cengiz return from the bathroom and stare at her. His look gradually turned to an eerie smile perhaps hoping some secret bond had developed between them. Inci closed her eyes hoping to return to sleep but found it impossible as she tried to not think about what her captors might have in mind for her.

11. Fragments

Davud Kurvesh and his two accomplices once again entered the lobby of the Istanbul Holiday Inn. In an effort to avoid the security barrier inside, they bypassed the revolving door and entered through a smaller, manual one. They walked beside the metal detector and nodded to a security guard who seemed disinterested in his surroundings. Once they were in the centre of the lobby, they smiled to themselves, quietly pleased at the lack of security in this hotel.Kurvesh told his partners to wait while he placed a call to Francis Sun's room. He would meet them in the bar.

"I do not know about you, but I am extremely hungry," Kurvesh said.

He summoned the waitress and placed a food order for a club sandwich and a beer. Kwok and Seleng ordered the same and as the waitress departed, Francis Sun entered the restaurant.

Kurvesh stood and extended his hand in greeting. Ignoring it the Oriental sat down slowly in one of the tub style chairs. His eyes expressed signs of exhaustion. He was consumed with finding his son and thought about nothing else since he arrived in Istanbul. For the first time in his life he felt weak. He was not working from a position of control. He also believed he had employed people unable to handle this job. He was frustrated and displeased.

"Ask your men to sit somewhere else. I want to speak with you alone." Francis Sun spoke slowly but there was no mistaking his meaning. Both Kwok and Seleng looked at each other and then turned to Davud Kurvesh. He nodded, and they moved to another table.

Davud Kurvesh was nervous. The only reason he could imagine Francis Sun wanted to be alone with him was in order to fire him from his assignment. It was a justified concern, for he had not accomplished the task he had set out to do. It was, however, an event that had never before happened in his career.

"I want you to tell me everything that has taken place," Francis Sun said, slowly. "Leave nothing out." He had just finished speaking when the waitress returned with a plateful of food. She had a puzzled look on her face when she noticed vacant chairs where the two guests had sat.

"They are there," Kurvesh said, nodding to a corner in the bar. The waitress did not question it. She placed one of the sandwiches and beer on the table and went to serve Kwok and Seleng near the window.

Davud Kurvesh began a detailed account of the events which had taken place. He left nothing out, including the assassination of the girl in the administration room of the Dolmabahçe Palace. He had always found it better to be up front with his employers, no matter what had taken place. This created a trusting relationship between the parties involved. He knew the type of man Francis Sun was and presumed he would not be happy if a detail, no matter how minute, had been omitted.

"Did you feel it was necessary to shoot the woman?" Francis Sun asked, upon completion of Kurvesh's story.

"Yes." It was a simple answer, which needed no further explanation.

"The two people who are also looking for my son are with the United Nations?" Kurvesh nodded affirmatively. With elbows resting on the arms of his chair and fingertips pressed together in front of his face, the Oriental pondered what he had heard. As a waitress passed he made a slight motion with one hand and said, "A cup of tea please."

"Apple tea or normal tea?" the waitress, asked.

"Regular tea." Francis Sun waited for her to leave before continuing his conversation. He closed his eyes and inhaled deeply. "I sincerely hope the Americans are mistaken about my son; however, his recent actions have led me to believe that quite possibly they are not. If he is associated with the group who call themselves the 'Children of the Sultan', he may very well be involved in terrorist activities." He paused a moment before continuing. "I want you to understand something." He lowered his hands and shifted his weight into a more upright position. "Make no mistake about my intent. If he is involved, it is a concern I will deal with, but above all, he is my son and I do not want him taken away from me by anyone, for any reason."

"If Mustafa and his men take him into their custody, I will never hear from him again. They will convince him to join their band, and he will be lost to me forever. If the Americans capture him, I could perhaps bargain for his safety." He inhaled again before speaking. "You see Mr. Kurvesh, I have little choice, but to find him myself."

The waitress returned with the tea and placed it on the table before Francis Sun. Would you care for milk or lemon," she asked.

Francis Sun shook his head and leaned forward, picking up the tea to enjoy a sip of its distinct flavour. Then he continued, "It is my intention to rent an airplane and fly to Nevsehir in an effort to make contact with the man who is responsible for the abduction of my son. I will pay him what he wants and my son will come back to me."

"What if he does not want the money?"

Francis Sun looked up from his teacup into the eyes of Davud Kurvesh. "Everyone wants money, Mr. Kurvesh, everyone."

Kurvesh nodded. "I suppose you are right."

"I wish for you to accompany me." Kurvesh was relieved at the request. He was not to be dismissed after all. "I do, however, want you to ask your accomplices to return home. Make whatever financial arrangements you wish, but I do not trust their ability."

Davud Kurvesh was about to dispute the allegations; however, he thought better of it and did not want to jeopardize his present position. He believed it would not take much for the man across from him to release him of his duties as well.

"I will make the arrangements immediately," Kurvesh said.

"Rent an airplane and have it ready to leave tomorrow morning at nine o'clock. I will meet you here at eight."

Francis Sun pushed his hands on the arms of his chair and forced his weight up until he was in a standing position. He slowly walked away from the table without looking at Seleng and Kwok who had silently kept their eyes focused on the two people.

Kurvesh waited for Sun to leave before joining his associates. "The job is over. We are finished," he simply said.

There was a look of surprise on the faces of the two men, but it quickly disappeared, as each of them had anticipated the action after being recalled from the ferry docks an hour and a half ago. "Did he give a reason?" Seleng asked.

"He believes we should have found his son by now."

"That is a little unjustified."

"I agree, but there is no point in arguing with him. As you know, he is a man of few words when his mind has been made up."

"What will you do next?" Seleng asked of Davud Kurvesh.

"I will remain in Turkey and try to relax for a little while. It is time for a vacation." He lied without detection. He gave no indication that he was to remain on the assignment.

"How does this equate to our financial arrangements?" Kwok asked.

"It will not be unchanged. You will receive the money we spoke of earlier. It will be deposited in the usual manner in one week's time."

Kwok looked surprised. "Why one week?"

"Mr. Sun desires it to be so. He feels his son is in grave danger and wishes to ensure that we will not speak of this matter to anyone. I would recommend you cater to those requests. You are to fly home immediately, and speak to no one of this entire incident. The money will be deposited in your account in one week's time."

"I am a little uncomfortable with that," Kwok replied.

"This choice is not mine and the decision has been made." Davud Kurvesh wanted to set his ally at ease. "You have worked with me long enough to know you can trust me. I will make certain you receive your money. Let us make the flight arrangements."

He stood and began to walk away. "I will return shortly." He left the lobby bar heading toward the front desk of the hotel.

"I am not pleased with this arrangement," Kwok said.

"I see nothing wrong with it," Seleng replied. "We are paid what we are owed and we have done very little work."

"We are not paid yet, my friend."

Davud Kurvesh greeted the attendant behind the front desk of the hotel. "I would like to make arrangements for two flights leaving as soon as possible please. One is to Manila, the other to Hong Kong. We will pick up the tickets at the airport. I will be in the bar with my associates. Please let me know the minute you have confirmation."

"When would you like to leave?" the girl behind the desk asked.

"As soon as possible." Kurvesh returned to the lobby bar and sat at the table with Kwok and

Seleng. "She is making arrangements and will call us in a few moments." He rubbed his hands together as if a feat had just been accomplished. "I think I would like another beer," he said, and summoned the waitress to take his order. Kwok and Seleng joined him. The conversation among the three, dealt with issues not associated with the Francis Sun affair.

Several minutes had passed and most of the beer had been consumed when the front desk attendant arrived at their table. "I have made the arrangements for your requested flights." She spoke in English. "There are two flights which leave about the same time." She referred to the piece of paper on which she had scribbled the information given her by the airlines.

"What time do they leave?" Seleng asked.

"In about three hours," she replied, courteously. "You can pay for them at the airport"

"That is perfect," Davud Kurvesh said. "Thank you for your assistance." The attendant departed.

Seleng looked at his watch. "I suppose we should be leaving shortly. Customs and immigration are always slow in this part of the world." He leaned forward and finished the remainder of his beer. Kwok agreed and did the same. Davud Kurvesh stood and reached into his pocket removing enough money to cover the bills at both tables. He laid the currency on the plate before him and walked with his associates, through the hotel lobby to the front door. Again they bypassed the magnetic metal detector and waited for a taxi to drive to the front door. The driver jumped out, looking for luggage and was pleased to see there was none. The two men stepped into the rear seat of the cab and, as the driver returned, he sped the taxi along the laneway exiting the hotel. Davud Kurvesh returned to the lobby and decided he would have one more beer before retiring for the evening. On his way to the bar, he made arrangements to check in for the night.

Kwok yawned noisily as the taxi sped along the major thoroughfare on its short journey to the airport. They arrived at a traffic circle and followed the flow of other vehicles. The taxi came to a halt at a red light and Seleng noticed a billboard, larger than most, displaying the famous Marlboro cowboy advertising that brand of cigarettes. As he turned to look out the side window of the taxi, he noticed the muzzle of an automatic machine gun pointed directly at him. It was the last vision he would see in this life. Kwok was unaware of what was happening and heard a loud crack as the taxi window's glass shattered. He turned to face Seleng and was sprayed with fragments of flesh as the bullets ripped his companion's head to pieces. He was about to scream when the window on his side of the car shattered and a series of bullets streamed into the vehicle, killing him instantly.

The driver of the taxi emitted an ear-piercing scream when he realized what was taking place.

In the confusion, he failed to notice the cars on both sides of him roll up their windows and continue driving forward. It would be another unsolved crime for which the local police force could find no motive.

Davud Kurvesh poured the cold beer into a tall glass. He enjoyed a long swallow and looked forward to the task, which lay ahead. He felt he would enjoy working with Francis Sun and appreciated the faith the Oriental man had in him. As he finished his beer, he made his way to the elevator for a restful night's sleep, unaware that his two companions had just been assassinated through an arrangement made by his new accomplice, Francis Sun.

12. Amr El Hab

The telephone rang three times before Phillip Wright realized it was not his alarm clock. He shifted slightly as Lana flipped the switch on the bedroom lamp, beside the bed.

Phillip immediately awoke, and his first thought was concern over Quentin's well being. He grabbed the telephone from the night table and answered it.

"Phillip, this is Peter Alexander." Phillip felt panic develop within his body, for he knew Peter would not contact him in the middle of the night unless it was extremely urgent. He waited for his superior to continue. "I just received a call from Amr El Hab."

Phillip suspected a problem. Amr El Hab was the head of the Mid East sector of ISIS. Phillip had known the Egyptian for most of his career. They had completed their basic training together and had become friends. Amr was very thorough in performing his tasks, and his results proved to be quite successful. The mere mention of his name by Peter Alexander indicated to Phillip that the secret involving Quentin in Turkey had no longer been contained.

Peter Alexander continued. "Amr is quite upset. He has just received a telephone call from someone in Turkey. The message was from our correspondent there, Inci Arzu. It read something to the effect that she had been kidnapped and was on her way to Nevsehir. The message also had the word Mustafa written on it."

Again the words 'Children of the Sultan' raced through Phillip's mind. If they were the culprits who had captured Inci, he was sure that Quentin's life would also be in jeopardy.

"We also have a report of a violent killing," Peter continued. "This one is in an historic landmark known as the Dolmabahçe Palace in Istanbul. Two men held a number of the administration people hostage and were interrogating them. Apparently the man in charge refused to answer the questions and one of the women who worked with him was brutally assassinated."

Phillip's heart went still as Peter began to unfold the details of what had occurred in Istanbul. For some reason, he began to suspect that Peter Alexander laid the blame for these incidents with Phillip. He knew it had been his idea to keep a lid on what had happened but the murder of this woman and the kidnapping of the agent had happened long before Phillip was involved. When the decision to keep this incident quiet had been made, Peter Alexander had been aware of the exact same facts Phillip was privy to.

"The facts remain the same since the last time we spoke," Phillip said. "The death of this woman verifies what Quentin said about his suspicions of being followed. We knew about Mustafa and Inci Arzu's capture." Phillip paused a moment. "This changes nothing."

"This changes everything," Peter Alexander replied. "Amr is involved and it is his territory. I'm turning things over to him as of right now. Is Quentin expected to phone you?"

"He said he would," Phillip replied. Although he was not pleased with Peter Alexander's move, he knew there was no alternative. If it were the other way around, Phillip would have been furious at having been left out of the loop. Phillip fully understood and agreed with his superior's action although he had trouble accepting it.

"When he contacts you, tell him to immediately call Amr. This has become a major, international incident and the risks are very high. We already have one agent in danger. I do not want to lose a second because of pride and ego."

Phillip understood the directness of Peter Alexander's statements. He rose from the bed as quietly as he could hoping not to disturb Lana, although he knew she was fully awake. "I'm just going into the den for a while. I better think this through and will probably telephone Quentin."

"Trouble, huh?"

"It appears so. Nothing has really changed except now I'm no longer involved, which means I don't know what will happen to Quentin."

Lana sympathized with the anguish her husband was feeling. She had become quite fond of her stepson, since their meeting, and she too was concerned for his safety.

Phillip manoeuvred his feet into his slippers, picked up his robe, and silently headed out of the room causing Abernethy, who routinely slept there, to stir. Although it was the middle of the night the room was flooded with moonlight. Waiting at the door for Abernethy, who decided to join him, the two made their way downstairs to the study where Phillip turned on a lamp and headed to a small table holding a crystal container of gin and several glasses. Picking up a glass he poured a shot of the clear liquid forgoing the formalities of ice and vermouth. He walked to a corner of the room and allowed his body to fall into the comfort a large, leather chair.

The walls of the room were covered with

oak panelling and book shelves filled with various books displayed in no particular order. Several framed photographs lined the walls depicting events in the lives of Phillip and Lana Wright. A large oriental, green and beige rug filled the centre of the floor and a brass telescope, mounted on an antique tripod, stood before one of the windows.

Full of artifacts, gathered by Phillip over the years, the comfortable room could have easily looked cluttered. It didn't. Lana was responsible for organizing the collection. Phillip conceded a long time ago that her eye for such matters was far superior to his.

He debated his next move and knew he had no alternative but to contact Quentin to relay what had happened. He also decided to phone Amr and discuss possible actions with his friend.

He took a swallow of the gin, hoisted himself from the chair and walked to the roll-top desk. Opening one of the drawers, he removed a small address book and looked up a number. Picking up the portable phone, he dialed the number, returned to his favourite chair, and waited for Amr El Hab to answer. Giving no thought to the time, he knew it wouldn't matter.

After three rings the Egyptian answered the phone. "Amr, this is Phillip Wright."

"Phillip, my friend. How are you?" Amr replied, genuinely glad to hear from his old friend.

"I understand we have some problems in Turkey?"

"So it seems," Amr replied. "How much did Peter tell you?"

Phillip relayed the information he had received from Peter Alexander.

"That seems to be all of the information I have as well. I know you have been in touch with your son. If there is anything you can add, I would appreciate it."

Phillip explained what he knew of the situation, sharing everything Quentin had told him, including what he had learned of the 'Children of the Sultan'.

"They are an organization which has been causing a great amount of grief lately," Amr replied. "Their leader, Mustafa, is wanted by many agencies. He is extremely difficult to find."

"How well do you know this girl Inci?" Phillip asked.

"She is extremely good. She has been with us for at least half a dozen years. Maybe more. Why do you ask?"

"When Peter told me he received a note from her, I wondered about the nature of her capture."

"What do you mean?" Amr asked, inquisitively.

"Well, I thought if she had been captured and had somehow got a note out, her captors could not be watching her too closely."

"Meaning what?" Amr interjected.

"Meaning that perhaps she had an opportunity to escape but decided not to in an effort to locate the whereabouts of Mustafa or possibly infiltrate his organization."

"That is interesting," Amr replied. "Your comment makes a great deal of sense." He paused a moment before continuing. "She is a well respected agent who does an excellent job. She has been in tight situations before and has always managed to get out of them." He thought a moment. "Perhaps you are right."

Phillip went on to talk about Francis Sun. Like Phillip, Amr had been unfamiliar with the man or his organization. Phillip gave him what few details he had.

"It has developed into quite an interesting situation," Amr added. "It would be safe to assume the men following your son and Inci work for this man, Francis Sun."

"Everything seems to point in that direction. The thing that concerns me is that his wealth and his desire to get his son back. He could probably do more damage than any of our agents."

Amr was silent, but agreed with Phillip's statement.

"What do you propose we do?" Phillip asked.

"I would defer to you for assistance, my friend," Amr said. "I would recommend we recruit several agents and try to release Inci. We should also develop a second network to neutralize the people who are allegedly working for Francis Sun."

Amr paused a moment. "Do you think we should pull Quentin out?"

Phillip thought deeply about Amr's suggestion. "Believe me, my friend, I would like nothing more. I feel, however, if we were to do that it could shatter Quentin's self-confidence and make him uncertain in future assignments. I am concerned about his safety from a father's perspective, and realize it's the wrong approach to take."

"I agree with you. We will leave him in; however, he will work with the team and take his directions from an experienced agent."

"Do you have anyone in mind?"

"I do not. However, I will do some investigating and appoint someone immediately. Where can I reach Quentin?"

Phillip gave Amr the necessary information including Quentin's hotel and telephone number. "Do me one favour, my friend?" Phillip asked.

"Anything. Name it."

"Let me know everything that happens."

"Of course. I understand your concern."

Phillip pushed the off button on the telephone and took a moment before making the next call. Knowing there would be opposition from Quentin to this latest turn of events. He knew he had to step up to the responsibilities of his higher ranking position and out of his role of father. With the direction this case had taken he had no choice. There were too many lives at stake, and there was too much at risk, for his inexperienced son to lead this operation. Dialing the number he hoped Quentin would understand.

The telephone rang twice before Quentin answered it. "Woke you up, huh?" Phillip said, humorously.

"No not really. I was laying here waiting for somebody to call." With his sense of humour, Quentin's response was quick.

"Well I've certainly got news for you. Whether it's great or not is up to you." Phillip inhaled deeply before he began. "We are going to bring in some help." Phillip waited for a response but none came. "Apparently, Inci is on her way to Nevsehir to meet with Mustafa."

"He is the leader of the 'Children of the Sultan', isn't he?" Quentin asked.

"Yes, he is."

"How do you know this?" Quentin asked.

"Peter Alexander just called me a few minutes ago and told me that Inci had managed to sneak a message out from a hotel room. It had her name on it, the words Nevsehir, Mustafa, and a telephone number, which of course is the number for Amr El Hab."

"When did this happen?" Quentin asked, impatiently.

"Very recently. I just spoke with Amr and he's going to make a few changes."

"What kind of changes?"

"He is sending in two teams. One to work with you to find Inci and Thomas Sun, the second to track the guys who are following you."

"Are there any options for me?"

"No. Peter Alexander has made a decision and it won't change. I know what you're thinking, but this is way out of hand. We're dealing with one of the most dangerous terrorist organizations in the world in an area where you don't even speak the language. You're being pursued by someone who controls a giant criminal conglomerate and you're partially involved in a murder."

The word murder stopped Quentin from responding. He thought a moment. "What do you mean murder?"

"Apparently, the guys who were chasing you caught up with some administration people in the palace that you were in yesterday. They were looking for the same information which you were given and when they didn't get it, they killed somebody."

Quentin was astounded by the news. He could not believe someone could be that callous. He kept his comments to himself. It was an indication to him, however, that perhaps he was in over his head. "Do you have any idea who was killed?" Quentin asked.

"No. I believe it was a woman, but I have no further details."

"What's the next move?" Quentin asked.

"You are to call Amr El Hab for further instructions."

Quentin noticed a distinct change in Phillip's

voice. His tone had become cold and his words sounded calculated. He had dissociated himself from the personal aspect of this mission and was now acting as he would with any other agent.

Phillip gave Quentin Amr El Hab's telephone number in Cairo and was about to say goodbye.

"Dad," Quentin said. "Thanks for your help."

"I want you to do me a favour," Phillip said. "Keep me posted as to what happens."

"I will."

"And Quentin, be careful."

Phillip replaced the portable telephone, finished the rest of his drink, and walked toward the kitchen to satisfy Abernethy's nagging for a quick trip outside. He disarmed the security system beside the rear door and let the dog out.

The haunting rays of the bright moon washed the backyard with an eerie glow. The autumn perennials were in bloom and took on different hues under the strange light. Phillip gazed across the well-manicured flower garden, but was oblivious to the visions before him. His mind was in a distant world -- a place of disorder and ruthlessness -- a place with which he was all too familiar.

Quentin did not immediately dial the number his father gave him. He wanted to be fully awake before speaking to Amr El Hab. Although his father had spoken of the section head from the Middle

East sector of ISIS many times, Quentin had never met him and wanted to be certain he did not make the wrong impression. He stumbled toward the bathroom and squinted as he flipped on the light. Splashing cold water on his face, he grabbed a towel and returned to the phone where he dialed Amr El Hab's number from memory.

The telephone only rang once before it was answered. "Amr El Hab please," Quentin said, speaking rather softly in the event he had disturbed the Egyptian.

"Speaking. Who is this?"

"My name is Quentin Wright. I believe you were just speaking with my father." Quentin was trying not to sound defensive. He had done nothing wrong and was proceeding on a course he felt to be correct. He thought perhaps Amr would be upset about Inci's capture and consequently blamed him.

"Ah, Quentin. How are you?" Amr sounded genuine when he spoke.

"I suppose I've been better. My dad said you're going to send in some people."

"Yes. There is far too much risk for one person to deal with."

Quentin was pleased that Amr used generalizations when speaking, rather than insinuating that it was too much for him to handle. "I am in the process of putting together two small teams. One to accompany you in the pursuit of Thomas Sun and Inci. The second to locate and neutralize the men who are following you." Amr paused before continuing. Born in Cairo, but educated in England, his English was perfect. He and Phillip were the same age and had gone through ISIS training together. Starting as a field agent, his outstanding leadership abilities and calm approach to any situation, he quickly advanced to his present position as Section Head of the Middle East.

"What can you tell me about the men who are pursuing you?"

Quentin thought for a moment. "I was never certain they were pursuing me until my father told me of the murder in the Dolmabahçe Palace."

"Yes. That was most unfortunate. I do not believe that it could have been avoided."

Quentin was glad he was not being held responsible for the murder in Istanbul. "I can't tell you very much. We only saw the men on videotape. They were quite far from the camera so a printout was not very helpful. From what I could see there were three men. Two were Oriental and one looked as if he could have been Turkish. I wouldn't rule out Italian, Spanish or Greek, either but definitely from a Mediterranean or Middle East country. They hung around the lobby of the Dolmabahçe Palace for quite some time and looked as if they were waiting for someone. Inci and I believe it was for us, but as I said, it could have been coincidence. If you talk to the guard responsible for security in the Dolmabahçe Palace, I'm sure he'll be able to verify descriptions."

"That is good to know. We will send someone out there immediately to get the information." Amr El Hab paused as he made notes of Quentin's account. "Tell me about Thomas Sun and the way he made his getaway from Istanbul."

Quentin went on to explain about the car running out of gas and Inci's abduction from the parking lot of the hotel in Bursa. A thought occurred to him as he was speaking. "I understand Inci managed to get a note out for someone to call you?"

"Yes she did. That is how I became aware of this situation; not exactly the proper channel I might add."

Quentin deserved the statement. He knew he should not have contacted his father. The rules are very clear. All reports are to be made to the person heading up the sector. "I understand. It won't happen again," he said assertively not in the mood for a scolding.

Amr El Hab sensed Quentin's feelings and did not pursue the matter. He firmly believed judgement had to be used by agents in the field. If judgement continued to be wrong, then the person would be replaced. He was not a great believer in using hindsight to judge actions.

"What can you tell me about the note?" Quentin asked.

Amr thought a moment before responding. "Not a great deal. It came from a hotel in Ankara. It had my telephone number written on it and the words Mustafa and Nevsehir."

"What was the hotel?" Quentin asked, trying not to sound anxious.

"Why do you want to know?"

"Well it makes sense for me to go there and see if she's still there. There is no reason why they would have left, especially since they wouldn't have known about the note."

"I am not certain that is a good idea," Amr replied.

"Why not?" Quentin asked, rather aggressively. "I'm right here in Ankara. You don't even have a team together. I can go over and find them. I know the car they're driving. I'll wait for them. I have a cellular phone so as soon as your team is organized, tell them to contact me and I'll meet them exactly where they are."

Amr El Hab could not challenge Quentin's plan. Amr paused then said, "Perhaps it will be all right. The call came from the Merit Altinel Hotel." He went on, "I want you to call me the minute you arrive and if they are there I want no heroics. There are lives at stake—lives very dear to me. Do I make myself clear?" He spoke very distinctly.

"Absolutely." Quentin assured Amr El Hab he would keep him informed and hung up the phone. He checked his watch. It was only four in the morning but he was awake and had new enthusiasm so he showered quickly and dressed. While checking out of the hotel he asked for directions to the Merit Altinel Hotel and a map of the city. He thanked the assistant and went out to his car.

Checking the directions, Quentin exited the hotel parking lot and was thankful there was very little traffic. It only took about twenty minutes to arrive at the hotel and his heart beat increased noticeably when he spotted the grey sedan parked near the entrance to the hotel.

For a split second, he debated whether or not to enter but decided against it, as he felt it would be better to follow the guidelines imposed by Amr. There may be more to this assignment than he understood, and he did not wish to jeopardize Inci's life.

He immediately removed the cellular telephone from its charging adapter and dialed the number of Amr El Hab.

"It is plain to see I am not going to get any sleep this evening," Amr said, jokingly.

"I'm at the hotel. The car is here, so I assume the people are inside."

"That is excellent news." Amr sounded genuinely pleased at Quentin's quick thinking and positive action. "I have assembled two teams and they are en route to Turkey. The one you will be working with is led by Ole Pcdersen. Ole is from Denmark and has been with us for at least ten years. He has been briefed on the situation and I will give him your cellular number so he can contact you the minute he arrives in Ankara."

"What time do you expect him to arrive?"

"His plane should land in about an hour and a half. He is flying in from Athens and will have three people with him, also ISIS agents. Together, the five of you will follow the perpetrators. It is important to understand you will take your direction from Ole." Amr El Hab maintained his pleasant voice, but Quentin knew he was not to be challenged.

"I understand," Quentin replied. "I'll wait here until I hear from him." Quentin went on to give Amr his cell phone number and a description of the rented vehicle he was driving. Amr thanked Quentin for his information and said he would look forward to meeting him once this matter was behind them. Quentin disconnected the phone line and again contemplated entering the hotel.

He was disturbed by a comment Amr had made which suggested they should pursue Inci and her captors. It was evident their intention was not to free her but to use her as bait in an effort to locate the man who headed up the terrorist organization.

Quentin was uneasy about the decision but knew the mission was all that mattered. He felt, after his conversation with Amr, that capturing Thomas Sun was no longer the objective. It was now clear they would be pursuing a Kurdish terrorist group known as the 'Children of the Sultan' and its leader, a man called Mustafa.

13. Konya

Davud Kurvesh waited for Francis Sun in the hotel's restaurant. He helped himself to a heaping plateful of breakfast from the generous buffet. Nervous and excited at the prospect of working with this highly respected businessmen, he did not consider Francis Sun to be a criminal.

Kurvesh worked for Francis Sun once before, several years ago. The two, however, had never come face to face. The assignment involved locating someone who had stolen money from Francis Sun. The culprit had escaped to the Mediterranean shores of Turkey, and Kurvesh had been responsible for the entire operation. He had been thorough and quick, and had apprehended the man within three days. Francis Sun had been extremely pleased. The financial rewards had been generous, but not as gratifying as the compliments paid him by the Asian crime syndicate leader himself.

Kurvesh spent many years establishing a network of trustworthy, reliable men. They included seasoned, crime veterans with good connections to established criminal families. They were professionals with extensive experience with explosives, extortion, assassination, theft, gambling, and information and security infiltration. Like Francis Sun he maintained complete control over his operation by ensuring that none of his employees was familiar with any other's activity.

He had amassed an empire which he could view from a distance, no longer needing to be directly involved. This case, however, was an exception. Francis Sun was one of the most powerful men in the world and Davud Kurvesh was adamant about completing this task to perfection.

The Asian was more demanding because his son was involved. Under other circumstances, he would have been quite pleased with Kurvesh's progress. The involvement of the underworld king's son made matters different. It caused impatience and great anxiety within Francis Sun -- anxiety noted by Davud Kurvesh.

Kurvesh was not concerned about working directly with Francis Sun. He was, however, unfamiliar with the man's methods and what he expected. He was beginning to feel more like a hired gun tagging along with the mastermind than head of his own syndicate.

He felt slightly agitated at being requested to return his accomplices to their homeland. They were good men and had performed their jobs well. He had used both Seleng and Kwok several times in the past and had always been pleased with their results.

As the years had progressed, Kurvesh's network had spread to other parts of the globe. Initially, he had created an excellent reputation throughout the Middle East, but as borders changed and increased travel made the world appear smaller, he had found it necessary to expand to different lands. The Orient was one of these areas. It was there, many years ago, that he had an opportunity to work with Rudy Seleng and Wu Fung Kwok.

Both men had served him well without question. He knew their egos would be damaged by the recent change in plans and could see it in their faces. Neither of them wanted to abandon their mission and return home. It had been, however, not an option for Davud Kurvesh. His role was to carry out the orders of Francis Sun. He felt confident Kwok and Seleng would be paid in full for the work they had performed and believed Francis Sun to be a man who kept his word. His reputation was that of being demanding but fair.

Kurvesh continued to dwell on his thoughts,

so it took him a moment to realize Francis Sun was approaching. "How are you this morning?" Kurvesh asked.

"I am well." Francis Sun sat in a chair directly across from Davud Kurvesh. He leaned forward, lifted the stainless steel coffee urn and filled his cup. Kurvesh lifted the milk container and was about to pass it to Sun when the large Oriental held up his hand to decline. He took a sip of the strong coffee, feeling its flavour tingle throughout the inside of his mouth.

Francis Sun glanced around the room and focused his attention outside the large, plate glass windows. The sun was rising slowly and a heavy dew covered the recently trimmed grass. From the restaurant, he could see the outside wading pool surrounded by beautiful rose gardens. In the distance, at the perimeter of the grounds, was a wall of flowering bushes, beyond which lay the deep blue waters of the Bosporus Sea.

The blue and cloudless sky, held forth the promise of an enjoyable day. The exterior colours flooded into the restaurant area where the tables were set with pale blue and white cloths matching the uniforms of the staff.

Looking around the room Francis Sun was surprised by the number of camera carrying, casually dressed, tourists. He hadn't realized Turkey was such a popular tourist destination.

His peaceful thoughts were interrupted by the arrival of a waitress, prepared to take his order. He had declined the buffet and had asked for eggs, sausages, and brown toast. The waitress explained, in broken English, that all these items were available from the buffet, but Francis Sun simply said he wished to order from the menu. The waitress did not argue, for she understood by the look on this man's face that he was not to be questioned.

The server retreated to the kitchen and Francis Sun took another sip of his coffee. He slowly raised his head and stared into the eyes of Davud Kurvesh. "Did you arrange an aircraft for us?"

"Yes, I have." Kurvesh lifted a forkful of egg from his plate. "It is waiting for us at the airport and will fly us to Konya."

Francis Sun's face had a look of surprise. "I thought we were going to Nevsehir?"

"Konya is only one hour's drive from there. It would not be wise to fly an airplane where the terrorists are hiding. They would see us immediately."

Francis Sun nodded, and was about to ask the time of the flight, when the waitress arrived with his breakfast. Holding his plate to one side, she picked up his napkin and draped it on his lap then carefully placed the plate in front of him. He thanked her and she departed.

"What time do we have to leave?"

"The plane is ready when you are. I told them we would be there around eight-thirty." Kurvesh looked at his watch. "We have plenty of time. It is only seven-thirty and it is no more than a fifteen minute drive. The aircraft is ours for the day."

"Can the pilot be trusted?"

"Absolutely." Kurvesh spoke with conviction. He felt very confident about the people who worked for him. "I've known him for many years and have used him many times."

Francis Sun nodded as he studied his breakfast. He dipped the brown toast into the soft, yellow yolk of the eggs and took great pleasure in enjoying its taste. "Have you made arrangements for someone to meet us in Konya?"

"Yes I have. It is someone who knows the area very well. We will meet at the airport and drive to Cappadocia."

Francis Sun looked up inquisitively.

"Cappadocia is the central area of Turkey," Kurvesh explained, aware of his employer's unfamiliarity with the region. "It is a mountainous area settled by early Christians in the fifth and sixth centuries. When you see its landscapes and strange formations, I think you will be impressed."

"We are not here on a sightseeing mission. Let us not forget my son is out there somewhere."

Kurvesh lowered his head, realizing he had spoken with too much familiarity. He waited patiently, in silence, for Sun to finish his breakfast. When they had completed the meal, Francis Sun left enough money on the table to cover both of the bills. The two men stood, walked toward the spiral staircase, and made their way to the lobby. Francis Sun walked to the desk to check-out.

"I will go and secure a taxi for us." Kurvesh said, and began to walk to the lobby door, again bypassing the security system.

When Francis Sun settled his account, he joined Davud Kurvesh, who was already seated in the rear seat of the small, yellow taxi.

"Did your two associates get to the airport all right?" Francis Sun asked.

"Yes. They left yesterday after we spoke." Kurvesh looked at his watch. "By now, they are most likely at home."

Francis Sun did not indicate his awareness surrounding the fate of Rudy Seleng and Wu Fung Kwok. He knew this mission would be over by the time Kurvesh received the news of their untimely death. Hopefully his son would be at his side.

The two passengers in the rear seat of the cab, remained silent for the duration of their short journey to the Istanbul airport. Davud Kurvesh was careful not to say anything which might offend or anger his superior. Francis Sun gave no thought to the man beside him. His concerns were with his son.

The harsh noise of Cengiz slamming the bathroom door startled everyone in the room. Inci had been asleep in the chair and although she had not slept comfortably, she had managed to doze off for a few hours. As she moved she felt a slight pain develop in her muscles as a result of the uncomfortable sleeping position she had maintained throughout the night.

Thomas Sun rubbed his face briskly as he tried to stretch his arms. He had awoken once during the night and had removed his jacket, carefully placing it over one of the two chairs beside the bed. He glanced around the room and said nothing. Slowly he swung his legs over the side of the bed and stood, stretching again as he did so. He slowly walked across the room and entered the bathroom, closing the door behind him.

"I am very hungry," Cengiz said, rubbing his stomach as he began to yawn.

Inci was disgusted with the man's mannerism. As he yawned, she could see a small bead of saliva stretch between his upper and lower lips. She detested him and vowed that if he ever touched her, she would make every effort to kill him.

"That is an excellent idea," Yalcin replied. "Let us get organized and we will eat in the restaurant downstairs."

"What are you saying?" Thomas Sun asked, as he re-entered the room.

"I am sorry, my friend," Yalcin said, this time speaking in English. "We were just discussing breakfast and decided we would eat downstairs."

"Do you think that is wise?"

"I do not think we have to worry. Our little friend will not try anything as long as we have these with us." He raised his semiautomatic and held it for Thomas Sun to see.

The Asian was not impressed by the gesture of superiority. "I was not concerned as much about her, as I was about her accomplice who is out there somewhere."

"He has no idea where we are. For all he knows, we are still in Bursa."

"Please do not underestimate our enemies." Thomas Sun spoke slowly and deliberately, a trait he had learned from his father.

"You worry far too much, my friend," Yalcin replied. "No one knows we are here and certainly not where we are going."

"I hope you are correct." Thomas Sun was not comfortable with Yalcin's lack of concern for the surrounding events. He agreed with some aspects of the Turk's words and felt it could have been difficult for the other agent to follow them; however, he had always learned never to assume the unexpected would not take place. He decided he would keep his eyes open and remain alert throughout the duration of this venture.

Yalcin led the way out of the room and along the musty hallway to the small elevator that finally delivered them to the lobby. They headed for the small dining area and stood beside a sign asking then to wait for an attendant. Not wanting to attract attention Yalcin stood patiently until a waitress came and seated them.

The restaurant, like the rest of the hotel, was in need of updating and repair. Well worn booths with chipped, green Arborite tables lined the wall. The dirty ceramic floor with missing tiles and walls covered with soiled, red and gold, smoke dingy, flocked wallpaper clearly proclaimed its age.

"A table for four please,"... a harried waitress finally came.

As the foursome waited for the waitress to return, both Inci and Thomas Sun were disgusted at the surroundings. Cengiz and Falcon grabbed menus and began scanning them hoping to quickly satisfy their hunger.

The waitress took a long time returning and when she finally arrived, brought an urn of coffee, but forgot the milk and sugar. She automatically filled the cups to capacity, assuming everyone drank coffee.

"I would like tea, please," Thomas Sun replied.

The waitress did not understand and Yalcin translated the request. She spoke in Turkish and departed.

"It appears she does not like working here. She is not too excited about getting your tea; however, I believe she will comply."

Inci took a sip of the coffee, and was shocked by its strength. Although she enjoyed strong coffee, it had stood for quite some time and this was beyond her pleasure. "Where is it we are going?" she asked.

"You certainly are an inquisitive one,"

Yalcin said. "I suppose there is no harm in telling you."

"I do not agree," Thomas Sun replied. "There is no need for her to know anything."

"Again, my friend, you are far too cautious. Let loose and live a little." Yalcin chuckled loudly as he spoke.

Cengiz looked around at other patrons in the restaurant and had no idea of the conversation which was taking place.

"As I mentioned earlier, we are on route to meet our old friend Mustafa. We will be driving to Nevsehir and then on to central Cappadocia. We will meet our friend later this evening and dine with him at his home in Avanos.

Inci had not visited this area in quite some time, but remembered seeing the fairy chimneys as a child. They were strange constructions of rock, which had formed as a result of erosion caused by wind and rain over many thousands of years. They had begun as small mountains with very hard, crusty caps. Over time the wind had slowly worn away the sides, but the caps stayed intact causing the remaining structures to take on a mushroom shape giving them their unusual name.

The area was further enhanced during the fifth and sixth centuries when the Christians began living in central Turkey. As they continued to preach their religion, they made enemies with the Muslim tribes to the south and east. As time progressed, Christians were constantly attacked and began carving holes in these chimneys. Over several hundred years, a massive series of underground cities were created which became a refuge for the Christians during attacks. They used the sand, which they dug from the caves, to build structures which resembled existing fairy chimneys, therefore, making it virtually impossible to be discovered by their attackers. This went on for three hundred years and the underground cities developed into architectural splendours. Large churches were carved out of the sandstone and were decorated with murals, which depicted the Christian scenes.

The rooms of the cities were linked with small corridors, creating a complex maze, which made it impossible for strangers to find their way.

Inci could understand why someone like Mustafa would use the area as a home. It would be difficult for him to be discovered by authorities or anyone else. He would have every opportunity to hide and from what she remembered from her history lessons, the underground cities of Cappadocia could easily hold three to four hundred people for a number of months. The area was now a tourist attraction, but ninety percent of it had still remained untouched.

Inci's thoughts were interrupted by the return of the waitress, carrying an aluminium teapot filled with hot water. She neglected to bring a cup and when Cengiz asked her about the cream and sugar for the coffee, she sighed and appeared to sneer at him. She took their food order, committed it to memory, and left.

"Perhaps you have heard of our dear friend, Mustafa?" Yalcin asked.

"No, I do not believe I have." Inci purposely lied to gain more information. She was familiar with the name and knew only that he was the leader of a terrorist group allegedly responsible for many criminal acts both in and outside of Turkey.

"Mustafa is our great hero. With him we will return Turkey to the strong power she once was." Yalcin said. "He has shown us how the Western pigs will stop at nothing to ruin our lives and that we must show them we will not be pushed around like cattle."

As he spoke, anger built up in his face, causing tiny veins to protrude near his temples. He stopped abruptly when the waitress arrived with their food and Inci decided she would not pursue this line of conversation. It stirred emotions rooted deep within Yalcin. She had no desire to cause this man more frustration, for his anger would surely be directed toward her.

She also noticed that none of the plates resembled anything that was ordered. But it was food and Yalcin and Cengiz were hungry enough to eat anything. Looking disgusted, Thomas Sun pushed his plate away and took another drink of tea. He decided to remain hungry.

It was only because Inci was raised in Turkey that she ventured to eat the pita bread and humus.

Cengiz, unable to understand the English conversation could see the anger in his partner's face. Thomas Sun also picked up on the raw emotions being unleashed. "I surely wish you would speak of something else," he said. "This can, in no way, help our cause." It was the first time, since Inci had met him, that he spoke with determination.

The small troop continued their breakfast in silence. Upon completion, Yalcin left enough money to cover the bill, but no tip. He felt the service had been unworthy of such a gesture.

While Yalcin made arrangements for departing the hotel, he told Cengiz to watch over Inci and to wait in the lobby with Thomas Sun.

The lobby was still empty, and the checkout procedure did not take long. It was dark when the foursome stepped into the parking lot. An autumn dampness had blanketed the surrounding area and left coolness in the air. The sky was a deep blue, not yet bathed in sunlight. The morning had the makings of another beautiful day as Yalcin led the four toward the car to continue their journey from Ankara to Nevsehir in the central region of Turkey, known as Cappadocia.

14. Bashing

Quentin slouched in the driver's seat of his automobile in the early hours of the morning as he waited patiently for something to happen. Now he was part of a new team and his objective was clear: locate, follow, and wait. On his own Quentin might not have followed this procedure but he was now guided by Amr El Hab and did not wish to counter his superior's directive. He was cold and damp, hungry and growing impatient. He was tired and he knew he was becoming drowsy.

As he replayed the events of the past twenty-four hours he realized things had really not gone as he expected. He was shocked when he heard about the murder at the Dolmabahce Palace and did not anticipate any of the events that changed the direction of this mission.

As thoughts flashed between Ankara and Istanbul, he suddenly grasped the scene unfolding before him. Four people stepped through the doors of the hotel into the parking lot. They stopped and glanced cautiously in several directions and it was only when Quentin focused his vision, that he realized one of them was Inci. He could not believe his eyes. She was alive, in fact, she appeared to be all right.

Quentin was relieved when he saw her. She was no more than twenty metres away from him and he realized how striking she looked. Her hair was slightly messed but the morning rays of golden sun bathed it in a reddish lustre. She appeared to be unharmed.

Quentin thought Thomas Sun looked tired and his suit had a slept-in appearance. The jacket was wrinkled and the collar was turned up, an antidote against the morning chill.

The two accomplices in charge appeared dishevelled and untidy. Quentin immediately recognized them as the two men who had met Thomas Sun at the ferry docks last evening. The tall one appeared to lead the group toward their parked vehicle. Their hands were in their pockets reassuring the security of concealed weapons, no doubt aimed at Inci.

Quentin was thankful the parking lot was full and that he was able to position his car so he had a clear view of the grey sedan, at the same time making it unnecessary for them to walk past him to get to it. In order for the four to leave the hotel parking lot, they would have to manoeuvre several metres in front of Quentin. A move, which would give him enough time to start his car, follow them onto the road, and still not be seen.

He wanted desperately for Inci to notice him so she would know she was not alone. On several occasions, while on route to their car, Inci glanced around the parking lot and looked in the direction of Quentin. For a split second, he thought she had noticed him. He felt she had allowed her eyes to dwell momentarily on his vehicle. He was, however, mistaken as she continued to scan the parking area for any sign of familiarity.

The tall man, leading the group, started the engine and guided the car from the parking lot on to the side street. Quentin waited long enough to ensure he would not be spotted before starting the engine. He cautiously manoeuvred out of the lot, following the grey sedan at a safe enough distance to avoid being spotted.

He kept his eyes on the car, thankful for daylight, as it would have been extremely difficult to pick out the vehicle in the dark of night. The car carrying Inci turned onto the main road and veered in a southeasterly direction. Quentin knew he was headed for central Turkey, but had no idea where

Nevsehir was. He had isolated it on the road map, but could not determine how long it would take to get there. He decided his only chance for success would be to stay in close pursuit of the car in front of him. Should he fail he would surely lose credibility within ISIS.

Inci again sat in the back seat of the grey sedan, next to Cengiz. The small, dishevelled Turk lit a cigarette, but refused to open the window, annoyingly puffing smoke in her direction. He had tied her wrists again using the same twine as the previous day, and Inci's hands were quickly becoming numb as the rope cut off her circulation.

She cast the pain from her mind and felt elated at what she had seen in the parking lot of the hotel several minutes earlier. Although she could not be one hundred percent certain, she felt confident she had seen Quentin slumped in an automobile, not far from where she was walking. She had to look twice, for she did not recognize the car, but found it odd that someone would be sitting in a vehicle at six-thirty in the morning -- especially someone who resembled Quentin Wright.

She wanted to take another look but did not dare, for she was concerned if it was Quentin and she acknowledged his presence, his fate would surely be sealed. It was for that reason she did not turn her head over her shoulder and look through the rear window of the vehicle to see if they were being followed. She knew it was a pale blue, compact car and would keep an eye out for it at every opportunity.

"Could you please ask him to open a window?" Thomas Sun said to Yalcin, as the cigarette smoke caused him to choke.

"Why do you not open yours?" Yalcin asked.

"It will draw the smoke even closer to me. Just ask him to open his window." Thomas Sun was irritated by the insubordination of these two supposed protectors.

He did not wish to oppose them, for even though they were on his side, he felt they would just as soon shoot him as help him. He did not trust these men and felt their loyalty was non existent. He was nervous about his future and wondered if he had taken the right direction.

He detested walking in his father's shadow. He had never been recognized for his own ability, but always as Francis Sun's offspring. His father had dictated every move he had ever made without allowing him any input into his schooling or his future. He respected his father for his accomplishments and certainly had no ill feelings about the type of business he conducted, but had longed for an opportunity to prove himself based on his own ability and merit, and not that of his father's.

It was while he was in school that Thomas Sun had become involved with several people attracted to him as a result of his connections with the criminal syndicate his father had organized. He never volunteered information about his father for fear it might lead to his incrimination or even death. Somehow the men who had befriended him in his last year in college knew a lot about his father's business. They were students from Europe, perhaps Greece, but they had been extremely tight-lipped about events concerning their background. At one point, Thomas Sun was convinced his new-found friends were Iraqis who had escaped from the violent clutches of Sadam Hussein.

It was shortly after graduation that the drama unfolded. Typical of any graduating class, there had been parties in every corner of the campus. Thomas Sun had gone to a few but when this group of new-found friends invited him to an off-campus hotel for some supposedly 'wild' times, he was curious and decided to join them.

He arrived at the upscale hotel and, as he entered the lobby, was greeted by a youth approximately the same age as Thomas Sun who escorted him toward the elevator. As they went upstairs Thomas recalled his heart beating with anticipation. He had heard of wild graduation parties where liquor and women were abundant. Somewhat shy he had no experience with the opposite sex and secretly he hoped that such an encounter lay ahead.

He recalled his disappointment when he arrived at the suite. The room was not crowded and filled with young, carefree people dancing gaily to the beat of modern music. Instead it was tastefully decorated with antiques and expensive furniture and was occupied by only three of his friends, accompanied by a stranger.

He was offered a drink and declined, as liquor had never been of interest to him. On the rare occasions that he had accepted an alcoholic beverage, his face had immediately gone red and perspiration had formed on his forehead. He was quickly overcome by dizziness as the effects of alcohol took their toll. It was for those reasons he had abstained from drinking.

"Perhaps a soft drink would suit you?" one of his friends had asked. Thomas Sun accepted and a Coca-Cola with ice was prepared for him.

"We would like you to meet someone," another member of the group said, motioning to the guest seated in the high-backed chair beside a small table in another area of the suite. One of Thomas's friends said, "come and meet our good friend, Mustafa. He comes from Anatolia, you now call it Turkey.

Thomas saw the man sitting in another area of the suite and was struck by his quiet, calm appearance. The man did not speak but smiled. His smooth, tanned skin and compelling deep set, brown eyes accentuated a somewhat long but straight nose. Thick eyebrows matched his black hair which fell into curls at the back of his head. Sideburns, longer than stylish framed a beardless oval face.

Thomas remembered staring at the tall, quiet stranger wondering who this man called 'Mustafa' was. He appeared older than his friends and was dressed in an expensive business suit. He sat quietly holding a crystal glass, which Thomas assumed held either whiskey or scotch.

"Mustafa is our friend and the saviour of our cause," one of his friends said confidently introducing them. He is here on a important mission to recruit people who feel as we do about the world and the lack of respect certain governments have for its survival."

Thomas remembered staring into the dark, brown eyes of this man known as Mustafa. The meeting ended shortly after it began, but left a deep impression with Thomas Sun. It would not soon be erased from his memory.

It was several days after the meeting that a second gathering had been arranged. Only Thomas Sun and Mustafa were present. Mustafa had described what the western world had done to his country and its citizens. After a two-hour conversation, Thomas Sun had been mesmerized by the words of this Middle Eastern stranger. He had at last found an opportunity where he could rise beyond the parameters which his father had carefully set all these many years. It had been a chance to chart his own course, and accomplish a feat which would give him the same respect his father had earned over the years. It was a challenge to which Thomas Sun could rise and show the world that he was also a man who could be counted on to follow through with plans.

The sound of the car window as it was opened created a rushing noise, jolting Thomas

Sun from his daydream to the reality of the present moment. He glanced around to see if anyone had noticed him engrossed in his thoughts. It appeared no one had.

Yalcin concentrated on his driving while Cengiz sat quietly in the rear, keeping a close watch over his captive. Thomas Sun could not see Inci without turning directly around and he had no reason to do so. The past few hours had given him an opportunity to think about the enormity of the thing he had done.

He recalled how he had been asked to rent a boat, a specific boat. He was then ordered to anchor it in the harbour off the coast of Long Island. For two weeks, his boat sat patiently in the water while Thomas Sun awaited orders from his superiors. It was a flat boat and he had no idea of its purpose. With the passing of each day, he hoped something would happen which would enlighten him to the reason for the requested action.

After two weeks of patient waiting, his queries were finally answered. A pleasure craft pulled up beside him and made contact. His instructions, when he rented the boat, had been very clear: address no one unless they mention Mustafa's name. It was the first word spoken by the stranger aboard the adjacent vessel. Thomas Sun had replied and the pleasure craft moored next to the large, flat boat.

Several wooden cases were transferred without conversation or instructions and the boat disappeared as mysteriously as it had arrived. Thomas Sun had not been given any instructions. He was curious about the contents of the crates and the purpose of the delivery.

It was the next evening when a second boat, a smaller one pulled up. Again secret passwords were exchanged and more cartons were delivered; however, this time two men remained on board Thomas Sun's boat.

The two strangers had worked for four full days assembling metal components, which had been contained within the crates. It was not until they were halfway through their task that Thomas Sun realized the men were assembling a rocket. It was a long, sleek, silver coloured object twice the height of a man. The small cone at the front was painted orange and had not yet been attached to the base. The electronic components of the launchpad were complex and Thomas Sun was impressed by the wizardry with which the two men assembled each vital section.

At last the rocket had been assembled and it appeared ready for launch. It had been hidden from view by a small storage building near the centre of the water craft and Thomas Sun remembered the anxiety he had felt when a government patrol boat, belonging to the coast guard, rode past. The soldiers appeared disinterested in Thomas Sun and his watercraft and departed without incident.

Thomas Sun had no idea about the nature of the scheme he was involved in, but enjoyed the thrill of the adventure as he played out the role he had been asked to perform.

Several days later, another boat arrived. The two men, who had become his only contact with the outside world, departed and were replaced by a team of three others who, Thomas Sun assumed, were there to carry out the final tasks of the objective.

The next evening, around seven p.m. all unanswered questions Thomas Sun had would be answered. The specialists checked control after control and continually entered data into the computer system inside the boat's cabin. After a long moment of silence, the leader asked Thomas Sun to stand at the rear of the boat.

The Oriental youth obeyed and watched carefully as data was again entered. After a short time, they paused and stared at the missile. Thomas Sun also looked out onto the boat. He jumped as he was startled by a loud, thunderous, sound. With a fiery thrust and an earth shattering blast, the rocket released its grip of the launchpad and slowly made its way skyward. It seemed to pick up speed at an incredible rate and Thomas Sun could not believe his eyes when only seconds later, he saw the rocket explode in mid air, not far from where his boat was anchored.

As he stared skyward in an effort to grasp what had taken place, he failed to see the small pleasure craft pull up beside him. Three men boarded his ship and quickly dismantled the remains of the launch pad used to detonate the killing projectile only moments before. All pieces belonging to the weapon were tossed overboard and the men departed as quickly as they had come.

Thomas Sun stood alone on the deck of his rented watercraft. The fire in the sky, caused by the impact of the rocket, had vanished, and although Thomas Sun did not know exactly what had happened, he assumed the missile had made contact with an aircraft. He went inside the cabin of the boat and poured himself a glass of wine. He felt the effects immediately as the adrenaline, which flowed through his veins, mixed with the alcohol.

He knew he had a job to do and if he was to avoid being implicated in this crime, he had to perform it quickly and with perfection. He started the engine of the boat and made his way along the U.S. coast. He waited until morning and docked the boat in the marina from where he had rented it three and a half weeks earlier.

It was not until he had returned to his apartment that he understood the full implication of what he had done. A passenger airliner had mysteriously exploded, the newspaper had read. All two hundred and thirty civilians on board were dead.

Once again, Thomas Sun awoke from his daydream as the car encountered a bumpy section of the road. He recalled the nauseous feeling which developed in his stomach after reading the newspaper report three months ago. Many times during the past few months he felt more like a petty criminal than a crusader trying to make the world better. Raised to oppose terrorism it was not something he could ever tell his father and he was not proud of what he had done. After hearing nothing from any of the others, he felt deserted by he people who had asked him to brutally slaughter innocent victims. It was not until eight weeks after the event, when a school chum still refused to meet with him and he threatened to tell the authorities, that a meeting with Mustafa was arranged.

It was for that reason that Thomas Sun made his way to Turkey. He had been visited several times in New York by investigators who questioned his use of the rental boat. He had become afraid and could not, as in the past, turn to his father for help. He decided he had no choice but to make his way to the homeland of the terrorists who had employed him.

As the car sped along, Thomas Sun wondered if he had done the right thing. Constantly overcome by guilt over the deed he had performed, he wished he could somehow reverse the clock and erase the evil actions which had taken place.

"You are very quiet, my friend," Yalcin said. Thomas Sun ignored him.

"Perhaps he is becoming afraid of the destiny he must face," Inci added.

"You had best be quiet," Yalcin said, directing his attention to the girl in the back seat.

Cengiz again was excluded from the conversation as he lacked the ability to understand

English.

"Are you becoming nervous?" Inci asked, provokingly. "One thing I have pondered over the last few hours," she continued, addressing Thomas Sun, "is whether or not you are on their side. It seems to me they would kill you without hesitation?" Thomas Sun did not reply to Inci's question, but deep in his mind he had often wondered the same thing.

Inci adjusted herself to a more comfortable seating position, which kept her as far away from Cengiz as possible. She wanted to glance through the rear window for signs of Quentin, but did not dare make a move, afraid of attracting attention.

The car sped along a freshly paved road on route to central Turkey. "I believe we will arrive in Nevsehir at about eleven o'clock. We must, however, stop for petrol very soon." As Yalcin spoke, both Inci and Thomas Sun peered at the gas gauge on the dashboard of the automobile. The small, amber light was illuminated indicating the car was in need of fuel. "We will stop ahead. There is a petrol station not far from here," Yalcin said. He then switched to Turkish. "You stay with the woman, Cengiz. Do not let her out of your sight. We will stop for coffee and a toilet break."

Cengiz smiled and Inci felt a sickening feeling develop in her stomach as she thought of her earlier incident with him in the washroom of the hotel in Ankara. She was pleased, however, at the prospect of stopping, for it would enable Quentin an opportunity to catch up. It would also set her mind at ease about the deep rooted concern that perhaps she had been mistaken in the parking lot of the hotel this morning. Perhaps it had not been Quentin waiting in the car. She hoped it was and was grateful she would soon have confirmation.

Quentin drove hard and guided his car carefully along the road in close pursuit of the grey sedan, approximately half a kilometre before him. He was careful to avoid narrowing the gap, at the same time being cautious not to lose sight of the vehicle which held Inci.

A wave of concern surged through him. He contemplated what might happen if he reached his destination before contact with the other ISIS agents had been made. He forced the thought from his mind and continued on. He squinted when he saw what he believed was a brake light on the car in the distance. The sun was now high in the sky and flooded the countryside with brightness. It caused a glare to develop on the road ahead, making visibility difficult. It took several seconds to realize the car ahead was turning off the main road entering a service centre. The action subconsciously caused Quentin to glance at his gasoline gauge and determine that he was also low on fuel. He debated filling up with gasoline at the same place as the car he was pursuing and wondered if he could be recognized. He raced through the recesses of his mind and concluded there had never been a time when the culprits in the car ahead had spotted him. He decided he would chance the opportunity.

Quentin drove slowly as he neared the entrance to the service station. He approached the pumps carefully, watching the passengers of the grey sedan as they left their vehicle. He was thankful it was not a self-serve station, an American concept that was not yet popular in Turkey. He slouched in his seat slightly finding comfort in knowing the people he was surveying had no idea of his whereabouts. He was relieved and exhaled a deep, thankful sigh when he saw Inci walking toward the bathroom. He was glad she had not been harmed during her ordeal over the last twelve hours.

Quentin rolled down the window as the attendant approached and asked the unshaven man to fill the gasoline tank.

Quentin saw one of the terrorists wait outside the small, concrete lavatory building as Inci entered. He could not help wonder if she had noticed him sitting casually in his rented vehicle.

The other terrorist, the one who appeared responsible for the group, walked toward the service station. He was followed closely by an Asian man whom Quentin assumed to be Thomas Sun.

As they entered the building, Quentin realized there was a small restaurant in the service centre. The thought of a steaming cup of coffee was appealing but he dared not jeopardize the situation through his own selfishness. The image of the hotel in Bursa remained extremely clear in his mind. He did not wish a repeat of those circumstances.

A sudden thought bolted through Quentin's mind as he assessed the situation. Thomas Sun and the tall terrorist were inside the restaurant while Inci was in the bathroom. The only person visible was the shorter of the two bandits and he seemed preoccupied by his thoughts as he casually guarded the entrance to the women's washroom. Quentin realized if an opportunity ever presented itself, this would be it. His mind raced quickly as he tried to develop a plan which would result in freeing his new-found friend and accomplice. He scanned the area closely to ensure Thomas Sun and the driver were safely inside the restaurant.

Quickly, Quentin swung open the car door and raced in the direction of the women's washroom. He stunned the terrorist who lifted his head in surprise as Quentin approached. The man was not prepared and Quentin lashed out his fist with full force catching the man square in the jaw. It was a devastating blow which hurled the guard into the concrete wall of the small building. Quentin instantly thrust his fist into the semiconscious man and grabbed him by the lapels, shaking him vigorously and, at the same time bashing his head against the concrete block wall. He realized, after what seemed an eternity, that the man was unconscious and would not wake for several hours. He thought how strange it had felt to inflict such forceful destruction on a human body and felt slightly nauseous when he saw a thin coating of fresh blood smeared against the grey, cement wall.

Quentin did not hesitate a moment and banged loudly on the door of the women's washroom. "Inci!" he yelled. "It's me, Quentin." Again he banged on the door but there was no response. His hand immediately reached for the handle and was discouraged when he found it to be locked. He knocked again but there was no response.

Suddenly, he felt relief when he heard a noise from inside the bathroom and saw the door handle begin to turn. Quentin heard a shout from behind and turned to see the taller of the two terrorists running toward him. He panicked and could not decide what his next move would be. He hoped Inci would exit the restroom and the two of them could make a mad dash to his vehicle, It was not to be. The bathroom door did not open and Quentin knew the second terrorist would be upon him in seconds. He had no choice but to run and did so away from the scene of activity. He raced in a circle behind the bathroom and made his way to the rear of the restaurant. He continued to run without looking over his shoulder, hoping he was not being pursued all the while not being aware of the activity in front of the service centre.

As Yalcin reached Cengiz, the bathroom door opened and Inci stood in a state of shock finding herself face to face with the scene of destruction.

"Come with me!" Yalcin yelled. He did not wait for Inci to respond and grabbed her by the arm as he dragged her toward his car.

Thomas Sun was running from the restaurant toward the restroom, unsure of what had just taken place. He was shocked to find Cengiz slumped on the ground and saw a small pool of blood forming at the base of his head. He saw Yalcin dragging Inci toward their car and watched as the tall Turk flung her in the back seat and removed his gun keeping it poised for action.

"Grab Cengiz," Yalcin yelled, at Thomas Sun. The terrified gas station attendant watched the entire event, awaiting payment for the fuel he had just funnelled into the tank of the grey sedan. The response was not the one he expected, for Yalcin greeted him with the barrel of the gun pointed directly at his face. "Get back to your building!" Yalcin commanded. The attendant nervously obeyed not wishing to partake in any segment of this treacherous event.

Thomas Sun lifted Cengiz from the pavement and dragged him toward the vehicle. As he approached the car, Yalcin started the engine and manoeuvred the automobile slightly ahead in order to make it easier for Thomas Sun to lift the motionless body of Cengiz inside.

"Come, come. We must hurry," Yalcin said, as he glanced around the service centre looking for Quentin. He turned his attention to Inci. "If you try to flee, I will surely shoot you, for you mean nothing to me. It is because of you that we are experiencing this grief."

"You are the one who kidnapped me. Remember?" Inci was furious with Yalcin. She was angered with herself for having locked the bathroom door. Had she left it unlocked, Quentin would have been able to free her from her captors.

She recalled entering the bathroom and locking the door to avoid duplicating the lecherous treachery that Cengiz had put her through in the hotel only hours ago. In fact, when she had heard the door handle rattle, her body had tensed and only after it was too late, had she realized it was Quentin who was trying to gain access and not Cengiz. As she sat in the rear seat of the car, watching Thomas Sun throw the near-dead body of Cengiz beside her, she contemplated jumping out and running. She knew Yalcin was beyond idle threats when he had said he would surely kill her. She had seen the anger in his face and had watched the tension grow as a result of the uncertainty of the events that were taking place around them.

Thomas Sun slammed the door shut and the car immediately sped away from the service station, barrelling along the road on its way to Nevsehir.

Quentin's body trembled from a combination of fear and exhaustion as a result of his mad sprint around the rear of the service centre. He cursed himself for not having acquired a firearm, for surely he would have been able to shoot the tires of the grey sedan as it left the parking lot.

He sprinted to his car, paid the astonished

attendant, and departed, taking the same route as the grey sedan only seconds before.

He now had developed an additional fear; surely the gas station attendant would have telephoned the police and given a description of the two vehicles. As he drove, he continued to feel his inadequacy at this job. He thought of the botched attempt at freeing Inci and wondered if he had jeopardized her life further. One thing he knew for certain; he had alerted the two terrorists and Thomas Sun to his presence and they would take extra precautions to ensure he would not catch them.

Thomas Sun was the first to break the silence. "Who do you think that was?"

"No doubt it was the other agent. The accomplice of our friend, here," Yalcin replied. He looked in his rear view mirror to get a glimpse of Inci. "Is that not true?" he asked.

Inci did not answer; instead she stared out the window. She could not help but glance over her shoulder to see if Quentin was in pursuit. Things were happening too fast and their speed was exceeding the limit imposed by the government. She could not see any cars behind her and wondered how Quentin would deal with the situation.

She looked at the still body of Cengiz and thought that perhaps he was dead. Blood was flowing freely from the rear of his skull and she was curious about the cause of the wound. She felt no remorse at his unfortunate condition and was, in fact, quite pleased with the infliction he had received. It was one less matter for her to be concerned with.

"Here, take this." Yalcin handed Thomas Sun his semiautomatic pistol. "Keep it pointed at her. If she tries anything, pull the trigger."

Thomas Sun reluctantly accepted the killing weapon from the man driving the vehicle. He nervously pointed the gun in the direction of Inci. It was immediately evident to her that he was unfamiliar with such weaponry.

"The trigger is very sensitive," Yalcin said, as he realized Thomas Sun's apprehension. "The slightest squeeze will put a bullet through her head." Yalcin smiled at the prospect of Thomas Sun killing Inci. He would have gladly done the deed himself if it were not for the important information she would bring to the equation, once Mustafa interviewed her.

Yalcin glanced in his rear view mirror several times as he forced the car to hurry along the road at an unprecedented speed.

The ringing of his cellular telephone interrupted Quentin's nervous concentration. He jumped slightly, startled by the screeching noise. He reached to the seat beside him, picked up the phone and spoke into the unit.

"Quentin Wright?" the voice from the other end of the telephone asked.

"Speaking."

"Quentin, my name is Ole Pedersen. I believe you are expecting my call?"

"Yes. I am." Quentin's speech was curt. Too many things had gone wrong. He was now faced with the prospect of speaking to a man who would replace him as a result of his superior's perception of Quentin's inability. It was a perception which he had recently proved to be accurate.

"What is your position?" Pedersen asked.

"I am following the car with our agent and am about halfway between Ankara and Nevsehir."

"Is she all right?"

"She appears to be." Quentin did not have any intention of relaying the events which had taken place at the service centre. The senior agent on the other end of the line would already be aware of Quentin's niaveté and the fact that this was his first assignment.

"I have three agents with me," Pedersen continued. "We are on our way to Nevsehir and should arrive there in about twenty minutes."

"As we arrived in Istanbul," he continued, "we learned that Francis Sun had chartered an aircraft and was heading for Konya. He has with him a man named Davud Kurvesh. We believe him to be the man whom you spotted at the museum in Istanbul. He is the one who has been following you. It may interest you to know that his two accomplices were brutally murdered in the back of a taxi last evening on their way to the airport. We believe Francis Sun is responsible." Quentin was shocked by the statement and was again surprised by the ruthlessness of the people he was dealing with. Secretly, he was beginning to feel somewhat more secure having the additional agents at his side. "Two of the men with me are going to remain in Konya and deal with Francis Sun and Davud Kurvesh. The other agent and I will make our way to Nevsehir as quickly as we possibly can and connect with you."

"How will we find each other?" Quentin asked.

"In Nevsehir there is a hotel called the Dedeman. It stands in the open, and is fairly new. It is quite a large complex and everyone knows of it. We will reserve rooms there and await your contact. The first opportunity you get, call us. I will expect to be there about three hours from now."

Quentin checked his watch and recorded the time. It would bring their rendezvous to nearly noon. Quentin's impression of Ole Pedersen was changing. He had formed an image in his mind of a ruthless man who would step over him and forge ahead. Instead this man gave Quentin the impression of wanting to work as a team.

"Quentin," Pedersen continued. "I must tell you, we are extremely impressed with the way you have handled this case. It was not easy to track someone with the little information you had, and then follow him all the way to your present location. It will be a pleasure to meet you and work with you."

Quentin placed the phone on the seat beside

him and thought about what Pedersen had just said. He hoped it was sincere and wondered if it had been at the direction of Amr El Hab. Regardless, he was glad to hear them and right now he needed a boost to his confidence.

15. Assistance

The small, single engine plane pounded along noisily in the clear skies over Istanbul as it headed for Konya. Davud Kurvesh sat in the front seat with the pilot leaving Francis Sun as much room as possible in the small cabin behind. The aged aircraft did not come close to offering first class seating. No one spoke as the irritating noise of the engine made it impossible for anyone to hear.

As the small craft made its way over the picturesque countryside and into the mountains of central Turkey, turbulence became very noticeable and the occupants were jostled around. The weather was growing colder and this time of year snow was not uncommon in this mountainous region.

Davud Kurvesh knew the city of Konya quite well. It had always been a centre for the Muslim faith in Turkey and although the government had outlawed the fundamentalists, it was the one city that had defied authority, and many of the people still dressed in traditional, black garb.

Konya was also the birthplace of the world famous Whirling Dervishes, a four hundred year old tradition started by a monk named Mevlana. It was believed that a state of ecstasy could be achieved by continuously whirling in circles. Through the use of mind altering drugs, ancient priests would go into a trance and spin in circles for hours at a time. It was another ritual which had been abolished by the first government of modern day Turkey in 1923.

Although Kurvesh was slightly irritated by the abolition of some of the ancient customs, he was generally quite pleased with the manner in which life had progressed in his homeland. Turks now drove cars, watched television, and drank Raki. There were far more opportunities for a better life and with the added mixture of the remaining ancient customs made for a complex society of deep-rooted individuals.

Kurvesh knew there were problems, but he also understood they were being resolved and the country was now more prosperous than it had ever been. He was proud to call himself a Turk and was glad he lived in the land of his birth.

He found it interesting to be traveling to Cappadocia, the homeland of the terrorists known as the 'Children of the Sultan'. He had always wondered about their way of living. He disagreed with their archaic beliefs and felt they had no future in a modern, westernized world.

Although this was just another assignment, a simple job of freeing one individual from the hands of these criminals, it would certainly not bother him if several of these terrorists were eliminated in the process.

Francis Sun sat in the back seat of the aircraft and stared blankly out the window. He turned his head slowly to the pilot when the aircraft entered a gap in the atmosphere and dropped several feet. The pilot appeared to ignore the movement, and continued to manoeuvre the plane through the cloudless sky toward its destination.

The airplane dipped again, this time a little further, causing Francis Sun's stomach to tingle slightly. It took several moments before the large Oriental realized the plane was beginning to descend.

Francis Sun had not developed a plan, an act he would normally have concentrated on at great length. His intent, this time, was to meet with Mustafa and offer him money in return for his son. He would refuse to listen to any discussion the terrorist would surely present in an effort to obtain a higher price for the release of his son.

Francis Sun could understand that his son might have misconceptions about these terrorists but he knew that a man like Mustafa used his son as a pawn in a game of corruption directed at prosperous victims around the world.

He decided not to bargain. The amount of money was a secondary factor for the safe release of his son. He felt extremely confident money would resolve his dilemma. It was the one thing everyone needed, especially underfunded terrorists.

Francis Sun was jolted from his daydream by the sudden approach of the land below which now appeared much larger than it had only moments before. He glanced forward and stared over the shoulders of the pilot and Davud Kurvesh, and could see a small airstrip directly ahead. As the plane neared its resting place, small airport buildings became visible with aircraft parked along each side of the runway.

With a sudden, sharp jolt, the airplane's wheels made contact with the uneven pavement of the runway. Strong winds caused the pilot to misjudge the distance between the aircraft and the ground, resulting in an uncomfortable landing.

It was evident by the look on Francis Sun's face that he was not pleased with the flight and was thankful to be safely on the ground. Although silent, Kurvesh had spoken not a word, he shared similar sentiments.

The small, royal-blue, rented automobile sped

through the streets of downtown Konya. The driver's name was Robert Wallace. He had been with ISIS for six years and was considered a reliable agent that could be depended on. After traveling for three straight days, he was tired. Hoping for a few day rest, he was whisked away to Turkey at the request of Ole Pedersen. In Istanbul, Wallace had been introduced to Ken Myers, the man beside him. Wallace and Myers had been sent to Konya where they arrived only a short while ago. Their mission had been clear: to locate an Oriental named Francis Sun and his accomplice. They were to follow them, and avoid being detected

"That could be the plane right there," Ken Myers said, as he pointed to a small, blue and white aircraft which had just landed on the runway at the airport in Konya.

"You might be right," Wallace replied. "I've got the markings here." He fumbled through his inside jacket pocket continuing to concentrate on his driving. He removed a small, white piece of paper with writing on it and passed it to the man sitting next to him. Ken Myers had removed a pair of binoculars from the glove compartment.

"Where did you get those?" Wallace asked.

"I'm a resourceful agent," Myers replied, jokingly. Myers glanced through the binoculars in the direction of the aircraft, which had just landed. "That's it," he replied.

The two agents were about half a kilometre away from the airport and Wallace slowed the car to ensure they would not be spotted. "What do you know about this guy, Francis Sun?" he asked.

Ken Myers shook his head. "Not a thing. I've never heard the name and I have no idea what he's done."

"I wish they'd tell us something once in a while," Wallace said, squinting, as he spoke, to avoid being blinded by the late morning sun which shone directly through the front of the car window. Wallace expertly parked the vehicle amid a row of cars. "What do you want to do?" he asked.

"Why don't we wait until they get out of the plane. Then we'll follow them. I don't really want to start anything in the middle of the airport," Myers replied.

Wallace nodded in agreement and turned off the car engine. He reached inside his jacket pocket and removed a small, Browning automatic checking to ensure the clip was full of bullets and inserted properly in the handle of the gun. Myers instinctively patted his side to confirm his firearm was also in place.

Ole Pedersen had arranged for the weapons to be given to them in Istanbul. Neither man had worked independently with Ole before but was familiar with his reputation, and respected him for his leadership abilities and the professional manner in handling assignments.

"What's that over there?" Myers asked. In the distance a black limousine approached the aircraft as it came to a halt at the end of the runway.

"Looks like our friend ordered a taxi."

The two agents slowly watched the limo approach the aircraft. As the stretch vehicle came to a halt, the driver, accompanied by another man, stepped out. Wallace and Myers could see both men stood at least six feet tall and were dressed in blue suits. They stood erect, their hands folded in front of them, awaiting the occupants of the aircraft.

"What do you think?" Wallace asked.

"I think they're big," Myers replied, smiling as he spoke.

The pilot was the first to exit the plane. He walked around the aircraft and opened the door on the passenger side. Davud Kurvesh stepped out and assisted Francis Sun in de-planing.

"The big guy must be Francis Sun," Wallace said. The two ISIS agents watched through the front windscreen of their rented automobile. Francis Sun and Davud Kurvesh stepped into the luxury limousine. The two men dressed in blue suits closed the doors and entered the front. Moments later, the car's engine started and it drove away, reflecting the bright sun from its darkly tinted windows.

"Let's go," Myers said. Wallace started the engine and backed the car out of the parking space. He drove along the parking area and around the beige coloured building, which housed various aircraft services. They remained close behind the black limo, for they were uncertain of its destination.

"I guess we'll have to wait to see if they

split up," Myers said.

"Or at least until we get Sun alone," Wallace replied.

"Let's just follow them for now and see where they go." It did not take long for the black car to reach the outskirts of the city of Konya.

"He obviously knows where he's going," Wallace said, finding it a challenge to keep up with the black limo as it made turns through the small streets at the edge of the city. It was not long before they found themselves on a quieter road heading in a northeastern direction. "Where does this road go?"

Myers pushed the small, black button to unlatch the glove compartment and removed the road map. As he unfolded it, he continually glanced forward, maintaining constant surveillance of the vehicle they were pursuing. As he opened the map on his lap, he scanned his finger across the red lines in an effort to locate their present position. When he found the small, yellow area and saw the name Konya, he traced his finger along a red line, which he believed to be the road they were on. "What's the name of this road?" he asked.

"I think it's called route 260," Wallace replied.

"Here it is," Myers said, as he located the route they had taken. "It heads to a town called Nevsehir. Looks to be about an hour." He again studied the map closely. "There doesn't appear to be anything in between."

"I wonder if that's where they're heading."

"Time will tell."

"Maybe you'd better phone Ole and let him know where we're going."

Ken Myers nodded his head in agreement and removed the cellular phone from inside his breast pocket. He flipped down the mouthpiece and dialed a number that was scribbled on a small piece of paper.

The phone rang twice before it was answered. "Ole, Ken here." Wallace glanced at his partner beside him as if subconsciously indicating he should also be mentioned in the phone conversation. Myers continued. "We saw Sun and Kurvesh at the airport and are presently pursuing them along Route 260 heading toward a city called Nevsehir." Again Wallace looked over at Myers who listened attentively to Ole Pedersen.

"That's interesting," Myers said, nodding his head as he spoke. "I'll do that." He flipped the small, grey mouthpiece of the telephone set which disconnected the signal and replaced the unit in his pocket.

"What's interesting?" Wallace asked.

"He wanted to know if I was taking good care of you." Myers laughed as he spoke. "Seriously though, he's on his way to Nevsehir. He's supposed to meet an agent there. The one that started this whole thing."

"I must have missed part of this story," Wallace said, frowning slightly.

"Apparently there were two ISIS agents following someone in Istanbul. One of them got captured and is being transported to this place called Nevsehir. The other agent is on his way there, and Ole is his backup."

"Looks like we'll all party together," Wallace said.

"Ole wants us to make sure that this Francis Sun guy doesn't get there."

"How did Ole get involved?"

"From what I understand," Myers explained, "a problem arose and there were no agents to assign to it. London called whomever they could find. Ole Pedersen flew from Greece or somewhere near there and Dave Parliament came in from London. I think they flew to Istanbul and then rented a charter to take them to Nevsehir."

"Do you know these guys?" Wallace asked. "I'm concerned about laying my life on the line with people I don't know."

"I've known of Ole Pedersen for years. He has a great reputation. I'm sure whomever he brings with him will be equally as good." Myers paused. "He picked us, didn't he?" The red faced man smiled.

"You're making my point," Wallace replied, jokingly, as he eyed his partner up and down.

"Oh, that's nice," Myers replied.

The small, blue, rental car carrying the two ISIS agents sped along the road as they continued their pursuit of the large, black limo transporting

Francis Sun and Davud Kurvesh to Nevsehir and the home of the 'Children of the Sultan'.

Quentin maintained his speed, as he entered the perimeter of Nevsehir. He skirted around the centre of the city and wound his way up a slow, steep grade, which ran for about a kilometre, climbing endlessly toward the sky. The view in the distance was spectacular and Quentin allowed his mind a moment's rest. The sun working its way toward the horizon was partially covered by streams of clouds. The green, fertile ground was beginning to turn amber as autumn reminded the countryside to ready itself for the oncoming winter.

The road curved slowly and Quentin passed an army base protected by a large, metal, barbed-wire fence. Sentries were posted every ten metres and as Quentin approached, he noticed they all had automatic machine guns poised at their sides ready to be used should anyone enter illegally. The road continued on and the grey sedan hugged it securely. Quentin maintained a safe distance and could not help, but wonder if the people ahead knew he was behind them.

Again the road turned and a tall building appeared in the distance. Quentin thought if perhaps it was the hotel Ole Pedersen had mentioned. As he continued, the structure grew in size and Quentin felt a tremor of excitement when he saw the 'Dedeman' logo displayed boldly at the top of the building. For a few seconds, he hoped Thomas

Sun and his accomplices were planning on spending the night there. That would be too coincidental, Quentin thought.

His wish evaporated as he watched the grey sedan pass the driveway to the hotel. Quentin wondered if Ole Pedersen was already there and decided to make a telephone call in the event the ISIS agent had intended to accompany him.

Wondering how to contact directory assistance for the number of the hotel Quentin noted the grey sedan began to slow down and turn into another hotel. He decided not to follow the car but pulled off to the side of the road shortly before the entrance and stopped. Keeping his eyes on the vehicle as it made its way through the parking lot, he dialed the operator requesting the number of the Dedeman Hotel and in a few moments was put through to Ole Pedersen's room.

Pedersen answered and Quentin explained where he was. "Excellent," Pedersen replied. "It must be the Hotel Peri Tower. It is the only one in the vicinity." Quentin studied the large, grey building in an effort to see a marking, which indicated the name. He could find none but, as there were no other hotels in the area, he assumed Ole to be correct. "Why don't you stay where you are and I will come out and meet you. You can probably do with a rest and my partner will relieve you while you update me as to what has happened."

Quentin replaced the telephone receiver in the pocket of his brown, leather jacket. He let out a long, deep sigh as he tried to relax and exhaust some of the tension, which had accumulated during the long drive from Ankara to Nevsehir.

He decided to call his father. He was uncertain of the next time he would have a few minutes to spare. As he dialed the number, he maintained his surveillance of the hotel entrance. He was thankful the road was not heavily traveled and only a few cars had passed him. He assumed, by the lack of police activity, that the service attendant had not telephoned the authorities. He probably had no desire to become involved in an incident which would only create problems for him.

"Hello," Phillip said, as he answered the phone.

"Hi, it's me," Quentin replied.

"Quentin. Where are you? Are you okay?"

"Yeah. Everything's great. I'm in a town called Nevsehir and have made contact with Ole Pedersen." Quentin went on to explain about the phone call he received from Ole and the planned rendezvous. He talked about the fiasco at the service centre explaining that he had omitted the ordeal from his conversation with Pedersen.

"It's important to follow orders," Phillip said.

Quentin agreed and, after farewell greetings, replaced the telephone in his pocket. An automobile pulled up directly behind him and through his rear-view mirror Quentin could see two men inside, both of whom left the car at the same time.

Quentin also stepped from his vehicle so he could meet the men halfway between the two automobiles.

"Quentin Wright?" one of the two men asked, as he extended his hand in the form of a greeting.

"Yes I am." Quentin accepted the gesture of friendship and smiled in a formal manner at the two men standing before him.

"My name is Ole Pedersen and this is David Parliament." Parliament was a tall man in his mid forties with no hair on the top of his head and the sides were cut short. His ears were larger than normal and stuck out extremely far from the side of his head. He nodded as he was introduced to Quentin but did not say anything. "David is one of your fellow countrymen," Ole said.

"It's always nice to see someone from Australia," Quentin replied. Although he was born in the U.S. he considered himself to be Australian. He had spent the majority of his life in the 'Land Down Under'.

"Actually, I'm British," David Parliament replied. "I thought you were as well." There was arrogance and an air of superiority surrounding him that Quentin found intimidating.

"I live in England now," Quentin said, forcefully in an effort to overcome his feeling of inferiority. "Are you going to keep an eye on them while we go back to the hotel?," Quentin asked, as he looked toward the grey, concrete structure in the distance.

"That would probably be the best idea," Ole Pedersen answered Quentin's question. "I'll drive back with you. If that's all right?" he added.

"Of course."

Quentin and Ole Pedersen stepped into the vehicle which Quentin had rented, while David Parliament returned to his. Quentin took the cellular phone and placed it in his pocket, at the same time clearing the maps from the passenger seat.

"He doesn't say much, does he?" Quentin said, as they entered the vehicle.

"Not much of a personality, I agree. He's very good at what he does though."

Quentin nodded and Pedersen smiled. Quentin had not met many field agents, but Pedersen looked exactly as Quentin pictured him. His skin was fair and his hair was blonde and although it was thinning, it was wavy and slightly tousled by the wind. Quentin figured him to be in his late thirties. He was in good shape and it was evident by the way he carried himself that he was very well disciplined.

"I think perhaps these light clothes are a little too thin for this climate. I did not realize it would be this cold." Pedersen briskly rubbed his hands together as Quentin turned the car toward the hotel he had passed only a few moments before.

"Are you getting hungry?" Pedersen asked.

"You want to believe it."

"I have an idea. Why don't we hit the bar,

get something to eat, and enjoy a cocktail while we discuss what has taken place here in the last two days."

"That sounds good." Quentin had forgotten about food but the mere mention of it caused his taste buds to tingle. He felt comfortable talking with Ole Pedersen and was no longer concerned about being viewed as a failure, incapable of performing his job.

16. Cappadocia

Yalcin left the motionless body of Cengiz in the car and told Thomas Sun to keep a close watch on Inci. The three left the vehicle and entered the lobby of the Hotel Peri Tower.

The massive, concrete building, although an architectural feat, was not pleasing to the eye. It resembled a fortress or perhaps a bunker where one would run to escape an air attack.

"Wait here," Yalcin said to Thomas Sun, pointing toward the seating area.

Sun acknowledged the command, and motioned for Inci to take a seat on one of the beige-coloured couches surrounding the glass-topped coffee table.

The coldness of the exterior of the building continued into the lobby with its vaulted ceiling and bare, cement, grey walls. Tropical plants in ornate, wrought iron stands were scattered about without thought and multicoloured carpets were spread throughout the huge area in traditional Turkish style but did nothing to enhance the austere surroundings.

Yalcin walked to the marble covered counter to arrange accommodations for the evening. Thomas Sun remained watchful of Inci who sat obediently on the small, cloth-covered sofa. He sat directly across from her, allowing him to keep his gun trained at her.

"What exactly is it you are wanted for?" she asked.

He ignored her question and turned his head to check on Yalcin's progress. He quickly looked back when he thought she made a movement but was relieved that he was mistaken. "It is none of your concern."

"You know they are just using you," Inci said, feeling slightly more at ease in spite of the gun trained on her.

"Be quiet. I do not wish to speak with you." Again Thomas Sun looked quickly toward Yalcin wishing the tall Turk would complete his business so he would not have to be alone with this woman whose motives he did not trust.

Inci contemplated making a run for it but,

under the circumstances, felt it would not be a wise move. The distance to the lobby door was too great and if Thomas Sun could not find the courage to shoot, Yalcin surely would. Her thoughts were interrupted when Yalcin returned.

"There has been a slight change in plans." Thomas Sun looked up at the tall, unshaven man. "Mustafa has requested we meet with him this afternoon."

"This afternoon?" Thomas Sun asked, somewhat surprised. "Why this afternoon?"

"Perhaps he is very eager to thank you for all the help you have been to him and our cause." It was evident to Thomas Sun that Yalcin did not know the reason for the sudden change in plans. The Turk's mockery did not add comfort to the insecurity he was feeling.

"What about Cengiz?" Sun asked. "Surely he is not in any position to travel."

"No, he is not. Mustafa is sending men around to meet us and to take care of our friend."

"Who are these men?"

"They are 'Children of the Sultan'," Yalcin replied. He smiled as he spoke. "I do not know why you are so concerned. We are not enemies, you and I."

Somehow Thomas Sun could not help but feel ill at the thought of having a great deal in common with the bandit who stood before him.

"What about me?" Inci asked.

Yalcin turned his attention to his captive

and smiled as his eyes scanned her from top to bottom. He visibly showed signs of admiration as he studied her shapely figure, which was even more pronounced by the tight blue jeans she was wearing. "Ah, yes. You are an entirely different matter." Yalcin continued. "We are uncertain what is to become of you. If it was up to me, I would surely dispose of you; however, Mustafa seems to have other plans."

"What plans?" Thomas Sun interjected.

Yalcin looked at him inquisitively. "Why should you care?"

Inci could not understand why Thomas Sun was concerned about her well being. She felt that perhaps he was becoming rapidly disillusioned by the organization in which he had chosen to participate.

"It is my understanding Mustafa wishes to get as much information as he can from her. He has ways of getting information, you know." Again he smiled, showing yellow stained teeth. "I am certain when he is finished, you will bring a handsome reward from some of our friends in the Arab world."

The words sent shivers down Inci's spine. She was very familiar with the black market slave trade which had taken place for hundreds of years. She decided she must act quickly, for she certainly did not wish to be a part of it. She had known people who had been kidnapped and taken to the Middle East for just such a purpose. She knew they had never been heard from again and their fate was surely worse than death itself.

"What is our next move?" Thomas Sun asked.

"Let us retire to the bar. It is there we will meet our contact."

"When will this happen?"

"It should not be more than forty-five minutes."

Yalcin began to walk in the direction of a hallway at the far end of the lobby. He was followed closely by Thomas Sun who stepped directly behind Inci, keeping his gun aimed yet concealed in his pocket.

"It is unfortunate," Yalcin began, directing his words at Thomas Sun, "that we are not spending the night here. I am extremely tired and would enjoy a nice, long rest."

Thomas Sun did not share his sentiments. Although he was tired, he wished this entire ordeal was over. He had not given thought to where he would go or what he would do at its completion.

Francis Sun sat quietly in the back seat of the limo as it made it's way to Nevsehir. The driving was slow as they passed through several small towns where sheep and cattle on the roads were a common site and easily outnumbered the inhabitants. With its grandeur, size, and heavily tinted windows, the limo presented a strange sight and along the road, people stared as it passed by.

The women tending the herds of sheep and

cattle covered their heads in the standard Muslim tradition. Most wore long, brightly coloured skirts and sweaters with heavy shoes and socks to keep them warm from the chilly autumn air.

Davud Kurvesh sat across from Francis Sun in the rear compartment of the limo and also gazed out the window at the passing sights. Very little had been said by the two men since their meeting, and Kurvesh assumed it was the nature of Francis Sun to speak only when necessary. Several times the Oriental's telephone had rung, and the conversations had been extremely short and to the point.

The two bodyguards sat in the front seat and were concealed from the rear by a darkly tinted window. They had their instructions and knew how to carry them out. They had been on similar assignments many times in the past, and had been recruited through Davud Kurvesh's network. They were unfamiliar with the two men they were transporting to Nevsehir.

"These men are reliable?" Sun asked.

"Yes. Very much so," Kurvesh replied.

"Do they understand their tasks?"

"Yes. They are to protect us at all costs." Davud Kurvesh was a close friend of the person responsible for supplying the two bodyguards. They worked together for many years and he knew his ally could be depended upon. They were well paid and, in turn, they did what they had to do. Not only were they skilled but would gladly lay down their lives to protect whomever they were ordered to look after. It was not because of heroism or a cavalier outlook on life but because they knew, should they fail in their task, they would also die.

The few words spoken would be the only ones for the remainder of the ride. Davud Kurvesh sat back and tried to breathe deeply, taking in what little rest he could. He was on edge, a condition he was not familiar with, and one he did not enjoy. He thought to himself how glad he would be when this ordeal was over, so he could return to running an operation in a manner to which he was accustomed.

Francis Sun also sat back and looked out the window at the passing sights. To him, they were a blur as his only thoughts were with his son and his upcoming meeting with Mustafa. He wished matters had gone differently, and deep down blamed Kurvesh for not having secured his son's release from the men who were escorting him to the central region of Turkey.

Quentin and Ole Pedersen were seated in a private corner in the bar of the Hotel Dedeman, only moments away from the building where Inci, Thomas Sun, and Yalcin had checked in only an hour before. Quentin enjoyed a cold Heineken while Ole Pedersen had a coffee and a cognac. They ordered a light lunch and were waiting for its arrival. Quentin was anxious to sink his teeth into what, on the menu, had been listed as a club sandwich. He somehow expected it to be different from what he was used to, but didn't care, as it had been a while since he had eaten.

"How long have you been in this business?" Quentin asked.

"About nine years." Ole took a sip of his coffee. "It is hard to believe. Time has certainly sped by." Quentin smiled. "And how about you?"

"Well, I've been with ISIS for two years but this is actually my first assignment." Ole nodded and Quentin thought he noticed a look of reflection back to the early days of his own career.

"How did you ever get into this business?"

"My father's been in it for twenty years." Quentin was about to continue but Ole had an inquisitive look on his face.

"Your father?"

"Yes. His name is Phillip Wright." Quentin paused a moment as he took a sip of his beer. "I thought you knew that?"

"No. Of course I know your father, but never realized you were related. Unfortunately I wasn't briefed on very much pertaining to this case. None of us were. We had just finished an assignment and were actually expecting a few days rest. We got the call rather urgently and didn't have time to meet with anyone for an outline."

Quentin nodded. "Well, my father started in South America and eventually ended up running that sector. He was transferred to England five or six years ago and is now responsible for Europe."

"I know the name but I have never actually

met him. You know the secrecy we have. I also believe the agents who were working the field back then were different types of people. They didn't have the resources we have today. It must have been much more frustrating."

"I agree. And listening to some of the stories my father tells, the only resources he had were his own. Money was a lot tighter, but crime wasn't as rampant as it is today."

"You're absolutely right."

The neatly dressed waiter interrupted their conversation as he approached with their food and placed it on the table. "Enjoy your dinner," he said as he left their table to look after other guests.

"I suppose the many stories you've heard from your father were enough to get you interested in this business," Ole said, as he took a bite of the pita sandwich stuffed with crabmeat.

Quentin paused a moment while he swallowed, "Not exactly," he said. "I lived in Australia with my mother."

"Of course," Ole interrupted. "I should have guessed the accent immediately."

Quentin nodded. "I only went to live with my father a few years ago. While I was visiting him one of the local residents was kidnapped. The police weren't too interested so, with my father's help, I followed up some of the leads. Next thing I know, I was involved in a fairly major ordeal. That's when I really got the taste for this type of work." Quentin took a bite of his sandwich. "How about you?"

"I was recruited. I was a police officer in Copenhagen and a few of us were chosen. Scandinavia had never been a high crime area, so an opportunity like ISIS was exciting.

"The other man with you, is he reliable?"

"Very much so. He has been doing this for a long time. I know he has no personality but he is very good at what he does.

There are two other agents in Konya. They are locating Francis Sun and taking care of him."

"He must be quite a man. I understand he is quite wealthy and has built an incredible organization around the world."

Ole nodded as he enjoyed his pita bread. "On a different matter, tell me about the present situation. How it came to be, and what you think we should do next."

Quite astounded at Ole's request for his opinion, Quentin was flattered and relayed the facts, intentionally omitting the incident at the service station.

"That sounds like a fairly simple matter," Ole said, at the conclusion of Quentin's summary.

"I don't understand why we can't just go in there and get Inci and Thomas Sun out. Surely one terrorist is no match for the three of us."

"I thought you said there were two terrorists?"

Quentin realized he had slipped. He had omitted the part about the accident Cengiz had suffered at his hands at the service centre hours earlier. "Sorry, I meant two terrorists." Quentin felt he had recovered from his slip. A thought occurred to him. It could be that Cengiz had recovered and was now back on his feet again.

"I think perhaps you are right. We could very easily overtake them, but I do not want to risk either our agent's life or the life of Thomas Sun. It is also a great opportunity for us to try and capture Mustafa."

Quentin nodded, for as he expected the ultimate goal had changed from capturing Thomas Sun to finding the leader of the terrorist group. "Now, I think it is best if we leave David Parliament to watch the entrance to the hotel, and follow these people, should they make a hasty exit. It will give us a good opportunity for a little relaxation, something I'm certain we are both in dire need of."

Quentin smiled but it was superficial. He did not want to relax. He wanted to secure Inci's safety -- a situation for which he still felt responsible.

"It looks like Ole was right," Ken Myers said. "It seems we're on our way to Nevsehir." He studied the map as the car continued along the route, which could lead nowhere else than the region of Cappadocia.

"I guess it's time we phoned Ole and told him what we know," Robert Wallace said.

Myers agreed and removed the cellular telephone from his pocket. He dialed the number and was immediately connected to Ole Pedersen. "Ole. It's Myers. We're on our way to Nevsehir. We're about half a kilometre behind Francis Sun who is in a black limo. There are three people with him."

"He seems to know where he is going. If you continue on the road you are on, you will pass by the Hotel Dedeman. Keep going about half a kilometre and you will come to another hotel. Our man, David Parliament, is posted outside. He is parked on a main street right by the entrance to the hotel grounds. I believe Francis Sun will go to that hotel in an effort to locate his son. When he arrives, I want you to make contact with our agent. We will then take him out."

"That sounds great. What happens if he doesn't go there?"

"Then you simply phone me and tell me where he is going and we will arrange to meet you."

"Sounds good."

"You say there are three men with him?"

"Yes," Ken Myers replied. "One guy looks kind of puny, the other two are about the size of a building."

"It is better then to wait until we're are all together. How long until you arrive in Nevsehir?" Ole asked.

"I think about half an hour."

Ken Myers replaced the telephone in his pocket and relayed the information to Robert

Wallace. Both men agreed with the senior contact's decision. The two men continued to keep their distance behind the black limo ahead.

"What was that all about?" Quentin asked, as he finished his meal.

"Those are our two agents in Konya. They are trailing Francis Sun. He is headed in this direction and it looks like he has inside information; otherwise I doubt if he would be coming to Nevsehir."

"So what does that mean?"

"I told them to follow Francis Sun. I believe he is heading for the Hotel Peri Tower to retrieve his son. David Parliament will team up with our two agents and eliminate Francis Sun once and for all. This will happen before Sun gets to the hotel."

"Shouldn't we help them?" Quentin asked, with concern in his voice.

Ole Pedersen finished the remainder of his food and took a swallow of his coffee before answering. "Absolutely not. If something goes wrong and our men get killed, I want to make certain there will still be two of us left to follow and get Thomas Sun back. You never know what can go wrong in a situation like this."

Quentin nodded and agreed with Ole's recommendation. It made sense and again he wished he had thought of a similar idea. He assumed time would give him the wisdom to create decisions which the veteran agent, sitting across from him, was now making. "What do you think we should do?" he asked, as a youth would of his teacher.

"We do not have to do anything at this point. Our three agents will take out Francis Sun, and we will wait patiently for Thomas Sun, Inci, and the two terrorists to leave the hotel. I am certain they have checked in for the night, and I doubt if anything will happen until morning. If it does, I will call you immediately and we will take up the chase."

The plan sounded solid and Quentin nodded his agreement as he wiped his mouth with the cloth napkin.

Ole Pedersen motioned to the waiter for the cheque and held his hand out as Quentin objected to him paying. "Don't be silly. It is the least I can do for all the help you have given us to this point." He placed a sizeable amount of cash inside the leather folder and closed it. "I guess that is all we can do for now. I do not know about you but I'm tired. I think I'll go to my room, perhaps watch a movie and have a rest. It must be night time somewhere?"

"That sounds good," Quentin replied. "I think I'll do the same." He felt strange not being more useful; however, Pedersen was his superior and he did not want to disobey.

The two men walked from the restaurant down a hallway to the elevators. Ole confirmed Quentin's room number and assured him he would contact him should anything happen.

Quentin was pleased with the arrangement and was the first to leave the elevator. Deep down, he was glad he was no longer alone. He hadn't bargained for anything this big and for the first time since he had begun this venture, he felt confident that perhaps soon everything would be resolved, and Inci would be safe again. He walked down the hallway to his room to go over the facts which he had accumulated so far on this mission.

17. Cutthroats

The bar in the Hotel Peri Tower was just as busy as the one in the Dedeman half a kilometre down the road. Thomas Sun was enjoying a cold soda water and Inci had ordered a coffee. Yalcin left them alone for a few moments while he went to check on Cengiz's condition in the parking lot.

Inci spoke little, and her thoughts were searching for an opportunity to escape. She knew Thomas Sun was nervous but was also aware his hand was fixed tightly on the semiautomatic pistol in his jacket pocket. She could tell by the direction of the muzzle that it was pointed straight at her. She knew the gun had been fixed with a silencer and would probably not be heard by anyone in the secluded corner of the bar. The people at the nearest table were rowdy and constantly laughing, which would drown out any sounds made by the muffled firearm.

Inci hoped Quentin was still trailing them. She was glad about what he had done to Cengiz as it made her odds of survival better. The shorter Turkish terrorist was more of a threat than Yalcin was. She felt more comfortable with Thomas Sun guarding her. She knew he would not hesitate to shoot her, but it would be from panic, not calculation. If she remained calm and did not upset him, her safety would be secure -- at least until they reached Mustafa.

She was pleased her message from the Hotel in Ankara had reached ISIS. It not only meant they knew where she was, but it also ensured agents would be sent to assist Quentin. She assumed they would be en route and would either have caught up with him by now or were very near. She knew the countryside and was aware they were no more than forty-five minutes to an hour's drive from the supposed hiding place of the leader of the 'Children of the Sultan'.

The waiter approached their table and asked if they wanted refills on their drinks. Both declined. Inci was frustrated, for she could have seized the opportunity of the waiter's presence to make a run for it. She had been engrossed in her thoughts and had not stayed in tune with her surroundings. The opportunity came and went for, as soon as the waiter departed, Yalcin returned.

"It appears our friend Cengiz is not doing too well. He is still bleeding from the head and is unconscious."

"Perhaps you should call a doctor," Inci said.

"I think you would like that. No," he paused a moment. "I think we will wait. Our comrades will not be long and they will take care of him."

"What if he dies?" Thomas Sun asked.

"It would be the price to pay for a cause."

Thomas Sun was having second thoughts. He was beginning to understand the ruthlessness of the people he was dealing with and wondered if he had made a mistake. He also knew there was no turning back. Still he felt he had to lay low and the opportunity of hiding in central Turkey under the umbrella of Mustafa would surely give him some time to examine his future. He tried to tell himself not to judge the organization by the events of the last two days or the two men he was with.

He fully understood terrorism was ruthless, not only because it had to be, but also because of the type of people it attracted. The latter was the major reason his father had shied away from it during the course of his business.

"Well, look who it is," Yalcin said, speaking in Turkish, as two men approached the table. He stood, embracing the first of the two men and planted a kiss on each cheek. He then repeated the motion with the second man. He welcomed them and asked them to sit at their table.

"This is our very good brother, Thomas Sun," Yalcin said, motioning to the Oriental man sitting quietly, watching the new arrivals. He had no idea what Yalcin had said and, at the mention of his name, assumed there would be introductions.

The first of the two Turks extended his hand in a gesture of friendship. Thomas Sun took it with his left hand, for he did not want to release his grip on the firearm still pointed directly at Inci.

"He is guarding our prisoner," Yalcin explained. "Do you speak English," he asked of his ally. The man shook his head and stared at Inci. He was tall, thin and had short, dark hair. His face was covered in scars caused by acne from his youth. He had a thick, black moustache, which hovered above his upper lip, and wore a plaid shirt, blue jeans and a brown sports jacket.

"She is an agent of the Turkish government," Yalcin said.

"No, she is not," the Turk replied. Yalcin had a strange look on his face.

"What do you mean?" he asked.

"I know this woman. Our paths have crossed once before. I forget her name but she is with the United Nations. ISIS, I believe you call it."

"What is ISIS?" Yalcin asked.

"It is a United Nations organization that deals with illegal immigrants who are linked to crimes."

Inci vividly remembered meeting the man before. It had been in the early days of her career six or seven years ago. His name was Murat Zeynep. He had been involved in a low-level auto theft operation and she had been responsible for escorting him from Southern Turkey to Istanbul. Although the trip only took a day, it was an intense time as she was naive in her work and was being very careful not to make a mistake. His face remained clear in her mind's eye, and seeing him now, standing directly before her, was as if a ghost had reappeared from within the deep confines of her memory.

"What is the problem?" Thomas Sun asked.

"Our comrade, Murat, seems to know our friend here." Yalcin pointed to Inci. "He tells us she is with the United Nations." It almost seemed as if Yalcin took pleasure in causing grief to Thomas Sun. He knew his worry had very little bearing on the present situation, but it was evident by the expression on Thomas Sun's face, the news did not sit well with him.

"What do you mean, the United Nations?" Sun asked. He did not wait for an answer but turned his attention to Inci. "Who exactly do you work for?" He fondled the gun in his pocket and Inci could see the barrel move. She became slightly afraid, not knowing what this latest jolt of anxiety would do to the man who held her life in his control.

She decided not to answer, instead turning

her attention toward Yalcin and speaking in Turkish. "You are making him nervous. Be careful he doesn't shoot his leg off."

Yalcin laughed at Inci's comment, causing greater frustration to build within Thomas Sun.

"Be careful with the gun," Yalcin said, reminding Thomas Sun of the killing weapon he held in his hand. "We do not want to be discovered here. Only use it, if she tries to escape." He paused a moment as he lit a cigarette, offering one to each of his two new companions. "It makes no difference whom she is with. The fact that she is with the United Nations only means that more people are aware of who you are and what you have done. It does not bring anyone closer to finding us. In fact, if anything, it puts us in a better position because we now have someone with tremendous knowledge. Perhaps someone we can use to bargain with in exchange for some of our brothers held in prisons around the world."

Unfortunately, Inci realized Yalcin was correct in his summation of the facts. It would only secure her well being until they arrived at the headquarters of Mustafa. She was relieved to see a slight relaxation, blanket over Thomas Sun.

"We must go," Murat said.

"We have a minor mishap," Yalcin said. "One of my men is in the automobile in the parking lot. He is badly injured and needs medical attention immediately."

"Give Mostel the keys to the car and he

will take care of it. I will drive you to Avanos."

Yalcin described the car to the second of the two men as he passed him the key. The shorter one took the keys and nodded. Yalcin went on to explain about Quentin and the confrontation at the service station.

"Perhaps you should leave by the back exit," Murat said to his bearded friend. "Just in the event they were followed here."

The man nodded and left the hotel in an effort to tend to Cengiz.

"I was unaware there was a back entrance to this hotel," Yalcin replied. "Had I known that, I certainly would not have come in through the front."

"Can we trust our Chinese friend?" Murat asked.

"I think so," Yalcin replied. "He is new to this type of work, but has proven himself in past actions." Murat smiled at Thomas Sun who had no idea of the conversation which had just taken place. He turned his attention back to Yalcin. "Take care of the bill here and we will be on our way."

A much more refined and capable individual than Yalcin, Inci knew immediately that Murat Zeynep was now controlling the situation. He carried himself well and spoke intelligently. With his good education, Inci was surprised that he could not speak English.

Yalcin paid the waiter, again using money which he had taken earlier from Inci. He smiled discreetly at his captive and winked as he caught her attention. She swung her head the other way, not wishing to partake in the mind games being played.

The four walked from the bar to the hotel lobby. "You wait here. I will go and check the parking lot to make sure no one is there. I will also see how our friend is progressing with your injured man," Murat said. Yalcin agreed and watched as he walked through the exit doors of the hotel.

Murat Zeynep walked in a direct and stately manner as he approached the parking lot. His eyes scanned every direction, glancing at each parked automobile. He walked back and forth in a grid-like fashion and was pleased when he saw nothing suspicious. He made his way to the grey sedan where Mostel was tending to the injured Cengiz. He rolled down the window of the vehicle.

"How is he?" Murat asked.

"He is not good. I do not think he will live."

"Do not worry about him. You know where to drive the car. If he is alive when you get there, they will look after him. If he is not... so be it." The man nodded at his superior's words. "Be sure you take the back exit. The front may be watched." The man again nodded, stepped out from the car, and sat in the front seat. He placed the key in the ignition and Murat stepped back as the car pulled away and disappeared around the corner of the concrete building.

Scanning the parking lot he walked slowly

to his vehicle and stood beside it for a few moments to see if anyone followed the grey sedan. When he felt relatively secure that no one had seen them, he opened the door of the brown mini-van and drove to the front door of the hotel. Leaving the engine running he went to the door and motioned to Yalcin to bring Thomas Sun and Inci.

"I would prefer it if you would sit in the back seat with the girl," Murat said.

"Of course," Yalcin agreed. He explained to Thomas Sun what Murat had said and took Inci by the arm pushing her toward the second seat in the mini-van.

Once everyone was seated, Murat pulled the car forward through the parking lot, and along the long drive which lead to the main road.

"Should we not also go out the back entrance?" Yalcin asked.

"No. If you were followed, then perhaps they would post someone at the back entrance. If that were the case, we would look much more suspicious going that way than out the front. They would have no reason to suspect this vehicle." Murat's statements made sense to Yalcin, and the van continued on.

As they approached the main road, a blue car was visible just past the entrance on the shoulder. "Get down," Murat ordered. He motioned to Thomas Sun who did not fully understand what he was saying. It was only when Sun saw Yalcin push Inci's head down that he realized he should get out of sight.

As the car turned the corner, heading northeast, Murat acted naturally so as not to attract the attention of the man seated in the automobile only metres away.

Inci had also seen the car parked along the road and was excited at the prospect of it being different from the one Quentin had driven earlier. It indicated to her that he had received help and she would soon be free.

Murat glanced constantly in his rear view mirror and was relieved when the blue automobile did not make any effort to follow. "We have done it," he said, smiling as he spoke. Yalcin also smiled, and Inci noticed a look of relief on Thomas Sun's face. The car continued on to the small village of Avanos, deep in the heart of Cappadocia and the land of the fairy chimneys.

The telephone rang loudly in Quentin's hotel room, startling him from his relaxed position stretched out on the bed. His heart began to pound as he made a dash for the phone, thinking immediately that something had gone amiss, and Ole was contacting him for assistance. He grabbed the telephone receiver, almost knocking the base from the table onto the floor. "Hi," he said.

"Quentin?"

Quentin was shocked. "Dad?" he asked, totally surprised to hear his father's voice at the other end of the line. "What's the matter?" he asked, inquisitively.

"Thank God you're all right," Phillip said.

"Why wouldn't I be?"

"Something's gone wrong," Phillip began. There was anxiety in his voice mixed with relief at Quentin's well being. "Ole Pedersen and David Parliament have been found murdered in a car just outside of Heathrow."

"What?" Quentin interrupted. "How can that be. I had lunch with Ole a few minutes ago."

"That wasn't Ole. We suspect Francis Sun arranged this. Ole and Parliament flew to London together. Somehow Sun knew about it and not only took them out, but replaced them with two of his own men."

"They sure were convincing," Quentin said. "All the time we had lunch, he carried on a pretty persuasive conversation. He even mentioned that he'd heard of you."

"I guess so," Phillip replied. "If he worked out of Denmark, he'd report to me."

It was a thought that had not occurred to Quentin. Of course he knew Denmark was in Europe, and his father was responsible for Europe. It had just never occurred to him when Ole was speaking. How could he have been so stupid? "What about the other two guys?"

"They're legit. They flew to Istanbul on their own. Neither of them has ever worked with Pedersen or David Parliament and therefore did not know them. They, like you, assumed the impostors to be actual agents."

"This is unbelievable," Quentin said.

"It happens, but it's quite unfortunate. Ole Pedersen was a good man. I've known him for a long time." Phillip had remorse in his voice. "Where are those two other agents now?" he asked.

"I believe they're on their way here. They're trailing Francis Sun." The thought occurred to Quentin that Inci's safety was in jeopardy once again.

"I spoke with Amr and he's arranging back-up for you; however, I think it will arrive too late."

"I know where Parliament, or whatever his name is, parked his car. He's at the hotel where Inci, Thomas Sun and the terrorists are held up. I'm going to boot over there and see if I can get to Inci before they do."

"You'd better be careful. There are more of them than there is of you."

Quentin slammed down the receiver, grabbed his jacket, and ran from the hotel room. He tapped his foot impatiently while he waited for the elevator to arrive. At long last it came and as he stepped inside, he fumbled through his jacket pocket for his car keys.

He noticed several people staring at him as he hurried through the lobby at a faster pace than the patrons were accustomed to. He put his jacket on as he stepped across the parking lot, and jumped in the car immediately turning the key.

Thoughts raced through his mind about the

things Phillip had told him. He knew Inci and Thomas Sun, along with Inci's captors, were in the hotel for the remainder of the night. David Parliament's impersonator was held up outside, awaiting further instructions. Francis Sun was on route to Nevsehir, closely followed by two ISIS agents who were unaware they were being led into a trap. The immediate question was where was Ole Pedersen, or the man who was pretending to be him.

As the thought passed through Quentin's mind, he wished he had knocked on Pedersen's door or at least telephoned his room in the event the blonde haired man would not be with David Parliament's impostor, awaiting the arrival of Francis Sun. As Quentin thought it through, he realized the intention would be for Francis Sun's entourage to storm the hotel and free his son. Inci's life would be considered expendable, as would that of the two Kurdish terrorists. He hoped he would arrive in time to come to the aid of the ISIS agents trailing Francis Sun. He had no idea how he was going to intercept them, but he was in dire need of the assistance they could give him.

A wave of panic flared through his body as he came closer to the entrance to the Hotel Peri Tower. He saw the car which Ole Pedersen and David Parliament's impersonators had driven. A royal blue car was parked directly behind it, but no one was about. Quentin could not halt the stream of questions surging through his head, but realized, as he pulled the car up behind the two vehicles, that he was too late. He could see the two, slumped bodies of the ISIS agents lying motionless in the front seat of the car.

Quentin rushed carelessly from his vehicle. He looked through the window and saw, as he suspected, the murdered bodies of Robert Wallace and Ken Myers. He opened the car door and a feeling of nausea permeated his stomach. The body of Wallace fell sideways onto the gravel shoulder of the road. Quentin immediately saw the bullet wound to the side of the head and was repulsed by the crimson liquid which was splattered on the windscreen, ceiling, and throughout the rest of the interior of the automobile.

Ken Myers had been shot in the stomach. His eyes were open and he had a look of surprise on his face. It appeared to Quentin that he almost seemed as if he was smiling. It was a vision, which was now imprinted permanently on Quentin's mind. He would not forget the sight.

His thoughts turned to Inci whose life was still in jeopardy, more so now than ever. He assumed Francis Sun and his accomplices were at the hotel in an effort to release his son. Quentin knew he had to somehow come to the aide of Inci who, partially due to his carelessness, had been apprehended by this band of cutthroats.

He was about to return to his automobile and head down the driveway to the hotel when he saw a car approach in the distance. He realized he could not leave the body of Robert Wallace lying lifelessly beside his vehicle. He bent over, put his hands under the arms of the large agent, and with great effort, returned him to an upright position behind the steering wheel. As he removed his arms, Quentin felt the hard bulge of a gun tucked in a holster underneath Wallace's jacket. Quentin removed the Beretta 84 and checked the clip. He was relieved and thankful when he discovered it was full.

He quickly closed the door, returned to his car, and backed up enough so he could enter the driveway to the Hotel Peri Tower. He drove quickly as the oncoming car approached, for he did not wish to be seen near the scene of this crime. If the local police caught him, he would never have an opportunity to free Inci.

Francis Sun and Davud Kurvesh were joined by the two bodyguards and the two men who had impersonated ISIS agents only minutes before.

"You should have killed the boy," Francis Sun said, speaking to the blonde man whom Quentin had known as Ole Pedersen. His real name was Stefan Johansen and although he was from Denmark, he certainly was no agent of any government. He was a contract killer who had worked for Francis Sun many times in the past. He had always been dependable and loyal. Although he had been paid well, he had always performed any task to the utmost. The other impersonator was British and also a member of Francis Sun's criminal network.

He was a quiet man who treated his work as a job. He had a wife, several children and lived in a small town north of London. His wife assumed he was a businessman who traveled regularly. Neither she, nor any of their acquaintances, had any indication that the quiet, mild-mannered man they were so familiar with, was in actuality a hired killer.

"I did not think it was necessary," Stefan Johansen replied.

"Why would you think that," Davud Kurvesh asked. "We have just killed two ISIS agents. One more would not have made a difference."

"I disagree with you," Johansen said.

Francis Sun looked inquisitively at the Dane and waited for him to continue his explanation. "The boy we dealt with is Quentin Wright." Francis Sun frowned slightly as he was unfamiliar with the name. Johansen continued. "He is the son of Phillip Wright the man who heads up the European sector of ISIS. Eliminate the boy and the father will use all resources at his hands to hunt us down. I do not think any of us wish to have that sort of threat constantly hanging over our heads."

"I do not agree," Davud Kurvesh said. "We have a job to do and we should not be intimidated from doing it."

Francis Sun looked at the men beside him. He inhaled deeply before speaking. "Johansen is right. We do not need any added aggravation." He paused. "Where is this agent now?"

"He is in his room at the hotel where I left

him."

"Is there any chance he will suspect something?"

"None whatsoever. He is fully convinced we are all ISIS agents and are working together to try and save his partner as well as your son."

At the mention of Thomas Sun, the large Oriental reflected again on the void in his life created by the sudden disappearance of his son. "Let us proceed with our task," he said and took the lead toward the entrance of the Hotel Peri Tower in an effort to accomplish what they had set out to do.

They approached the counter and Francis Sun placed both hands, palms down, on the marble surface. The two bodyguards remained silent during the entire trip and now stood on each side of the Oriental to ensure no harm would come to the man who was paying them handsomely for their protection.

The man behind the desk looked up and was surprised by the sight before him. The six men who were standing directly across from the counter looked as if they had a purpose and he was astute enough to realize he did not wish to become the target of their visible anger.

"How may I help you?" the uniformed attendant asked, courteously. He spoke in English, for it was obvious to him that the people before him did not speak Turkish.

"We are looking for a group of four people," Johansen said. "One is a girl, one is an Oriental of about twenty-five and the other two are Turks. They would have checked in about an hour ago. We want to know what room they are in." Johansen was pleased at having retained the information relayed to him by Quentin.

The attendant behind the counter shook his head and frowned. "I do not know the people of whom you speak, sir." He thought deeply for he did not want to antagonize the party confronting him. "I will check with my associate." He walked along the counter and spoke with a girl who was entering information into a computer. She shook her head, exchanged several words, and the clerk returned to the front counter.

"I am sorry sir, but no one has checked in fitting that description."

"Let me see your list of check-ins in the last hour," Francis Sun said, in a way that was not to be challenged.

"One moment sir," the clerk said. He entered several digits on the keyboard and waited patiently as the printer did its work. As he tore the sheet of paper from the top of the print roll and placed it on the counter, he mumbled how irregular this procedure was. Francis Sun paid no attention and turned the piece of paper around, glancing at the list of names. There was nothing to indicate his son's presence, and only a small handful of people had arrived in the last sixty minutes.

"Perhaps you could try the bar, sir," the

clerk said, at the same time motioning with his hand in the direction of the entrance to the lounge.

"Maybe that is where they have gone," Johansen said. "Maybe they had no intention of staying the night."

Francis Sun was visibly angry and did not reply to Johansen's statement. Instead he marched into the lounge followed by his henchmen. He approached the bar and gave a detailed description of his son, explaining he was with two other men and a woman to the bartender who nodded and said he believed the people were there only moments before. He called the waiter who had served them and asked Francis Sun to address his questions to him.

"I am looking for some people," Francis Sun repeated, but this time speaking to the waiter. "I understand you may have looked after them." He again described his son.

The man frowned, and it became evident he did not understand English. Francis Sun turned to Davud Kurvesh and motioned for him to translate immediately. Kurvesh did and Sun was relieved when the man nodded confirmation to the description. The man replied, and Kurvesh translated back to Francis Sun.

"He says they were here a short while ago. There were, however, only three of them. A man, a woman, and someone who fits the description of your son. While they were here, two men joined them and they all left together."

"How long ago did they leave?" Francis Sun asked. He waited patiently for Kurvesh to translate but was growing short of patience when the waiter took his time in responding.

"He says it was only a few minutes ago."

"Did they leave the hotel?"

Again the translation process took its time. "Yes. The waiter said he thought they all left through the front door."

Francis Sun nodded. "Pay the man," he said abruptly as he turned and walked away heading for the door and the limo waiting outside. His entourage followed. After rewarding the waiter for his assistance, Kurvesh caught up with them.

The two, silent bodyguards stepped into the front seat of the limo. Johansen and Parliament's impersonator joined Francis Sun in the rear. Kurvesh came running and closed the door behind him as the limo departed the parking lot.

18. Fairy Chimneys

Quentin was dealing with the shock of the massacre and realized he must act quickly or he would be too late. He jumped in his car, turned it around and drove to the Peri Tower hotel.

As he entered the driveway he noticed a black limousine drive by but his mind was preoccupied and he paid little attention. Driving to the front door he stopped at the curb and ran into the lobby. Approaching the front desk and not waiting for the clerk to address him, he described Inci, Thomas Sun, and the two men he believed to be David Parliament and Ole Pedersen.

Fortunately the front desk clerk's English was well beyond acceptable and Quentin had no problem in understanding him. "They must be very popular people," the uniformed attendant said.

"Why do you say that?" Quentin asked, impatiently.

"Those people were here only moments ago."

Quentin was elated with the news and felt excitement surge throughout him. "What do you mean they *were* here? All of them? Even the last two?"

"Yes. I was just speaking with my colleague." The clerk motioned to the waiter who was staring at the front desk after his interrogation by Davud Kurvesh.

"The first group of people you spoke of were in the bar and left nearly thirty minutes ago. The others departed within the last few minutes."

"Did you see them leave?" Quentin asked, anxiously, slightly confused by the number of people.

The clerk turned to the waiter and spoke to him in Turkish. A moment later, he turned his attention to Quentin. "My associate here said he watched them leave. They were driving a large, black, I forget how you call it." The man rubbed his chin in an effort to recall an English word.

"Limousine," Quentin said. It was a statement, not a question. His mind flashed to the limo he had just passed upon his entrance to the hotel.

"That is it. Yes. Limousine."

Quentin thanked the man and immediately dashed out of the lobby, returning to his car. He jumped behind the wheel, hurriedly manoeuvred the vehicle through the parking lot, and guided it along the driveway. When he reached the main road, he turned right and was surprised that no police officers had arrived at the scene of the crime. He assumed the murder had not yet been discovered and therefore no one had reported it. Quentin forced the automobile to exceed the speed limit. He calculated he was about five minutes behind the limo.

"Why are we stopping here?" Yalcin asked, as Murat halted the brown mini-van in the small parking lot of a public toilet facility in central Cappadocia.

"Our contact is here. We are to wait until we are met. We will then be escorted to our rendezvous with Mustafa."

Thomas Sun was becoming frustrated at his inability to understand the language spoken by the two men.

"Why are we stopping?" he asked. Yalcin smiled and apologized for their rudeness.

"As Murat explained to me, our instructions were to wait here and we would be told when Mustafa can see us."

"When will that be?" Thomas Sun asked.

"That, my friend, We do not know."

Inci sat quietly in the rear seat of the van next to Yalcin who continued to keep his gun poised at her. She was feeling extremely tired, hungry, and generally worn out. Her emotional state had also taken a beating. She was not used to being a pawn and did not function well when she was not in control.

She wondered how Quentin was faring on his own, and was slightly relieved when she remembered he had the assistance of other agents who had been flown in to help him. Inci realized there had been several opportunities for a rescue attempt, and she began to understand why they had been passed up.

It was becoming very clear that she was now being used as bait in this game of international intrigue. An opportunity for ISIS to capture the infamous Mustafa and discover the headquarters for the 'Children of the Sultan' was a far greater prize than the capture of Thomas Sun.

A rusted lamp hung suspended from a post beside the deteriorating brick framework of the public toilet facility. Under it, an attendant sat on a wooden chair and continually eyed the mini-van, which had stealthily entered his domain, and sat lurking as if waiting for something to happen.

Murat became aware of the attendant's constant gaze and felt it wise to explain their presence. The very last thing he wanted was to alert was the suspicious mind of a passer-by that would surely warn authorities.

As he approached the man, he removed a small amount of cash from his pocket and handed it to him in exchange for use of the facility. Murat smiled at the man and spoke briefly about the weather.

Yalcin stretched his arms forward and quickly brought his gun back, pointing it at Inci as he realized he was becoming far too relaxed with his prisoner. Thomas Sun sat quietly in the front seat of the mini-van and glanced at the haunting silhouettes of the caves, fairy chimneys, and strange rock formations.

Square, stone houses had been built into the cliffs where people had lived for hundreds of years. Many of the rock formations had holes carved in front and had been hollowed out as caves for the living quarters of the ancient Christians.

Murat returned from the bathroom and explained to the attendant that they were waiting for someone and would not be very long. The man smiled and nodded. Murat gave him another bank note and returned to the mini-van.

"There is no sign of Mustafa yet," Yalcin said.

Murat looked at his watch and realized the predetermined rendezvous time had passed. He became nervous, but did not dare show his anxiety to the people with him. "I am certain they will be here shortly."

He had no sooner spoken the words when a small, black automobile approached. The four members of the party inside the mini-van quietly stared at the oncoming vehicle, in anticipation of meeting the famed leader of the Kurdish rebel group.

As the car came to a stop, the door opened and a dark skinned woman dressed in jeans and a black leather jacket walked around the front of the mini-van. As she approached the driver's side, Murat rolled down the window and smiled.

"You are Murat?" the woman asked. Her voice was harsh and deep and, if it was not for her facial features, she could easily have been mistaken for a man.

"I am," Murat replied.

"Follow me. I will take you to Mustafa." The woman did not smile nor show signs of emotion as she again walked around the front of the mini-van and entered the vehicle she had come in. She manoeuvred her car in a circle and exited the parking lot. Murat followed closely, unaware of their destination.

Thomas Sun shifted in his seat to gain an upright position. "Where is it we are going?" he asked, having been unable to understand anything spoken between Murat and the woman in the black car.

"We do not know. Mustafa's hideout is a very well kept secret. He has sent the woman to take us to him." Thomas Sun nodded and was pleased Murat had told Yalcin to be open with him. Although the Turk seemed a great deal more intelligent than Yalcin, Thomas Sun was still disappointed by the calibre of people who consider themselves part of the group known as the 'Children of the Sultan'. He had been familiar with the clientele his father entertained -- well-to-do people who were intellectual executives. They were people motivated by money. The pirates he was now dealing with included religious fanatics, petty thieves, and individuals who would gladly lay down their lives for their cause.

Thomas Sun felt ill at the prospect of having to spend the rest of his life with this sort of people. He also knew it would be impossible for him to return to the way things had been before his involvement in the downing of the passenger aircraft. As he continued to rethink his earlier decisions, he realized he had no choice but to follow the destiny which now lay before him.

Quentin pushed the car to its limits and was angry with himself when he realized in his haste to leave the hotel room, he had forgotten his cell phone. He was tired and found it difficult to see off in the distance. He was thankful there were no side roads for the limo to turn on and he presumed it was ahead.

Heading for central Cappadocia he realised he was getting closer when he saw the countryside change from rolling hills into an area of strangely eerie, red and green rock formations.

It occurred to him that he did not have a plan. He knew he was drastically outnumbered and subconsciously reached for the security of the Browning automatic in his pocket.

He squinted as he saw an automobile in the distance ahead. As he drew nearer, his heart began to beat faster when he realized it was indeed the black limo.

With the concern of locating the black limo now in his past he began to plan his next move. Putting the events in perspective, it occurred to him that Francis Sun had information which was unknown to him. He wondered if Francis Sun knew where the Turkish terrorists were taking Inci and his son or if some kind of deal had been made with the thugs. He concluded that Francis Sun would soon make contact with the people holding his son.

Suddenly, another more menacing thought occurred to Quentin. What if Francis Sun had made an arrangement with Mustafa which would secure his son's freedom? If that were the case, there would be little chance to retrieve Inci from the hands of these terrorists.

The more he thought about his latest realization, the more he began to believe it to be the case. He had no idea how to tackle those circumstances. He knew he would never be able to walk into the stronghold of the 'Children of the Sultan' and simply leave with Inci.

The thoughts played in his mind and caused frustration to build within the young, inexperienced agent.

The drive to Avanos did not take long and Murat

trailed the small, black automobile with expertise.

Avanos, a small village hidden deep within Cappadocia, was shrouded in history dating back to the time of Christ. Its residents lived in small mud, brick buildings, most of which were the facades of ancient caves constructed over the last twelve centuries. The inhabitants were mostly goat herders and carpets weavers who meticulously wove rugs of bright red, green, and cream coloured fabrics dyed with herbs, plants, and minerals from the local area. The rugs hung colourfully along the walls facing the roadway.

The ancient dwellings were in direct contrast with the few modern buildings found along the roadway. The black limo slowed and turned into a brightly coloured blue and yellow service station with a restaurant and toilet facilities.

Murat followed and drove his brown coloured mini-van into the parking spot beside that of his leader's emissary.

"Now what?" Yalcin sighed.

"I guess we can never be too careful," Murat replied.

Thomas Sun shifted nervously in his seat. Inci too turned and stared out the window nervous and unsure of what was to come.

The foursome watched as the black leather clad woman stepped from her vehicle and motioned for them to follow her into the restaurant.

"This is stupid," Yalcin said. "Are we to walk in there with our guns visible?"

"Keep your gun in your pocket and do not

release hold of your charge."

Yalcin slid the door of the mini-van back, took hold of Inci's arm and stepped from the vehicle. He pulled the ISIS agent with him and waited for Murat to close the door before walking toward the restaurant. The woman lined up at the self serve counter, and Murat suggested Yalcin take Inci into one of the booths and he would get lunch for them.

He accompanied Thomas Sun to the long, modernized counter and stood before the glass lined compartments which contained prepackaged food.

The restaurant was as brightly decorated on the inside as on the outside. Blue and yellow booths took up most of the seating area. Bright, white tiles reflected a cleanliness not common to that part of the world.

"Why are we stopping here?" Murat asked, as he approached the woman who had led them to the rest stop.

"We are to wait here until two o'clock. Precisely at that time, I will take you to Mustafa. He is expecting us at two-fifteen and we are not far." Her answer was short and to the point and did not leave Murat with any unanswered questions.

The black woman accompanied by Thomas Sun, and Murat ordered food and paid for it before joining Yalcin and Inci who were seated in a booth located in the corner of the building. Thomas Sun sat opposite them and the woman who represented their host joined him. Moments later, Murat arrived carrying a tray for himself and Inci. He placed the food on the table and slid into the seat directly beside the captured ISIS agent.

"Where I am from we do not feed our enemies," the woman said, vindictively. The coldness of her voice caused a shiver to make its way up Inci's spine.

"And where is that?" Murat asked, politely.

"I am from a small village on the slopes of Mount Ararat."

"What is your name?" Yalcin asked.

"I am called Zeliha," she replied, brushing her hair back from her face in an effort to look more presentable. She was conscious of her appearance in the presence of the dishevelled, yet attractive Inci. As she removed her jacket her breasts heaved forward allowing their fullness to press against the thin, black material of her shirt. The movement caused Yalcin to stare lewdly.

The woman dismissed the action, for she was accustomed to dealing regularly with men. She gave the appearance of being able to handle herself in any situation, and was not the least bit afraid of advances made toward her by the men she worked with.

The group devoured their lunch in silence. No one was in the mood to converse. Thomas Sun was deeply embedded in thoughts surrounding his future. Yalcin chewed away at his food as if it was the most important thing in his life, while Murat planned the remaining leg of their journey in an effort to ensure nothing would go wrong. Inci contemplated the events ahead as well as her own welfare and was becoming concerned with ISIS's ability to get to her in time. She hoped Quentin and the agents who came to help him were close behind. There seemed no other hope for survival. She knew that at this stage of the game there would be no opportunity for her to attempt an escape. If the woman known as Zeliha was any indication of the temperament of the terrorist they were about to meet, any attempt at gaining freedom would be met with certain death.

As the limousine drove through the hilly terrain of Cappadocia, Francis Sun solemnly stared through the window in anticipation of events that were about to occur. Stefan Johansen, also stared out the window at the passing scenery, wondering what lay in store for him under the direction of Francis Sun.

Davud Kurvesh was fidgeting; he had been sitting in automobiles far longer than he cared to. He also felt he was no longer in the foreground of his superior's plans and was surprised when he found his thoughts drift to images of Kwok and Seleng. He wondered if they had felt that way about him at any time during their business association. "What exactly is your intention?" he boldly asked. His question caused Francis Sun to turn his head in Kurvesh's direction, at the same time raising an eyebrow in surprise at the directness of the Turk's request.

"My intention is to free my son, Mr. Kurvesh." The Oriental spoke softly but with determination.

"And how are we to do that?" Kurvesh asked. He was becoming tired of not knowing the plans evolving in the mind of Francis Sun. He had decided that if he was to be part of this plan, he should be made aware of every detail. If the Oriental did not agree, he felt he would rather not be part of the team.

It was as if Francis Sun sensed the inner emotions of Kurvesh. "I will tell you what my intent is," Sun began. His comments caused the two impostors to perk up and stare in anticipation at the large Oriental man still dressed in the grey suit. "We are going to visit with the leader of a terrorist group known as the 'Children of the Sultan'. His name is Mustafa and he resides somewhere in these hills." As he spoke, he used his hand to motion toward the window as if pointing at the surrounding countryside. "I have made an arrangement with this man to exchange my son for an undisclosed amount of cash." He sighed as he spoke, and Kurvesh wondered if, for the first time since he had met him, Francis Sun was unsure of the result of the action he proposed. "The reason I am telling you this now, is because I wish to formulate a plan which will utilize the talents of each of you, as well as of the driver and of his assistant, in freeing my son."

"Do you think they will hand him over if

you offer the cash?" Kurvesh asked.

"These men are animals and do not play by the same rules we are accustomed to." Sun paused a moment, "I am accustomed to," he corrected.

"How exactly do you propose to make the exchange?" Stefan Johansen asked.

"When I spoke to Mustafa, he instructed me to take my car to a small rest area. It was the only one of its kind on this road. We should not have any trouble in locating it. We are to arrive no sooner than two fifteen. A representative of this group will meet us. Someone will escort us to a specific place where the transaction will take place. I was adamant about dealing only with Mustafa and no one else. He agreed, and that is all I know."

The three men sat back, digesting the new information.

"Where is the money now?" Johansen asked.

Francis Sun was hesitant in his reply. "It is in this vehicle," he finally admitted. His concern was due to his natural lack of trust of anyone. The substantial amount of funds, which was securely locked in the trunk of the limousine, might change the motives of his accomplices. He feared they might seek methods of obtaining the bounty for themselves. "Perhaps," Johansen continued, "the money should remain in the car while you go inside and negotiate. Bring Mustafa and your son into the limousine, and make the exchange here. Tell him he can bring several men with him, if he so desires."

Francis Sun nodded slowly as he thought

about the words Stefan Johansen had spoken. "There is merit to your plan," he slowly said.

The vehicle began to slow its speed as it pulled into a long, winding drive which led away from the thoroughfare. The limo stopped in a small, gravel filled parking area near an adjoining building. A sign reading 'public facility' was posted clearly for all to see.

"Now we wait," Francis Sun said slowly, "Now we wait."

Quentin nearly missed the black limousine as it turned away from the main thoroughfare on to a side road. From the corner of his eye, he caught a glimpse of the red tail lights of the limo several hundred metres to the side. He quickly steering wheel around guiding the vehicle into a meadow, securing its position behind a cluster of trees. He hoped he had not been spotted and turned off the ignition. He opened the door and walked from the car. His mind raced in every direction possible looking for answers to questions pounding at his brain. He had no idea where he was or why the limo ahead had stopped. Perhaps Francis Sun did arrange a meeting with Mustafa. Could this be the hideout of the famed leader of the 'Children of the Sultan'.

Quentin walked cautiously along the side of the road ensuring he was well hidden by bushes and shrubbery. He came to a parking lot and noticed an attendant seated on a wooden chair outside a building which was obviously a public toilet. Chuckling to himself he decided this was probably not Mustafa's hideout. Perhaps Francis Sun merely had to use the facility. He immediately discounted that theory when none exited the vehicle. The longer he watched the more he realized it was a rendezvous. Crouched in the bushes he hoped his car was well hidden and checking his watch several times he wondered how long he would have to wait to discover, whatever it was, to happen next.

19. Pottery

Murat and Zeliha left the restaurant, followed closely by Yalcin who maintained a firm hold on Inci's arm. Thomas Sun brought up the rear and glanced around the building as if he subconsciously felt it would be the last time he would see it.

"How long a drive is it?" Murat asked, directing his attention to Zeliha.

"It is not long. Perhaps ten minutes or less."

As they neared the two vehicles, Zeliha walked to the passenger side of the mini-van. "Follow me. When we arrive, do not leave your vehicle until you are instructed to do so." She spoke with authority and dominance, traits which had been developed during a lifetime of insecurity and violence.

Murat nodded and entered the mini-van. Again Yalcin and Inci took their places in the back seat and Thomas Sun joined Murat in the front. Zeliha had been correct. It was not much further when the vehicle came to a halt on the shoulder of the road directly in front of a series of buildings.

Murat obediently stayed in his van as he watched Zeliha walk from her car along a pathway and then disappear through trees. Inci, Thomas Sun, and Yalcin stared through the windows in an effort to see what lay beyond the shrubbery.

Several moments later Zeliha returned, this time followed closely by two men carrying automatic machine guns. They approached the mini-van and as Zeliha opened the door, the men stood in an action stance, hands on their killing weapons, legs slightly apart, each glancing cautiously in all directions to ensure there would not be any problems.

"Come," Zeliha said.

Murat stepped from the mini-van and waited for Yalcin to open the back door. As soon as he did Zeliha, reaching past him, grabbed Inci by the arm.

"We will take care of her now." She tugged at Inci's sleeve and the two women momentarily exchanged glances. Their eyes were filled with hatred for each other. It was an emotion which seemed to bring Zeliha pleasure.

As the auburn-haired ISIS agent stepped from the van, her movement caught the attention of the two guards posted outside. Simultaneously they stared at the tightfitting jeans and enjoyed the curvature of her buttocks as she made her way clear of the mini-van. Zeliha pushed Inci into the arms of one of the guards who held her secure, awaiting further instructions.

"You," Zeliha said, directing her attention to Thomas Sun. "Come with me." Thomas Sun obeyed and followed the woman as she began to walk along the path.

"What about us?" Yalcin asked, concerned about being left behind.

"Go with the guards. They will give you food and drink. When you have rested, you can be on your way." Yalcin stared at Murat and somehow expected to be included in the meeting with Mustafa. Murat shrugged his shoulders. Realizing nothing could be done about the arrangements; the prospect of a fine glass of Cappadocian wine sounded intriguing. One of the guards led them along a different path in a direction which appeared to be a side entrance to the same building where Zeliha had taken Thomas Sun.

"Where are we going?" Thomas Sun glanced at the surroundings

"Finally you are to meet Mustafa. You must be tired after your journey?" It was the first time she had spoken English and for some reason, Thomas Sun hoped there was sincerity in her voice.

Perhaps he had misread her harshness, and it was only the guttural sounds of the Turkish language which had caused him to think her to be abrupt.

A weatherworn, wooden sign with Turkish letters printed on it, hung above an opening in the ivy-covered white, stucco building. A large part of the building was decorated with ferns, flowering bushes, and shrubs. As they entered a small hallway, Zeliha was greeted by two men who were carrying a set of ceramic dishes. It took Thomas Sun a moment to realize the building was a pottery factory. Multicoloured ceramic plates lined the walls and small shelves held teapots, vases, and ornamental figurines. The hallway extended to a larger room, which again was filled to capacity with clay items.

The room, as well as the adjoining hallway, had been carved out from the sandstone and it occurred to Thomas Sun that the entrance was merely a façade to a cave which had been hollowed out to create a series of small chambers interwoven with square tunnels.

They continued their trek through the maze and entered a larger room where several youths sat around a table carefully painting intricate scenes on freshly-baked clay platters. Thomas Sun watched as the delicate fingers of the young artists applied their trade meticulously without so much as a glance toward the strangers who had just entered their domain. Several kilns lined a wall and shelves containing rows upon row of unbaked clay figurines waited patiently for their turn to be beautified by the young, talented artists.

Zeliha continued on, followed closely by Thomas Sun. To the unsuspecting tourist, the surroundings would appear merely as a place where pottery was manufactured. No doubt, this false front, which served as a mask for an intricate terrorist organization, was unto itself, a profitable entity.

Zeliha continued on and led Thomas Sun through another corridor, longer than the others. They wound their way along several curves and the hallway began to shrink in size. As they neared the end, Thomas Sun had to lower his head to pass through the opening and then found himself in a long, narrow room filled with benches covered in dark, red-coloured carpets. "I will leave you now," Zeliha said. Thomas Sun looked at her and nodded. He was confused by the surroundings and felt very much alone when Zeliha departed the room.

He sat quietly on one of the benches and felt a cold chill overcome him from the dampness of the cave's interior. The dank sensation mixed with the perspiration that had formed on his clothes, caused by the anxiety and partial fear he felt since entering this strange place. Before him stood a potter's wheel and several shelves with dark, brown-coloured, clay teapots, which had recently been molded. As he continued to glance around the room, he saw a young girl enter carrying a tray with glasses as well as a bottle of wine. A kerchief had covered her hair and face and she bowed respectfully as she placed the tray on a small table before the first row of benches. She then backed out of the room as silently as she had entered and Thomas Sun stared at the door realizing he was becoming more and more anxious about his own safety. He knew what these men were capable of and did not feel a part of them. He studied the bottle of wine, which had been carved from the local rock and saw that it took the shape of the fairy chimneys, which dotted the surrounding countryside. The cream-coloured bottle looked unique and Thomas Sun wondered if it was manufactured within the walls of the building in which he sat. There were two glasses and Thomas assumed one was for Mustafa, the other for himself.

He waited patiently and was surprised that he had only been inside the pottery establishment for a few minutes. He heard a shuffling noise and directed his attention to the opening which the mysterious servant had recently used. A moment later, a man entered the still chamber.

Thomas Sun was relieved when he saw the face of the man before him. It was the same clean-shaven, lean face of the man he had met in New York nearly five months ago. It was the man who had been introduced to him by his school chums, the man who had arranged for Thomas Sun's role in the downing of TWA Flight 800. It was the man with whom Thomas Sun felt a familiarity. It was a familiarity which eased some of the tension building within him.

"My dear, dear friend Thomas. How are you?" Mustafa asked, speaking robustly and extending both his arms as if he was about to hug his new guest.

Thomas Sun immediately rose and forced a small smile to his lips. As the man approached he wrapped both his extended arms around his body and embraced him vigorously. "It is so good to see you again."

"I did not think I would ever see you again," Thomas said softly.

"Ah, life is full of surprises." The man smiled and noticed the tray with wine glasses and accompanying bottle. "Let us have a beverage to celebrate the success of your mission."

"I do not drink," Thomas Sun said.

"Of course," Mustafa replied. "Some tea perhaps." Thomas Sun nodded and Mustafa picked up a small bell, which sat on a table in the corner of the room. He chimed it and seconds later the servant girl returned. Mustafa spoke to her in Turkish and she retreated to the darkness of the corridor.

"Ah, some fine Turkish apple tea will do you good." Mustafa said. "So tell me," he continued. "How have you been?"

"Well, thank you. I have been concerned about the uncertainty of my future."

"That is all behind you now. You are among friends. You have proven that you are worthy to become a member of the 'Children of the Sultan', and you will be looked after for as long as you shall live." There was confidence in Mustafa's voice and Thomas Sun began to feel easier.

"What is it you have in mind for me?"

Mustafa looked at his watch." I would like you to wait here for a short while. Have some tea, and relax. I will call for you in about thirty minutes and we will take you to your next destination."

Thomas Sun looked confused. "My next destination?" he asked.

"Yes. You cannot stay here for it is a temporary meeting place. As you can see, it is a pottery factory which is open to the public. We must take you underground and keep you away from the people who are seeking to bring you to trial."

"How much more traveling will I have to endure?" the young Asian asked, despair in his voice.

"Not much more. Soon you will be in the comfort of your new home." Mustafa stood and walked from the room.

Thomas Sun breathed a long sigh of relief at the prospect of ending his constant relocation in an effort to avoid capture by Western authorities. The thought of peace and a good night's rest created a feeling of comfort and serenity within him.

At the sound of the oncoming car, Quentin dove into the bushes beside the road. He was thankful there was shrubbery in the immediate vicinity as it gave him cover whenever he required it. He crouched beneath several bushes and watched a small, black automobile approach in the tracks the limousine had taken thirty minutes earlier. Quentin wondered if the car approaching was the contact for Francis Sun. He waited for the automobile to pass and, when he felt confident he would not be seen, made his way to the edge of the road where the limo was parked.

He hid behind several trees at the edge of the parking area and had a clear view of the black car as well as the limousine. He held his breath when he saw the driver's door open. He watched a dark-skinned woman dressed in a leather jacket and blue jeans step out. She did not leave the vicinity of her car, instead leaning against it, crossing her legs at the ankles, and folding her arms. It was as if she were waiting for the inhabitants of the large limousine to come and greet her.

A moment later, the front doors of the limo opened and two bodyguards stepped out. One of them stood guard by the door while the other met with the woman. They conversed for a few moments and the large, muscular man returned to the limo and opened the rear door. He leaned forward and spoke to the people inside. He opened the door further and along with his partner, stood guard while the people from inside the limo came out.

Quentin dared not move and kept his gaze fixed on the scene before him. He was surprised when he saw the two men whom he had believed to be Ole Pedersen and David Parliament step from the limo. A large, Oriental man, whom Quentin assumed to be Francis Sun, followed them. Quentin watched as a fourth man exited the automobile. His mind raced in all directions and he tried desperately to stay focused. The fourth man was the one he had seen on the videotape at the palace, which now seemed to be an eternity ago.

He had no idea who the woman was, but assumed she must represent the terrorist group. Quentin's heart began to beat faster at the anticipation of possibly being close to where Inci was being held captive. He hoped an opportunity to free her would present itself and he desperately wished he had some assistance. He studied his opponents and knew he would be no physical match for these men. Without more information he could not formulate a plan. All he could do at this point was to watch, listen, and follow. His attention focused on the woman as she spoke.

"You are Francis Sun?" she asked, directing her attention to the large Oriental.

Sun nodded and although he was large in stature, he appeared dwarfed, as the two bodyguards stood directly beside him to ensure their leader would not be harmed by anyone.

"You are to come with me," the woman said.

"We will all join you," Sun replied.

"My instructions are very clear. I am to bring you alone."

"Your instructions may be so but we will all follow you in my car." Francis Sun spoke slowly and deliberately with an air of authority that was not to be questioned. "If this is not acceptable to you, we will simply leave and you may discuss the consequences with your superior." He did not wait for a reply and returned to the limousine. One of the bodyguards immediately opened the door for him and he stepped inside. Davud Kurvesh and the two impostors closely followed him. The two bodyguards returned to the front of the vehicle and closed the doors.

Quentin watched and was amused by the expression on the woman's face. She returned to her vehicle and slammed the door shut. An instant later, she engaged the engine and turned the car completely around. As she departed the parking lot, the limousine inched its way forward following her closely. Quentin tucked himself securely behind a tree and waited for the cars to pass. As soon as he felt certain he would not be seen, he quickly made his way to his own vehicle. Jumping into the driver's seat, he started the ignition. Ramming his foot on the accelerator, the wheels began to spin in the soft, fertile soil and the car did not move. Cursing his stupidity he reversed the engine and rocked the car enough to set it free.

It was not long before he saw the cars in the distance. He could feel anxiety building within him and he knew his adrenaline was flowing.

Quentin slowed the car when he realized the gap between himself and the vehicles was narrowing. They were slowing and eventually came to a halt behind a brown mini-van parked alongside the road.

Keeping a safe distance he stopped his car beside a vacant building where he hoped he would not be seen.

The woman dressed in black stepped from the vehicle and was immediately greeted by half a dozen men armed with automatic weapons. Like bees around honey, they swarmed the black limousine, guarding every possible corner in the event of an unforeseen attack.

A moment later one of the rear doors of the limousine opened, causing the guards to jump slightly and point the muzzles of their weapons in the direction of the large, Oriental man who was emerging from the luxury automobile. No sooner had Francis Sun stepped from the vehicle than his two bodyguards immediately opened the front doors and joined him. The guards were poised ready for attack, but both remained calm and stood at the side of their leader.

"You will come with me. Everyone else stays here," the woman said.

"These men go where I go." It was a statement, not a request. Francis Sun spoke with dominance and unchallenging determination. The woman said nothing and turned, leading the way along the path, through the shrubbery and bushes, and into the building where less than half an hour before, she had delivered Thomas Sun and Inci.

They walked through the same passageways

and halted when they came to the room where the youths were creatively decorating the earthenware. "Wait here," the woman ordered. "I will return shortly."

Francis Sun and his bodyguards glanced around the room at the craftsmanship taking place. None of them spoke and were consequently ignored by the artists performing their tasks.

Quentin was growing impatient and decided he would take a chance and move closer. He had no idea how to approach the building. It was heavily guarded and he could not walk by unnoticed. He knew he would be immediately recognized by the two men who had earlier impersonated Ole Pedersen and David Parliament. At one point, the thought of firing a bullet into the guards around the black limousine flashed through Quentin's mind, thinking it would create confusion, perhaps even resulting in the two forces attacking each other. He quickly discounted the idea as ludicrous and most impractical. He decided there was nothing he could do outside. He had to gain access to the interior of the building.

As he approached the area he checked the surroundings and decided he would stand a better chance if he crawled through the bushes. At the entrance to the building he was surprised at the absence of guards. A sign over the door read 'Çanak Atölyesi'. He entered cautiously, and immediately realized he was in a pottery factory of some sort.

He stealthily followed the long, dimly lit corridor pausing several times when he though he heard voices coming towards him. Further along he could see light streaming out of a room into the hallway and could detect the movement of shadows made by the people inside. Just ahead of him was a small corridor which let into darkness. Quentin paused at the dark hallway for suddenly he heard voices coming from the room.

"It is good to finally meet you. My name is Mustafa." The leader of the terrorist group extended his hand in a greeting to Francis Sun. "You have met my compatriot Zeliha. I hope she has taken good care of you."

Francis Sun returned the greeting but said nothing.

"Come with me," Mustafa continued. "We will meet in more private surroundings. You do not need your associates to join you. You can see I am alone as well."

"These men go where I go," Francis Sun said.

"As you wish." Mustafa led the way and Francis Sun, accompanied by his bodyguards, followed. The terrorist leader looked at Zeliha. "You need not come with us. Join the others and enjoy some refreshments."

Zeliha nodded and left the room by the same door Mustafa used to enter. The Turk led the way, retracing the steps Francis Sun and his bodyguards had taken moments earlier.

Meanwhile Quentin could hear noises coming toward him and was concerned that the man known as Mustafa would lead Francis Sun in his direction. He headed along a dark corridor which ended at a wood barrier. In the darkness, Quentin felt planks which were nailed together to form a crude door. He was relieved when his hand touched the bottom of a small handle. Removing the Beretta from his pocket he made sure the safety was off then pulled back the lever allowing a bullet to enter the chamber.

Quentin flipped the lever on the door and was glad when it gave way. Cautiously, opening the barrier he saw only darkness. He listened carefully and heard nothing not even his own breathing. He was alone. It occurred to him there might not be an exit from the room and if Mustafa and Francis Sun did enter, he would surely be caught. He tried desperately to see his surroundings but found it impossible as the room was filled with darkness. He assumed there was a light switch but did not wish to chance illuminating the area.

Quentin wandered around the chamber and realized it was quite small. He stumbled against what he thought was a chair and table and walked toward one of the walls. As he groped in the dark, he used his hands as his eyes and searched the perimeter of what felt like a crate. It seemed to be at least a metre long and a metre high. As he continued to search, he came across a second crate leaning against the first. He decided it would be a place to hide should anyone enter the room.

He returned to the door and closed it all but three or four centimetres, enabling him to hear any sounds from approaching people. The silence was abruptly disturbed by the shuffling noise of feet as they made their way along the sandstone floor. Quentin could hear people speaking and decided someone was heading in his direction.

He silently closed the door and held the latch with his fingers until it was locked in place, ensuring it did not make a sound. Retracing his earlier steps, he made his way around the table and chairs, and when he found the crates, worked his way behind them, crouching down into concealed position. As he quietly sat, he saw a light shine under the door and presumed a hall lamp had been switched on.

It did not take long until he heard the door open, and light from the illuminated hallway flooded into the room. The chamber became even brighter when a switch was flipped and lights were turned on. Quentin glanced up to confirm he was well hidden from view; he felt relatively secure in his hiding place, knowing they would not be looking for him. He also suspected their time would, no doubt, be precious. He listened carefully to the conversation taking place around him.

"Please, have a seat," Mustafa said, motioning to the empty chairs. "Would you care for a beverage?"

"No, thank you." Francis Sun sat as his bodyguards remained standing. One walked toward the door and stood beside it, as a sentry. The other began to walk toward the crates which were piled along one wall. When he reached them, he turned around and faced his master in the interior of the room.

Quentin's heart skipped a beat when he heard the guard walking in his direction. He thought for certain he would be discovered and was only somewhat relieved when he heard the man stop and turn.

"I want my son returned to me."

"All in good time, my friend." Mustafa was polite and smiled as he spoke. He knew he was in control and had every intention of maintaining the upper hand. "Let us talk about the arrangements." Mustafa paused a moment and stared at the two bodyguards, again smiling slightly. "Do you have the money?" he asked, redirecting his attention to Francis Sun.

"I have it. Do you have my son?"

"Yes. I do. He is well taken care of. You will have him as soon as I have the money."

"You misunderstand my intentions. You will have the money as soon as I have my son." Francis Sun spoke calmly, and it was evident to Mustafa, he had a flare for negotiation.

"You understand, my friend, I cannot hand your son over to you until I have the money. Once you have him, there are no assurances for me that you will keep your end of the bargain."

"I am a man of honour. I have made a living by that honour. I believe the shoe is on the other foot. You are the one who is not trustworthy."

Mustafa was visibly upset by Francis Sun's statement. "I resent that. I believe if we are to negotiate a successful transaction, we must have each other's trust."

"That is my point exactly," Francis Sun said, softly. "You bring me my son, I will give you the money. What more trust could a man ask for?"

Mustafa knew he was not getting anywhere. He decided to try a different approach. "Where is the money?"

"It is in safe keeping. You will have it the minute my son is released."

"I have an idea," Mustafa said, as if a new thought had just entered his mind. "You go and get the money and return here. I will get your son and do the same. We will then make the exchange at the same time."

"Your idea has wisdom and I would agree except for one minor detail."

"What is that?" Mustafa asked, inquisitively.

"I will go and get the money and I will wait for you in my vehicle. You bring my son into the car and we make the exchange there."

"I am not that stupid," Mustafa said, slightly offended. "You have men in your car. As soon as I arrive, what is preventing you from shooting me, taking the money, and your son?"

"Listen to what you are saying," Francis Sun said, sternly. "You have men positioned around my vehicle. How far could I possibly get? If you feel that way about it, why not bring some men with you. There is room for three people in the car plus my son."

Mustafa pondered Francis Sun's suggestion and decided it was a worthwhile idea. "So be it," he finally said. He stood to leave, leading the way toward the door. Francis Sun followed him, and the two bodyguards brought up the rear. They walked along the corridor and wound their way to the main hallway. Mustafa guided Francis Sun in the direction of the entrance to the building. He looked at his watch. "It is three-fifteen. I will be in your vehicle in fifteen minutes. Be sure to have the money ready, for I will have your son. Do not do anything foolish, as I will have a gun pointed directly at him."

"One more thing," Francis Sun said, before leaving. "Does my son know of these arrangements?"

"No. He believes we are taking him underground into hiding."

"I see," Francis Sun said, solemnly.

"It is a problem you will have to deal with. You are his father and no doubt responsible for his present situation."

The words rang deep into Francis Sun's emotions. He had an inner desire to lash out at the man who had just spoken but knew better -- partially because the action would cause nothing but problems, but also because, deep down, he knew that Mustafa's words were true.

The large Oriental, accompanied by his two bodyguards, departed from the hallway and walked toward the safety of his vehicle. Mustafa stepped in the other direction to make arrangements for reuniting Thomas Sun with his father.

Quentin knew he had very little time in which to act. As soon as he felt the coast was clear, he stood from behind the crates and walked through the well-lit room toward the exit.

He opened the door slowly and glanced in the hallway to ensure no one was there. Thankful the lights had been left on, he decided to turn left, away from the entrance. He knew Inci was somewhere in the building and, although it was a maze of tunnels and chambers, he had no choice but to locate her. He knew she would be of no use to the terrorists and hoped dearly that she was still alive, for if she was not, he was not sure if he could handle the responsibility. It would have been a direct result of his inexperience.

He made his way along the hallway arriving in a large room occupied by people who sat at tables painting pottery and ornaments. He was surprised that no one looked up when he entered. He assumed these people, engaged in their daily employment, were accustomed to strangers constantly in the area.

There was only one exit to the room, other

than the one through which he had come. Quentin decided to take it. It was another corridor. This one led in a winding fashion to a set of steps. As he walked along the stairs, he heard the noise of footsteps coming toward him. He quickly made his way to the bottom of the steps and jumped into a small alcove at the side of the hallway.

Seconds later, he saw a form pass directly in front of him. He pressed his body hard against the indentation in the corridor. As the person passed, Quentin instantaneously recognized him as one of Inci's captors. It was the man from the service centre and he felt his heart begin to pound. He had a split second in which to make a decision and allowed instinct to take control of his actions. He jumped out, placed his arm around the man's throat and embedded the barrel of his gun deep into the man's ribcage.

"If you make a sound, it will be your last," Quentin whispered into Yalcin's ear.

It was evident by Yalcin's trembling that he was taken by surprise and at this point was unsure of who it was holding him from behind. "Who are you? What do you want?"

"You are holding an ISIS agent here. I want to know where she is."

"I have no idea what you are speaking of," Yalcin said, unconvincingly.

"We both know better. My gun is cocked and ready to fire. Do not make me use it."

"If you use it, you will never get out of here

alive."

"At this range, the gunshot will be muffled. I doubt if anyone would hear it. One thing will be for certain; my fate will not yet be determined, where as you will surely be dead." He waited a moment and allowed the words to sink in. "Now move," he said, forcefully.

"It is this way," Yalcin said, and began to return in the direction from which he had come.

"Wait," Quentin ordered. He released his grip from around Yalcin' throat and searched the man's torso for a weapon. When he found a gun securely placed in its holster, he removed it, disarming the Kurdish terrorist. Quentin nudged Yalcin with his semiautomatic and the man began to move. He walked through the corridor passing several doors. As they continued, the hallway became larger. Quentin had a sense they were heading underground and wondered if he would ever find his way out, assuming he would first locate Inci and secure her safety.

As they continued on their trek, Yalcin began to slow as distant voices became more audible. Quentin tugged on the man's collar, signalling him to stop. He leaned forward and whispered in the terrorist's ear. "Where are the sounds coming from?" he asked.

"A room down the hall. The door is open and it is filled with people."

"Is she in there?"

"No. She is just beyond."

Quentin assumed Yalcin was telling the truth, for he appeared to be the type of person who valued his life more than anything else.

Quentin thought for a moment and decided he had no alternative but to continue walking. "I will walk beside you. No one knows me, so no one will question who I am. If anyone says anything, shrug it off. The slightest cause for alarm and you will be dead. Don't think that I care what will happen to me because if I die, I will not go alone." Quentin spoke convincingly, even though he knew his threat was idle. Even if he did kill Yalcin, nothing would be achieved. He would surely be shot himself, along with Inci, and it would all be in vain.

As they approached the opening, the noise became louder and from the sound created inside the room, Quentin assumed there to be at least half a dozen people.

They walked past the opening and neither of them looked in.

"Yalcin!" Murat yelled from inside the room, as he watched Quentin and his captive pass.

Quentin nudged the barrel of the semiautomatic pistol forcefully into the side of Yalcin, causing the man to cringe slightly. Yalcin raised his hand in the feeble form of a greeting and continued on. They walked along the corridor and passed several closed doors, causing Quentin to wonder if Inci might be secured behind them.

At last Yalcin stopped directly before a

wooden door which appeared slightly larger than the previous ones. The lock was a deadbolt; however, it had a flip latch from the outside, allowing anyone to enter. It was evident to Quentin that this was a makeshift prison.

Quentin was about to put his hand on the handle when he heard a man shouting in Turkish from behind him. "Yalcin, where are you going?" It was Murat. He had grown slightly suspicious when he saw Yalcin accompanied by a stranger.

"Ignore him," Quentin said, quietly, with determination. As he spoke, he placed his hand on the doorknob and turned it. He heard a familiar click as the lock released its hold on the latch.

"Look out!" Yalcin yelled, in Turkish. "It is a trick!"

Quentin saw Murat's eyebrows turn into a frown and knew he had no options left to him. He slipped his hand inside the trigger guard of the semiautomatic pistol and gently squeezed the small, metal object with his forefinger. The gun went off but the sound was not loud. The flesh of Yalcin's abdomen muffled most of the thrust.

Murat was taken by surprise, as the events unfolded with extreme haste, and before he had a chance to react, Quentin allowed Yalcin's lifeless form to slump to the ground. At the same time, he raised his pistol in the direction of Murat and fired a second shot. The bullet hit its mark and caught Murat squarely in the chest. Quentin knew he had only seconds before the rest of the people in the area realized what was happening and would pursue him.

He swung his gun into the opening of the door and pointed it toward the interior. Something was wrong and he immediately realized the room was empty, causing his heart to fill with despair. Yalcin had lied! Inci was not here. She was somewhere else. Quentin knew he would now be trapped, and it would all have been in vain.

He debated returning to the hallway and felt it was the only option left open to him. As he was about to leave, the door suddenly swung shut, as if pushed from behind, and forcefully caught him on the side of his body hurdling him against the doorframe. The act caught Quentin totally off guard and it caused his gun to fall from his hand. In the split second during which the action occurred, Quentin had lost control. He tried to regain it and bent forward to retrieve his semiautomatic. He saw, from the corner of his eye, a shape emerge from the shadow. As he turned his face, he was met with a sharp jolt caused by the shoe of the person who emerged from behind the door. He looked up in a blur and was about to be greeted by a second kick when he realized that it was Inci.

At the same moment, she recognized Quentin and froze in total shock. "Quentin, it is you!"

"Yes." It was all Quentin could say. He was glad to see her but his face was in excruciating pain. He raised his hand to his mouth and felt the warmth of blood seeping from the wound.

"I am so glad to see you," Inci said.

Quentin, still massaging his face said, "why don't you kick me again and show me how much you really missed me."

"I am sorry. I did not realize it was you."

"We'll talk later." Quentin sprung into action and grabbed his pistol from the floor. He reached into his belt and removed the one he had taken from Yalcin earlier. He passed it to Inci who, upon receiving it, unlocked the safety and checked the chamber.

The entire activity inside the small room had lasted only seconds. As Quentin stepped into the hallway with his gun poised for action, he came face to face with Zeliha. As he looked in her eyes, he saw a look of surprise. She did not know who this stranger was. As soon as she looked past him and saw Inci, she realized what was happening. She did not have the opportunity to react, for Inci had fired a shot from around Quentin's side, catching her square in the face. The woman bolted backward, landing flat on her back on the floor of the corridor.

"Which way?" Inci asked. She thought Quentin might have been familiar with the layout of this underground catacomb.

"This way," Quentin said, pointing in the direction opposite to the one from which he had come. They raced along the corridor, opening each door they came to, in anticipation of finding a hiding place or an exit.

It took several tries and at last one of the doors led to a room which, unlike the others, was flooded with daylight. Quentin quickly scanned the area and realized the source of the light was a window located on the upper part of a wall directly across from the door. "This way," he ordered, and immediately took the lead. Using the back of his gun, he pounded twice against the windowpane causing the glass to shatter. Again using the gun as a hammer, he broke away a small piece of the glass which remained sealed in the wooden frame. Inci had the foresight to close the door behind them in an effort to throw their pursuers off the scent.

"Here, quickly." Quentin held his hands clasped together in order to make a step for Inci. She understood immediately, walked toward Quentin, raised her foot into the makeshift stirrup, and lifted herself up, using the window ledge for support. She forced herself through the window opening, being careful not to cut her flesh on the jagged pieces of glass which remained lodged in the frame. As soon as she was through, she glanced around to ensure no one was there. She reached in and extended a hand to assist Quentin. He tucked the gun into his pocket and hoisted himself up to the window frame.

"There is no one here," Inci said, answering a question visible in Quentin's eyes.

It did not take long and, with help from Inci, He found it was quite easy to make his way through the opening.

Once outside, he again grabbed the security of the Beretta and he attempted to gain his bearings.

"What is happening?" Inci asked.

"It's a long story, but right now, Mustafa is taking Thomas Sun to his father."

"To his father?" Inci said, surprisingly. "What does he have to do with this?"

"His father made a deal with Mustafa to exchange money for the return of his son."

"Interesting." Inci felt that from what she had learned of Thomas Sun, he was not in any position to desire a reunion with his father.

Quentin started to walk through the foliage in the direction he believed led to the main road. "Come on," he said. "We don't have much time."

Inci caught up to him and the two ISIS agents, once again united, made their way toward the front of the pottery factory. Their guns drawn ready to take immediate action, should the necessity arise. They made their way along the wall and each time they reached a corner, wondered if there was ever an end to this maze of concrete and sandstone.

The dark, green leaves on the shrubbery provided an excellent cover as the two made their way to the end of the brick building. It was a small clearing, which provided them with a view of the front entrance and the road beyond; still shielded by the leaves and bushes, they would not be seen. They had a clear view of the activity taking place before them.

20. Pawn

"It is time to go," Mustafa said, as he entered the room where Thomas Sun sat patiently waiting. The youth jumped to his feet, for he had long awaited this moment.

"Where are we going?" he asked, inquisitively.

"Come with me. I have arranged for your safety and security."

Thomas Sun was excited at the prospect of a new future. Mustafa led the way out from the small room, along a corridor. They walked through the room where the artists were busily painting the pottery and made their way toward the entrance of the building. As they walked over a flagstone path, leading to the road, he noticed the black limousine and guards surrounding it.

"This is all for me?" he asked.

"But, of course," Mustafa said. "We do not wish to take any risks."

At last Thomas Sun felt he was being given the importance he deserved. He had played a major role in an international terrorist act, and had felt all along that his pride had not been adequately rewarded.

When they arrived at the limo, Mustafa ordered him to wait for a moment. The terrorist leader walked toward his guards and spoke to them in Turkish. Thomas Sun could not understand what they were saying. There were six guards standing around the black automobile and four of them moved back when Mustafa finished speaking. The other two walked toward Thomas Sun and stood on each side of him.

"We will make certain nothing happens to you," Mustafa said, as Thomas Sun looked at the guards who were now standing next to him. "Come with me," the leader of the 'Children of the Sultan' said.

As they arrived at the black limo, the bodyguard seated in the front passenger's seat, stepped out and opened the rear door. One of Mustafa's guards entered, and a second one pushed Thomas Sun through the opening. The guard followed and Mustafa quickly entered the stretched automobile. The bodyguard returned to the front seat and the limousine immediately began moving.

"What are you doing here?" Thomas Sun asked when he saw his father sitting directly across from him.

"Say nothing," Francis Sun said.

As soon as Mustafa felt the car moving, he immediately looked concerned. His guards also realized something was going amiss. They lowered their weapons but Stefan Johansen along with David Parliament's impostor were prepared and had already drawn their guns in readiness.

"Where are we going?" Mustafa asked.

"We are driving off so that each of us can fulfil our bargain." Francis Sun sat back and stared at Thomas who was fidgeting nervously across from him.

"What you do mean we are going to keep our bargain?" Mustafa asked, slightly upset by the change in arrangements.

"We are going to drive a short distance from here. Away from your guards. You, my son, and myself will leave this vehicle which will then depart. We will go our separate ways, each with our own packages."

"You mean the money?" Mustafa said.

Francis Sun nodded.

Thomas Sun looked up at Mustafa and then again at his father. "You mean you are exchanging me for money?" he asked.

"I said, say nothing," his father ordered.

The men sat in crowded silence as the limousine drove along the main road of the small, Cappadocian village of Avanos.

Quentin and Inci watched as the vehicle moved down the road. "What will we do now?" Inci asked.

"Come with me," Quentin said and began running through the bushes toward the area where he had left his car. They arrived several metres down the road and Quentin removed the keys from his pocket. Inci looked at him and smiled.

"How resourceful." She smiled as she spoke and Quentin nodded.

"Try and stay with me this time?" he said, laughing as he spoke. The two agents jumped into the automobile. Quentin started the car and moved it in the direction of the black limousine. He pulled out of his parking spot slowly so as not to attract the attention of the guards in front of the pottery factory.

"I guess they are not aware of what has happened inside," Inci said. "How did you ever find me?"

"It's a long story," Quentin said. He turned his head toward Inci and slowly smiled. "I'd like to tell you about when we have some time."

"That is good," Inci said. "How do you say in your country? That is a very smooth line."

Quentin smiled as he piloted the vehicle along the paved road in pursuit of the black limousine. He did not wish to drive too fast, for the last thing he wanted to do was be discovered by Francis Sun or Mustafa, and their entourage of guards.

Stefan Johansen sat with his back to the driver's compartment of the limousine. He raised his semi-automatic pistol and tapped three times on the smoked glass. The vehicle began to slow and came to a halt in an area surrounded by cotton fields.

"Why are we stopping?" Mustafa asked.

"This is where we will stop," Francis Sun answered. "You, Thomas and myself will leave the automobile at this point."

"Do you have what I want?" Mustafa asked. Francis Sun picked up a briefcase and patted it with his hand. "Do you mind if I look at it?" the terrorist asked.

"Not at all. It is a reasonable request." Francis Sun opened the briefcase and showed the currency to Mustafa. The Turk's face beamed with excitement at the sight of the crisp neatly stacked bills. "I trust this meets with your agreement?" Francis Sun asked.

"Yes indeed," Mustafa replied.

Thomas Sun, intimidated by his father, dared not speak. He felt as if his entire world had just caved in. He had set out to prove himself and his ability to act without his father's constant intervention and here, after his first attempt, his father had again entered his world, established all the rules, and taken control of his life as well as his destiny. He was filled with anger, but knew he could do nothing. He dared not speak for he could no longer trust Mustafa. He had been used as a pawn to secure financial gain for the terrorist. He felt foolish and immature, and knew it was only his pride which kept him from breaking into tears.

"Leave your gun here," Francis Sun ordered. "I will do the same." As he spoke, he removed a semiautomatic from under his jacket. He placed it on the floor of the limousine and waited for Mustafa to do the same. The Kurdish rebel leader removed his weapon and laid it beside the other firearm.

"Let us go," Francis Sun said. Stefan Johansen opened the door to the limo, never once taking his eyes off Mustafa's guards.

Francis Sun was the first to step out of the vehicle, followed immediately by his son. Mustafa stepped on to the pavement and Stefan Johansen closed the door.

Quentin and Inci pulled over and stepped from their vehicle as they watched the actions ahead. They both removed guns from their secured positions and ensured the safety catches were off. As they neared the scene where the three people had stepped from the limousine, they crouched into the field and stooped, hiding amid the white, puffy, cotton flowers.

"I wonder what's going on?" Quentin asked, quietly.

"It looks like they are making a trade," Inci replied.

"Why is the limo taking off?" Inci did not respond, for she had no answer. "I think this is the only opportunity we're going to get," Quentin said. "Let's go." They hesitated for a brief moment -- enough time to create a safe distance between them and the limousine.

They jumped through the cotton fields toward the spot where Thomas Sun, Francis Sun, and Mustafa stood. Quentin saw the large Oriental man hand the briefcase to the Turkish terrorist leader. He felt it would be as good an opportunity as any for him to intervene.

"Freeze!" he yelled, as he stood up amid the cotton.

All three were taken by surprise when they saw the two ISIS agents standing in the field with their guns pointed directly at them.

Thomas Sun was the first to speak.

"What are you doing here?"

"Who are these people?" Francis Sun asked, totally baffled by the events taking place around him.

"They are ISIS agents," Mustafa replied. "How did you escape?" he asked, directing his attention at Inci.

"Never mind that now. Bring the suitcase over here." She directed her comment at Thomas Sun who nervously did not know what his next move should be. Quentin was about to restate Inci's directive when the sound of gunfire came from an area just down the road.

"What was that?" Mustafa asked.

Inci and Quentin looked at each other briefly, neither of them knowing what the gunshots represented. A moment later, their questions were answered when they saw the black limousine return.

Quentin did not wait for the limo to arrive and stepped forward, grabbing Thomas Sun by the collar. "She said, come with us!" he commanded. "Did you not hear her?" He dragged the youth toward his vehicle but knew he would not make it in time to avoid the arrival of the black limo.

As the large limousine came to a stop, Stefan Johansen was the first to jump out. The two bodyguards from the front seat, and the man impersonating David Parliament also stepped from the car. Francis Sun put up his hand, and the four men halted.

Mustafa stared at the doors of the limo and waited for his men to come out. He realized, when no one exited the vehicle, that the previous gunshots were directed at them.

"You have tricked me," he said, speaking to Francis Sun. The large Oriental said nothing and redirected his attention toward Quentin.

"Let the boy go," he ordered. "You can see you are outnumbered." Quentin raised his semiautomatic weapon to the temple of Thomas Sun.

Inci jumped in front of Thomas Sun. "You will not see your son alive if you do not let us leave," she said. She cautiously guarded their hostage and made it very clear to Francis Sun that if anyone was to shoot, the boy would be killed.

As Quentin dragged Thomas Sun back toward his vehicle, Stefan Johansen and his accomplices could do nothing but look on helplessly.

As their gaze was sternly fixed on Inci and Quentin, they failed to notice Mustafa reaching behind him to remove a semiautomatic weapon. The Turk quietly raised his gun and pointed it at the four men beside the limo. He fired three times in rapid succession. Each bullet found its mark and the two bodyguards along with David Parliament's impersonator fell to the ground. Stefan Johansen was the first to respond and removed his gun, instinctively firing in the direction of Mustafa, causing the Turkish leader to fall to the ground. Inci squeezed the trigger on her weapon, which was directed at Johansen. The first bullet missed its mark and Johansen swung around in order to release a round in her direction.

"Wait!" Francis Sun yelled, for fear his son would be injured. Johansen fired and the bullet grazed past Inci's head embedding itself within the skull of Thomas Sun. Quentin felt the weight of his hostage's body go limp. He pointed his weapon at Stefan Johansen and squeezed the trigger. The bullet made its mark and caught Stefan Johansen in the chest. The Danish impostor fell to his knees and smiled sadistically at Quentin. He fell forward, laying face down on the pavement and, after several twitches of his left arm, lay motionless on the ground.

Francis Sun ran toward the lifeless body of his son. Both Inci and Quentin kept their guns trained on him. "He is dead," Francis Sun cried. "My son is dead. His tears were visible, and he made no effort to hide them.

Quentin felt pity for the man, for he knew how his father would feel under similar circumstances. "There is nothing more you can do here," Quentin said. "I suggest you get in your car and leave." Francis Sun slowly stood and stared at Quentin Wright. His eyes were glazed and tears were running down his cheeks.

"This is my son." Francis Sun looked down at the motionless body lying on the ground before him. "I did not have an opportunity to tell him that I loved him."

Quentin's emotions were beginning to take over, and he had to fight hard to keep them recessed so as not to interfere with any necessary action. He glanced at Inci and noticed her eyes were also glossy as they filled with tears.

"Do you have a cell phone with you?" Quentin asked, directing his attention to Francis Sun.

The large Oriental man remained squatted as he hovered over the body of his son. He slowly turned to look at Quentin and acted as if he had not understood his request. Finally he spoke. "There is one in the limousine," he said, slowly.

Quentin nodded and motioned Inci to ensure her gun remained trained on Francis Sun. Although the man posed no immediate threat to the two ISIS agents, Quentin did not wish to take a chance, for he knew Francis Sun's reputation and did not want to underestimate him.

As Quentin walked toward the limo, he looked at the bodies of the two impersonators and the two, muscular bodyguards. Their faces appeared less threatening, as they lay motionless. Their eyes stared into the blackness of death. As he stepped over them, he looked back at Inci to make sure she was in control of her situation.

He stepped into the limo and saw the telephone lying on the seat. There was no possible way he could have seen the body of Mustafa, several metres away, shift slightly. The Kurdish leader slowly manoeuvred his weight to his side and glanced in the direction of Francis Sun and Inci. Although the man was severely wounded, he somehow found enough energy to raise his semiautomatic and squeeze the trigger.

Quentin heard the loud crack from the killing weapon as it echoed throughout the vicinity. His first thought was that Inci had shot Francis Sun. With telephone still in hand, he immediately jumped out of the limo and glanced toward the place where Inci and Francis Sun were standing. When he saw Inci lying motionless on the ground his body was riveted with shock. He ran to the scene and levelled his Beretta at Francis Sun who was still squatted beside the body of his son.

Quentin was confused, for he did not see a

gun in Francis Sun's hand. He trembled with anger. The Oriental must have realized what was going through Quentin's mind and pointed in the direction of Mustafa.

Quentin did not understand, but as he followed Francis Sun's finger, he saw the Kurdish rebel leader desperately attempting to raise his gun and fire a second time. Quentin squeezed the trigger of his Beretta and the gun barked twice. The bullets hit their mark and Mustafa moved no more.

Quentin looked at Inci and a feeling of nausea built up in his stomach. He was sick at the sight and, as he knelt down he saw the blood seeping from a fresh wound in her side. He was about to check her throat for a pulse when she moved her head slightly.

He tried to remain as calm as he possibly could and kept his gun pointed at Francis Sun. With his other hand, he used the telephone and dialed the ISIS emergency number.

The phone was answered immediately. Quentin explained the situation and included his location. The dispatcher confirmed that an ambulance would arrive very shortly. He was put on hold. While Quentin waited he took hold of Inci's hand and held it tenderly. He felt her respond with a gentle squeeze, which sent a ray of hope throughout his devastated body. He looked at Francis Sun. The shock of the events, which had happened, was too great for the man to contain, he was now openly weeping.

A moment later Amr El Hab was on the line. "Quentin, this is Amr. What has happened?"

Quentin explained what had taken place and how Inci was now laying before him.

"How is she?" Amr asked.

"I don't know. She's not moving."

"Is she alive?"

"I don't know. I can't feel a pulse." Quentin tried desperately to check her vital signs by placing his fingers on her wrist. He felt no response.

"Where is Thomas Sun?" Amr asked.

"He's here. He's dead."

"What about Francis Sun? Was he shot as well?"

Quentin heard the sirens of the ambulance approach from the distance.

"No. As soon as the shooting started, he jumped in the limo and took off." Quentin was not sure why he lied but the scene of this man openly weeping over his son's body touched his heart and clouded his mind.

Amr continued. "I would suggest you get out of there before the ambulance and the police arrive. "I want you to stay in Turkey and lay low for a few days."

"Why? Why can't I return to London?"

"There are too many people looking for you. Apparently you left quite a trail, from stolen cars to an incident at a service centre only a few hours ago. They will be looking for you at customs. We will come up with a new identity to get you out of the country, but it will take several days. I am also certain you could use the rest." Rest was the last thing Quentin wanted. The thought of Inci being dead after all he had gone through to free her left him feeling disgusted and he wondered if he'd ever get over it. He was hoping he would get another assignment immediately to take his mind off his weary burden.

"I want you to go to Antalya. It is a seaside resort community on the southern coast of Turkey, about a three-hour drive from where you are. There is a hotel, which we use called the Cender. Check in under an assumed name and leave your rented automobile parked in the parking lot. We will expect you to be there some time tonight and we will arrange to have the vehicle picked up. Be careful because the police will be looking for that car. They know you rented it."

"What am I supposed to do while I'm there?" Quentin asked.

"Relax a little and enjoy the scenery. It is a beautiful resort and the Mediterranean should still be warm. We will be in touch with you shortly."

The telephone went dead and Quentin slowly closed the cover. He released his grip of Inci's arm and felt sick at the scene around him.

His gaze drifted toward Francis Sun who was staring directly at the mannequin face of his son. "I suggest you get in your car and get out of here," Quentin said.

Francis Sun looked up at the dark-haired

youth beside him. Quentin's statement came as a surprise. He fully expected to be arrested.

"Why are you letting me go?"

Quentin thought for a moment before answering. "I'm not sure. Perhaps I'm not cut out for this business but I know you've suffered enough. My job was to find your son and nothing else. I have done that and although the end is not what I had hoped, I see no need to arrest you as well."

Francis Sun slowly shook his head. "You are a man of conscience," he said, slowly. "My son brought this on himself. I fully understand that. I would like you to know that I respect you for your actions and the way you handle yourself. I am certain our paths will never cross again; however, if they should, I will remember you and the kindness you have shown me today." Francis Sun extended his hand and Quentin shook it.

The young ISIS agent maintained a strong grip on his Beretta as he shook the hand of Francis Sun. He did not wish to be taken by surprise for he did not fully trust the man who seemed to have opened his heart to him.

His suspicions were incorrect and Francis Sun sadly walked toward the limousine. He turned around and paused a moment. "You will ensure my son's body is returned to me?"

"I'll do what I can." Quentin watched as Francis Sun stepped into the driver's side of the limousine, and manoeuvred the car onto the road. Inci lay motionless amid the fresh cotton. Her face appeared relaxed and was void of pain. Quentin leaned forward and placed a farewell kiss on her still forehead. He went to his car, turned onto the road, and drove. As he pulled away, in his review mirror he could see the flashing lights of an ambulance and police cruisers and over head a medical helicopter approached. He would drive to Nevsehir and then on to Antalya.

As he was clear of the scene where the activity had taken place, he decided he would call his father and enlighten him on what had just happened. In the event he was being watched he used Francis Sun's cellular phone to eliminate detection. He dialed the numbers and glanced in his rear view mirror to ensure he was not being followed.

"Quentin!" Phillip replied. "God am I glad to hear from you. How are you? Where are you?" Phillip could not hide the enthusiasm and excitement he felt the sound of his son's voice.

"I'm okay. It's over." Quentin sighed as he spoke the words, realizing for the first time that the ordeal had indeed ended. He went on to share the events with Phillip and explained that Amr El Hab had asked him to remain in Antalya for a few days. Quentin expressed his displeasure with the idea, and Phillip understood.

"It's common practice to lay low after an event, especially if you're still in the country where it took place. We have a good rapport with most countries; however, from time, to time we push the rules just a little. I think this may be one of those times."

"I suppose you're right." Quentin asked about Lana and explained that he would not be able to call for the next few days.

"Not to worry, I'll know where you are. We do have a good internal network," Phillip said.

After a few more words of encouragement, Quentin thanked his father and closed the lower half of the cellular phone. He suddenly slowed his speed when it dawned on him that he wasn't in a rush. He thought of Inci and had to admit he probably had grown more fond of her than he realized. His thoughts then drifted to Francis Sun and his enormous grief at the loss of his son.

He rolled down the window and allowed the wind to blow through his hair and cool his face. The rushing sound was a welcome sensation and it helped to drown out the sorrowful thoughts racing through his mind.

Epilogue

The hotel in Antalya was indeed beautiful. Complete with swimming pool, ocean view, and a courtyard fashioned around the semi circle of the building. Each balcony faced onto the blue waters of the Mediterranean.

Quentin had obeyed the rules meticulously and had not ventured from the hotel in the three days he had been there. He spent his time swimming and reading, and took most of his meals on the balcony overlooking the Sea.

Amr El Hab was true to his word and the rented automobile was picked up about an hour after Quentin arrived. He read the only available English newspaper and saw no signs of any of the events which had taken place. There was no mention of the incidents at the Dolmabahçe Palace or in Avanos. He had watched television regularly, paying special attention to CNN International and again, nothing had been reported.

Although the evenings were chilly, Quentin enjoyed sitting on the balcony, watching the ships sail past and the tourists walking in the courtyard. It saddened him to see people walking hand in hand, as he envied their companionship and began to realize what his father had meant when, he told him how lonely this job could be.

Quentin had not been contacted by anyone since his arrival at the hotel, and was understandably startled when the telephone rang. At first he was uncertain whether he should answer but after the fourth ring decided that it had to be for him. No one else knew he was there.

He stepped from the balcony into the room and walked to the telephone on the table between the two twin beds.

"Hello," he said, cautiously, unsure of what to expect.

"I thought you were going to let the telephone ring all night," the voice at the other end of the line said.

Quentin was silent for a moment as he could feel his heart begin to pound against his chest wall. "Inci?" he questioned softly, as if not daring to say her name out loud.

"Of course it is me. Although I do not know why I am calling you after you abandoned me in a cotton field in Avanos."

"But... I..." Quentin stammered, not knowing what to say.

"I was only teasing. Are you all right?" Inci asked.

"Yes," Quentin replied, beginning to realize he was not dreaming. "I'm fine but... the question is, how are you?"

"Much better, thank you."

"What happened? I thought you were dead."

"I can see we have to give you a refresher course in first aid," She laughed. "The bullet missed any vital organs. I lost a lot of blood but there was no serious damage."

"Thank God," Quentin exclaimed. "You can't believe how happy I am that you're all right."

"Well I am still in a lot of pain. Chocolates and a nice conversation would probably make me feel better."

Quentin smiled at Inci's words and was truly glad that she was all right. "Where are you now?"

"I am in a hospital in Konya."

"How long will you be there?" he asked, his mind racing as to how he could make plans to see her.

"They expect me to be released tomorrow."

"Tomorrow? That's great. What are your

plans?"

"Amr wants me to take a few days off. He suggests I go down to Antalya. We use a beautiful resort hotel there right on the Mediterranean. Perhaps you have heard of it. It is called the Cender."

Quentin smiled. His eyes noticed the hotel name on the small pad of paper beside the telephone in his room. "That'd be great," Quentin said. "I can't wait to see you."

"I am looking forward to it. Sunny skies, ocean breezes, and the relaxation will do me good."

"And me," Quentin said. "Don't forget. I'll be here too." He smiled as he spoke.

"Oh yes. I almost forgot," She said, mockingly. There was a moment of silence on the line and Inci was unsure whether she had hurt Quentin's feelings. "I was only kidding," she said. "You are the main reason I am coming to Antalya."

"I'll be here!" Quentin said happily. They said good bye and he was truly overjoyed at the prospect of Inci being alive and en route to see him. He had not realized how fond he had grown of this girl in the few hours they had spent together. Perhaps it was the abruptness of their separation or the turmoil they shared together, but he felt truly elated when he thought of them being together.

He walked out onto the balcony and again pondered the events of the past few days. This time, however, the shroud of despair had been lifted. He felt he had failed in his mission by not bringing Thomas Sun back alive; however, it was a minor detail which had been overlooked because of his infiltration into the headquarters of Mustafa and his band of terrorists. He had completed the entire task without the assistance of any other members of ISIS. He was pleased with his accomplishments, even though visions would continue to haunt his mind for quite some time: visions of Cengiz laying in the parking lot of the service centre with his head split open, Francis Sun crying over the body of his dead son, the bullet ridden bodies of Bob Wallace and Ken Myers, and the slaughter beside the cotton fields of Avanos. His thoughts of Inci subdued the pain and cleansed him with a feeling of contentment.

     He stood on the balcony of the white, stucco hotel and listened to the waves lap the shore. Only now he smiled as he watched lovers walking hand in hand through the courtyard below in this beautiful resort on the southern coast of Turkey.